Murder

at

Netherfield

by

Jann Rowland

One Good Sonnet Publishing

By Jann Rowland

PRIDE AND PREJUDICE ADAPTATIONS

Acting on Faith
A Life from the Ashes (Sequel to *Acting on Faith*)
Open Your Eyes
Implacable Resentment
An Unlikely Friendship
Bound by Love
Cassandra
Obsession
Shadows Over Longbourn
The Mistress of Longbourn
My Brother's Keeper
Coincidence
The Angel of Longbourn
Chaos Comes to Kent
In the Wilds of Derbyshire
The Companion
Out of Obscurity
What Comes Between Cousins
A Tale of Two Courtships
Murder at Netherfield

COURAGE ALWAYS RISES: THE BENNET SAGA

The Heir's Disgrace

Co-Authored with Lelia Eye

WAITING FOR AN ECHO

Waiting for an Echo Volume One: Words in the Darkness
Waiting for an Echo Volume Two: Echoes at Dawn
Waiting for an Echo Two Volume Set

A Summer in Brighton
A Bevy of Suitors
Love and Laughter: A Pride and Prejudice Short Stories Anthology

MURDER AT NETHERFIELD

Copyright © 2018 Jann Rowland

Cover Design by Marina Willis

Published by One Good Sonnet Publishing

ISBN: 1987929926
ISBN-13: 9781987929928

To my family who have, as always, shown
their unconditional love and encouragement.

CHAPTER I

*I*t is an inescapable truth that when a single man of good fortune moves into a neighborhood, he immediately becomes the focus of attention for the young ladies and matrons who live there. But when several murders occur at the man's house within a few months of his moving there, the interest is quashed quite quickly.

Now, it is not the purpose of this work to cast aspersions on Mr. Bingley or accuse him of something so heinous as murder. He was also known to be a fine, happy man of impeccable manners and a happy disposition. Such benefits of character must necessarily include the assumption that he was completely incapable of anything underhanded. But then again, he must also be considered a suspect, for the murders occurred at his house and under his stewardship. Therefore, he could not be absolved without understanding the facts, which would serve to exonerate or damn him in the eyes of the law.

Sadly, when the gossips of society hear of anything salacious, innuendo is followed by tales told, becoming more outlandish by the moment, until the subject's reputation is ruined. Whether the events at Netherfield were to result in this pitiable state of affairs remained to be seen, though gossip would undoubtedly ensue. This, of course, would not free any of the other residents of the estate from speculation.

But perhaps we should start at the beginning, for the ending would only confuse the reader without the proper foundation. And it *is* possible that Mr. Bingley might be acquitted, should the full circumstances be known.

Netherfield Park, the estate in question, had long stood empty — or at least long in the eyes of the younger generation. Those who had lived long enough in society would remember the grand balls the previous owner had held, the likes of which none of them had seen since. The estate was the largest in the vicinity of the small market town of Meryton, more than twice the size of the next largest estate. The new owner — though he had owned it for several years — had no use for the property and had tried to let it for some time before finally attracting Mr. Bingley, a young man whose father had left him a large fortune amassed in trade. He was eager to fulfill his father's wish and purchase an estate. Fortunately for him, his good friend convinced him it would be better to lease the estate for a year and learn to manage it properly before taking such a step as using his life savings on the purchase.

Netherfield's nearest neighbor was an estate by the name of Longbourn, which was also the next largest to Netherfield in both size and income. The family at Longbourn, the Bennets, who had held the estate for several centuries, were typical country folk, not rich enough to engage much of their time in London, and blessed — or cursed — with a succession of five daughters, with not an heir to be had. This was particularly pitiable since the estate was entailed on a distant cousin whom none of them had ever met.

Mrs. Bennet, the estate's mistress, was herself the daughter of the local solicitor who had made a fortunate marriage when she had come to the attention of the estate's young master. He had married her in haste, having been enchanted by her good looks and vibrant character. Unfortunately, what may be entered with haste may be repented at leisure, for Mr. Bennet soon found that his wife's good humor and beauty hid the character defects of an illiberal mind, mean understanding, and an inability to discuss anything other than fashion or gossip. Mr. Bennet, though he repented heartily of his choice, possessed an unusual philosophy, which allowed him to take his amusement where he could — usually at his wife's expense — and retreat to his bookroom when her nerves became too much for him to tolerate.

It was unfortunate, but the longer their marriage progressed, the more prevalent Mrs. Bennet's nerves became. The primary culprit of this change was the aforementioned entail. Mrs. Bennet's dowry, a mere five thousand pounds, would in no way be sufficient to provide for her when her husband passed on, and she lived in fear of being forced into the hedgerows when the unknown heir arrived to claim the estate. Her silliness thus increased apace, rendering her an ever less tolerable companion for her husband. Combine this with an insatiable desire to see her daughters wed and with the silliness of two youngest girls—Kitty and Lydia—and their incessant giggling, carrying on, and loud talking, and it was a wonder Mr. Bennet ever came out of his bookroom.

It should not be a shock that the arrival of a young man of good fortune should cause palpitations on the part of the mistress, indeed, such that she was forced to call for her smelling salts several times in the days after his arrival became known in the village. Dreams of this man providing the means for their salvation flashed before Mrs. Bennet's eyes, leading her to declare him the property of her eldest and most beautiful daughter, Jane, long before any of them had actually made his acquaintance. Jane's younger sister and closest confidante, Elizabeth, watched her mother's enthusiasm with annoyance, though she fully agreed with the idea that Jane was the dearest person in the world. Any man would be a fool not to fall in love with her. The middle daughter, Mary, contented herself with her favorite little homilies, to which, as usual, no one paid any attention.

While Mrs. Bennet dreamed and schemed, and her daughters participated to varying degrees, it remained a fact that none of the Bennet ladies had ever laid eyes on the young man. As such, they were dependent upon the account of their good friend, Charlotte Lucas, who informed them she had seen him from a distance and thought him tall and well favored. Their first glimpse of the elusive man came at the assembly they attended not long after Mr. Bingley's arrival in Hertfordshire.

"He is, indeed, a handsome man, is he not, girls?" giggled Mrs. Bennet when the party was shown into the room.

"He is," agreed Charlotte, who stood with them, having pointed out which one of the party was Mr. Bingley.

"Who are the other members of his party?" asked Elizabeth, noting the presence of two other gentlemen and two ladies.

"The tall, dark one is Mr. Darcy, apparently a friend of longstanding. The ladies are his sisters—the taller is the younger, Miss Caroline Bingley, while the elder is Mrs. Louisa Hurst. Mrs. Hurst is married to the other gentleman."

"How convenient," exclaimed Elizabeth, turning a grin upon her oldest friend, "that the plain, stout man would be the one who is already married! The single gentlemen are quite handsome, indeed, and will be much sought after, I dare say."

Charlotte smiled. "I am certain you are correct, Lizzy. Perhaps you will even catch the eye of one of the gentlemen yourself."

"If I can pry their attention away from Jane," replied Elizabeth, noting that Mr. Bingley was already looking in their direction and at her elder sister in particular.

A few more moments' time proved Elizabeth's supposition, for the party made their way toward the assembled Bennet ladies, Sir William leading them while speaking and gesturing in his expansive manner. Mr. Bingley strode alongside him, apparently eager, while Mr. Darcy was slower to follow. The ladies and Mr. Hurst only continued to stand by the door, and in their manners, Elizabeth thought she saw haughtiness and disdain.

"Mrs. Bennet," said Sir William when he and Mr. Bingley had reached them, "Mr. Bingley has expressed a wish to be introduced to you and your family."

"Thank you, sir," replied Mrs. Bennet with a low curtsey. Sir William performed the duty with his usual civility, and Mr. Bingley bowed along with his friend and said all the usual niceties. But his next action succeeded in proving Elizabeth's earlier thoughts.

"Miss Bennet," said he, "I would be pleased if you would do me the honor of standing up with me for the next."

"Thank you, sir," replied Jane, a rosy hue already working its way over her countenance."

"Excellent!" cried Mr. Bingley. Then he seemed to remember something, turned to Mr. Darcy, who was watching them all with an unreadable expression, and gave him a pointed look. Whether they had previously spoken of the matter, Elizabeth could not be sure. But Mr. Darcy, though he did not appear to be enthused in the slightest, obliged, addressing Elizabeth.

"Would you care to dance, Miss Elizabeth?"

Though a perverse portion of her mind thought to refuse his application, given the unwilling nature of his offering it, she had no wish to sit out for the rest of the evening. Thus, Elizabeth gave her assent, and soon they proceeded to the dance

Whatever she had expected, Elizabeth would not have thought the man would be determined to remain silent throughout their time together. It was clear to Elizabeth that he was a reticent man, though she could not quite make out whether he thought himself above his company or was excessively proud. But for the first fifteen minutes of the set, she found herself despairing of ever having any conversation with him.

"Do you plan to stay long in the neighborhood, Mr. Darcy?" asked she, finally desperate to have any, even the most banal of conversations with this man.

"I believe I shall likely stay until at least early December," replied Mr. Darcy.

Though she waited for him to elaborate, it turned out to be a futile expectation, for Mr. Darcy once again fell silent. In fact, Elizabeth thought she detected a hint of displeasure about his mouth and the way his eyes narrowed ever so slightly. That, of course, set her once again to annoyance. It was not as if she had asked him the income of his estate, inquired regarding the size of his fortune, or requested the keys of his vaults!

"I hope, then, that you enjoy your time at leisure." Having said that much, Elizabeth intended to say nothing more, for there did not seem to be the possibility of intelligent exchange with this man. Then he surprised her and spoke again.

"The purpose of my visit is not my leisure, Miss Bennet. As this is Bingley's first chance to manage an estate, he has asked me to be of assistance to him."

"Then that is commendable, Mr. Darcy," said Elizabeth. "But I suspect Mr. Bingley does not wish to be consumed with estate matters at *all* times. Autumn and winter are times on the estate when the amount of work is lessened, and a wise estate manager must use the time effectively to refresh himself for the work which must be done the following spring."

Mr. Darcy smiled at Elizabeth's comment, the first time she had ever seen such a thing from the man. She had begun to wonder if he was even capable of truly smiling. "You are quite correct, of course. Hurst is much more interested in sport, so I assume there will be much of that. I am fond of riding, and as my friend is too, I dare say there will be many opportunities for leisure. However, Bingley has much to learn, and as my purpose is to facilitate this, I would be a poor friend if I did not direct him back to it on occasion."

"A conscientious landowner," said Elizabeth, her respect for the man rising a little. "I hope Mr. Bingley proves to be an excellent student."

Mr. Darcy again smiled, though Elizabeth could easily detect the wry quality it contained. "My friend is quite intelligent and has the best of intentions. Unfortunately, he *is* easily distracted on occasion. But I shall persevere."

They parted soon after with little else passing between them. Elizabeth was not certain what to think of the man, for he avoided conversation for the rest of the evening, speaking only to the members of his own party. He did dance twice more—once with each of Mr. Bingley's sisters—but Elizabeth thought his performance was nothing more than duty, rather than engaging with them out of pleasure for the activity or their company.

He was an enigma, a puzzle she could not quite understand. He seemed to be a stiff man, though whether that was the strict adherence to proper behavior, discomfort, or a sense of superiority, she did not know. Most of those to whom she spoke commented that he had danced with her out of all of them, but most seemed to think it was because of what his friend had expected of him. Though she could not say she was looking forward to his acquaintance, she was interested to see if she could make him out any further.

While Elizabeth had difficulty in sketching Mr. Darcy, the same was not true of the rest of the party. Mr. Hurst was a bore, rarely saying anything at gatherings and always sitting in a position which afforded easy access to the refreshments. Mrs. Hurst and Miss Bingley thought highly of themselves and meanly of their neighbors, and while they seemed to take a liking to Jane, they rarely had anything other than a sneer for anyone else in the neighborhood.

But Mr. Bingley, by contrast, was a genial man, open and eager to be included in their company, happy, garrulous, and everything gentlemanly. But the greatest point in his favor was the fact that it was soon clear that he preferred Jane's company to anyone else's. There were several other activities in the ensuing days, including dinners, parties, card parties, and even a meeting or two on Meryton's streets. Mr. Bingley's preference was clear for all to see, for he did nothing to hide it. Jane, however, was quite different, and it took one with knowledge of her to divine her preferences. As such, Elizabeth took it upon herself to ensure Jane left Mr. Bingley in no doubt of her growing feelings.

"Do you wish me to show Mr. Bingley more affection than I feel, Lizzy?" asked Jane in that mild manner of hers when Elizabeth brought the subject to her attention.

"You know very well I advocate no such behavior, Jane," replied

Elizabeth. "I only inform you that you are quite the reticent creature, and as such, it would behoove you to make your regard known to him." Elizabeth paused and shot her sister a mischievous smile. "Or am I mistaken about your regard for the gentleman?"

Jane blushed, but she did not avoid the question. "No, Lizzy, you are not mistaken. Mr. Bingley is one of the finest men I have ever known, and I like him prodigiously."

"Only like?" asked Elizabeth, laughing when Jane turned the color of a ripe apple.

"I have not known him long," cried Jane. "How can I know at this early juncture if I feel more for him?"

"You cannot, dearest," replied Elizabeth. "And I understand. I only speak this way as I am not certain you will be allowed to take your time to come to know him. You may be required to discover your feelings in a more expeditious manner."

A frown settled over Jane's pretty face. "Surely you do not think our mother would push me more than I am comfortable."

"While I consider our mother capable of almost any behavior which would result in any of us marrying sooner rather than later, I do not speak of her." At Jane's uncomprehending expression, Elizabeth sighed, wishing her sister was not quite so eager to ascribe the best motives to all and sundry. "Jane, surely you must see that Mr. Bingley's sisters—and perhaps his friend—do not favor his attentiveness to you."

"I have seen no such thing," replied Jane, a defensive note entering her voice. "Mrs. Hurst and Miss Bingley have been very kind to me."

"Yes, Jane, they have been." Elizabeth sighed. She did not like opening her gentle sister's eyes to the sins of others, but it was necessary that Jane was aware of the obstacles which Elizabeth was certain would threaten her happiness. "I know they are your friends and that you esteem them. It is to your credit that you feel that way. But I would not have my sister unaware of the other side of their characters which they do not show to you."

"Of what are you accusing them?" asked Jane, appearing as if she wished to conclude this discussion as soon as may be.

"I do not know the specifics of what they think, Jane. But I *can* tell you that they have no good opinion of Meryton or anyone in it. They are not friends of their brother's interest in you, for I have often seen them when they think no one is watching. I am not asking you to throw them off as friends, Jane, nor do I ask you to confront them. All I ask is that you remain watchful and that you do not allow them to deceive you."

"You think they will persuade their brother against me."

Elizabeth gave her sister an affectionate smile and patted her hand. "If you show Mr. Bingley your true feelings and leave *him* in no doubt, I do not think his sisters will have anything they can do to prevent him from following his heart. I cannot say if they will attempt anything dishonest, but a true knowledge of your feelings should negate it if they do."

Jane seemed to think on this for a few moments before she nodded her head slowly. "I can do that, Lizzy. I will still consider them my friends, but I will watch for anything which suggests they are not truthful with me."

"That is all I can ask."

Had Elizabeth been privy to a conversation which was happening at that moment between the subjects of her conversation with Jane, she would have been positively smug. Having seen their brother's interest in Miss Jane Bennet, the Bingley sisters gathered together late that evening, intent on discussing the situation between themselves, without husbands or brothers overhearing.

"What do you think of this one?" asked Caroline, directing an expectant look on her sister.

Louisa only sighed and shook her head. "It is impossible to tell. Some of his past interests I might have said he pursued with more fervor than he does Miss Bennet. But there seems to be a . . . depth of feeling present when he speaks with Miss Bennet that I don't recall with any of the others."

"It is possible," said Caroline, thinking on the matter and wondering how she could pull her brother away from his latest interest. "If Charles would only fix on a suitable woman, we would not need to take such steps. But he seems to have a knack for finding the poorest ladies of the most wretched situations. I know not how he accomplishes it."

"Oh, come, Caroline. They have not all been that bad."

"It seems like they have," snapped Caroline.

In her frustration, she went to the sideboard where a bottle of her brother's fine brandy sat with several glasses. She unstopped the decanter and poured herself three fingers worth before placing it back on the tray. Then she sighed at the scent of the heavenly liquid which lay within and took an experimental sip. It was her one guilty pleasure. Most ladies chose something more proper, such as wine or sherry, but

Caroline preferred the feelings engendered by brandy, and she often indulged.

"Oh, Caroline," said Louisa with a sigh. "I truly wish you would not drink so much of that harsh beverage Charles prefers. It is not ladylike, you know."

Caroline glared at her sister, even as she took another deliberate sip of the heady liquid. "I am every inch the lady in everything I do. Mr. Darcy will not care if I have a sip or three of his brandy every so often."

Though she shook her head, Louisa did not comment any further. The discussion had played out many times before, and Louisa had learned not to push the matter, lest she provoke an argument. Caroline did not know why men kept this wonderful drink to themselves, and she would not allow it in her home.

"Let us see," said Caroline, holding up the fingers of her free hand as she counted Charles's improper loves. "There was Miss Standish, the parson's daughter; then Miss Jones, the tradesman's sister; after that it was Miss Derry, the woman whose father was stricken with poverty, followed by Miss Taylor, whose situation was much the same as Miss Bennet's. And do not forget Miss Strickland—no one could forget the woman who claimed five thousand pounds was a substantial dowry. There were more, but I cannot remember them all."

"I do not know what you mean to accomplish by naming them," said Louisa.

"I simply wish to remind us both from what we are saving our brother," replied Caroline. "They were each, in their own way, unsuitable, and we did well to persuade Charles against them."

"You are misstating the matter, Caroline," said Louisa, her tone admonishing. "Charles eventually lost interest in each—it was nothing *we* did to dissuade him."

"I am certain we played a part," replied Caroline with an airy wave. She sipped at her drink again, relishing the burn as the liquid flowed down her throat. "It was our protests which set his disinterest in motion."

Louisa again shook her head. "You may believe what you like, Caroline. But, eventually, one of these ladies who has turned Charles's head will keep his interest. And there will be nothing either of us can do about it."

"There must be!" cried Caroline. She lifted the glass and drank the rest, pouring herself another portion without thinking. "If only we could redirect him to a woman of good fortune and connections in London. But though he is his usual self among them, he never becomes enamored with one. It is as if he is determined to disappoint us."

"I doubt he has anything other than his own happiness in mind."

"Louisa," said Caroline, her annoyance with her sister climbing to intolerable levels, "can I count on your support when the time comes?"

Louisa grimaced, but she did not hesitate. "I no more wish Charles to marry Miss Bennet than you do, Caroline. I am only pragmatic when considering our chances of influencing him."

"Good," said Caroline, choosing to ignore the second part of her sister's response. "For now, I think it is sufficient to watch and wait. When the time comes, we may need to strike quickly."

"Agreed," said Louisa. "We will do what we can, as we have always done."

With those words, Louisa excused herself to return to her rooms, leaving Caroline alone with her thoughts. It should not be too difficult, she mused. If everything else failed, perhaps Miss Bennet could be proven to be improper in some way, lessening her allure in Charles's eyes. It would not be the first time Caroline had acted against a woman to whom she thought Charles was becoming too close. It would likely not be the last.

Either way, now was not the time to consider the matter any further. Caroline stood, a little unsteadily, and made her way to her room. Perhaps everything would be clearer after a good night's sleep.

CHAPTER II

WWhile Jane's budding romance with Mr. Bingley seemed to be proceeding apace, Elizabeth was able to gain no more clarity regarding Mr. Darcy than she had before. He was at the same time aloof, yet kind, and proper—though not friendly—when he was induced to speak. He was intelligent but not personable. He was confident in society, but reticent when speaking. He was the most maddening subject she had ever studied!

At times, Elizabeth thought him on the verge of censuring them all. At others, he seemed amused by what he saw. It was a surprise to Elizabeth that the presence of Lydia and Kitty were equally likely to provoke either response in him when she might have expected he would consider them ill-bred and wild. Elizabeth *herself* felt that way about her sisters.

They continued in this manner through October and halfway through November when an event occurred which prompted much rejoicing at Longbourn. Though there had been talk, primarily from Mr. Bingley, of a ball to be held at Netherfield, the sisters always appeared as if they would much rather be drawn and quartered than host the cream of Meryton society. It seemed, however, that Mr. Bingley finally prevailed. But no one—not even his sisters—could misunderstand the gesture he made by delivering the invitation in person. Nor could they deny what happened next.

"Excellent!" cried Mr. Bingley when Mrs. Bennet gave her assurance, in a voice as giddy as those of her younger daughters, that they would be happy to attend. Then he turned to Jane. "If I may, I should like to take this opportunity to solicit your hand, Miss Bennet, for the first sets."

While Jane blushed with pleasure, Elizabeth watched the superior sisters and was not reassured by what she saw. They wore matching pinched expressions which would have curdled milk. If Elizabeth was to guess, she thought they had suspected their brother's intentions and had felt powerless to stop them.

When they departed, Elizabeth was left with her sister and was privy to all Jane's pleasure and her hopes and fears for the future. She provided a willing ear for Jane to vent all her thoughts and was not disappointed by what she heard.

The days before the ball at Netherfield would not have been remarkable had it not been for the coming of a most unexpected visitor. The invitation for the ball had been delivered on Thursday, which sent the Bennet ladies—particularly the mother, in the company of her youngest—into a frenzy of preparations. Therefore, when the rumble of a gig on Longbourn's drive announced a new arrival, it went quite unnoticed by her mother. Elizabeth, who had been sitting near the window, looked out and, seeing the approach of the vehicle, frowned and decided to approach her father when she saw a tall man alighting from it.

"A visitor, you say," said Mr. Bennet, apparently as perplexed as Elizabeth was herself. "I was not expecting anyone."

"The gig has already stopped in front of the entrance, Papa," replied Elizabeth. "The man was dressed in clerical garb, from what I could see."

That piece of information seemed to bring no greater clarity to Mr. Bennet. But he rose and motioned Elizabeth from the room, regardless.

"I suppose we should see what he wants."

When they exited the house, they met the man who was at that moment approaching the door. Behind him, the gig which had delivered him was already making its way back up the drive and toward the village. The man directed a smile at them and bowed so low, it almost seemed he considered her father to be a duke.

"Mr. Bennet," said the man, "I am exceedingly happy to be in your presence, sir, for I have wished these many months to look upon the face of my closest relation."

It seemed that declaration induced recognition in Elizabeth's father, for he regarded the other man with some interest. Elizabeth could only stare at the man. He was tall, but heavyset, a distinct paunch decorating his midsection. His hair, what she could see of it under the wide-brimmed black hat he wore, was dark as night, though with a faint shine common to hair which had not been washed in some time. He was not precisely homely, though Elizabeth thought him rather plain. But he was also not appealing in any physical sense.

"I am sorry, sir," replied Mr. Bennet, "but I do not believe we are acquainted. Might I know your identity?"

"I would have thought my words would have spoken to my identity," replied the man. "Be that as it may, I have no objection to stating it. I am William Collins, a name which must be known to you, I suspect, for I am to be your heir."

Comprehension flooded Elizabeth's mind. Though her parents had rarely spoken of the man—other than Mrs. Bennet's lamentations concerning the entail—she had known his name and had heard from her father that he was studying at a seminary to be a clergyman. It seemed he had attained that rank, given the dress he now wore.

"Your name *is* known to me," replied Mr. Bennet. "But I cannot account for your presence, sir."

"Is it not understandable that I would wish to view the estate over which I am to be master?" asked Mr. Collins. "Of course, I wish it. And in the words of my great patroness, Lady Catherine de Bourgh, familiarity with the lands which will soon be mine cannot be obtained quickly enough. I must have intimate knowledge of it since I shall someday be responsible for it."

"How sensible for you to have thought of it," replied Mr. Bennet. Though Mr. Collins preened at her father's words, Elizabeth could hear the mocking quality in his voice, which told her he thought Mr. Collins anything but sensible. "What I am asking you, sir, is why you are here now? I have received no letter from you and have issued no invitation. I cannot even be certain of your identity."

"That is no impediment," said Mr. Collins, waving Mr. Bennet's protest away as if it were nothing more than smoke on the wind. "I am a clergyman, sir, and as I inhabit that exalted sphere, I believe I understand the rules of conduct for one in my position. As for my identity, surely, as you knew my late honored father, you must see some resemblance to him in my countenance."

"I suppose that is correct," was Mr. Bennet's grudging reply.

"Then no impediment exists." Elizabeth thought Mr. Collins's tone was rather smug.

Mr. Bennet regarded Mr. Collins for several moments, seemingly considering the matter. Elizabeth, who knew her father, suspected he saw the potential for amusement in Mr. Collins's visit. Therefore, he did not send the man away as she had hoped and invited him in.

"Since you are here now, there is no help for it. As we have had no word of your coming, I hope you will excuse us if the guest room has not been readied."

"I assure you, Mr. Bennet, that I am able to adapt quite quickly. As long as the bed is made and is clean, I shall be comfortable."

They led the man inside, Elizabeth noting with interest that he had not spoken any words to her. He did, however, comment on the vestibule as they passed through, seeming satisfied with its size, layout, and many other details Elizabeth herself would not have considered. He commented that the doors were perfectly serviceable and would not have looked out of place in his parsonage and that the floors were polished nicely.

"None of this matches the home of my patroness, Lady Catherine de Bourgh, of course," said he as they approached the sitting-room. "Rosings Park is, you must understand, one of the great estates, and perfectly situated on a bit of rising land, surveying all about it like an angel on a cliff. I am sure there is not its equal in all of Kent if not all of southern England!"

Mr. Collins, apparently, saw himself as possessing the soul of a poet. Elizabeth was already coming to the conclusion the man was nothing more than ridiculous. Mr. Bennet seemed to feel the same way, as he grinned at Elizabeth and lifted an eyebrow when he noticed her watching. Elizabeth shook her head — after only a few moments in his company, she could already see how trying the ensuing days would be. And he had not yet mentioned how long he intended to stay!

Upon entering the sitting-room, Mrs. Bennet finally seemed to realize they had a visitor, for she looked up and frowned at the man. Mary and Jane had returned to the sitting-room in the interim — they had both been absent when the carriage arrived — so the whole family was present. Mr. Bennet, seeing he had all his daughters in attendance, lost no time in making the introductions.

"Mrs. Bennet," said he. "As you can see, we have been blessed with a visitor." Then a thought seemed to cross Mr. Bennet's mind, and he turned to Mr. Collins. "I do not believe you have mentioned how long you intend to stay, sir."

"Let us see what comes of my visit," replied Mr. Collins, a fatuous grin adorning his countenance.

It was the height of rudeness, not only to invite oneself but to voice one's intention to stay for an indefinite period. But Mr. Bennet seemed to see there was no reason to trade words with such a dull specimen, for he only nodded.

"Mrs. Bennet, this is Mr. Collins, who, as you know, is my heir. Mr. Collins, my wife, Margaret Bennet, and my daughters, Jane, Elizabeth, Mary, Catherine, and Lydia."

"Madam, Miss Bennets," said Mr. Collins, giving them the same low bow he had shown to Mr. Bennet previously. "I am vastly pleased to be here. I thank you with all my heart for your unstinting welcome and your willingness to allow me entrance into your home. I hope, in time, we shall become true relations and intimates."

It seemed to Elizabeth that her mother was on the verge of one of her infamous nervous attacks, for the sight of the future master of Longbourn must bring to her mind the image of the hedgerows as her future place of residence. But though she had never had the opportunity to welcome him into her home, she seemed to latch onto the last bit of his statement even more quickly than Elizabeth had.

"You wish to become better acquainted with us?"

"But of course, Mrs. Bennet," was Mr. Collins's lofty reply. "It is Christian to forgive the grievances of the past and look toward the future. Furthermore, it is the particular wish of my patroness, Lady Catherine de Bourgh, who, in her boundless generosity, charged me with this reconciliation. 'You must initiate it, Mr. Collins,' said she, 'for it is your duty due to your profession. And if, when you meet your cousins, you find that an olive branch may be extended, why you should seize the opportunity. Your cousin and his progeny might be lower gentry, but they are gentlefolk. A man in your position cannot expect too much.'"

While the younger girls giggled at the man's ponderous manner of expressing himself and Mary looked on him with something akin to approval, Jane and Elizabeth exchanged a glance, and Elizabeth was certain they each understood what the other was thinking. Jane was, no doubt, thanking the Lord on high that Mr. Bingley was already showering his attentions on her. Elizabeth, on the other hand, was fervently wishing he would not turn to her.

Mr. Bennet, on the other hand, was watching the spectacle, amusement shining from his very being. It was possible the prospect of Mr. Collins's continued absurdity might be enough to draw him from his bookroom more than was his wont. No doubt, should the man choose to pursue Elizabeth, Mr. Bennet would only watch and laugh as she attempted to put him off. Luckily, Elizabeth was also certain her father would support her should she be required to refuse a proposal from their cousin.

No one in the family had expected the Netherfield party to visit again before the ball the next week. Surely there must be many things to accomplish in the days before the event was scheduled to take place. But they were all surprised when the day after Mr. Collins's arrival saw the two gentleman—for Mr. Darcy had accompanied Mr. Bingley—riding down Longbourn's drive.

They were welcomed with the same enthusiasm as ever, and they received it with their usual response. In other words, Mr. Bingley beamed at the welcome and immediately sat down at Jane's side, while Mr. Darcy responded with his typical thanks, but remained more reserved. What none of them could have predicted was Mr. Collins's response to the introduction to Mr. Darcy.

"Can it be that I am in the august presence of Mr. Fitzwilliam Darcy of Derbyshire?"

Mr. Darcy's surprise was clear. "You seem to have the advantage of me, sir."

"Indeed, I do," said Mr. Collins, clearly taking Mr. Darcy's response as an affirmation of his question. He was also quite quivering with excitement. "In fact, I am in possession of the living at Hunsford, which, as you must already be aware, is under the authority of Lady Catherine de Bourgh, who I suppose must be your aunt."

"Yes, she is," replied Mr. Darcy.

"What an incredible coincidence this is, Mr. Darcy!" cried Mr. Collins. "I could not have imagined that a visit to my cousin's house would admit me to the unmitigated honor of obtaining your acquaintance! I should like to inform you that your lady aunt and her daughter were in the best of health only yesterday, for I saw them before I departed from Kent."

Mr. Collins sidled closer to Mr. Darcy, and in a voice more than usually obsequious, said: "As you can imagine, I am very attentive to her ladyship and grateful for her generously offered condescension. I could not depart from Kent before paying my respects to her and accepting those final few tidbits of wisdom which she did not stint in bestowing upon me."

It was with a remarkably straight face that Mr. Darcy replied: "I can imagine her words to you, sir. You are fortunate in your situation, it appears."

"Oh, yes, indeed I am! The most fortunate man in all England, I assure you. Not only am I in possession of that wondrous gift of Hunsford and her ladyship's condescension, but I am also the heir to this estate. I feel my good fortune, exceedingly, I assure you."

No one missed the improper nature of Mr. Collins's words, least of all Mr. Darcy. To speak of such things in mixed company was beyond the pale. But Mr. Darcy, showing himself to be a gentleman, ignored that which was ridiculous and replied with nothing more than a nod of his head. Mr. Collins accepted it as if it was commendation from the king himself.

Elizabeth, finding herself nearby Mr. Darcy, looked at him with some amusement, wondering if he would deign to speak to her after such a spectacle. It seemed that day the more personable Mr. Darcy was in attendance, for he glanced at her, and showed her a slight smile, which for anyone else would have been a hearty laugh.

"What a strange coincidence this is, Mr. Darcy," said Elizabeth in a soft voice. "Who could have predicted that such a connection would exist here, of all places?"

"I cannot account for it myself, Miss Elizabeth," replied Mr. Darcy.

His gaze returned to Mr. Collins, and hers followed. His toadying to Mr. Darcy apparently a success in the parson's mind, he had turned his attention to the rest of the company, and he was now watching Mr. Bingley and Jane closely. It seemed that what he saw did not please him, for a frown settled on his countenance. A moment later, however, he seemed to nod to himself, and his attention turned elsewhere.

"It seems Mr. Collins has recognized Mr. Bingley's interest in my sister," said Elizabeth, not sure if she should be speaking of such a thing. She did not know what Mr. Darcy thought of the matter, after all.

Mr. Darcy positively started, and his eyes quickly found them. "Do you have an . . . expectation of my friend, Miss Elizabeth?"

"Expectation is a strong word, Mr. Darcy," replied Elizabeth. She chose to answer his question honestly and without rancor, for she did not sense any disapproval in his manner. "It is clear to me that Jane enjoys his company. I will not say that she is in love with him, for it is too early for her to know, I think. But I believe she could be, with very little provocation."

"I had not seen that in her," said Mr. Darcy, though he nodded slowly.

"She is reticent, Mr. Darcy. Much like certain others I could name."

Mr. Darcy smiled and turned to her. "Touché, Miss Elizabeth. I suppose I must bow to your superior knowledge of your sister. As for Bingley himself, I cannot say what his feelings are. He has had a habit of paying attention to the newest pretty face in the past. But his fascination with her has already lasted longer than any of those."

"Only time will tell. But do not assume Jane will accept him for reasons of prudence, or that anyone else will have any say in her decision. *If* he ever comes to the point, she will respond according to the contents of her heart."

"I am glad to hear it," replied Mr. Darcy. "I wish only for the best for my friend, you understand. He is his own man and may make his own decisions."

Satisfied with the result of her conversation with Mr. Darcy, Elizabeth turned her attention back to the rest of the gathering, only to see Mr. Collins's eyes on her and Mr. Darcy. It was clear by the censorious glare he was bestowing on her that he was not amused, though she could not understand why he might be offended. Then something else caught his attention, and he turned away.

"Excuse me, Mr. Bingley, but am I to understand you have invited my cousin's family to a ball at your estate?"

"Yes, I have," replied Mr. Bingley, tearing his eyes away from Jane. "It is to be held Tuesday next, and we are much anticipating their attendance."

Mr. Bingley's gaze returning to Jane's face told anyone who was watching *whose* attendance would be most agreeable to *him*. Mr. Collins did not miss it either. His eyes darted to Elizabeth and then back to Mr. Bingley. It was no surprise then when he spoke again.

"What a wonderful notion, Mr. Bingley. I assure you that I am not one of those members of the clergy who considers a ball anything other than an innocent diversion, especially when it is given by a man of good character. As I have heard your residence in the neighborhood is short, it is understandable you would wish to further your acquaintances by hosting them all in this manner. I hope, sir that you are to live here in the future, for I would count it a blessing to have such an affable neighbor as yourself."

Several of the company winced as Mr. Collins showed his lack of sense by again referring to the entail. Mr. Bennet was not one of them, for he only watched his heir and seemed to be clutching hold of his mirth by the tips of his fingers. Mrs. Bennet, by contrast, was watching the parson with something akin to terror.

"You are, of course, invited to attend with the rest of the family," said Mr. Bingley, eager to be finished with Mr. Collins's civility and return to his conversation with Jane.

"I do appreciate your generosity, sir," replied Mr. Collins. Elizabeth saw a hint of a smirk curving his lips, which seemed to suggest he had obtained what he wished. "I thank you for it and accept your graciously offered invitation. I shall be happy to attend."

Then Mr. Collins turned and faced Elizabeth. "Please allow me, my dear cousin, to solicit your hand for the first sets of the evening."

No one was more surprised than Elizabeth by Mr. Collins's application. But while she wished for anything other than to be the focus of this man's lovemaking, there was no choice but to accept. The way Kitty and Lydia giggled at her predicament, Elizabeth thought some retribution might be in order, but they paid no heed whatsoever to her scowl of disapproval.

"Excellent!" cried Mr. Collins when Elizabeth gave her disinterested consent. "I am sure we shall have a lovely evening. I am confident you are anticipating our dance as much as I am myself!"

Elizabeth did not know how he could be so confident in the face of her tepid reply, but it appeared Mr. Collins was a man who saw whatever he wished. Mr. Darcy, by contrast, was well aware of her hesitation, and he shot her a sympathetic smile. He did not speak, however, and Elizabeth was grateful; she did not think she could speak to him with equanimity, given what was passing through her mind at present.

"The Bennets possess an oddity of a relation, do they not?" said Bingley as he and Darcy rode away from Longbourn.

"I do not know that 'odd' is precisely the term I would use, my friend," replied Darcy. "But I have been privy to the kind of man with whom my aunt prefers to surround herself, and while Mr. Collins is perhaps eccentric and not a little extreme in his manners, he is no different from the rest of them."

Bingley laughed. "The droll way in which you portray your aunt is quite amusing, Darcy. Though I know she has no wish to sully herself with an acquaintance such as myself, I cannot help but hope that I someday become known to her."

"If I were you, Bingley, I would wish to postpone the pleasure indefinitely."

Again, Bingley let out a great guffaw. "Perhaps that would be best. I shall be guided by you, my friend."

They rode on, and while Darcy gave the appearance of giving his attention to his friend's continuing conversation, in reality, he was thinking of the words he had exchanged with Miss Elizabeth. As they had sat in company, he had endeavored to watch Miss Bennet carefully, prove her sister's assertions of her character. In the end, Darcy was forced to acknowledge that everything Miss Elizabeth had said to him about her was nothing less than the truth.

Which realization altered Darcy's intentions. He had seen, as had they all, Bingley's increasing interest in Miss Bennet, and while Darcy had never been required to insert himself into Bingley's business before, he had thought it might be necessary to do so this time. But he would not come in the way of Bingley's happiness, especially if the woman was as drawn to Bingley as he was to her. In this case, Miss Bennet was clearly coming to esteem Bingley more as time went on, and with Miss Elizabeth's assurances of her trustworthiness fortifying him, Darcy was content in allowing Bingley to come to his own conclusion.

Why Darcy should trust Miss Elizabeth to that extent, he was not certain. She was a forthright woman, he decided, not in the habit of deception to obtain that which she desired, unlike some other women he could name. She had existed on the edges of his consciousness since he had come, his interest in her intellect, which he thought was prodigious, never extending beyond that, though he could readily confess she was a handsome woman. Somehow, she inspired trust; whether it was sensible or not, Darcy could not help but trust her.

"I am very happy to have Miss Bennet's hand for the first dance," said Bingley, drawing Darcy's mind back to his friend's continuing speech. "For a moment there, I almost thought you would ask Miss Elizabeth for the first set. Then that strange cousin of hers managed it before you could."

"Why would I ask Miss Elizabeth for the first dance?" asked Darcy. "You know I rarely dance the first."

Bingley only gazed at him slyly. "Perhaps because it would assist you in avoiding my sister's less than subtle appeals for the same? Besides, you have danced with her before. The only lady, other than my sisters, with whom you have danced since we came to Meryton, as I recall."

"That is true," replied Darcy with an absence of thought. "But I only did that because you asked her sister to dance, and it would have been churlish to refuse to dance when you had already made yourself agreeable."

"I never thought anything different," replied Bingley. "But you should consider the woman a little more, Darcy. You have always claimed that women who try to attract you with exaggerated deference annoy you. With Miss Elizabeth, you would ever need to fear for such behavior."

It was the truth, Darcy thought. Perhaps he would dance with her again. But he would not raise her expectations by asking her for the first or the supper. She was a fine woman—he was becoming more convinced of that by the moment. But she was not for him. His future lay with a woman of society.

CHAPTER III

The next day, the rain, which had been threatening and falling in intermittent spurts the previous day, began in earnest, restricting the family to the house. While Elizabeth did not dislike rain in general, except for the way it curtailed her activities out of doors, in this instance, she thought it would prove to be a bother. Having been awoken by the sound of the light tapping on the pane of her window that morning, Elizabeth rose and wrapped a blanket about her as she went to look out onto the landscape. Already the ground was soaked, and little puddles had begun to form, rendering the outside world dreary, and her spirits, depressed.

With a sigh, Elizabeth stepped away from the window, annoyed that she would have no refuge from Mr. Collins other than the room she currently inhabited. She settled in her bed again, drawing the coverlet about her, considering her predicament with morose irritation. She had little doubt of Mr. Collins's focus on her, and while she would have preferred to refuse the honor of his fatuous lovemaking, she was relieved *she* was the sister who would have the duty of denying his proposal. She knew that other than Lydia, none of them would possess the fortitude necessary to provoke their mother's displeasure.

As a young woman who was often awake with the sun, it was not in Elizabeth's nature to return to sleep, and she was not disposed to lie in bed doing nothing. She indulged in a book for a short time, after which she found it necessary to arise from her bed. The grey day induced her to choose a dress which was much like her mood—a dull lilac gown she had often thought more fitting for half mourning than a normal morning dress. She then called the maid to attend her, and moments later was descending the stairs to break her fast. It was with surprise, then, that she was witness to Mr. Collins entering the house from the front door.

He was wet and bedraggled, his wide-brimmed black hat dripping water and his overcoat divesting little rivulets which pooled on the floor under his feet. Elizabeth glanced at the water, annoyed at the extra work the man had just created for the maids. But her attention was drawn away from the mess and to the man's person, as he regarded her as if suspecting she had appeared that way only for him.

"Good morning, my dear cousin! I was not at all aware that you were prone to waking this early in the morning. I must count it among your many perfections and assume this is evidence that you are an industrious and useful sort of person. For as my great patroness, Lady Catherine de Bourgh has said: 'To rise early is to be godly, Mr. Collins. Let not sloth tie you to your bed in the mornings, for much can be accomplished in the early hours.'"

To Elizabeth, who had obtained an image of Lady Catherine as a pompous and stupid woman, Mr. Collins's quote almost sounded something like sense. But as curious as she was, she was not at liberty to ignore his coming in out of the rain on such a day.

"I believe I might agree with her ladyship's position, Mr. Collins, for I have no liking of lying in bed in the mornings myself. Does her ladyship's wisdom also extend to advising you to walk in the morning in inclement conditions?"

Mr. Collins laughed as if Elizabeth had just related some hilarious joke. "It seems to me you are quite witty, Cousin. An excellent trait, to be certain, though I am confident the respect for Lady Catherine's rank will prompt silence when you finally meet her."

For the moment, Elizabeth ignored his reference to her ultimate meeting with his patroness. "That does not resolve my confusion, Mr. Collins. Should you not have chosen a more appropriate day for a constitutional?"

"You have mistaken my purpose, Cousin. I did not walk the grounds of Longbourn, beautiful though they are. In fact, this morning

I was engaged in walking to Meryton for the purpose of sending a letter to my patroness."

"But you only left Kent two days ago," said Elizabeth.

"That is true." Mr. Collins assumed an expression of such mindless adoration that Elizabeth might have wondered if he was experiencing some sort of religious ecstasy. "Lady Catherine, her wisdom so boundless and without equal, expects daily reports of my activities here in Hertfordshire. With such boundless condescension as she pays me, such assistance and advice, how could I possibly stint in following her instructions to the letter?"

"How, indeed?" echoed Elizabeth, feeling quite fatigued, though it was yet early in the day.

"I see you see the situation in the same way as I," said Mr. Collins, satisfaction seeping from his tone. "That bodes well for the future, indeed."

Then Mr. Collins turned and, whistling tunelessly, climbed the stairs toward his room. Suddenly bereft of an appetite, Elizabeth waited until she heard the sound of his door closing before making her way back to her room. Even boredom could not be worse than giving even a perceived hint of welcome to this man's efforts at wooing.

Elizabeth did all she could to avoid Mr. Collins during the next days, though at times it proved nigh impossible. For one, Longbourn was not large, and whenever she left her chambers, Mr. Collins would be nearby with his peculiar brand of civility and cloying attentions. For another, her mother, seeing Mr. Collins's intentions, had latched onto them as a means of saving the family from being destitute. So, while they all prepared for the ball, Elizabeth was treated to a constant litany of her mother's commentary.

"I think this cream dress will do for the ball," said she on one occasion, rummaging through Elizabeth's closet as if it was her own. "When Mr. Collins sees you in this, I am certain his eyes will pop out of their sockets."

While Elizabeth did not care if Mr. Collins should be rendered blind for the rest of his life, she did not wish it to be because of the sight of her. But she knew that to speak would be to provoke an argument with her mother, and she did not wish to do that until necessary.

On other occasions Mrs. Bennet would direct Mr. Collins to sit by Elizabeth, or hint of *her* enthusiasm for the match. On one occasion, she even referred to it in a manner Elizabeth could only term as gauche, for she said, though speaking to herself softly: "If Mr. Bingley can be induced to propose to Jane, perhaps we may have a double wedding."

Something in Elizabeth's countenance must have betrayed her distaste for the notion, for Mrs. Bennet directed a fierce glare at her second daughter. "I am aware that Mr. Collins is not what you would have chosen in a husband, Lizzy, but he is what is before you. I suggest you accept him with whatever grace you can muster."

The inference that Elizabeth would not be allowed to refuse him was not misunderstood, but again she declined to invite argument. Elizabeth was well aware that she possessed a much greater understanding of her father than her mother did. He would never force her to marry so objectionable a man.

Thus it was that Elizabeth was relieved when the day of the ball finally arrived, and it was not only because she was anticipating the amusement. Her mother, eager as she always was to display her daughters to their best advantage, was distracted. Elizabeth had thus far avoided or ignored Mr. Collins—it was the combined efforts of them both that was fatiguing her.

When she exited her room that evening and descended the stairs to join the family in the vestibule, she became aware that her mother was quite correct in her assertions regarding Mr. Collins's reaction to her choice of finery. But while Elizabeth had seen appreciative glances aplenty during her time in society, there was something in Mr. Collins's looks that she could not like. That he found her attractive was obvious. But there was a leering quality in his gaze which made her uncomfortable. It was as if he was undressing her with his eyes.

Though it was difficult, Elizabeth put him from her mind. The family entered the carriage, though Mr. Bennet was forced to ride on the box with the driver, and soon they made their way to Netherfield. When they arrived, Elizabeth was eager to enter the house and lose herself in the crowd for the moment. As such, she made her way through the receiving line as quickly as she could, and entered the ballroom, looking for Charlotte.

"How happy I am to see you, Charlotte!" exclaimed Elizabeth when she had found her friend. She could hear the note of hysteria in her own voice and knew her friend recognized it as well.

"Eliza," said Charlotte with a grin. "Can I assume your mother was especially trying today?"

"She was, indeed. But I can handle my mother. It is the presence of Mr. Collins who has provoked my current despair."

"Mr. Collins?" asked Charlotte with interest. "I am not acquainted with a Mr. Collins."

"You should consider yourself fortunate," muttered Elizabeth. "I apologize, Charlotte. I had forgotten he has only been in residence for three days. It has seemed more like three years."

"He is a houseguest at Longbourn?"

"My father's cousin and heir," said Elizabeth. "He is also stupid and servile, of suspect hygiene, and he seems to think I am the perfect woman to live with him at his parsonage, with his meddling termagant of a patroness watching our every move."

Charlotte laughed at Elizabeth's characterization. "He seems to be quite the specimen, Lizzy. I am anticipating making his acquaintance."

Unfortunately for Elizabeth's state of mind, that moment came much sooner than she would have wished. Before long, the man had joined her as she stood with Charlotte, his mouth full of little nothings and silly compliments.

Obliged, as she was, to dance the first with him, Elizabeth allowed herself to be led to the dance floor when the music floated over the company, expecting no pleasure in the ensuing half hour. She was not surprised, as such, when it turned out to be a disaster. Elizabeth did not know in what circumstances Mr. Collins had been raised, but his education on the dance floor was sadly lacking. He turned the wrong way, stepped on her toes more than once, and spent the entire dance apologizing for his ineptitude. When it was finally over, Elizabeth bolted from him, eager to be free of his odious company.

Matters improved after that, for Mr. Collins was distracted by the need to pay attention to the other young women in attendance. Though many were her friends, Elizabeth was not at all sorry that they were required to endure his civilities. Should the pain of his presence not be shared among them all?

For a time, Elizabeth lost herself in the pleasure of the evening. She had always been a popular partner at these events, and that evening was no different. Jane was enjoying herself with Mr. Bingley, and even Mary was seen to have stood up for more than a single dance. That one of those dances was with Mr. Collins, Elizabeth decided not to examine too closely. Even Kitty and Lydia, who had obviously dipped into the punch deeply and were behaving in a manner which was guaranteed to embarrass, could not diminish Elizabeth's enjoyment of the evening.

And so it continued until Elizabeth was once again approached by a man she might have expected to avoid the activity altogether. And when he bowed to her, his intentions were revealed.

"Miss Elizabeth, if you are not already engaged, will you dance the next with me?"

Feeling some asperity as to this man's continued ability to defy her attempts to sketch his character, Elizabeth, on the impulse of the moment, responded with teasing. "I do not know if it is wise, Mr. Darcy."

The man regarded her, perplexity written on his brow. "I do not understand."

"Why," said Elizabeth, "should we dance again, it would mark the second time we have danced since you arrived in the neighborhood. And as, by my count, you have danced with no other young lady not of your own party, those in attendance might consider us as good as engaged. You know what it is like in a small neighborhood such as this, do you not?"

Belatedly Elizabeth wondered if the man might be offended by her words, but Mr. Darcy only grinned. "Surely you overstate the matter, Miss Elizabeth. It is nothing more than a dance, after all."

"I see you possess a great fortitude then. If you are willing to endure what must ensue, I shall accept. But do not say I did not warn you."

His grin became wider, and the thought struck Elizabeth that while she had always thought him handsome, it was when he smiled that the true devastation of his looks was unleashed. She allowed him to take her hand, however, and soon they were engaged in the steps of the dance.

"I believe, Miss Elizabeth," said he a few moments later, "that you have a gift for hyperbole and a tendency to express positions contrary to your own."

Elizabeth laughed. "That is ungenerous, sir. Do you believe that nothing of truth passes my lips?"

"Indeed, not," replied Mr. Darcy. "You have a light disposition and a talent for putting others at ease. I have rarely seen your like in all my years in society."

Strangely flattered, Elizabeth turned away, grateful the dance had taken them apart, allowing her to regain her composure. When they met again several steps later, she thought she was better able to meet him with composure.

"I thank you for the compliment, sir, though I will own that I wonder at your making it."

"I do not flatter needlessly, Miss Elizabeth."

"Never would I have suspected you of it, sir," replied Elizabeth drily. Mr. Darcy seemed to understand, for he allowed a slight smile. "Rather, I believe that many would find my manners impertinent and not at all suitable for the higher echelons of the ton. Surely what you call a talent for putting others at ease, others would refer to as an unserious disposition. Such as Miss Bingley, for example."

"You will find, Miss Elizabeth," replied Mr. Darcy, his tone as dry as Elizabeth's had been before, "that my opinions rarely align with hers. If you will pardon my saying it, Miss Bingley does not know high society nearly so well as she believes. *She* has little experience there, and though I do not say it to aggrandize myself, her entrance therein is entirely because of her brother's friendship with me, and her place is tenuous, at best."

"I am not surprised to hear it, sir," replied Elizabeth. "Nevertheless, I thank you."

Mr. Darcy nodded, and they continued to dance, though silence had fallen between them. But it was not an awkward silence, one of those with each partner uncertain of what to say to the other. Rather, it was akin to that which ensues when all which must be said has been.

Toward the end of their dance, however, Elizabeth witnessed a strange change in Mr. Darcy's demeanor. Mr. Darcy was, though not precisely genial, at least good-humored as they continued to dance. But suddenly, as they made a pass by each other, he stumbled slightly before continuing the form, and when he was standing across from her, his gaze was fixed on a point across the room. Perhaps the strangest thing was his countenance, which had been pleasant, was now overset with a coldness the likes of which Elizabeth had never before seen.

"Is everything well, Mr. Darcy?" asked Elizabeth as she turned her head, attempting to catch sight of whatever had disturbed him.

Mr. Darcy started, but he quickly recovered. "Yes, Miss Elizabeth. Everything is quite well."

Though Elizabeth gazed at him, doubtful of his assertion, she knew not to press the matter. The set ended only a few minutes later, and Mr. Darcy, taking her hand, led her to the side of the room. There he left her with a hurried bow and a murmured apology. Elizabeth could not understand what had happened to induce such a sudden change in him.

There was nothing for it, however, so she continued to enjoy the evening as much as she was able amid her swirling thoughts. Her next partner came and collected her, and for a time she was lost again in the movements and conversations in which she was engaged.

Later, toward the supper hour, Elizabeth was approached by one of the officers, a Lieutenant Denny by name. Though the man was a great favorite of Lydia and Kitty, Elizabeth did not know him well, only having exchanged a few words with him. By his side stood another man of the militia, his insignia showing him to be of equal rank. But this man was unknown to her.

"Miss Bennet," said the lieutenant, flashing her a grin. "My friend here has requested an introduction to you if you will allow it."

"Of course, Mr. Denny," said Elizabeth, looking to his companion with interest. He was tall, slender, dark of hair and eye, and was, outside of Mr. Darcy, possibly the handsomest man she had ever seen.

"Mr. George Wickham, my friend, lately of London. Wickham, please allow me to introduce Miss Elizabeth Bennet of Longbourn."

"Have you been with the regiment long, Mr. Wickham?" asked Elizabeth. "I do not believe I have seen you at any other gathering."

"I have only been here for a few days, Miss Bennet," replied Mr. Wickham. Even his manner was gentlemanly and his voice melodious. "This is the first event of society in which I have partaken. It is fortunate that Mr. Bingley issued a general invitation to the officers, else I should not have had the opportunity to attend this evening."

"That is fortunate, indeed," replied Elizabeth. "But even had he not, I am sure Mr. Bingley would not have protested your presence. He is a man fond of company, and a note asking for your inclusion would have been successful, no doubt."

"I have every confidence in Mr. Bingley's congeniality," replied Mr. Wickham. "But I do not like to beg for my inclusion in such things. It makes one seem grasping. Do you not agree?"

"I suppose it could be construed in such a way, though I doubt one would believe it of you. But welcome anyway. I hope you have enjoyed your time in Meryton, however brief it has been."

"Everything has been lovely, and the people most obliging. I have made several acquaintances already, including your sisters, I believe. I am quite charmed by everything I have experienced."

They talked for several more moments about nothing in particular. Mr. Wickham, Elizabeth discovered, possessed the ability to speak of any subject and make it seem like the most interesting thing in the world. Mr. Denny, though he stood with them for a short time, soon bowed and left, looking for other amusement. Mr. Wickham then asked Elizabeth to dance, and though her next set was spoken for, she was pleased to offer the one after. When her next partner came to collect her, she spent the entire dance anticipating the next with Mr. Wickham, and as such, found it difficult to focus.

It was only a few moments into her dance with Mr. Wickham when he leaned toward her during a pass in the steps and spoke in a low voice: "It seems we have drawn an audience to us, Miss Bennet."

Elizabeth followed his gesture with her eyes, and she caught sight of Mr. Darcy. It was clear that he was, indeed, watching them and, furthermore, if the scowl he directed at them was any indication, he was not pleased with what he saw. It was another facet to add to the already difficult Mr. Darcy. She could not understand him; why would he care who she chose to accept an offer to dance? Or was he displeased that *she* was dancing with Mr. Wickham?

"Ah, Darcy," said Mr. Wickham, his tone carrying hints of sad amusement. "I see he is putting his best foot forward, as he usually does in most neighborhoods he visits." Mr. Wickham was obviously attempting to put a humorous note in what he was saying, though the sarcasm was clear for Elizabeth to hear. "Unfortunately, I have never known him to behave any other way."

"You know Mr. Darcy?" asked Elizabeth.

"All of my life, in fact. You could not search for someone who has more knowledge of the Darcy family than I."

"That is interesting, sir. When I caught sight of him just now, it seemed to me he was displeased about something."

"When is Darcy not displeased? Sometimes I think it is his purpose to go through life being discontented about everything. He is not at all popular in town, you know, for the majority of those in society consider him to be unapproachable and proud."

Elizabeth digested Mr. Wickham's words with a sense of astonishment, tempered by the fact that she had just made his acquaintance and knew nothing of his character. Surely she had been confused about Mr. Darcy, and she had seen some of Mr. Wickham's assertions in her own study of the man. But he was not always thus.

"I see I have confounded you, Miss Bennet," said Mr. Wickham, drawing her attention back to him. "In fact, I am sure you are aware, at least a little, of Darcy's position in society. His connections are such that few will risk his displeasure openly. But trust me when I say that he is not well liked at all in town."

With a shake of her head, Elizabeth glared at her dance partner. "I do not know why you are telling me this, Mr. Wickham. What is it to me if Mr. Darcy is praised or reviled in society?"

A mournful expression came over Mr. Wickham's face. "I do apologize, Miss Bennet. I have done it again, it seems. I try to tell myself over and over that I should not speak of Darcy when I have nothing good to say of him. But my outrage overcomes my determination, and I cannot stay silent. Had his offenses been confined to poor behavior in society, I might have been able to ignore them. But the wounds between us are simply too deep."

In spite of herself, Elizabeth was interested. But she would not ask, for she knew it was not proper. It seemed, however, that Mr. Wickham had little compunction in sharing his woe, for he allowed only the time in which they separated due to the dance steps before he once again spoke.

"You see, Miss Bennet, I was to have received a valuable living from the Darcy family by the express wish of his father. But while Darcy knew of it — had been informed by his father — he chose to withhold it from me. Thus, I am as you see me now — forced to make my way in the world, when my future should have been secure."

Elizabeth gasped. "But had you no hope of satisfaction in the law?"

"The elder Mr. Darcy trusted his son, Miss Bennet," was Mr. Wickham's somber reply. "As such, the matter was only referred to obliquely in his will. A man who had not heard of it from his father's lips or chose to misinterpret what was written therein might do so without anything to deter him."

"But surely an appeal to him would bear fruit. I am sorry, Mr. Wickham, but while I am nothing more than a minor acquaintance to Mr. Darcy, I have always thought him strict in his adherence to duty. If his father wished you to have the living, I cannot suppose Mr. Darcy would not know. And if he knew of it, I would think him honor bound to act in accordance to his father's instructions."

"Dear Miss Bennet," said Mr. Wickham, "it seems you know little of the world of great men. Those such as Darcy are accustomed to having whatever they want. Darcy is only bound by duty when he feels it is worth his while to be so bound. I am nothing to him — merely an annoyance with whom he would prefer to dispense. Furthermore, Darcy is well aware of which of us his father preferred. All these things motivate him to push me as far from his life as possible."

Elizabeth was skeptical. Though she had never had the highest opinion of Mr. Darcy, she had never thought him malicious. Mr. Wickham's words painted the picture of a corrupt character, indeed. Furthermore, there was the question of why he was saying this to her now. It was hardly a subject to be canvassed less than an hour after making one's acquaintance!

Before she could reply, however, a disturbance appeared on the far side of the dance floor near the main entrance. She could hear the sound of raised voices, and wondered what it could mean.

Chapter IV

The sight of George Wickham at Bingley's ball surprised and disgusted Darcy. The sight of Wickham dancing with Miss Elizabeth Bennet made Darcy want to call the libertine out. It was not enough he had left Georgiana a broken girl, depressed and silent, but he now intruded on Darcy's presence yet again. Was it by chance or design? Darcy could not say, but he had learned never to discount Wickham's ability to cause havoc wherever he went.

While Darcy watched, he could see that the man was likely plying Miss Elizabeth with the story of his history with the Darcy family — or at least his version of it, which contained enough truth mixed with falsehood to mislead the unwary. Darcy thought Miss Elizabeth was intelligent enough to separate the truth from the falsehood. But he could not be certain. As such, Darcy determined to find Miss Elizabeth after the dance, if only to ensure she was not caught unaware of George Wickham's true character.

Subsequent events, however, rendered Darcy's resolve impossible. For as the dance was coming to a close and Darcy was considering how he might approach her, a disturbance arose at the entrance to the ballroom, and he could hear a strident voice over the music. It was a voice he knew well.

"Where is Darcy? Where is my nephew? I will see him at once."

How the blazes had Lady Catherine known where to find him? And why had she come? Lady Catherine was entirely capable of insulting everyone in attendance within moments of her arrival. Thus Darcy sought her out immediately, intent upon silencing whatever tirade she had come to deliver.

A ring of gawkers and whispering masses had formed around the lady's entrance, and while the woman looked this way and that, demanded in her loudest voice and most offensive tones for his attendance, she seemed to have insulted no one yet. And when Darcy forced himself free of those who were standing and whispering, he noted Fitzwilliam's presence by her side. A sigh of relief escaped his mouth, for he knew his cousin would be a great help in controlling her.

"I am here, Lady Catherine," said Darcy, approaching her and fixing her with a frown. It would be necessary to ensure she did not see a crack in his armor, for if she did, she would strike with the ruthlessness and precision of a master swordsman. "Why have you interrupted my friend's ball?"

"Why?" demanded Lady Catherine. "Why, indeed. I should have thought you would know in an instant why I have come."

"Yes, Darcy," said Fitzwilliam, smirking in his insufferable way. "Why else would your aunt travel miles and miles at night on the hunt for you? I cannot imagine that you cannot guess her purpose."

"Really, Fitzwilliam," said Lady Catherine testily. "This is not helping."

For perhaps the first time in his life, Darcy found himself agreeing with his aunt, a most curious sensation, to be certain. But Lady Catherine was already speaking before Darcy could think to answer.

"I have come to protect my daughter's interests, of course! I received word only two days ago that there was some Jezebel in residence here who is attempting to distract you from your duty. It cannot be allowed!"

"Let us move this conversation to another location," said Darcy, frustration with his aunt threatening to make him lose his temper. "There is no reason for us to declare our family's private business where all may overhear."

It was a wonder that Lady Catherine allowed Darcy to lead her away. Usually, she would not have worried about the opinions of others, one reason why her brother, who abhorred scandal, could not tolerate the woman. Darcy caught Bingley's eye, and when his friend nodded toward a parlor not far from the ballroom, he made for it, being certain to close the door behind him. Or at least he attempted to do so, for the person of the woman's toadying parson was at the door and called out to Lady Catherine before Darcy could shut the door.

"Mr. Collins!" cried Lady Catherine. "Come in here at once."

"Yes, your ladyship," said the groveling parson. He scampered toward her, bowing every two or three steps, mumbling words of obedience and praise which were quite unnecessary to the situation. "I am here, your ladyship."

"I can see you are," said Lady Catherine, her voice hard and unfriendly. "Now, Mr. Collins—did you or did you not inform me that a young lady of the neighborhood was usurping my daughter's position?"

Darcy glared at the man, and Mr. Collins licked his lips, seeming to feel the heat of it. "I do not think I put it precisely in that fashion, your ladyship."

"You claimed he was on the verge of losing his head over one of your cousins! How can this be misunderstood?"

"I believe, your ladyship, that I only . . . That is to say . . ."

"Your foolish parson has led you here under false pretenses, Lady Catherine," said Darcy, glaring at the parson. "I am not courting anyone, nor have I fixed my attention on any young woman. You are wasting your time, and you have brought infamy on the family for no purpose at all."

"Is this true, Mr. Collins?" asked Lady Catherine, eyes narrowed. The parson appeared too frightened to move. "Well?"

"I would not say that, Lady Catherine. Mr. Darcy seemed quite close, indeed, to my cousin when he visited, and he danced with her this very evening. It is my understanding that she is the only young lady of the neighborhood with whom he has danced since coming to Hertfordshire. Since she is to be my intended, I was concerned."

"It sounds as if your parson used what he knew of your wishes for Darcy to remove whatever competition he might have thought he had for the hand of the fair maiden." Fitzwilliam snorted, his look at Mr. Collins contemptuous.

The very thought of this odious toad making love to a jewel like Miss Elizabeth filled Darcy's throat with bile. But he mastered himself and focused on Lady Catherine, ignoring the ineffectual parson.

"Nothing has occurred between Mr. Collins's cousin and myself, Lady Catherine. Yes, I have danced with her, but I have given her no special notice, nor has she sought it. As Fitzwilliam said, it seems your parson has played on your well-known eagerness to broker a marriage between Anne and me."

Lady Catherine regarded him, suspicion alive in her eyes. In front of her, Mr. Collins had broken out into a sweat, but while he appeared eager to speak and defend himself, one glance from Lady Catherine silenced him.

"Then I have your word that you do not mean to offer for this woman."

"Is my word required?" asked Darcy, fatigued already by this woman's presence. "I am my own man, Lady Catherine, and may act as I see fit."

"You are engaged to *my* daughter." Lady Catherine's tone might have shattered bricks.

Though he did not wish to incite an argument here of all places, Darcy was not about to allow his aunt to assert such things when she had repeatedly been told that Darcy had no intention of marrying Anne. Anne was no more amenable to the suggestion than Darcy was himself.

"Please desist, Lady Catherine. You are well aware that no betrothal agreement exists. My father denied your request when you asked. I am *not* engaged to Anne, nor will I ever be, by her will and mine. I will not speak on this matter again."

While he might have expected an explosion of temper, Lady Catherine only glared at him. He knew she was attempting to gain the upper hand and cow him, as she might have done when he had been naught but a lad. But Darcy was a man full grown and had faced down those who were much more fearsome than his elderly aunt. It was a confrontation she would not win, though she likely possessed supreme confidence in her ultimate victory.

"Mr. Collins," said she, turning to the parson, "it seems you were not overstating the danger. For your actions, I thank you heartily."

"Of course, Lady Catherine," said Mr. Collins, sounding like he was about to faint with relief. "I am your humble servant, as always."

A regal nod was the lady's answer, after which she turned back to Darcy. "Since it is clear I must stay and sort this matter out, you will inform your friend I require two rooms—one for myself and one for Anne."

"You brought Anne, and you left her in the carriage?" demanded Darcy.

"Of course not," snapped Lady Catherine. "Anne is resting in a chamber not far from the entrance, as the journey fatigued her excessively."

Darcy shook his head. "I will ask Bingley, but I believe you will need to depart in the morning."

"I am not leaving until I have the assurances I require. If I cannot obtain them from you, then I shall have them from your little paramour."

With those final words, Lady Catherine let herself from the room, Mr. Collins following behind her like an obedient dog. Darcy watched her go, wishing for what seemed like the thousandth time that he was not connected to her. His sainted mother had been fond of her, but she had become much more irascible and unreasonable as she had aged.

"Am I to meet this wondrous creature to whom you have lost your heart?" asked Fitzwilliam. Darcy turned and glared at his cousin, which prompted nothing more than a responding grin. "Or at least your head, anyway."

"What is your role in this farce, Fitzwilliam?" asked Darcy, ignoring his cousin's intended witticism.

Fitzwilliam shrugged in his usually insouciant way. "Lady Catherine entered my father's house this morning as if she were a northern gale, screeching of betrayal, disloyalty, and treachery, and demanding his assistance. You know Father—he responded to her demands in as insulting a language as possible and flatly refused to interfere in your affairs. Lady Catherine held some hope of persuading him, even in the face of this, but by late this afternoon, even she was forced to acknowledge defeat.

"I only came along to protect Anne. Since Lady Catherine was essentially frothing at the mouth, I thought it likely she would kill her daughter with neglect in her zeal to prevent your marriage to another woman."

Darcy sighed. "I truly wish you had managed to detain her for another day. It is a deuced inconvenience to Bingley to have her here. You know his origins. She will offend both Bingley and his sisters within an hour of making their acquaintance."

"On the contrary, old man," replied Fitzwilliam, "I suggest you *owe* me for my assistance. You have not spent the past five hours in a carriage with Lady Catherine ranting the entire distance. There were times when I considered the merits of simply throwing her from the conveyance and driving on."

Darcy could not help but chuckle at Fitzwilliam's jests, though there was truly nothing of this situation about which to laugh. Trust his cousin to always see the humorous side of any trouble and see that Darcy laughed about it at least once.

"I'll see you are shown to a room, Fitzwilliam. I am certain you are fatigued."

"I am quite well, indeed. In fact, I think I shall attend the rest of the ball if Bingley will allow it. I am quite curious about this neighborhood, for I understand there are some beauties in residence."

Fitzwilliam grinned and slapped Darcy on the back. "Perhaps I shall find that elusive heiress for whom I have been searching these past years."

A snort was Darcy's response. "Then you will hope in vain. There is little wealth to be found in this neighborhood."

"Then I suppose I shall simply enjoy the company."

With a hand on Darcy's shoulder, Fitzwilliam exited the room, leaving Darcy by himself. He did not know how he could manage to keep Lady Catherine from offending everyone in the neighborhood. At least that evening she seemed intent upon finding the bed in her room. Thank heavens for small miracles.

After Elizabeth made her escape from Mr. Wickham—and escape it was, as the man's tale had made her decidedly uncomfortable in his presence—Elizabeth made her way closer to the door in an attempt to discover the reason for the sudden furor. In this, however, she was disappointed, as whatever had caused it had disappeared. Many who had been in the vicinity were now gossiping about the matter, but she had no time to stop and listen to gossip.

"You should have seen it, Lizzy!" cried Lydia a few moments later. It seemed her youngest sister had also been nearby, though Lydia's account must be considered suspect. "It was a grand lady who entered the room, followed by another man. She demanded to see Mr. Darcy and fairly insisted on his attendance when he could not immediately be found."

"And did Mr. Darcy appear?" asked Elizabeth. In fact, she already suspected the identity of the lady, though she could not say anything about her reason for coming in such a state.

"Yes. Between them, the two gentlemen led the lady from the room. They have not returned yet."

At that moment, one of Lydia's favorites among the officers approached, and Lydia lost all interest in gossiping with her elder sister. Soon she darted away with him, laughing in a raucous fashion, creating a scene wherever she went. Elizabeth grimaced, wondering yet again if there was some way to restrain the girl. Perhaps Mr. Bingley had some rope she could use.

The dinner hour was soon upon them, and as Elizabeth had been busy with her sister, she was not available to be asked to dance it, and it had not been previously secured. As such, she watched the dancing, swaying along with the music, and avoiding Mr. Collins when he came too close to her. She did not have a partner when she stepped into the dining room for dinner and was thus content to sit near Jane and Mr. Bingley, enjoying their closeness. At the same time, she tried not to fix Mr. Bingley's sisters with a smug grin—it was apparent they were not enjoying the scene as much as Elizabeth was herself.

During dinner, the talk mostly centered around the appearance of the lady, and Elizabeth heard no less than ten theories as to why she had come. Her mother was as engaged in speculation as any of the other ladies. At least she was not crowing about Jane's good fortune or her expectations for the rest of her progeny.

It was not until after dinner that Elizabeth saw Mr. Darcy again, and when she did, he was with another man. His companion was a veritable mountain of a man, standing taller than Mr. Darcy, with broader shoulders, and thick, powerful arms. He was dressed in the typical suit of a gentleman, but he carried himself erect as a soldier. And while he was not so handsome as Mr. Darcy, he appeared good-humored, and she soon discovered his mode of address was most definitely that of a gentleman.

"Miss Elizabeth," said Mr. Darcy, leading the other man toward her. "My cousin has requested an introduction to you."

It seemed to Elizabeth that Mr. Darcy was performing this duty as if he was being led to the gallows, and she wondered at it. Was she so much of an embarrassment that he would not have wished to introduce her to anyone in his family? Elizabeth forced such a thought away and determined not to judge him, not knowing what he was about, and gave her consent.

"Fitzwilliam, this is Miss Elizabeth Bennet, a resident of Longbourn estate which lies directly to the west of Netherfield. Miss Elizabeth, my cousin Colonel Anthony Fitzwilliam, the second son of my uncle, the Earl of Matlock."

Elizabeth curtseyed to Colonel Fitzwilliam's bow, bemused at her introduction to the son of an earl. To the best of her knowledge, she had never known anyone of such an exalted state.

"Miss Bennet," said Colonel Fitzwilliam, bowing over her hand, "it is my pleasure and honor to make your acquaintance. I hope you are enjoying the ball this evening."

"I am, sir," replied Elizabeth. "But then again, is not an opportunity for fine food and drink at no cost to be relished?"

Colonel Fitzwilliam caught the teasing tone in her voice and guffawed. Even Mr. Darcy shook his head, a grin readily apparent, before excusing himself.

"You must know I meant enjoyment in the company."

"Then yes, I have no complaints, Colonel. These people are all dear to me, for I was raised among them."

"They are *all* dear to you?" asked the colonel, his raised brow suggesting he did not believe her. "Surely there are some amongst their number whose company you could do without."

"Oh, you are quite correct there," said Elizabeth, catching sight of Mr. Collins. Colonel Fitzwilliam noted her look and his gaze followed hers. Mr. Collins had been watching them with some exasperation when the colonel shot a glare at him. It seemed Mr. Collins was unable to withstand such displeasure, for he immediately fled.

"I find I must agree with you, Miss Bennet," said Colonel Fitzwilliam. "I have spent a matter of five minutes in Mr. Collins's company. I dare say he is entirely disagreeable."

"You do not know the half of it, Colonel," replied Elizabeth.

Grinning, the colonel leaned in and said: "I do not suppose you are an heiress, are you? I have been looking for one for these many years, and if you possess even a moderate fortune, I believe you will do very well, indeed."

"I am afraid not," replied Elizabeth, allowing a mournful note in her tone. "I am naught but the second daughter of five of a country gentleman. I dare say the son of an earl would expect fifty thousand, at least, and I, unfortunately, have only a fraction of that."

"Then I suppose a dance will have to do," replied Colonel Fitzwilliam, grinning once again. "If you will agree to it."

Elizabeth was entirely willing to dance with such a charming man, and soon he had led her to the floor. They spoke in a lively and sportive fashion throughout the first part of their sets together, much as they had when they were standing beside the dance floor. The colonel, Elizabeth decided, was a man she would like to have as a friend, for he was gregarious, always ready with a jest, and well able to make her laugh. Some time passed before their conversation became more serious.

"I am surprised you are here," said Elizabeth as they stepped around each other. "I do not recall your presence at the beginning of the ball."

"That is because I was not present. Surely you noted the late arrival of a rather loud and demanding guest?"

"I will own I remember something of that sort occurring," allowed Elizabeth. "But I apologize. I had not meant to pry."

"It is no trouble, Miss Bennet. In fact, it is providential that we have had this conversation, for I should warn you, as it will likely affect you in the future."

"How could it possibly affect me?" asked Elizabeth, quite perplexed as to his meaning. There was no jesting in Colonel Fitzwilliam's manner, and he regarded her with some appraisal. Elizabeth bore his scrutiny as best she was able, though she wondered at it. Had Mr. Darcy told him something of her of which he did not approve? She could not imagine him speaking to her in censure after so short an acquaintance.

"Your cousin, Mr. Collins, it seems, saw something in Darcy's behavior toward you and warned his patroness, who, as you must know, is Lady Catherine de Bourgh, aunt to Darcy and myself."

"Something in his behavior?" echoed Elizabeth, not understanding any more than she had a moment before. "Mr. Darcy has been kind in speaking to me on occasion, but there has not been anything else between us. And how could it affect your aunt?"

"It seems you are missing a crucial piece of information, Miss Bennet," replied Colonel Fitzwilliam. "You see, Lady Catherine has asserted for many years that Darcy is engaged to her daughter, Anne."

Elizabeth grimaced. "You have clarified matters admirably, sir. When Mr. Darcy came to Longbourn the day after Mr. Collins's arrival, I did share some conversation with your cousin. Mr. Collins, as he is a zealous supplicant of your aunt—"

"Lost no time in informing her ladyship," finished Colonel Fitzwilliam.

"Idiot," muttered Elizabeth, prompting Colonel Fitzwilliam to laugh. "I had wondered why he felt it necessary to send a letter to your aunt, even walking to Meryton in the pouring rain to ensure its delivery."

"Indeed," replied the colonel, still smirking at her epithet toward the ineffectual parson. "Lady Catherine can tolerate no hint of Darcy's interest to another woman, and, as such, she hastened here to 'protect her daughter's interests.' As I happened to be at my father's house when she came and was on leave, I decided to accompany her, thinking I could render Darcy assistance."

"I am certain your offer is much appreciated, Colonel," said a distracted Elizabeth. This Lady Catherine would be difficult to tolerate, Elizabeth knew, especially since she had a reason—created out of whole cloth by her stupid parson—to suspect Elizabeth of ulterior motives. At least she was not in residence in the same house as the virago.

"So, I suppose I should ask you now," said Fitzwilliam. Elizabeth could hear the hilarity in his tone. "*Do* you have designs on my cousin?"

Elizabeth directed a saucy wink at him, prompting his chortle again. "I cannot inform you of that, now can I, Colonel? No lady likes to forewarn one who might be in opposition."

"I dare say Darcy deserves you, Miss Bennet." The colonel shook his head and wiped at his eyes. "He requires a lively lady to keep him on his toes, and I am certain you would be good for him."

"Colonel!" gasped Elizabeth. "Do you not think you should refrain? I already have no good expectations of your aunt's behavior."

"Do not worry, Miss Bennet. I do possess *some* discretion. I cannot say anything about my cousin's feelings on the subject, but he is a good man. You will find no better testimony of his character, for we have been friends since our childhoods."

A flustered Elizabeth could think of nothing to say, so she blurted the first thing that came to her mind: "Even better than childhood companions?"

A quizzical look was the colonel's response. "Have you met any who claim to be Darcy's childhood friend?"

"One," replied Elizabeth, now wishing she had not said anything. "There is a Mr. Wickham in attendance tonight, and though he had much to say of Mr. Darcy, it was not nearly as complimentary as what you have said."

In an instant, Elizabeth witnessed Colonel Fitzwilliam's genial countenance turn from bright sunlight to the darkest night. He seemed to feel some great anger, which he masked with some effort.

"And is Wickham here now?"

Elizabeth shook her head. "I do not know, sir. I have not seen him since before supper."

Colonel Fitzwilliam nodded. "I will attempt to find him, for where George Wickham goes, devilry must not be far behind. Do not give heed to his assertions, Miss Bennet, for the infamous behavior is all on Wickham's side."

With a nod, Elizabeth returned her mind to the steps of the dance, and within a few more moments, it had ended. The colonel escorted her to the side of the dance floor, and with a short bow, he excused himself. And then he was gone.

The evening continued, and as all things must end, so too did the ball come to a close. Elizabeth had not seen Colonel Fitzwilliam again that evening, nor had she caught sight of Mr. Wickham, which she suspected must be to the man's benefit. Of Mr. Darcy, she had only caught a glimpse. Also absent was Lady Catherine, for it seemed that she had decided to retire upon arriving, which was just as well, in Elizabeth's opinion.

One by one, the carriages of those in attendance were brought around, and Elizabeth's friends and neighbors departed. As the dwindling company waited for their conveyances, Elizabeth began to wonder when their carriage would come. A glance out the front doors showed that a heavy bank of fog had descended upon Hertfordshire, and she knew that if they did not begin soon, the hour would become truly late, and the fog would make travel hazardous.

A few minutes later, Phelps, Longbourn's driver, entered the house and made his way to Mr. Bennet for a whispered conference with him. Mr. Bennet listened gravely as the man spoke, his countenance betraying none of his thoughts. Not far from Elizabeth, she noted Mr. Bingley's sisters standing, clearly wishing them to be gone. As the last guests other than the Bennets departed, leaving them alone with the Netherfield family, Miss Bingley raised a hand to her face and produced a most prodigious yawn.

"I am so fatigued!" complained she to Mrs. Hurst, a clear and less than proper method of advising them all that their presence was no longer wanted.

"Mr. Bingley," said Mr. Bennet, rising from his conference with Longbourn's driver. Mr. Bingley looked up from his conversation with Jane. "It seems we have a problem. My carriage has developed a fault and will be quite unable to convey us to our home."

"Then let us call our carriage, Charles," said Miss Bingley, with more urgency than tact. "It can see the Bennets home readily."

"It will take some time for the carriage to be taken out of storage and the team made ready," replied Mr. Bingley. "I think it might be best to invite the Bennets to stay the night. They can then return to their home in our carriage tomorrow."

"Surely there is no call for that!" exclaimed Miss Bingley. At the same time, Mr. Bennet voiced his objections, stating: "We would not wish to intrude, especially after you have provided such excellent entertainment tonight."

"Nonsense!" said Mr. Bingley, choosing to ignore his sister for the moment. Miss Bingley was not insensible of it and clearly fumed that her brother was answering Mr. Bennet instead of herself. "It is hardly your fault that your carriage is having trouble tonight." He turned his eyes toward his sister, and they hardened slightly. "I am certain Caroline joins me in inviting your family to stay the night. It is the sensible thing to do, especially if any of us wish to find our beds before sunrise."

Though it was evident she was unamused, Miss Bingley sighed and conceded the point. "I suppose it does make sense. I will speak to the housekeeper. Fortunately, I have several rooms kept at the ready for visitors."

Thus, it was done. The housekeeper was summoned and assured them the rooms would be ready in a matter of minutes. A footman was sent to Longbourn to return with a selection of clothing for those staying the night. Then, an assortment of nightgowns for the ladies and bedclothes for Mr. Bennet and Mr. Collins were procured, and soon they were making their way above stairs to their rooms. Outside, Elizabeth noted through one of the windows that a few snowflakes had begun to fall. She hoped it did not amount to anything more than that. She had no wish to stay at Netherfield any longer than required.

CHAPTER V

"Oh, Louisa!" cried Caroline when they were finally alone in her room. "It is in every way horrible! Not only must we host those awful Bennets the night after enduring the entire neighborhood, but now Mr. Darcy's odious aunt has descended upon us as well."

A small part of Louisa Hurst's mind was amused at her sister, and she could not help but say: "To say nothing of Colonel Fitzwilliam's presence as well."

"Ugh. Do not remind me. He may be respectable as the son of an earl, but his flippant manners are absolutely dreadful."

Louisa nodded in commiseration, though in the back of her mind, she wondered at their hubris. Lady Catherine and Colonel Fitzwilliam were members of an old and well-placed family, nobility at its very finest. Caroline had hopes of attaching herself to the family, after all, by way of marriage to Mr. Darcy. But Louisa knew Caroline detested Lady Catherine because of that ridiculous cradle betrothal story and because the lady had denigrated their connections during their only previous meeting. As for the colonel, well Louisa could not imagine many of high society behaved in the same way he did.

"I do not suppose we will be successful in luring Charles back to town tomorrow with Lady Catherine in residence," said Louisa.

"I wonder why she came at all. She has never cared for our association with Mr. Darcy in the past."

Louisa knew that was not quite true. She knew that Lady Catherine had protested Mr. Darcy's friendship with Charles before, and she would not be surprised if she continued to voice objection to it whenever she had the chance. The fact of the matter was that she did not consider the Bingleys a threat to her precious daughter.

"At least we will be rid of the Bennets tomorrow," said Caroline. "If we can, we must induce Lady Catherine to leave and return to London ourselves."

"Or you may lose Mr. Darcy," added Louisa. "He seems to be more approving of Miss Elizabeth every day."

Caroline only snorted. "Mr. Darcy's discernment is far too developed to be taken in by the likes of Miss Eliza Bennet. I have no fear that she might be set up as a rival."

Though Louisa was not so sure of that, Caroline had taken up the brandy decanter and poured herself a glass. Louisa could not abide her sister's drinking the foul beverage, so she excused herself at once.

"Cheer up, Sister," said she, a last word of encouragement to the sister with whom she had always been so close. "I am certain something will present itself. We will remove Charles somehow."

Louisa did not know if Caroline made any response, for she turned and quickly let herself out of the room. When she obtained the sanctuary of her bedchamber, she sighed and threw her dressing gown over a chair, making her way to the bed. As she lay down, she could see little balls of ice impacting the windows, and she was lulled to sleep by the faint sound which reached her ears.

"You did not tell me that Wickham was here," said Fitzwilliam, his tone accusatory.

Darcy frowned. "It had quite fled my mind," replied he. "I was not even aware of his presence until earlier this evening."

"What could he be doing here?" asked Fitzwilliam as he paced the room. They had gathered for a bit of strategic planning after the guests—other than the Bennets, of course—had departed. The question about Wickham was the first topic of discussion his cousin had raised. "Do you think it likely he followed you here to cause more trouble?"

"I doubt it," replied Darcy. "He was in London those months after Ramsgate, as you know. Though I have had him discretely watched, I have not looked into his doings. Regardless, he was wearing the scarlet of the militia, so I assume he joined the regiment in Meryton, though I cannot fathom how he might have obtained the funds to purchase the commission."

A slow smile spread over Fitzwilliam's face, and it was not at all pleasant. "Well, well. Who would have thought you had it in you, Georgy Porgy? This is an opportunity to finally control him. It is possible I can use my influence to have him transferred to the front lines in Spain. I have no doubt our Georgy would look good with a French bullet adorning his gut.

"As long as he leaves me and mine be, I am quite content to return the favor," said Darcy.

"That is the problem, Darcy, if you will forgive my saying so. Sentimentality colors your perception when you consider that libertine. He has already begun to try to defame your name in this town."

"Oh?" asked Darcy, though his mind was on other matters. "It is not as if I shall be here long."

"And it does not concern you that his chosen target is none other than Miss Elizabeth Bennet?"

Darcy tried not to react, but his cousin's snort told him that it was an abject failure.

"Oh, yes," continued Fitzwilliam. "I know not what he told her, but it seems Miss Elizabeth had the sense to at least question his tale. I informed her that she should not believe anything Wickham said, but I am unknown to her. It would be best if you informed her of enough to allow her to defend herself and her family."

"I will not betray Georgiana's secret."

"I was not asking you to do so. Of course, you wish to protect Georgiana, and I might bludgeon you about the head if you spoke of Ramsgate to anyone not in the family. But Wickham's sins are enough that even a vague description of them should be enough to put her on her guard."

"Very well," replied Darcy. "I shall consider it."

Fitzwilliam put his feet up on the table between their two chairs. He sighed and rubbed his eyes, and then he gave a great yawn.

"I attempted to find Wickham after my dance with Miss Elizabeth, but I suspect he must have departed. In the morning I shall ride to Meryton and speak with his commanding officer. That should be enough to put a spike in old Georgy's wheel."

"Do you know the man?"

A snort was Fitzwilliam's response. "The militia officers' ranks are filled with men who have no stomach for war, and little in their heads but a pretty face and a gambling table. But *some* of the regiment commanders are decent men. Should the colonel of *this* regiment be of the other ilk, at least he will know that Wickham's actions could seriously affect his position and future advancement. If I must, I may take certain steps myself."

Again Darcy was uncomfortable with the direction of Fitzwilliam's thoughts. Wickham had been a thorn in his side as long as he could remember, but he *had* been raised and educated under the auspices of the Darcy family. In a way, that made him a Darcy family responsibility. Darcy would rather see him shipped off to Botany Bay or the Americas than see him in Fitzwilliam's sights. That sounded too much like murder for his taste. In the back of his mind, Darcy mulled over the story of King David, wondering if sending Wickham to Spain would make him no better than the ancient King of Israel.

"Well, I think I am for bed," said Fitzwilliam. "I bid you good night, Darcy."

Fitzwilliam stood, but as he was making his way toward the door, he glanced out the window. Darcy's eyes followed his gaze, and he noticed a buildup of snow around the bottom corners. Fitzwilliam drew closer to the window, as Darcy extinguished the candles, and peered out over the countryside.

"It seems the light snow that started as the ball ended has become something much more substantial. If this should continue, we shall be snowed in."

Darcy groaned. Snowed in with not only Lady Catherine, but Miss Bingley as well? What could possibly be worse?

It might have been the unfamiliarity of the bed or her surroundings. It might have been the knowledge that not only was she to be the focus of Lady Catherine de Bourgh's displeasure, but now she was staying in the same house as the virago. It might have only been the fact that the night had been full and Elizabeth's mind was, consequently, not prepared for sleep. Whatever the case, she found that her eyes remained stubbornly open after being shown to her room.

Reaching down, Elizabeth itched a location on her leg, thinking ruefully that it might be this nightgown she had been given. The size of it suggested that it belonged to Louisa Hurst, though Elizabeth thought, with asperity, the woman might now prefer to burn it, given how it had adorned the unfashionable Miss Elizabeth Bennet that night. She would not put it past either of the supercilious women.

After some time of this, Elizabeth gave up every thought of sleeping. Instead, she rose and took the dressing gown, intent upon finding the library. Surely there would be a book which would hold her interest long enough for her to become fatigued enough to find sleep. A light under the door of the room next to hers changed Elizabeth's mind, and she knocked, entering when the word was given. Elizabeth did not even notice the eyes watching her as she padded down Netherfield's hallway late that evening.

"Jane, dearest," said Elizabeth when she had entered the room and closed the door behind her. Jane was sitting up in the bed, but her mind was clearly far away, her gaze focused on some spot through the window. "Why are you still awake?"

"I might ask the same of you, Lizzy," said Jane, turning a smile on her younger sister.

Elizabeth did not hesitate in joining her sister on the bed, grasping one of her hands between her own. "Oh, I do not know that our reasons are precisely the same," said Elizabeth in a teasing tone. "I, after all, do not have a handsome man in the palm of my hand, paying me every possible deference." Even in the dim light of the single candle, Elizabeth could see her sister color. "But I could not sleep either. I do not know what prevents me, but I do not feel even a hint of desire for sleep."

"Then shall we share confidences under the moonlight?" asked Jane. "It has been some time since we stayed awake in such a fashion."

"And perhaps we will not have many opportunities in the future," replied Elizabeth.

Once again Jane ducked her head, but they were both surprised by a knock on the door. Elizabeth looked at Jane, who returned her query with a shrug. Rather than call out permission to enter, Elizabeth rose and went to the door. But when she opened it, she found a woman she had never before met on the other side.

"You are Miss Elizabeth Bennet, are you not?" said the other woman, timidity in her tone and posture.

"I am. May I help you?"

"I am Anne de Bourgh. I noticed you came in here not long ago and thought you were having some sort of conference. Do you mind if I join you?"

This young woman seemed nothing like her mother—or the picture Elizabeth's imagination had drawn of the woman, having never met her. Intrigued by her impulsive decision to ask for admittance,

Elizabeth readily gave it, drawing Miss de Bourgh back into the room. Jane, when she saw them, looked at Elizabeth askance, but Elizabeth only shook her head slightly, prompting Jane to subside.

"Miss de Bourgh," said Elizabeth, "this is my sister Jane. Jane, we have been joined tonight by Miss Anne de Bourgh."

"I apologize for my presumption," said the young woman, "but I find that I require a friend at present, if I may impose upon you."

"You are very welcome to join us," was Jane's kind reply. "Lizzy and I have often gathered together late at night. It is one of the benefits of having a sister to whom you are closer than anyone else in the world."

Warmth erupted in Elizabeth's breast at her sister's words; she had always felt the same way about Jane. Miss de Bourgh, however, ducked her head in embarrassment.

"I have never had such an experience, as I have no sisters." Then she released a nervous laugh. "Even if I had any, I am certain my mother would not approve."

Miss de Bourgh seemed to gather her courage, and she turned to Elizabeth. "I would like to apologize to you in advance, Miss Elizabeth. I know not if you are aware, but it is because of Mr. Collins's characterization of my cousin Darcy's actions toward you that we have come."

"I believe your other cousin, Colonel Fitzwilliam, mentioned as much to me last night."

A slow nod was the woman's response. "Yes, Fitzwilliam would have felt it necessary to warn you."

A sense of frustration came over Elizabeth. "I do not know what Mr. Collins has told your mother, Miss de Bourgh. But Mr. Darcy has paid me no compliments. There is nothing between us. I have no more notion of Mr. Darcy proposing to me than I have of accepting the same from Mr. William Collins."

Miss de Bourgh giggled at Elizabeth's statement. "Mr. Collins is . . ."

"Revolting?" finished Elizabeth, once again provoking Miss de Bourgh's giggling.

"Lizzy," admonished Jane.

"I apologize, Jane, but it is the truth. *You* are not the subject of Mr. Collins's idea of courtship. It is in every way objectionable."

"Be that as it may, Lizzy — Mr. Collins is our cousin and our father's heir. You are not required to like Mr. Collins. We should at least attempt to respect him."

"You do not need to concern yourself, Miss Elizabeth," said Miss de Bourgh. "My mother has spoken of her wishes for us for many years, but neither Darcy nor I have any interest in the other as anything other than cousins. Even if my mother were to coerce my cooperation, I doubt she would ever command Darcy. He is a . . . formidable man."

"That is not the point," replied a frustrated Elizabeth. "I was completely honest when I said there is nothing between Mr. Darcy and me. It is nothing more than a misconception conceived in our ridiculous cousin's vacuous mind."

"My mother does not see it that way."

"Which puts her sights squarely on me."

Miss de Bourgh gave a helpless shrug. "I am sorry, Miss Elizabeth. But I cannot say you are incorrect. She will not give in, and as such, she will see you as a threat."

"Come now," said Jane, inserting her calm tones into their exchange. "This is a subject to concern ourselves on the morrow. For now, shall we not come to know each other better?"

A shy smile was Miss de Bourgh's response. "I should like that very much. As you might expect, my mother has never encouraged my friendship with other young ladies—or at least those she has not chosen for me. And as I have always been of a sickly constitution, I have little experience in society."

Elizabeth's heart went out to this timid young woman. She was, Elizabeth judged, older than either Jane or herself, but in matters of experience in the world, she was as a child of ten.

"Of course, Miss de Bourgh. We will be happy to count you as a friend."

The beaming smile the woman directed at them made any number of uncomfortable experiences with Lady Catherine worth it. Or perhaps it did not—Elizabeth did not know quite what form the woman's displeasure would take, after all. Either way, Miss de Bourgh clearly needed a friend, and Elizabeth was quite willing to offer herself up in such a capacity.

The three ladies stayed in Jane's room for more than an hour, talking, laughing, sharing of themselves. As they spoke, Elizabeth discovered that there was more to Miss de Bourgh than she might have suspected in her cynicism. Miss de Bourgh was intelligent, but her hesitation in speaking her mind—at least in the early part of their conversation—suggested a woman who had not much experience in others actually listening to her opinion. From what Elizabeth suspected of Lady Catherine, she thought this was in direct response to her mother's domineering character.

By the end of their time in that darkened room, the two Bennet sisters thought they had made a firm friend. But their closeness was not destined to last, as Elizabeth was certain Lady Catherine would object to her daughter making such unsuitable acquaintances.

"Please," said Anne as her eyelids began to droop and fatigue to set in, "shall you not call me Anne? I would be pleased if you did."

"Of course, Anne," said Jane, instantly accepting Miss de Bourgh's overture without any thought. "I would be happy if you would call me Jane."

"And I am Elizabeth, though my family and friends usually call me Lizzy," added Elizabeth.

Anne beamed with pleasure. But that only lasted for a moment before a look of horror came over her.

"But only when we are alone!" exclaimed she. "Please do not act so familiarly when my mother is present."

Though Elizabeth agreed readily, Jane seemed shocked. She followed Elizabeth's example and agreed, to which Miss de Bourgh seemed relieved. Soon she let herself from the room to return to her own, leaving Elizabeth alone with her elder sister. Jane was pensive for a moment, and Elizabeth, who had seen her sister in such an attitude before, knew Jane meant to say something.

"There is something very dear about Miss de Bourgh," said Jane at last. "But I cannot fathom this reticence to be friendly with us in front of her mother. Would Lady Catherine not be happy her daughter has quickly obtained friends here?"

Elizabeth sighed. It was pointless to attempt to open Jane's eyes to Lady Catherine's character, though she already knew what kind of woman the lady was. "We should not ask her reasons, Jane. Let us simply be friends with her. I think she is very much in need of them."

"Of course," was Jane's immediate reply. With Elizabeth's suggestion, it seemed Jane quite put the matter out of her mind. It was better that way.

"Good night, dearest Sister," said Elizabeth, kissing Jane's cheek and exiting her room.

While she was preparing herself for sleep, Elizabeth considered the events of the evening, from their arrival, her dances with Mr. Collins, Mr. Darcy, Mr. Wickham, and Colonel Fitzwilliam, to the subsequent events which had led to their forced residence at Netherfield. Though she had attempted to put it from her mind, Mr. Wickham and his assertions once again came to her, followed by those of Colonel

Fitzwilliam.

Elizabeth could not know the truth of the matter — nor did she wish to. But every interaction with Mr. Darcy told her that though he was, at times, not the most pleasant of men, he was scrupulously proper. Mr. Darcy's reaction to seeing Mr. Wickham had not been feigned, nor had Colonel Fitzwilliam's. Therefore, Elizabeth decided to trust them and avoid Mr. Wickham.

A movement caught Elizabeth's eye, and she stepped to the window, noting the softly falling snow. Whereas the small pellets she had seen while waiting for the carriage had seemed like little enough, now the snow fell in great clusters of flakes, which were quickly piling up on the ground outside. Already, drifts were building, and a rich, thick blanket of white was forming wherever she looked. And it occurred to Elizabeth to hope that her family would be able to return to their home on the morrow.

In the blackness outside Elizabeth's room, a solitary figure moved in the shadows, taking care not to make any sound which might wake the residents of the estate. The hall was long and dark, with only a little light filtering in through a window at the end, coupled with whatever light was able to penetrate from the entrance hall.

Once the figure reached the end of the hall, it stopped and glanced out onto the night landscape, grimacing at what was revealed. "We have not seen snow such as this in an age. We will all be bound here for days if this continues."

With a shake of the head, the figure turned and made its way back toward the stairs. There was a sound, a ghostly whisper to its left, and the figure stopped, surprised at the sudden noise. When it was not repeated, the figure shook its head and once again walked down the hall, arriving at the stairs.

But just as the figure was about to attempt them, a shadow separated itself from where it was hidden in a small alcove, and as the figure's foot touched the first stair leading down, the shadow reached it, pushing with all its might.

Arms flailing to catch itself, the figure hurtled down the stairs, its cry of sudden fear cut short by the sickening sound of breaking bones. It tumbled to the bottom of the stairs and lay still.

The shadow, fearful the cry had been heard, melted back into the darkness of the alcove, waiting to see if anyone arrived to investigate. But all was quiet. The house and the world around it slept on, it seemed.

Gingerly, ready to flee at any moment, the shadow made its way down the stairs toward the fallen figure, eyes alight for any sign of movement. A few short moments later, it reached the fallen body lying on the floor below. Then, satisfied, the shadow bent down to confirm the identity of its victim.

The faint light entered the window and fell on the prone body, twisted limbs lying where it had fallen. And when the face was seen and recognized, the shadow was heard to utter two words.

"Oh bother!"

CHAPTER VI

A scream rent the air, jolting Elizabeth from a sound sleep. It was faint, though still audible, and she wondered at it, thinking it should not have woken her. When it fell silent, Elizabeth, with the muddled thoughts of one startled from sleep, thought to return to that blessed state. Then it sounded again, and she was forced into full wakefulness, wondering at the awful ruckus.

Grasping at her robe, she hurried to the door and opened it in time to see several of the other residents also investigating the sound, their figures moving down the still-dark hallway. Elizabeth judged it was still well before dawn. At the end of the hall near the stairs, one of the maids was shrieking, pointing down. Mr. Darcy and Colonel Fitzwilliam, the closest to the panicked woman, moved quickly to see what was wrong, and Elizabeth, along with several of her sisters and other residents of the house, moved to follow them.

"Hold, Mr. Bennet!" said Mr. Darcy in an authoritative voice. "Someone is lying at the bottom of the stairs."

Mr. Bennet, understanding at once, held Lydia, and Kitty back, refusing to allow them to go forward. Jane stopped abruptly where she had been walking, but Elizabeth — the one closest, gained the top of the stairway and looked down, her eyes following the cousins as they hurried down to the lower floor. There, at the bottom, as Mr. Darcy had said, lay the body of a man in Netherfield livery.

Elizabeth gasped and put a hand to her mouth. The body was a mass of limbs twisted in angles they were never meant to bend. Several servants, including the housekeeper, rushed into the room and the combined light of their candles allowed Elizabeth to see a pool of dark liquid around the man's head, glittering in so many points of light.

"It appears to be the butler, Mr. Forbes," said Mr. Darcy as he bent to investigate.

By his side, Colonel Fitzwilliam looked back up the stairs. "He must have tripped and fallen. Poor man."

"When did this happen?" Mr. Darcy turned to the housekeeper, Mrs. Nichols, and said: "When did you last see Mr. Forbes?"

"Perhaps an hour after everyone went to bed," said Mrs. Nichols in a shaky voice. "He was to walk the halls one last time to ensure everything was as it should be."

Mr. Darcy glanced about. "I do not see a candle."

"Mr. Forbes usually did not use a candle," replied Mrs. Nichols. "He felt the light from a candle blinded him in the darkness. He preferred to simply walk in the dark."

"That preference seems to have cost him his life," said Colonel Fitzwilliam.

"Let us have a few stout lads carry the body away," instructed Mr. Darcy. "Do you know if he had any family nearby?"

Mrs. Nichols shook her head. "He is not from the neighborhood and did not speak of his family. As far as I am aware, he was alone in the world."

Mr. Darcy nodded. "Then it will be up to Bingley to decide what to do with the remains. It would likely be best if he is interred in the local churchyard."

The housekeeper climbed the stairs, avoiding the place where the butler had fallen, and gathered the poor maid who had made the discovery to her. She was quickly herded from the area, while two footmen stepped forward. They arranged a makeshift litter and arranged the body on it before bearing it away. As Elizabeth watched the scene, she noticed Mr. Darcy looking after them, and though she could not see his countenance in the darkness, he seemed contemplative, and she wondered what he might be thinking.

"Lizzy!" called her father. "I think it is time we all returned to our beds."

Nodding, Elizabeth turned and made her way to where her father still stood with her three sisters. Of Mrs. Bennet, Mary, Mr. Collins, Lady Catherine and Anne, and the entire Bingley clan there was no sign. Mr. Bennet noted her curious look and shook his head.

"Your mother can sleep through a war, Lizzy—I am not surprised the maid's screams did not wake her. As for the others, I assume they either were not disturbed, or their rooms were too far away."

"Mr. Bingley will need to be informed in the morning," said Elizabeth.

"Mr. Darcy will assume that responsibility, I am sure."

As they began to make their way the short distance down the hall, Elizabeth could not help but wonder at the suddenly deceased man. He had seemingly made this trek many times in the past and knew the layout of the house very well. One false step could affect one for a lifetime, or even end one's life, she reflected ruefully.

"Ugh!" said Lydia in her usually loud voice. "A body. Who would have thought we would see a body during our stay at Netherfield?"

"I am sure I shall not sleep a wink for the rest of the night!" lamented Kitty.

"Lydia, Kitty," said Elizabeth, a warning note in her voice. "Have some respect for the dead. I am sure the poor man did not tumble down the stairs to inconvenience you."

Elizabeth thought Lydia would protest her admonishment, but she only huffed and hurried to her room. Kitty followed suit. Mr. Bennet turned to Elizabeth and winked at her before making his way to his room and shutting the door firmly behind him. This left only Elizabeth and Jane behind. Before she went to her room, Elizabeth looked back down the hall, hoping the gentlemen had not heard her younger sisters' thoughtless remarks. But she saw nothing.

Soon, she was once again in her bed. Unfortunately, sleep would be slow in returning.

There was something about the situation that bothered Darcy, though he could not quite put his finger on it. A fall down the stairs of a house was a common enough occurrence that it should not be wondered that it might have happened, even to a servant who was experienced and familiar with the house. Broken bones were common enough in such circumstances, especially on hard stairs, such as those that made up the grand staircase at Netherfield manor.

But while fatalities were not unheard of, the butler seemed to have many more injuries than a simple tumble down the stairs would suggest. Normally, when a person fell, a foot would slip out from

under them, or in the worst cases, the unfortunate might trip and fall
forward. But this man almost seemed to have pitched forward, his
momentum taking him much further down than might have been
expected. It was as if he had been running the moment he fell, which
would account for the momentum. But Darcy could not understand
why a staid and proper servant would be running toward the stairs.

Knowing this was a matter which could not wait until the morning,
Darcy knocked on the door of his friend's rooms, entering when there
was no response. He knew his friend was a deep sleeper, and as such,
he would need to be shaken awake. This Darcy did immediately.

"Darcy, what the deuce?" demanded Bingley, his words slurred,
his eyes still filled with sleep.

"I apologize for waking you, Bingley," said Darcy. "But something
of a serious nature has occurred."

Bingley produced a great yawn and rubbed at his eyes. "What has
happened? And why could it not have waited until the morning?"

"One of your maids discovered the body of your butler at the
bottom of the stairs, Bingley. He is dead."

For a moment, Bingley seemed to be unable to understand what
Darcy was saying. He blinked, looked up at Darcy, his mouth slack
and his eyes wide. Darcy watched as the clouds cleared from the
depths of Bingley's eyes, and he soon sat up straight in bed.

"Mr. Forbes has died?"

"I am afraid so, Bingley," replied Darcy. "It seems he fell down the
stairs sometime during the night and was discovered only a short time
ago."

Hastily, Bingley stood from his bed and began pacing the room.
"How could this have happened? It is inconvenient, indeed, to lose my
most senior male employee."

"Really, Bingley," reproved Darcy. "A man has died in this house
tonight. Have a little respect for the dead."

Chastened, Bingley shook his head. "I apologize, Darcy. I did not
mean it to come out in such an unfeeling way. I am simply shocked
that this has happened."

"As are we all," replied Darcy.

"What of the body?"

"A pair of footmen were tasked with taking the body to the cellar.
According to the housekeeper, he did not have any family nearby—
any family at all, that anyone knew. It would likely be best if you
simply had him interred in the local cemetery."

Bingley nodded distractedly. "I suppose that is best. I suppose I will have to promote one of the footmen to the position of the butler, at least in the short term."

"That would be best," agreed Darcy. "The position is important and should not be left vacant."

Darcy stayed with his friend for some minutes discussing the situation. As he had expected, Bingley did not wish to view the body at the late hour. When they had made some few decisions, Darcy bid his friend good night again and retired to his room.

For the rest of the night, the matter bothered Darcy, and he could not sleep again. He ended up sitting in a chair near the fire which had been built up in his room. At times, however, he took himself to the window to look out onto the world below. The snow had continued through the night, and if Darcy was any judge, was now several inches deep. No one would be leaving Netherfield any time soon, he thought.

When Elizabeth eventually fell into a fitful sleep, it was punctuated by nightmares, the sensation of falling, and chilling screams of terror, some she felt issued from her own throat, though no one came to investigate. But such was her fatigue that though she was woken several times by her night terrors, she would soon fall back asleep, only to have the pattern begin all over again.

At length, well after the dawn, Elizabeth woke from her bed and refreshed herself with the cold basin of water in her room. She dressed and took herself to the window to investigate the damage to the outside world. The storm, however, was still ongoing, as snow fell, though now it appeared to be whipped up by the wind, which whistled and shrieked, causing the manor to groan in response. Her bedchamber, situated in the front of the house, would usually allow a view of the drive. But nothing could be seen but endless white.

Breakfast was served late that morning, almost the time when luncheon would normally be served at Longbourn. As the night had been late, many of those in residence did not make an appearance until called to break their fast. For Elizabeth's part, she attempted to find something to read in Mr. Bingley's library, only to discover that the man's poor selection of books did not contain anything of interest. Elizabeth wished she had brought a book or two with her, though she knew it was nonsensical, given the reason for their attendance the previous evening.

When she was finally able to make her way to the dining room for the repast, she found that the entire company had gathered. Naturally, the conversation at the breakfast table was dominated by two subjects:

the storm outside and the death of the butler.

"It is nothing less than foolishness and carelessness," said Lady Catherine in her authoritative voice. "The servants at Rosings are better trained and know not to tumble down the stairs. I declare I have never heard such a thing."

Miss Bingley, Elizabeth suspected, had heard about the incident just before arriving and had been heard to voice her shock and sense of annoyance at the work this would cause her. It also seemed like Miss Bingley's well of tolerance for Lady Catherine was rapidly evaporating. She did not like being taken to task in her own home and for such a ridiculous reason.

"I hardly think it is a matter of training. The servants are not taught to walk, after all. They should already possess that accomplishment when they apply for a position."

"Well, perhaps you should consider it when next you hire," replied Lady Catherine. "Clumsiness is not a trait to be prized in a servant."

"Thank you, Lady Catherine," replied Miss Bingley, an edge in her voice. "I am sure I will take your advice and give it the consideration it deserves."

A regal nod, which suggested Lady Catherine had completely missed the sarcasm with which Miss Bingley spoke, was the woman's only reply. The company spoke for some little time concerning the disposition of the body of the late butler, his lack of family, and other such topics before the subject was changed.

"What have we planned for our guests' return to their homes?" asked Miss Bingley, peering at her brother. "Has the Bennets' carriage been repaired?"

"The Bennets will not be returning home today," said Mr. Bingley. "I have spoken with the groundskeepers. The roads are exceedingly hazardous, and more snow is piling up as we speak. It is much too dangerous to attempt to drive their carriage through such roads, whether it is repaired or not."

Miss Bingley was clearly not amused. "I am sure you are overstating the matter, Charles. Longbourn is no more than five miles away. I am sure they may go safely over such a short distance."

"Three miles, actually," interjected Mr. Bennet. "Unfortunately, I concur with Mr. Bingley, though I would prefer to be in my home again. This is the worst snow storm I have ever seen. I would not wish to gamble the safety of my family on our ability to push our way through the snow drifts."

"An eminently sensible decision," said Mr. Collins. "It is often said that discretion is the better part of valor, and in this case, it would be best to remain at the location which offers protection and sanctuary. And we must thank Mr. Bingley for his generosity in offering us shelter from the storm in our time of need."

"It is no trouble, Mr. Collins," said Mr. Bingley. "Of course, we would not wish to leave you to the elements or attempt an unsafe journey back to Longbourn." Mr. Bingley turned to Lady Catherine. "And you and your daughter — and Colonel Fitzwilliam too — are quite welcome to stay here until the roads are passable again."

"Of course, we must stay," replied Lady Catherine. "It is providential, indeed, for I have much to make right while I am here in Hertfordshire."

The little undercurrents around the table were fascinating to Elizabeth. Miss Bingley was annoyed with Lady Catherine, while Lady Catherine considered herself superior to anyone else at the table, with the exception of her daughter and two nephews. Colonel Fitzwilliam was watching his aunt's performance with a grin, and Mr. Darcy, with poorly concealed annoyance. Kitty and Lydia were giggling at each other, prompting glares from Mrs. Hurst, who was situated nearby, and Mary appeared to be watching the company with bated breath. No doubt she had memorized some little tidbit of wisdom and was waiting to insert it into the general conversation.

"Either way," continued Mr. Bingley, "we are quite happy to have all of you. About the only matter of concern is the clothing requirements." Mr. Bingley turned and regarded Mrs. Bennet with compassion. "Between Darcy and myself, we can likely clothe your husband, Mrs. Bennet, but my sisters are only two, whereas you and your daughters are six."

"One of the footmen was sent back to Longbourn with some clothes for us to wear today," replied Mrs. Bennet. "We do not have much, but we shall make do while we are here."

"Excellent!" replied Mr. Bingley. "If you require assistance, I am sure Caroline and Louisa have some dresses with which they may dispense."

It was clear that whatever Mr. Bingley thought, his sisters were not of like mind. It was a relief, therefore, when the sisters declined to respond to their brother's assertion. The way they glared at every Bennet lady seemed to dare them to ask for a single article of clothing. Two dresses had been delivered from Elizabeth's closet — Mrs. Hill, having seen the weather, had likely suspected their stay might be longer, and had planned accordingly. Thus, though a dress would need to be laundered every day, Elizabeth knew she would be kept clothed as long as she needed to be at Netherfield.

"You are very good, Mr. Bingley!" exclaimed Mrs. Bennet. "I am certain we will all be well. Happily, my Jane looks good in anything, for we only have a few dresses each."

What a mortifying statement! Miss Bingley and Mrs. Hurst carefully avoided all response to Mrs. Bennet's absurd words, but Mr. Bingley only smiled at a blushing Jane. "I cannot agree more, Mrs. Bennet."

After that, the company attended to their breakfast with a little more zeal. Conversation, while there were still some words exchanged between diners, was more banal in nature. For that, Elizabeth could not be anything but grateful.

At length, breakfast was complete, and the party made its way from the dining room and dispersed to their sundry activities. Though she would learn to rue the choice, Elizabeth joined several others in the sitting-room. With nothing to do at present, it was clear that all amusement would be had by sitting with other residents of the estate. Mrs. Hurst and Miss Bingley, clearly wishing their guests miles away, took themselves to the pianoforte. Elizabeth, however, joined Mr. Darcy, Colonel Fitzwilliam, the de Bourghs, Mr. Collins, Jane, and Mary in the sitting-room, and for a time, they sat in that attitude conversing among themselves. Of course, it was increasingly difficult to hold any conversation due to Lady Catherine's propensity to attempt to dominate any such discourse. Mr. Collins, of course, hung off every word which proceeded forth from her mouth, inserting his flattery whenever he thought he could do so without inciting Lady Catherine's ire. Elizabeth could cheerfully have continued in such a manner had she known what was to come next.

"Now, Mr. Collins," said the lady after discussing some nonsensical improvements to the latter's parsonage. Shelves in the closet sounded like a remarkably daft notion to Elizabeth. "I am reminded that I have come here for a purpose. Will you kindly point out which of the Bennet sisters has been attempting to turn my nephew from his duty?"

Mr. Darcy frowned, and Elizabeth glared at the parson, but before either of them could say anything, Mr. Collins had answered his patroness's question.

"It was Miss Elizabeth, your ladyship."

The bludgeoning weight of Lady Catherine's gaze fell on Elizabeth. "Miss Elizabeth, is it? I suppose I am not surprised, given what I know of your family. What have you to say for yourself?"

"I need say nothing, Lady Catherine," replied Elizabeth. "Mr. Collins has quite clearly misread the situation. Mr. Darcy has given me no such notice, nor have I attempted to solicit it."

"Miss Elizabeth speaks the truth, Lady Catherine," added Mr. Darcy. "Whatever your quarrel with me regarding your wishes, you need not involve Miss Elizabeth."

"Oh, do be still, Darcy," replied Lady Catherine with an irritated wave of her hand. "Allow me the greater understanding of the arts and allurements of young ladies. I have seen the likes of the Bennet sisters before. They are all minor gentry, possessing little but avarice and determination to entrap a man of fortune."

"I assure you that you are quite mistaken, Lady Catherine," asserted Elizabeth. "As I have said, Mr. Darcy and I have done naught but exchange a few words on occasions when chance has brought us together."

Lady Catherine considered Elizabeth for a few moments, slowly nodding her head. "It seems you now understand the folly of your ambitions. That is well. Then I require your promise, Miss Elizabeth. You will stay away from my nephew, and if he should, at some moment of infatuation, propose, you will instantly refuse him and resist all further entreaties."

Though Elizabeth was shocked at the lady's demand, she could not help but notice Mr. Darcy's sudden anger. By his side, Colonel Fitzwilliam was shaking his head, clearly not amused with his aunt's behavior. Anne, by contrast, was keeping her reaction carefully blank, though Elizabeth could not be certain that was because she wished to avoid angering her mother or because of some other reason.

"Lady Catherine," said Elizabeth carefully, "I have informed you I have no designs on your nephew. But I dislike having my freedom taken from me in such a manner, especially since Mr. Darcy and I are both to be confined to this house for who knows how many days."

"Miss Elizabeth," said Lady Catherine, her manner suggesting impatience, "if you have no designs on my nephew, you will give the assurances I require. What reason could you have to refuse, unless you are attempting to mislead me with falsehood?"

"No, Lady Catherine," interjected Darcy. "I will not allow this. You have made an unreasonable demand of Miss Elizabeth, and she has every right to refuse it. Please cease speaking of such a matter."

"It is clear *you* have lost your head over her," snapped Lady Catherine. "As such, I have no choice but to appeal to her sense of right. I will not retract my demand."

"Miss Elizabeth,' said Mr. Darcy, "if I might prevail upon you, can you please leave the room. I believe it is time we had a long overdue family discussion."

Elizabeth returned the man's gaze, unsure if she should leave in such a fashion. A part of her wished to give Lady Catherine the assurance she desired. After all, though Elizabeth had nothing against Mr. Darcy, she had no intention of ever accepting his overtures, even in the unlikely event he should ever offer them. Then again, such a request was impertinent and beyond the pale, and the other part of her wished to inform Lady Catherine of her opinion.

But Mr. Darcy looked at her with such a pleading, yet encouraging, expression that she felt she had no choice but to accede. "Very well, Mr. Darcy. I shall leave you to your family conversation."

"You shall do no such thing!" commanded Lady Catherine. "I have not finished with you, Miss Elizabeth."

"I apologize, Lady Catherine," said Elizabeth, "but at present, I am afraid you are. You have insulted me in every possible way, and I believe Mr. Darcy's suggestion is for the best."

Under the enraged eye of Lady Catherine, Elizabeth arose and, taking Jane's hand and nodding to Mary to follow them, left the room without looking back. She was relieved when the door closed behind her, and the lady had not spoken again.

"I cannot understand her ladyship," said Jane, eyes wide. "How could she behave in such a way?"

"The rich may act as they wish and offend whom they will," replied Elizabeth. "I only hope Mr. Darcy can talk some sense into her."

Though Jane did not reply, Elizabeth knew she fervently agreed.

CHAPTER VII

*L*ady Catherine was an elderly, meddling, irascible woman, accustomed to having her own way. The family, tolerated her for no other reason than she *was* family, and even then, they offered the bonds of familial affection only grudgingly. Darcy, because his mother had been fond of her sister, was one of the more tolerant members of the family, even going so far as to visit her every year at Easter to look over her estate books and deal with any matters which required a man's hand.

But that tolerance was quickly being put to the test—had been put to the test for some time, actually. As she aged, the woman appeared to be growing ever more cantankerous, ever more unreasonable, and exponentially more difficult to endure. This business with Anne and his supposed engagement to her had been quickly coming to a head, for Lady Catherine had suggested she would send notice to the newspapers, should Darcy not agree to the marriage soon. It was only his assurance that no newspaper would print it as he had already warned them that to do so would be to invite a lawsuit that had prompted her to subside.

"There will be no more assaults on the character of Miss Elizabeth," said Darcy at the end of a long discussion. "She has done nothing wrong. If you cannot refrain from bringing up the matter of my supposed engagement when you speak with her, then you will not speak with her at all."

"Darcy," said she, in a tone of exaggerated patience, "you do not know what such a woman may —"

"Enough!" snapped Darcy. Something in his tone must have warned Lady Catherine that he was not in a mood to be gainsaid, for she fell silent, though she glared at him with mutinous anger. "Remember, Lady Catherine, that I assist you every year at Easter. If you do not wish me to withdraw that assistance, you will oblige me now."

"You would throw your own blood over for that scheming little adventuress?"

"I am throwing no one over," said Darcy. "I am only resolved to protect a good woman who does not deserve your censure. I have nothing more to say on the matter. I am not engaged to Miss Elizabeth, and I have no intention of offering for her. That is enough for you."

Then with a final glare, Darcy let himself from the room. As he was departing, he heard Fitzwilliam's chuckle, and his words to their aunt before the door closed. "It appears you have finally pushed Darcy too far. Well done, Aunt. Well done, indeed."

For the rest of the morning, Darcy avoided Lady Catherine — avoided everyone else in the house. The library was his refuge, for while he knew Mr. Bennet might be within, and Miss Elizabeth was also a devotee of the written word, Bingley's library was so pitiful that no one of any interest in reading would consider it to be anywhere close to adequate.

In the early afternoon, he went looking for Bingley, wondering what his friend had been occupying himself with that morning. He found his friend with his cousin, laughing in Bingley's study. They fell silent when Darcy entered, and he wondered if they had been speaking of the situation with Lady Catherine. If they had been, Bingley should not laugh — Darcy suspected it would not be long before Miss Bingley also came to his aunt's attention, for her behavior, unlike Miss Elizabeth's, was truly objectionable.

"Darcy, come in man," said Bingley. "We were speaking of the weather. I sent several men out to test the roads, and they have returned, saying the drifts are several feet deep on the road into Meryton. I am afraid we are all confined here for the moment."

I did not expect anything different," said Darcy. "This much snow in this area is quite rare, though I have seen it many times in

Derbyshire."

"We experience the same in York," replied Bingley. "Though it usually does not stay long."

"It is a boon, is it not Darcy?" asked Fitzwilliam, grinning, likely about to make a jest. "The fair Miss Elizabeth Bennet is in residence with us, and you may take her measure in the following days. Of course, Lady Catherine's presence is a hindrance, to be sure."

"Fitzwilliam," said Darcy, holding his temper in check, "as I told Lady Catherine, I have not been paying any attention to Miss Elizabeth."

"No, I dare say you have not," said Fitzwilliam. "But I know you better than most, and I am certain the interest is there."

Bingley chortled. "That is what I have been trying to tell your cousin, but he has been stubborn."

"Oh?" asked Darcy. "I do not recall you attempting to educate me, Bingley."

Bingley only waved him off. "Would you prefer, perhaps, that I pushed my sister in your direction?"

There was no hiding Darcy's distaste for such a suggestion, and he did not even try. Bingley was well aware of Darcy's opinion of Miss Bingley, for they had discussed it many times, Darcy often suggesting that Bingley should control his sister better, lest she ruin him in society. Fitzwilliam chortled at Darcy's reaction, but Bingley shot him a rueful look.

"I do apologize, Darcy. I know my sister has been difficult, especially since we have come to Hertfordshire."

"It is no trouble, Bingley," replied Darcy. "In fact, I think we are even now, given Aunt Catherine is now in residence."

"That is nothing less than the truth!" said Fitzwilliam.

A knock on the door interrupted their hilarity, and for that Darcy could only be grateful. Bingley called out permission to enter, and the door opened, revealing the young man Bingley had chosen to replace the unfortunate Mr. Forbes.

"Yes, Mr. Campbell?"

"There is an officer of the militia here to see you, Mr. Bingley."

"An officer of the militia?" asked Bingley, a frown settling over his countenance. "Why would they send an officer here in all this snow?"

Darcy exchanged a glance with Fitzwilliam and noted his cousin's interest. "Did the officer leave his name?"

"No, Colonel," replied Mr. Campbell. He colored in embarrassment, realizing after the fact he should have asked the officer's name. It was an indication of his inexperience. "I do know he was in attendance last night, but I did not request his name."

"Surely it could not be *him*," said Darcy, a premonition suddenly coming over him.

Fitzwilliam instantly understood Darcy's comment, though Bingley appeared confused. "There is only one way to discover it," said Fitzwilliam, pushing himself to his feet.

As one, the three men followed the new butler from the room, toward the entrance hall. While Darcy knew that it was unlikely the officer was whom he thought, the suspicion would not leave him.

When they entered the entrance hall, the officer stood there in his red coat, his grey overcoat open down the front, the snow melting in rivulets down the shoulders and back. He was tall and slender, his hair a little mussed due to the snow and wind. Darcy would know that stance anywhere.

"Hello, Darcy," said Wickham, as he turned and caught sight of them. He regarded them with an insouciant smirk, much as Darcy had seen more times than he would care to remember. "And Fitzwilliam too. I apologize for not greeting you gentlemen last evening, but I really had nothing to say to Darcy, and I did not know Fitzwilliam was in attendance."

"What are you doing here, Wickham?" spat Darcy.

Wickham's grin only widened. "As charming as ever, Darcy. I understand you are sniffing around Miss Elizabeth Bennet. Take my advice and develop a personality—she is not a woman to accept the attentions of a cold fish."

With a growl, Darcy lunged at Wickham, only to be held back by Fitzwilliam and Bingley. While Wickham continued to regard him, sardonic amusement evident in his mien, Darcy thought he sensed a hint of apprehension in the man's detestable confidence.

"I suggest you say what you came to say and leave," said Fitzwilliam. He caught Darcy's eye, and when Darcy nodded, he released Darcy's shoulders and turned back to the libertine. "But let me warn you that if you taunt Darcy again, I will not hold him back. In fact, I will join him."

A sneer met Fitzwilliam's words, though Darcy noticed that Wickham did not say anything further to them. Instead, he turned to Bingley and bowed.

"At least there is a reasonable man here to talk to."

"I have no more care for you than my friends," said Bingley coldly. "If Darcy informs me your character is lacking, that is all I need to know. Now, please state your business."

With a nod, Wickham said: "Officers of the regiment have been sent to every estate nearby to ascertain the wellbeing of the residents in this weather."

"Oh?" asked Bingley, frowning at Wickham's assertion. "Why would Colonel Forster concern himself with such matters? Most estates are self-sufficient for at least some days."

"Because one of our number was sent to Longbourn to speak to Mr. Bennet and discovered that he and his family had not arrived home. The runners are to determine if the residents returned in safety last night and to try to discover the whereabouts of the Bennets and mount a search party for them if need be."

"The Bennets are at Netherfield," said Bingley at once.

At the same time, Darcy frowned. "That does not make sense. I know the Bennets sent to their home for clothing last night. The housekeeper, at the very least, must have been aware of their whereabouts."

"I know nothing of this," said Wickham. "I am only following orders." When Darcy made to speak, Wickham added: "I *did* hear that rumor, but Colonel Forster dispatched us, regardless."

Darcy turned to Fitzwilliam, a question in his gaze, and his cousin shrugged. "It is not unheard of for a regiment to take such an interest in the residents of a neighborhood."

"Your trust in me is positively heart-warming, Darcy," came Wickham's sarcastic response.

"I would not trust you for any reason, Wickham," snapped Darcy. "You are inherently untrustworthy, as you have proven over and over again."

Wickham snorted and turned back to Bingley. "It is good, then, that the Bennets have been discovered. The weather is growing worse by the hour. It was difficult to even make my way as far as I have, and providential, as well. I was instructed to return if they were not here, but as the colonel is concerned for his officers, he gave me leave to stay if I found them here."

"*You?* Stay here?" Darcy growled his disdain. "There are gentle ladies in residence at this estate, and I would not have you within fifty miles of them. You had best turn around and push your way through the snow drifts back to your barracks."

"We cannot make him return in this weather, Darcy," said Bingley.

"Yes, we may," replied Darcy. He turned to his friend and continued: "Wickham has no morals, and no bad behavior is beyond him. You have a sister in residence—she will be a target for Wickham's schemes and his need to acquire wealth, to say nothing of how he will prey on the Bennet sisters."

"Perhaps I have changed," came the unconcerned response of the man Darcy most detested in the world.

"Do not make me laugh," replied Fitzwilliam. "You have not changed since you were five years of age unless you consider your increased depravity a change."

"Either way," said Bingley, raising his voice to make himself heard, "I would not send a man to his death, regardless of his character, and sending him out in this weather may result in such."

"Thank you, Mr. Bingley," said Wickham.

"Of course, Mr. Wickham," said Bingley. "But I will warn you—we will be watching you while you are in residence. If you attempt anything improper with any of the ladies here—"

"Or any of the servants," interjected Darcy.

Bingley nodded. "Or any of the servants, then you will be removed to the stables where you may wait for the storm to abate."

"I have no intention of doing anything improper," said Wickham with a bow toward Bingley. "All I wish is a place to stay until I can leave."

"Very well. If you wait here, I will ask the housekeeper to assign you a bedchamber."

Again, Wickham bowed and murmured his thanks. Bingley instructed him to wait in the entrance hall until the housekeeper summoned him to go to his room. Though Wickham did not miss the inference that while he was a guest, he was not a *welcome* guest, he only regarded Bingley, sardonic insolence alive in his manner as he acceded to Bingley's instructions. Then Bingley led Fitzwilliam and Darcy back into the house. The butler had been waiting nearby, and the man acknowledged Bingley's instruction before leaving to make the arrangements with the housekeeper.

"I am not exaggerating the danger to the ladies, Bingley," said Darcy as they walked. "Wickham has no respect whatsoever for rank, and he considers any woman a challenge. Your sister's dowry will be an enticement to a life of ease, such as he has always desired."

Bingley's response was not what Darcy might have expected, for he fixed Darcy with a wry grin. "I should like to see him try with Caroline. She is a woman who has planned and schemed and attempted to become the mistress of Pemberley—can you see her falling for whatever charms Wickham possesses?"

While Darcy did not quite appreciate Bingley's jest—particularly given the events at Ramsgate the previous summer—Fitzwilliam could not help but chortle. "You have a point there, Bingley. I imagine Wickham will experience all the blasts of winter's chill should he attempt anything with Miss Bingley.

The two men grinned at each other, but Darcy only glared at them. "Fitzwilliam, you know Wickham's character firsthand. This is no jesting matter. And, if you consider who else is in residence, you may reconsider your jocularity. Can you imagine Miss Kitty or Miss Lydia Bennet resisting Wickham's charm?"

In an instant, both men returned to a sober demeanor. "We shall simply need to be watchful," said Bingley. "And perhaps it would be best to inform Mr. Bennet."

Fitzwilliam replied with a snort of derision. "Oh, yes, I am certain their father will be pleased that you invited a known libertine to stay at your estate."

"It was either that or send him out into the storm again, potentially causing his death."

"Believe me, my friend," said Darcy, "I am not at all certain which would have been the better option. Given what I know of Wickham, it is not at all clear."

That evening was utterly uncomfortable for Elizabeth, and she thought several other members of the party were in similar straits. She had not come across Lady Catherine again that day, and for that she was grateful. Whatever Mr. Darcy had said to his aunt, it seemed it had been effective to a degree, though the woman was not to be completely silenced. At least she did not speak to Elizabeth in particular, instead confining her comments to the entire company, though her meaning was completely transparent.

Of greater annoyance, however, was the presence of another guest, and one whom Elizabeth had not thought to see again so soon. When the party gathered in the dining room, she thought her eyes had betrayed her when Mr. Wickham entered the room, surveying it as if he thought it his own. When his eyes alighted on Elizabeth, he fixed on her, smirking in a manner most unpleasant, and turned his steps toward her.

"Miss Elizabeth," said he when he approached, favoring her with a bow. "How wonderful it is to see you tonight."

"Mr. Wickham," said Elizabeth with a gasp, finally finding her tongue. "Why are you here?"

Though her query was delivered with more shock than manners, Mr. Wickham did not seem offended by it. "Colonel Forster decided it was best that he confirmed the wellbeing of those in the neighborhood when it was discovered that your family had not returned to Longbourn. I was fortunate to be sent to Netherfield."

"I see," said Elizabeth, unsure how to take his current assertion.

"Yes, I am fortunate, indeed. For there is no other estate in the neighborhood in which there are so many beautiful and agreeable ladies in residence."

Elizabeth had heard flattery aplenty, but never had it been delivered with such smoothness, such utter assurance that the speaker would be believed that his words were nothing more than the truth. Of course, Elizabeth disbelieved and distrusted him in an instant. While he might find her attractive, she was certain he was speaking in such a manner for his own benefit.

Before she could speak, however, the obnoxious voice of Lady Catherine rang out over the group. "By my word, Miss Elizabeth, you *are* forward, are you not? Must you attempt to use your wiles on every man in the room?"

The scowl Elizabeth directed at Lady Catherine caused even that great lady to pause. "In case you did not see what is happening in this very room, Lady Catherine, Mr. Wickham approached *me*, not the reverse."

Then Elizabeth directed a glare at Mr. Wickham—which seemed to amuse him more than anything—and she stalked away from the man. Lady Catherine huffed at Elizabeth's tone, but she did not speak directly to Elizabeth again. Instead, she began speaking of matters dearer to her interests.

"It *was* clear to my dearest Anne and me that, even at a young age, our children were meant for each other. They were so close, you see, so much so that they doted on each other. My sister and I spoke about it many times over the years, and we knew it was nothing less than perfect; they are both descended from the same noble family on their mothers' sides, and while their fathers were not titled, they possess old and respectable family names.

"Indeed, who could stand between them?" Lady Catherine's eyes fell on Elizabeth to no one's surprise, but they soon switched to the person of Miss Bingley, surprising Elizabeth—she had not thought Lady Catherine so perceptive as to detect Miss Bingley's interest in Mr. Darcy so quickly. "No one can, of course. I have no doubt they will both do their duty in the end."

"Of course, they must" added Mr. Collins, his adoration for the lady evident in his vacant smile. "You are to be commended for your boundless wisdom and infinite care toward your family. I am certain when presented with such arguments, your daughter and nephew must agree with alacrity."

It was difficult to determine who was made crosser at Lady Catherine's pronouncements—Mr. Collins was ignored. Anne, who Elizabeth could acknowledge was still a new acquaintance, looked at Elizabeth and shook her head, then looked skyward, almost prompting Elizabeth to laughter. Mr. Darcy, by contrast, was glaring at his aunt, his angry countenance willing her to silence. Most of the rest of the party ignored her, but Colonel Fitzwilliam only watched her, amusement in his countenance and posture. When he spoke to vex his aunt, Elizabeth was not surprised at all.

"I have always been curious, Aunt," said he, "why you did not attempt to betroth Anne to *me*. Darcy already has an estate, after all. *I* am the poor soldier in need of an estate."

"Do not be foolish, Fitzwilliam!" snapped Lady Catherine. "You are your father's responsibility, and it is easily seen that you and Anne are completely unsuited. Furthermore, a union between Darcy and Anne would be great, indeed! They will create one of the wealthiest families in the kingdom. Why, even my brother's wealth will pale in comparison."

"So you have teased and tormented us with your dreams for these many years solely for your greed and dynastic ambitions?" said Mr. Darcy. It was obvious he was seriously displeased, for he glared at his aunt with the heavy force of contempt. "I will inform you once again, Aunt, that I have no interest in your ambitions, and neither does Anne. Keep your opinions to yourself lest you ruin the appetites of everyone present."

Elizabeth could only count it fortunate that the company was called to dinner at that very moment. Lady Catherine was instantly offended, but as Fitzwilliam rose and approached her, speaking in a soft but emphatic manner, she subsided. Mr. Collins, who could be counted on to support his patroness come what may, directed a censorious scowl at Mr. Darcy, but his reaction paled in comparison to Lady Catherine's. Her scowl in Mr. Darcy's direction could not be mistaken. It seemed, in this instance, the immovable object had been met by the irresistible force. Elizabeth could not imagine who would eventually prevail.

Soon, Lady Catherine was on Mr. Bingley's arm and Miss Bingley on Colonel Fitzwilliam's, and they made their way toward the dining room. As the ladies outnumbered the gentlemen, several of the gentlemen escorted two ladies, and as a result, Elizabeth found herself walking with her father and mother. Mr. Bennet, it appeared, was quite amused, for he spoke softly to Elizabeth as they walked.

"Is this not more diverting than comedy, Lizzy? I dare say Lady Catherine is so ridiculous that she will provide endless amusement until we are ready to quit this estate."

Mrs. Bennet stared at her husband, not understanding his jests. But Elizabeth glared. "Shall you not also censure the lady, Papa? She has been quite rude to me, for no reason at all, since her arrival."

"If I suspected you of being of little courage, I might," said Mr. Bennet, favoring Elizabeth with a wink. "As it is, however, I think I shall simply watch as you put her in her place."

Though annoyed with her father's propensity to seek amusement above all other considerations, Elizabeth knew that he could not be reasoned with when he was in such a mood. Her mother, her understanding of her husband ever less than perfect, appeared confused. The way she looked at Elizabeth suggested she had something to say. Elizabeth was grateful, however, when she subsided for the moment.

Unfortunately, the rest of the evening was little better than it began, though Mr. Darcy's outburst at his aunt directed Lady Catherine's attention back to him and away from Elizabeth. But while Jane seemed to enjoy her evening and was rarely separated from Mr. Bingley, the rest of the company was tense. The possible exception, of course, was Mrs. Bennet. For while she regarded Lady Catherine at first with annoyance, having heard Lady Catherine's remarks at Elizabeth, soon she was distracted by Jane and Mr. Bingley. And she was not the kind of woman to allow such welcome circumstances to pass without comment.

"Is it not wonderful the way Mr. Bingley and our Jane have taken to each other?" asked she of her husband before the soup course had even been cleared away. "They look so good together, too, and after such a short time! And I dare say they are good for each other!"

If she had spoken in a quiet tone, it might have passed the notice of the rest of the company. But Mrs. Bennet had never possessed the ability to moderate her voice. Miss Bingley and Mrs. Hurst kept their countenances admirably, but it was clear to anyone with the wit to see that they were displeased. Mrs. Bennet continued speaking in such a fashion, and Mr. Bennet acknowledging her words without commenting himself, which prompted her to continue speaking.

At another part of the table, Mr. Wickham had managed to seat himself close to Lydia and Kitty and was speaking to them in a soft voice, eliciting giggles and exclamations from the two girls. Elizabeth was too far away to hear them, but she knew they were not behaving with propriety. Then Mary would interject with some homily, to which no one paid attention, but which increased the cacophony about the table, especially when Lady Catherine continued to speak loudly, her words just short of berating Mr. Darcy. That gentleman simply ignored her.

"What a quaint company this is," commented Miss Bingley, at length adding her voice to the discord. "What delights await us in this neighborhood. What a wonderful thing it is that my brother has stranded us here."

The glare she directed down the table, accompanied by the sneer she liberally bestowed on the two youngest Bennets and their mother, gave meaning to her statements. Elizabeth knew she could do nothing about her mother, but Kitty and Lydia were another matter, and she resolved in that instant to ensure they did no more damage to Jane's chances with Mr. Bingley than they had already done.

The feeling of ecstasy which came over Elizabeth could not be described when it finally was time to retire. She made her way above stairs, fleeing to her bedchamber, eager to be alone with her thoughts, away from termagants, proud young ladies, silly ones, and libertines. Would that this stay at Netherfield would come to an end as soon as possible, for she now wished for the comfortable and familiar walls of Longbourn more than she had in her entire life.

As she reached the top of the stairs, she was confronted with the sight of Mr. Bennet facing an irate Lady Catherine. Of what they had been arguing she could not say, but she hoped her father had finally taken an interest in quelling Lady Catherine's censure of her in particular.

"You will oblige me, Mr. Bennet," demanded Lady Catherine, giving the lie to Elizabeth's hope.

"I shall not, Lady Catherine," retorted her father. "What you ask is unreasonable. I shall not yield."

Her father turned and without a hint of deference, entered his room. Lady Catherine huffed and turned away. She saw Elizabeth there and scowled, but she did not say anything, instead muttering under her breath at recalcitrant Bennets. Then she turned and stalked back down the stairs.

Elizabeth fled to her room, closing the door behind her. In silence, she divested herself of her dress, braided her hair, and readied herself for bed. When the light was out, she went to the window, hoping against hope that something had changed to allow her to escape from this house. But it had not. For outside Netherfield's walls, the wind howled, and the snow still fell.

CHAPTER VIII

By the next morning, the wind had abated, and while the snow still fell, Elizabeth was hopeful that it too would soon cease. Though she knew it might take a day or two before the conditions improved enough for them to depart, the sooner that happened, the better, in Elizabeth's opinion.

It was with a sense of purpose that Elizabeth rose and prepared for the day. With only one ladies' maid and one upstairs maid between six ladies, the sisters had long been accustomed to assisting one another to dress. That morning Jane and Elizabeth dressed together, but as Jane was distracted and Elizabeth determined, few words passed between them. Once she was ready for the day, Elizabeth set out in search of her younger sisters.

As they were not in their rooms, Elizabeth took herself below stairs, listening for the sound of their carrying on—always the easiest way to discover their whereabouts. It was not long before she located them in a small parlor. But they were not alone.

"Lizzy!" exclaimed Lydia when she entered the room. "Come and join us. Mr. Wickham has been telling us the most amusing stories."

Mr. Wickham, who had stood at her entrance, bowed, though not without an insolent smirk. "Yes, Miss Elizabeth—please join us."

"He has, has he?" said Elizabeth, keeping a tight rein on her temper. "That is tempting, but, unfortunately, Mr. Wickham, I must have words with my sisters. Please excuse us at once."

The way Mr. Wickham regarded her suggested he knew exactly of what she wished to speak, but he inclined his head and made to depart anyway. Kitty and Lydia, of course, protested his going, but he did not take any heed to their cries.

As he was passing by Elizabeth, he fixed his frivolous expression on her and said: "Your sisters are charming, Miss Elizabeth. I have rarely been so entertained in all my life."

"I would ask you, Mr. Wickham, to stay away from them," said Elizabeth. "I know what you are about, sir, and I know something of your history. I will not stand for you trifling with my sisters."

Mr. Wickham's amused smile never wavered. "Perhaps you should speak to *them*, Miss Elizabeth. They all but dragged me into this room." Then he turned and was gone, Elizabeth watching him as warily as she would an asp.

"Why must you always interrupt our fun?" demanded Lydia, with Kitty echoing her sentiments.

"Enough, Lydia," said Elizabeth.

She stalked to her sisters and glared down on them. Lydia huffed and made to rise, but Elizabeth pushed her back down on the sofa, her severity informing her sister it would go ill for her if she continued to protest. Both girls knew enough of their sister to know when she would not be gainsaid, and while that did not often lead to them heeding her, at least they subsided.

"Good," said Elizabeth. "I have several matters of which I must speak, and Mr. Wickham is one of them. I must insist you stay strictly away from Mr. Wickham, for he is not a good man."

Kitty gasped, but Lydia shook her head with annoyance. "You only say that because he was paying attention to *me* this morning instead of you. I do not intend to allow you to keep him to yourself."

"He was paying attention to me too!" cried Kitty, unwilling to allow her sister to outdo her.

Neither girl missed Elizabeth's scowl, and they subsided yet again. "In fact, I will be staying well clear of Mr. Wickham myself. He is quite obviously lacking in sense and has very little respect for propriety. Furthermore, I have been told by both Mr. Darcy and Colonel Fitzwilliam that Mr. Wickham is most certainly not a good man. You will stay away from him."

"How can you say that, Lizzy?" demanded Lydia. It was very

nearly a screech. "He is ever so charming and handsome and has such beautiful things to say."

"Mr. Darcy is just as handsome as Mr. Wickham, Lydia. A handsome countenance does not make a good man. It only makes one more dangerous for silly young gentlewomen."

Lydia glared mutinously at Elizabeth, but in the end, she chose not to speak. "I will be speaking with both Jane and Mary as well," said Elizabeth. "None of us has any business even speaking with Mr. Wickham, and Mr. Bingley will send him on his way as soon as the weather allows it. Until then we must share a house with him. But we will not give him our attention. You will both give me your promises now."

While she knew they were half-hearted at best, both girls eventually gave their promise. Though not satisfied with their sincerity, Elizabeth decided it was all she would receive at present and resolved to remain vigilant.

"The other matter of which I wish to speak is your carrying on when you should be speaking in a quiet and demure manner. Do not think I did not witness your behavior the night of the ball. At Longbourn, you may act that way and escape censure, but we are not at Longbourn now. You must start behaving as young ladies of your station!"

"There is nothing the matter with us," said Lydia with a sniff of disdain.

"Oh? There is nothing wrong with chasing after officers, carrying on in loud laughter, speaking in loud voices of subjects you should not?"

"I do not have to listen to this from you!" was Lydia's spiteful reply.

"Yes, you must!" spat Elizabeth.

She glared at her younger sister, stalling her attempt to rise and take herself from the room. By her side, Kitty watched with astonishment and no little trepidation. While Lydia herself was usually no less than fearless, it seemed Elizabeth's violent reaction had instilled a little of that emotion into her breast.

"Have you both not heard the cutting comments from Mr. Bingley's sisters and Lady Catherine? Have you not seen the censorious looks from Mr. Darcy, the shaken head of Colonel Fitzwilliam at your antics? Furthermore, have you not seen Mr. Bingley's attentions to your eldest sister?"

"What have Mr. Bingley and Jane to do with us?" This time Lydia's tone was more sulky than angry.

"What do you think will come of Mr. Bingley's attentions to Jane?"

Lydia replied with an uncaring shrug. Kitty, always the more governable of the two, said: "It appears he likes her very much. Do you think they will marry?"

"I hope so, for Jane's sake. But with such sisters as *you*, that is not at all certain."

Both girls' voices rose in protest, but Elizabeth quelled them with a sharp look. "Our society prizes good behavior, and you two do not have the comportment you need. Mr. Bingley is a good man, but he is also the son of a tradesman. He is rising in the world, but when he marries, he requires not only a wife who knows how to behave—which Jane does—but also connections who will do him credit. You are not those connections with your present manner of conducting yourselves.

"Furthermore, Miss Bingley is no friend to her brother's interest in Jane. Your continual poor behavior only induces her to strive against Jane with more determination. She does not wish to acknowledge relations who will embarrass her in every drawing room in London!"

"I cannot see how we have been so very bad," said a sulky Lydia.

"That is obvious, considering how obnoxious you have been." Once again, Lydia frowned, but she decided against saying anything. "If you wish to know how to behave, then watch Jane. You could do no better than take her likeness as an example.

"Do not ruin your sister's chances at happiness. If you must think of it in such a way, consider this: if Jane should marry Mr. Bingley, she would then be a part of society in London. At some time or another, *after you have proven you can comport yourselves properly*, she may invite you to stay with her. That will not happen if you provoke Miss Bingley to persuade her brother against Jane."

Lydia heaved a great sigh of frustration. "Well, I suppose if you put it that way," grumbled she.

"I do, indeed."

"Then I suppose we have no choice. We will behave ourselves."

By her side, Kitty seemed a little surprised, but she nodded her willingness.

"Good," said Elizabeth. "You may go to the breakfast room. I will meet you there shortly."

The girls exited the room much subdued, Elizabeth watching them as they departed. All the while she was wondering if it had been enough. They would not change overnight—they would still require constant supervision. She would speak with Mary, and between her sister and herself, they would keep a constant eye on them.

"You are incorrect in one way, Miss Elizabeth," said Darcy as he stepped into the room after the youngest Bennets vacated it.

It seemed she had been set in earnest contemplation, for she jumped when Darcy spoke. "I apologize, Miss Elizabeth," said he hastily, raising his hands in a placatory gesture. "I had not meant to alarm you."

"It is no trouble, Mr. Darcy," said Miss Elizabeth. "I am afraid I was not attending to my surroundings." She paused and looked at him, curiosity written in her expression. "Of what am I mistaken?"

"The influence Miss Bingley has over her brother."

Miss Elizabeth gasped. "You overheard us speaking?"

"Do not concern yourself," replied Darcy. "You said nothing improper, and I only heard a little at the end. I believe you and I have something of . . . an understanding of each other. I can see you mean nothing more than to see your sister happy, and while I might have been concerned if I had not heard you speak on the subject, your manners disarm suspicion."

"You would have been concerned?"

Darcy nodded, not without embarrassment. "I apologize, but your mother, in particular, does not inspire confidence. Her words last night might have led one to believe that her daughter would not be allowed to refuse a proposal from my friend."

A blush of mortification rose in Miss Elizabeth's cheeks, and the idle thought struck Darcy that it made her look fetching, indeed. As he watched her as she struggled to find the words to offer in response, he acknowledged to himself for the first time that she was a pretty woman, which rendered her other qualities of liveliness, intelligence, and forthrightness all that much more attractive. For the first time, Darcy felt the pull of her allure, and he wondered, even as he shunted it to the back of his mind if he truly wished to resist it.

"Thank you for giving us the benefit of the doubt, Mr. Darcy," said Miss Elizabeth at last. "My mother . . . She is concerned for our futures, and it sometimes leads her to be more eager than she ought."

"I have never doubted her affection for you all."

"No, though at times her way of showing it is not welcome. Jane will not accept anything from Mr. Bingley if she does not feel what she must for a husband. We Bennets can be a trying lot, but we are not lost to avarice."

"No, I never would have suspected you of it," replied Darcy. Then he paused and grinned at her. "And *my* family is not the best-behaved either, so in that sense, I believe we are equal."

Darcy was heartened by the sight of her grin. "That, I suppose, is nothing less than the truth, Mr. Darcy, though I would not cast aspersions on you." She sobered again. "I have warned my sisters away from Mr. Wickham and asked that they behave themselves. They have acquiesced, but I well know that they have not changed in essence. I hope you will assist—I do not trust your acquaintance in the slightest."

"I watch Wickham whenever he is near, Miss Elizabeth. You can be certain I will remain vigilant."

With a quiet word of thanks, Miss Elizabeth excused herself, no doubt to follow her sisters to the dining room. For the rest of the morning, he watched her, though he attempted to tell himself that he watched Wickham and the rest of the party as assiduously. It was fortunate that Lady Catherine was absent for breakfast, for Darcy had not the patience to endure her.

By the afternoon, the snow had lessened, though biting cold had descended over Netherfield. The thoughts of Miss Elizabeth, Miss Bennet, Bingley's situation, and that of Darcy himself continued with him throughout the day, and as the afternoon wore on, Darcy decided he had best speak with Bingley. The eldest Miss Bennets were estimable ladies, and while Bingley's attentions seemed fervent, he had seen the man's attitude in the past. He found Bingley ensconced in his study with Fitzwilliam and Hurst.

"Your aunt is the prickliest woman I have ever had the misfortune to meet, Darcy," said Bingley when he entered the room. "I know not how you have endured her all these years."

"A great deal of practice," jested Fitzwilliam.

Hurst and Bingley seemed to think this was hilarious, for they broke into laughter. Darcy could only shake his head.

"Has she done something else to make herself unwelcome?"

"She has been pestering my housekeeper all day long," said Bingley, his tone carrying more than a hint of annoyance. "It seems she believes the bedchamber to which she was assigned is not fine enough for her and wishes to be installed in one better."

"Dicked in the nob, she is," said Fitzwilliam. "She should be happy she has shelter at all. We might have been caught in that storm, left stranded in some little hovel, or frozen to death in the carriage, all because of her dynastic ambitions."

Darcy grunted at his cousin's echoing of Darcy's own words. She truly was a foolish woman.

"What of the weather?" asked Darcy. "It seems to me the snow has let up."

"It has to a certain extent," replied Bingley. "But my groundskeeper informs me that the snow is deep and the wind has hardened it. The roads are in no condition for travel. I am afraid we are all stuck here together for the immediate future."

"With that bit of cheerful news," said Fitzwilliam, before they could all settle into moroseness, "I believe I would like a game of billiards. Would any of you gentlemen care to join me?"

Hurst indicated his willingness at once, but Darcy and Bingley both refused. It worked well with Darcy's purpose that his cousin should absent himself anyway. When they were gone, Darcy turned his attention to his friend.

"I apologize for my aunt's behavior, my friend. But I thank you for enduring her as a houseguest. I have done it enough times myself to know how demanding she can be."

A wave of the hand was Bingley's response. "There is no help for it, even if I wished to throw her from the house."

"I cannot imagine that desire is far distant."

Bingley laughed. "There are times, my friend. There are times, indeed."

"I am curious, however," said Darcy. He was not certain how to approach the subject of Miss Jane Bennet and had determined that a forthright approach would be for the best.

"Yes?" replied a distracted Bingley.

"Your intentions concerning Miss Bennet."

Bingley frowned and turned his full attention to Darcy. "Is this the part where you warn me away from her as she is unsuitable?"

"Not at all," replied Darcy. "I know of no harm of the woman. She does not, I expect, possess much dowry, and there are certain elements of her family which are . . . trying. But if those factors are of no concern to you, then I shall not speak against them."

"*All* our families are perfectly well behaved, of course," was Bingley's dry reply. "My sisters, for example, or your aunt."

Darcy could not help but grin. "You are the second to point that fact out to me today, and you are no less correct than Miss Elizabeth was."

"Miss Elizabeth?" It almost seemed to Darcy like Bingley's ears perked up like a dog. "Why would you have any reason to discuss such a matter with her?"

"Because she has borne the brunt of Lady Catherine's displeasure," replied Darcy. He paused, toying with the idea of informing Bingley of her thoughts regarding her sister. Bingley watched him, apparently willing to allow Darcy to work through his thoughts, and it was this more thoughtful Bingley which led him to be explicit.

"In fact, Miss Elizabeth is convinced that her sister esteems you highly, Bingley."

A slow smile spread over his friend's countenance. "Miss Bennet loves me?"

"I said nothing of that," replied Darcy. "I am afraid you will need to discover the depth of Miss Bennet's feelings for you on your own, my friend. But I have spoken with Miss Elizabeth several times since her coming, and I am convinced she is honest and without artifice. She insists that her sister will accept nothing from you if she does not feel for you what she ought for a man who pays his addresses. The matter of Miss Bennet's preference is nothing more than her own opinion concerning her sister's feelings."

"But as her sister, she must know Miss Bennet better than either of us."

"That is the truth," replied Darcy. "Have you given thought to making her an offer?"

"There are times I have thought of little else."

Darcy sighed. "I do not wish to direct you, Bingley. Many would say it is foolish for you to offer for such a girl, who is penniless and whose family has been buried in Hertfordshire since the flood."

"My only thought is that I wish to be happy."

"Then your path seems clear. Only take care that your feelings for her are what they should be and confirm for yourself the state of *hers* without reference to her sister, your sister, or anyone else."

"As always, your advice is excellent, Darcy," said Bingley. He stood and clasped Darcy's hand, saying: "I do not know what I would do without your friendship. I thank you for it without reservation."

Then Bingley was gone, leaving a thoughtful Darcy behind. It was obvious that Bingley had made the decision to pursue Miss Bennet, and while Darcy might wonder at the wisdom of it, he could not say his friend's decision was incorrect. Then the memory of a pretty woman, with dark brown hair shining in the light, her beautiful eyes flashing with pleasure floated in Darcy's memory. Perhaps Bingley was more correct to follow his heart than Darcy had ever thought.

"Well, well, well," a detested voice interrupted Darcy's reverie. "If it is not Fitzwilliam Darcy, master of Pemberley and proud man with connections to the nobility. I never thought I would see the sight of you slumming in the country, Darcy. You have always been much too stuck up for such activities."

"Wickham," growled Darcy. "How utterly unpleasant to see you. You have somehow managed to mask the stench of your dissolute ways; else I would have detected your miasma long before you entered the room."

Far from being offended, Wickham only bared his teeth in a grin. "Charming to the last, Darcy. You have always had a way with words."

"As have you, Wickham. If only the truth would pass your lips on occasion."

"I must give you credit, Darcy," said Wickham, changing the subject. "When you choose to notice a woman, you choose the brightest one present. Then again, I could have predicted which one would catch your fancy in advance — we always have had similar taste in women. She *is* a beauty and possesses a fiery temper to match. It would be a privilege to attempt to tame that wild spirit of hers."

"I would suggest you be silent, Wickham," snarled Darcy. "She is a gentlewoman. I will not have you dishonor her."

"But you may wish to temper your admiration." Wickham sneered, sauntering about Bingley's study as if it was his own. "Lady Catherine has already seen it. If she knew her nephew, betrothed of her insipid daughter, was falling in love with the fair Miss Elizabeth, how do you think she would act?"

With a violence of motion, Darcy stepped forward and caught Wickham by the lapels. "You truly are a stupid specimen, Wickham. Bingley allowed you to stay, but do you not know that one word from me will result in your residence in the nearest snowbank?"

"Perhaps I should simply tell Miss Elizabeth what kind of a man you are," said Wickham, ignoring Darcy's threat.

"I believe she already knows," replied Darcy, amused by Wickham's threats. "But more importantly, she knows what manner of man *you* are. By all means, Wickham — attempt to ply your trade with her. I will enjoy how she puts you in your place."

Wickham wrenched his coat from Darcy's grasp and stepped away. "You are not so clever as you think."

"And you have ever overestimated your abilities," rejoined Darcy. "Do not test me, Wickham. You will not like the result. Now get out."

Though slowly, meaning to show Darcy that he was not intimidated, Wickham sauntered from the room. Darcy did not fear anything Wickham could do concerning Lady Catherine. But he would bear watching. If he had seen Darcy's budding admiration for Miss Elizabeth, he would not be above ruining one of her sisters for nothing more than spite.

CHAPTER IX

*T*urnabout, it seemed, was nothing more than fair play. Elizabeth had not intended to overhear anything. Her purpose was to avoid Lady Catherine, as she knew the lady would take the opportunity of Mr. Darcy and Colonel Fitzwilliam's absence to start berating her again. And as she had no desire to stay in her room, she had taken to walking the halls of Netherfield, mostly lost in thought.

That was when she heard raised voices emerging from one of the rooms she was passing. As a well-bred woman of her time, she knew it was not proper to eavesdrop on the conversation of others, and when the voices sounded angry, she had thought to step past the room and continue on her way simply. But then she heard the deadly cold words and thought she could taste the feeling behind them.

"And you have ever overestimated your abilities. Do not test me, Wickham. You will not like the result. Now get out."

The words chilled her, like a bucket of cold water being emptied over her head. But of more immediate concern, assuming Mr. Wickham did not stay to taunt whoever else was in the room, he would come across her. Hurrying to avoid being caught, she spied a door across the hall and let herself into a small room, pushing it to the doorjamb, but leaving a sliver open. Within moments, Mr. Wickham left the room. When he had attained the hallway, he stopped and peered back at the door, muttering imprecations under his breath. Then he turned and stomped away, still shaking his head in fury.

With a sigh of relief, Elizabeth waited until he had proceeded down the hall, and then left her sanctuary. She paused for a moment in indecision. The man in that room was likely in no mood to speak with another. But she knew his likely identity, knew that there was something terribly wrong with Mr. Wickham. And while she had no desire to know him any more than she already did, she felt a need to understand of what his sins consisted to better protect herself and her sisters. Thus, she firmed her shoulders and pushed the door open, entering the room.

From the resemblance it bore to her father's bookroom, Elizabeth thought this was likely Mr. Bingley's study, though it certainly did not contain the bookshelves, nor the books themselves, that her father kept. But it was large, airy, and commanded a fine view of the drive in front of the house, and down on the fields of Netherfield which provided its wealth. And there, in front of the window, looking down on the snow-choked fields, was a tall man, standing with his hands clasped behind his back.

"Mr. Darcy," said Elizabeth, startling him such that he whirled around. When he caught sight of her, he relaxed. She could see Mr. Darcy attempt a smile but noted that it was a miserable failure.

"Miss Bennet," replied Mr. Darcy with a bow.

Ensuring the door was left open for propriety's sake, Elizabeth stepped forward into the room. "You have my apologies, sir, but as I was walking past this room, I could not help but hear raised voices."

Mr. Darcy's countenance darkened, and he approached her, the concern alive in his eyes. "Did Wickham accost you?"

"No," replied Elizabeth. "I had the presence of mind to hide until he passed."

A nod, seeming in relieved distraction, was Mr. Darcy's response. "That is well. You should take care that you are not alone with him, Miss Bennet. No young lady should ever allow herself to be alone with him."

"That is just it, Mr. Darcy," said Elizabeth, some of her frustration seeping into her voice. "I have no knowledge of what he is capable. I appreciate you warning me of him and have taken steps to warn my sisters and avoid him myself. But I would wish to know exactly of what you accuse him."

Mr. Darcy paused, Elizabeth's request causing his countenance to become unreadable. "Is it not enough to simply know he is not to be trusted?"

"Perhaps it is, Mr. Darcy. If you will not inform me, then I suppose I must be content. But I would rather know it all, or as much as you can share with me. Your words inform me that he is a seducer of women, but I wonder if his depravities are more extensive than that."

"If you are asking if Wickham will attempt to . . . take your virtue by force, in that, at least, I believe I may acquit him, though there is precious little else he will not do." Mr. Darcy sighed, and his head drooped in defeat. "There was a time, Miss Bennet, when I considered Wickham to be among my closest friends. That was many years ago when we were still boys before he began to show signs of the character he possesses now."

When Mr. Darcy fell silent, Elizabeth, knowing it would be best not to press him, remained quiet herself. He seemed to appreciate this, for when he spoke, he did so with a smile, albeit one which did not quite reach his eyes.

"Mr. Wickham has always been in possession of fine manners which inspire belief. Thus, he can make his way through the world, amassing debts from those who should know better, and gaining the favor of those who would not associate with him if they knew his true character. Of course, he cannot hide it forever. Without fail, his excesses are exposed, and he is forced to flee. This has been the pattern in more than one location of which I have direct knowledge.

"As for his particular sins, those involve gaming, purchasing goods on credit without the hope—or intention—of paying for them, seductions, debaucheries, and cavorting with those of unsavory reputations. He fits among their number, I suppose, though usually not until those who gave him their trust have learned of his true nature. To his gaming, he pays particular attention, though he should eschew it, for he has never had much skill. Any of his other vices, however, will be a suitable substitute when the gaming tables are out of reach."

"Those are serious accusations, indeed," said Elizabeth, frowning. "We should, perhaps, take some thought of warning the shopkeepers in Meryton. He could cause much damage there if he is left to his devices."

"I thank you for believing my account, Miss Bennet. Fitzwilliam and I have taken some thought to that. If there is anything in my account which you find difficult to believe, or of which you would like proof, I can call on the testimony of more than one witness, and among that number is Fitzwilliam, who has been acquainted with Wickham since our childhoods. I also have receipts of his debts, which I purchased myself, should you wish to see them."

"I believe your word, coupled with Mr. Wickham's general behavior, is sufficient." Elizabeth frowned. "But I do wonder, with all this man has done and the heartache he has caused you, why he is not even now in prison. Given what you have suggested of his debts alone, I doubt he would ever emerge from it if he were imprisoned."

Mr. Darcy sighed and shook his head. "That, I suppose, is what, in part, has stayed my hand, though the fact that my father esteemed him is also a part of my thinking. Fitzwilliam believes as you do, Miss Bennet. But I have not told you all. For you see, Mr. Wickham also attempted to seduce my sister last summer with the intention of obtaining her dowry, which is quite substantial."

"Your forbearance is positively astonishing, Mr. Darcy!" exclaimed Elizabeth, gaping at him. "I doubt many of your station would forgive such an offense."

"I have not forgiven him," said Mr. Darcy. "My reaction to his presence at the ball is evidence of that. But there exists some possibility that Georgiana might be affected should Mr. Wickham choose to tell tales."

"The vengeful mutterings of a man in prison are not likely to be believed, Mr. Darcy, even if they were to make their way to society from such a place."

It seemed Mr. Darcy understood Elizabeth's chiding tone, for he nodded in obvious distraction. "It has also been several months since the event."

"Exactly. If he were to go to prison now, anything he says would be construed as the words of a bitter man trying to obtain revenge by any means."

Mr. Darcy nodded, though slowly. "I believe you are correct, Miss Bennet. I had not thought of it that way."

He turned his full attention back to her and favored her with a slow smile. Elizabeth felt butterflies take flight in her stomach at the sight — his countenance was made all the more handsome when he unleashed a devastating smile which was nothing less than genuine and delivered in pure happiness.

"You are a sagacious young lady, Miss Bennet. Perhaps Mr. Wickham will pay for his misdeeds much sooner than he ever thought."

They shared a suspiciously evil grin together, one fraught with a resolve to do whatever it took to see justice done. Then Elizabeth remembered what he said about his sister, and she began to feel a little mournful.

"How is your sister, Mr. Darcy? I cannot think that such an episode has not affected her."

"She is improving," said Mr. Darcy. "She has an affectionate heart, one which was persuaded to believe herself in love with Mr. Wickham due to her memories of him as a child. Furthermore, her companion, whom I had selected and hired, was discovered to be a confederate of Wickham's, with a prior acquaintance."

"Oh, Mr. Darcy," said Elizabeth, stepping forward and laying a hand on his arm. "It is clear you blame yourself for this. I cannot say what the circumstances were or how you came to hire this woman. But I will say that you cannot divine the purposes of others unless you can read their thoughts."

"Perhaps it is as you say, Miss Bennet," replied Mr. Darcy, his voice so quiet that she was forced to strain to hear his words. "But I recall my sister's tearstained face, and I must acknowledge my failures."

Moved by compassion, Elizabeth squeezed the arm she still held with her hand, and then pulled away. Something inside her was moved by the pure emotions Mr. Darcy was showing, which disproved any thought of his being incapable of them. But it would not do to be too familiar with him should someone come upon them in such an attitude.

"You must learn a little of my philosophy, Mr. Darcy." He regarded her with an expression of curiosity, which prompted her to wink at him. "Think of the past only as it gives you pleasure. While the lessons of the past are important for our continued growth, do not dwell on them. It is necessary to live in the now."

"That is remarkably wise of you, Miss Bennet," said Mr. Darcy, with no hint of patronizing. "It is not something at which I have excelled, but I shall do my utmost to follow your excellent advice."

Elizabeth sent him an encouraging smile and then excused herself. Mr. Darcy had given her much to think about, and if she was not mistaken, he had much to consider himself. Furthermore, Elizabeth knew it would be best if she warned her sisters with this new information Mr. Darcy had shared. She would not, of course, speak of Miss Darcy, though the heiress's situation was so different from that of the Bennet sisters that it did not matter. But she suspected that a lack of fortune would not protect them from a man such as Mr. Wickham.

* * *

When the company gathered for dinner that evening, the atmosphere was equally oppressive as the one previous. While there were several of the company for whom Elizabeth had little respect and no liking, she was forced to acknowledge Lady Catherine created most of the tension.

At dinner, first, she was heard to complain about virtually everything, from the beginning of the meal through to the end. "This soup is far too cold, Miss Bingley," said she soon after the soup was served to the company. "Send it back to the kitchen so that it may be warmed to the proper temperature."

"Oh, indeed," chimed in her faithful servant, Mr. Collins. "You should learn from Lady Catherine, Miss Bingley. The soup at Rosings is always served at the height of its temperature and is always a veritable treasure to partake."

"The soup is fine," rejoined Miss Bingley, ignoring Mr. Collins's contribution. "It is piping hot. Why, the steam rising from my bowl is enough to be seen clearly."

Lady Catherine narrowed her eyes at Miss Bingley from the other end of the table, but she did not comment any further on the soup. But when the next dishes arrived, her comments only increased and became much more mean-spirited.

"There is not enough salt on this pheasant," she would complain. "It is far too bland." On another occasion, she attacked Miss Bingley's menu. "Whoever heard of serving wine of this vintage with pheasant? You should have chosen better." On another, she referenced Miss Bingley's choice of dress. "That shade makes you appear positively sallow, Miss Bingley. Perhaps a nice rose would suit you better."

Through all this criticism, Elizabeth learned one thing about Miss Bingley. She had always thought the woman's greatest failings were her unreasonable pride and her overinflated sense of her importance in the world. In fact, it seemed Miss Bingley's greatest failing was vanity, for she could not simply ignore Lady Catherine. Miss Bingley, Elizabeth thought, had maintained the hope that Mr. Darcy's family would welcome her with open arms should she succeed in inducing him to propose, and this display of criticism infuriated her more and more as the dinner hour wore on. It prompted her to respond in kind to Lady Catherine's attacks.

"In fact," said Miss Bingley, when Lady Catherine mentioned the pheasant, "our cook is quite excellent in her knowledge of exactly the correct amount of seasoning. The pheasant is perfect." She made some comment about how the vintage of wine served had been present at other meals like this, and her own nephew, Mr. Darcy, had approved it. Her meanest statement, however, came when the lady attacked her dress.

"Considering," said she, "that some in attendance have dressed as if they are to enter a ballroom in London, I hardly think you possess the ability to cast stones."

Elizabeth thought the whole argument was patently ridiculous, as both women were rather overdressed for an evening. Lady Catherine, however, huffed in infuriated affront. "I will have you know, Miss Bingley, that as a member of the first circles, I am always dressed appropriate to the situation."

"As am I," replied Miss Bingley.

The two women glared at each other.

"It seems we have another grasping social climber in our company."

Lady Catherine's glare raking over Elizabeth informed the entire company—if they could be in ignorance—of who the *first* was, in Lady Catherine's opinion. Elizabeth, however, determined to ignore the woman, unwilling to be drawn into their argument.

"Let me be understood, Miss Bingley," said Lady Catherine, turning the force of her glare back on Miss Bingley. "You will never succeed in your attempts to become the mistress of Pemberley. No, never. Not only is Darcy engaged to *my* daughter, but he also would never be so lost to all that is decent by actually offering for a woman whose father was a tradesman. You are nothing but an avaricious social climber, and I am ashamed of you."

Miss Bingley's jaw might have been chiseled from stone. A scathing reply appeared to be poised on the tip of her tongue, but Colonel Fitzwilliam, who was seated by her side as dictated by propriety, leaned toward her and spoke earnestly. Miss Bingley's anger did not abate one iota, but she seemed to master it. She directed a withering glare again at Lady Catherine and then proceeded to ignore her.

For her part, Lady Catherine seemed to think she had scored a victory, for she nodded at Miss Bingley in a manner which was condescending and continued to speak. At least this time she made general observations about the entire company, most of which were laughable. In everything she said, of course, she was backed by her faithful lackey and parrot, Mr. Collins, who seemed to consider her higher than a deity. It was one of the silliest spectacles Elizabeth had ever seen.

It only became worse in the sitting-room after dinner, though

Elizabeth knew she felt that way because Lady Catherine's vitriol was directed back at her. She would never know how it had all occurred, but as Elizabeth was entering the room, she happened to be near Mr. Darcy, and he spoke to her in a soft voice:

"Thank you, Miss Elizabeth, for refusing to rise to my aunt's poor manners."

"It was no trouble, sir," replied Elizabeth. "I have no desire to draw her attention any more than necessary."

That was, of course, exactly what happened, for Elizabeth was startled by the sound of the lady's loud voice once again berating her. "Miss Elizabeth Bennet!" spat she. "What have I told you about continually trying to turn my nephew's attention to you? Must you be censured and despised by all for this egregious behavior of yours?"

"On the contrary, Lady Catherine," said Mr. Darcy, interjecting before Elizabeth could even find her wits, "it was I who spoke to Miss Elizabeth. She did nothing to try to draw my attention."

"Allow me the greater knowledge of young women of Miss Elizabeth's ilk," said Lady Catherine, her tone all airy unconcern. "She is a lady of little quality and no consequence in the world, attempting to raise herself by any means possible. In that respect, she is much like Miss Bingley, though of moderately higher birth and significantly less fortune."

It seemed that even such an insult was not enough to allow Miss Bingley to lose her superiority. She cast a sneer at Elizabeth, seeming to think she had gotten the better of the bargain. Elizabeth, who was by now, becoming incensed, ignored Miss Bingley altogether.

"Actually, Aunt," said Colonel Fitzwilliam, "I consider Miss Elizabeth to be of exemplary quality and a high degree of intelligence and worth, beyond what those foolish of society who measure others only by their physical qualities."

"Be silent, Fitzwilliam!" snapped Lady Catherine. "There is nothing of quality in such a mercenary woman as Miss Elizabeth Bennet." Lady Catherine's eyes raked over her form in disdain. "She is nothing. She never will be anything. I have seen her kind many times before."

"Lady Catherine," said Elizabeth in a voice which was nearly a snarl, "you are without a doubt the worst behaved, ill-tempered, unfeeling virago I have ever had the misfortune to meet." Mr. Collins gasped, even as Lady Catherine's face turned red with fury. "I think it best to be silent, lest you prove once and for all by your words that you are nothing more than a fool and a termagant!"

Lady Catherine screeched in offense, but Mr. Darcy reached her side, grasped her arm, and led her forcibly to a nearby sofa, where he sat close to her and spoke to her in words which were inaudible. But it was clear he was instructing her to behave in a manner which left no room for disobedience. Lady Catherine appeared as if she was not enjoying the experience of being berated by her nephew, but she was mercifully silent for a time.

"Cousin Elizabeth!" whined Mr. Collins, the other player in the drama who had yet to be silenced. "You will not disrespect Lady Catherine in such a manner! She is everything good and genteel and wise, and she is destined to be your future patroness!"

"I doubt she will ever be anything to me but a haughty, meddling crone with an opinion of her own nobility which is far from reality." Mr. Collins's eyes bulged at her, but Elizabeth turned away. "I have nothing further to say to you, sir. If you have any notions of pursuing me, I suggest you reconsider, for I will never have you."

After these altercations, the party was subdued for the rest of the evening. Lady Catherine could not be silenced forever, but when she began to pontificate in tones too loud or to speak to either Elizabeth or Miss Bingley, a frown from Mr. Darcy would silence her. She would scowl at him, but she did not push him. Mr. Collins watched Elizabeth, seemingly attempting to determine if she had been serious in her words to him. The Bingley sisters sat whispering, Bingley and Jane were inseparable, Mr. Bennet sat and laughed at everything he was seeing, and Kitty and Lydia giggled between themselves.

It was a relief, therefore, when the hour finally arrived that Elizabeth felt she could excuse herself for the evening. The Bennet sisters all departed at the same time, though not without some reluctance on Jane's part. It seemed the rest of the company was soon to break up as well, and Mr. Darcy and Colonel Fitzwilliam seemed eager to be away from Lady Catherine's toxic presence.

"You surely are in hot water," exclaimed Lydia. Though Elizabeth might not have been able to credit it, her youngest sister actually waited until they were well away from the sitting-room before her outburst. Elizabeth might have expected her to do it at a time when it could cause especial mortification.

"I cannot see how I am," replied Elizabeth, her tone studied nonchalance. "When the weather improves, Lady Catherine shall leave, and I shall never be in her company again. I care little what she says now."

Kitty and Lydia exchanged a glance and began to laugh again. "You know," said Lydia, "I think she is worrying for a good reason. It seems to me that Mr. Darcy *has* been paying much more attention to you of late."

Elizabeth turned and glared at her sister. "Do not say such things, Lydia. Do you wish Lady Catherine to overhear and become even more unendurable?"

Lydia only snorted. "She cannot overhear. And even if she should, there is nothing she can do."

"That is true. But I still do not wish to endure her continual harping on the subject. And Mr. Darcy does not have any interest in me. There is no reason to anger her when I am no threat to her daughter."

"If you will excuse me, Lizzy, I think you are protesting too much. It is clear to me that Mr. Darcy pays much more attention to you than you will confess. He *is* a handsome man, even if he is the most disagreeable man I have ever met."

With that, Lydia went to the door to her room and let herself in. Elizabeth's other sisters directed wry smiles at her, and then they, too, were gone. Elizabeth was left with entering her chambers and readying herself for bed. And she did wonder if she was denying the attraction which had suddenly appeared between herself and Mr. Darcy. And had Lady Catherine not been present, she wondered if she would be so eager to keep herself from the gentleman.

CHAPTER X

What relief the company at Netherfield could find was often found in the dead of night when they were all safely ensconced in their beds. Elizabeth was not the only member relieved at the ability to retreat from everyone else and regain a little of her composure. It was the third night of the Bennets' enforced stay at Mr. Bingley's leased home. While the company slept on, the snow, which had continued unabated for almost two days, had lessened and finally stopped, though there were still periods in which it fell, further complicating any thought of retreating from the estate.

But while most of the house slept, there was one who moved through the house on silent feet, moving carefully to avoid disturbing any of the residents who slept in their rooms. A sound disturbed the silence, the cry of an owl taking advantage of a break in the weather to search for its next meal. Heart pounding at the noise, the figure stopped, listening for anything more, but when it became aware of what had caused it, the figure continued to walk, its gait a determined step.

When it, at last, arrived at the correct door, the figure paused long enough to listen closely for any signs of movement. When there were none, it let itself into the room, taking care not to allow any screeching of the metal hinges. It then left the door open for a quick escape.

The room was dark, with only a hint of light filtering through the drawn curtains. The angle of what little light there was did not reach the bed situated in the center of one wall, instead spilling out over the floor in front of it.

On ghosted footsteps, the figure approached the bed and, upon spying the person within had knocked a pillow askew, and that it was lying halfway in their face, stepped forward with chilling intent. Grasping the pillow, the figure brought it fully down over the head, holding it there with gentle pressure. A few moments later, the person in the bed began to suffer from lack of air and began to clutch at the pillow.

Throwing all caution to the wind, the figure pressed down with every hint of strength it possessed. The sleeping person awoke and began struggling in earnest. But the figure held on grimly. After a few moments, the struggling weakened and then ceased. And with a smile of satisfaction, the figure hurried back toward the still open door and moved through, closing it firmly behind.

The morning after informing Miss Elizabeth Bennet of Wickham's sins, Darcy awoke feeling better than he had in many weeks. There was something about receiving the absolution of a good woman, though he supposed Miss Elizabeth herself would not consider it that way, which eased his guilt, washed away his lingering malaise. Georgiana was still on the mend, but Darcy finally felt her ultimate recovery was finally possible.

With an absence of mind, which in reality was nothing more than continuing thoughts of Miss Elizabeth, Darcy rose and, with the assistance of Snell, his valet, dressed and made his way to the dining room. It was entirely fortunate, in his opinion, that he met Miss Elizabeth in the hallway outside her room.

"Miss Elizabeth," said he, bowing, the gesture more a measure of respect at that moment than the social custom it was. "I hope you slept well."

"Adequately, Mr. Darcy," was her response, though she looked at him as if on the verge of some witticism. "I suppose I should not be surprised that you are an early riser. Unless, of course, something particular has drawn you from your room this morning."

"No, you should not be surprised," said Darcy, feeling the effect of a grin stretching his face. "When I was younger, perhaps I was in the habit of sleeping later, but that has not been the case for many years.

May I escort you to breakfast?"

"Of course, sir," said Miss Elizabeth, grasping his extended arm.

They made light conversation on their way to the dining room, speaking of matters of inconsequence. But her thoughts were quick and her responses equally so, and Darcy could not help but notice that the sparkle of enjoyment was in her eyes. A sense of pleased satisfaction entered his breast at the thought that *he* was responsible for putting it there.

They found they were among the first to arrive in the breakfast room; only Fitzwilliam and Mr. Bennet had arrived before they did. As Darcy entered with Miss Elizabeth, Fitzwilliam watched him with an expressive sort of glance, but one which suggested they would be speaking later. Darcy was not eager to relinquish the company of this exquisite creature, but he knew Fitzwilliam's motives — Aunt Catherine would be unbearable, should she descend and discover them in this attitude. Mr. Bennet only greeted them, a glance passing between father and daughter, the meaning of which Darcy could not fathom.

Inquiring after her preferences, Darcy offered to fix her a plate from the sideboard, which she accepted. Then they sat and began to partake of their meal. It was a companionable time between the diners, much more so than any Darcy had experienced since his arrival at Netherfield. The only other resident who disturbed them as they ate was Miss Bennet, and as she was well mannered and kind, it was no trouble to share the table with her. At least the most divisive members of the party were not present.

After breakfast, the diners decided to wait in the sitting-room for a time, and Darcy was only too eager to accompany Miss Elizabeth once again. He thought to offer her his arm, but Fitzwilliam caught his eye and motioned for him to stay, and Darcy reluctantly agreed. Miss Bennet and Miss Elizabeth went together with their father following behind.

"What do you think you are doing, Darcy?" demanded Fitzwilliam. "Do you wish for Miss Elizabeth to become even more of a target of Lady Catherine's spleen than she already is?"

"No, Fitzwilliam," replied Darcy. "But I . . ."

Fitzwilliam broke out into laughter. "I believe I see now. The great and stoic Fitzwilliam Darcy has been caught by a woman, and a country miss at that!"

Not knowing what to say, for he suspected it was nothing but the truth, he settled for glaring at his chortling cousin. Fitzwilliam, who had never been intimidated by Darcy's displeasure, continued to chuckle and shake his head.

"If that is all she was, I would continue to tease you," said he. "But she strikes me as an intelligent, worthy sort of woman, the kind who would do you good. As such, I will offer my services, Darcy. Go and pay court to your young woman. I will alert you should the dragon lady approach."

"Thank you, Cousin," said Darcy, eschewing his usual reproof at Fitzwilliam's characterization of their aunt.

"One thing, Darcy," said Fitzwilliam as Darcy turned to leave the room. "Make utterly sure she is a worthy woman. She seems to have courage aplenty, but you know she will need it all in society if you pursue this to its natural conclusion."

There was truly no need to remind his cousin that he was not even courting the woman, let alone engaged to her. He knew it would only increase Fitzwilliam's teasing. Choosing the easiest option of simply nodding, Darcy let himself from the room. Outside the sitting-room, however, he found Mr. Bennet loitering, and knew he was about to receive another well-meaning caution.

"Mr. Darcy," said Mr. Bennet, "It seems to me you have become much friendlier with my Lizzy in the past two days."

"I have had an opportunity to come to know her better than I did before," replied Darcy. "I assure you, Mr. Bennet, that I do not possess any dishonorable intentions."

"I never suspected you of any such. But you are aware of your aunt's character, and as Lizzy has already been a focus for her displeasure, I do not wish for you to further excite her anger."

"I understand, Mr. Bennet," said Darcy. "My cousin's thoughts are in line with yours. He has promised to alert me should Lady Catherine make an appearance."

Mr. Bennet seemed to consider that. "Very well. Perhaps if we all sat together, your aunt would have less reason for anger should she come upon us unaware."

Privately Darcy thought Mr. Bennet attributed a more reasonable attitude to Lady Catherine than she warranted. But he agreed to the man's suggestion, and they entered together. Miss Elizabeth and Miss Bennet were already seated on a sofa, speaking in quiet tones. Darcy might have preferred to have her attention all to himself, but he knew there was wisdom in Mr. Bennet's words. Furthermore, he *was not* courting her, though it was becoming more difficult for him to remember that fact.

"Come, Mr. Darcy," said Miss Elizabeth upon espying him entering the room. "Of what shall we speak? Or perhaps you would prefer a game? Charades?" Then she giggled. "Then again, perhaps not. Such a silly game is surely beneath your dignity."

Had Darcy thought she was speaking in censure, he still would not have been offended. Her arch smile and teasing tone rendered her comments above reproach. Rarely had he been teased in recent years, and he was finding it quite an interesting experience.

"I have played charades, Miss Elizabeth. But do you not think there are too few of us to play?"

"I have played with my sisters, and we are only five."

Miss Elizabeth turned her attention toward her father, but he knew the substance of her question before she asked. He chuckled and shook his head. "No, Lizzy, I think I shall refrain."

"Then perhaps we might play later," said Miss Bennet.

"This does not seem to be the sort of company which lends itself to such frivolity," said Miss Elizabeth, "though I have rarely seen a group of people more desperately in need of a laugh."

"If we can convince my aunt to retire early, it may be possible."

Miss Elizabeth responded with a delighted laugh. "That sounds suspiciously like censure of Lady Catherine, Mr. Darcy."

"Not at all," replied Darcy, vastly enjoying their irreverent discussion. "My aunt, you see, upholds the family honor, and though you mistakenly attribute the lack of dignity in such a game to *me*, in reality, it is my aunt who thinks in such a manner.

"But I assure you, Miss Bennet, that should Lady Catherine ever decide to lower herself to play such games, she would almost assuredly win them, for she has the talent and nobility to succeed wherever she directs her attention."

A laugh burst forth from Miss Elizabeth's lips, joined by Mr. Bennet and, in a more demure manner, from Miss Bennet, too. "You do attribute the ridiculous to your aunt, Mr. Darcy," said Miss Elizabeth. "Have you no respect for her elevated position?"

"Oh, no, Miss Elizabeth," replied Darcy. "In fact, I have that nugget of wisdom directly from Lady Catherine's mouth. I once heard her tell Georgiana that she must practice her pianoforte and that though Lady Catherine had never learned, if she had, she would have practiced constantly and become a true proficient."

The gales of laughter which ensued served as a balm to Darcy's sometimes troubled mind. What would it be like to have this woman with him, to hear that gay laughter every day for the rest of his life?

Though Darcy knew he still did not even know her well, it was at that moment when Darcy decided he wished to know her better. Perhaps now, when they were at Netherfield under Lady Catherine's watchful eye, was not the best time for a rapprochement. But Lady Catherine would leave eventually. Then Darcy would move forward in his designs with respect to this enchanting woman.

"Then we are agreed," said she, oblivious to his introspection. "This evening we shall attempt to convince your aunt that our acquaintance is no impediment to her designs and play charades when she has gone to bed. Perhaps if we feigned an argument?"

Darcy considered her suggestion, causing her grin to widen. "I doubt we could give her a performance convincing enough to induce her to believe it."

"And why would that be?" This time Miss Elizabeth's reply was more curious than teasing. Mr. Bennet snorted, and Jane watched her sister with a gentle smile, but neither spoke.

"Because, Miss Elizabeth, you and I are far too forthright to lie with any hope of convincing a suspicious woman such as my aunt."

Miss Elizabeth frowned and considered the matter, and Darcy used the opportunity of her silence to change the subject. Mr. Bennet was watching them, open appraisal in his look. It seemed that he had not misunderstood Darcy's understated inference that there *was* something between them, whereas Miss Elizabeth had not quite made the connection. Fortunately for Darcy, Miss Elizabeth shifted to their new topic with ease and did not press the matter.

They sat there for some time, discussing matters of interest to them both, Mr. Bennet and Miss Bennet adding their comments at times, but mostly content to listen. Miss Bennet, Darcy learned, was not as well read as Miss Elizabeth, but that lack came from preference rather than intelligence, for she was as sharp as her sister. Mr. Bennet's comments told him from where Miss Elizabeth had obtained her love of books, for his observations were well considered and intelligent. Darcy found himself enjoying their exchange immensely.

At times during the morning, they were joined by other residents. Miss Mary was the first, though she sat with a book herself and did not interrupt them. Soon Bingley, the Hursts, Miss Bingley, and the youngest Bennets all entered the room. But while the youngest girls sat together and spoke quietly, their discussion liberally interspersed with giggles, Miss Bingley narrowly eyed Miss Elizabeth, suspicion alive in her eyes. Darcy did not care for her opinion, so he ignored her. As for Mrs. Bennet, it seemed she was as adept as her husband at divining any interest in her daughters, for her look at him was full of confusion and hope. She did not speak, however, so Darcy was grateful for small miracles.

It was then that disaster struck. The discordant note which came over the house was not noticed by Darcy initially. His entire focus was on Miss Elizabeth's conversation, one he could not imagine enjoying more. But the noise soon attracted Darcy's attention, and he looked up, the sounds of shouting reached his ears.

It attracted Miss Elizabeth's notice as well, for she looked up and frowned. Darcy rose to go to the door when it was opened, and Fitzwilliam entered the room. His eyes were wild, alighting on Darcy, an uncharacteristic pallor making him appear naught but a ghost.

"Darcy, come with me, immediately."

Though Darcy was mystified, he followed, noting with an absence of mind that Miss Elizabeth rose also and followed them from the room. The disturbance was emanating from above stairs, prompting Darcy to hurry there and begin climbing.

"What the devil is happening, Fitzwilliam?" demanded he of his cousin.

Before Fitzwilliam could answer, the sound of a loud wailing voice echoed down from above, a counterpoint to the staccato tapping of their footsteps on the stairs. Several doors down from the landing, one of the bedroom doors was open, and outside of it, Mr. Collins was making a great deal of fuss in a loud voice.

"How could this have happened?" howled he. "This is not possible! It must be a mistake."

"What the blazes are you going on about, Collins?" asked Darcy irritably.

The parson looked around at Mr. Darcy with wild eyes, but it was Colonel Fitzwilliam who replied. "It is Lady Catherine, Darcy. She has passed in the night."

A gasp caught Darcy's attention, and he looked around to see Miss Elizabeth's shock at the horrible news. But Darcy had no notice to spare for the one who had been full of his thoughts only moments before.

"Passed? What are you saying, Fitzwilliam?" Darcy turned back to his cousin, pleading with him to share what he knew.

"Aunt Catherine is dead, Darcy. Her maid discovered her only minutes ago. She was worried when Lady Catherine did not call for her at her usual hour and entered to discover the body."

Without further thought, Darcy surged into the room, his cousin following close on his heels. The room to which Lady Catherine had been assigned did not have a sitting-room, which Darcy knew caused the woman much annoyance. But it was large, with a spacious closet on the near wall. Darcy had little interest in the room, however, and his gaze immediately fell upon the bed, upon which the unmoving body still lay.

Lady Catherine had knocked the bedcovers askew in the night, baring the nightgown-clad upper portion of her body to the air above, while the blankets lay around her hips. Her pillows were also haphazardly strewn about the bed, one lying on the floor near her head. The lady's face was slack, her eyes closed, and the rictus of some great emotion was still etched upon her face.

"Does Anne know?" asked Darcy, his faculties returning.

"Do you think she would remain ignorant with Collins's caterwauling?"

"How is she taking it?"

"She is stoic, as might be expected." Fitzwilliam paused and shook his head. "Even to her daughter, Lady Catherine was not precisely loveable. In some ways, Anne might even be relieved, though I am certain she knows nothing but shock at present."

Darcy grunted. Though it was distasteful to speak of such things, it was nothing more than the truth. "Do you think she expired because of an apoplexy or her heart stopping?"

"It is difficult to say. Perhaps a surgeon could determine the cause of death."

"There is nothing we can do now. Once the snow ceases, we should summon one and have him examine her."

"By then she may have been dead for several days. I am not sure a surgeon could make a diagnosis."

"You are likely correct," said Darcy. "But I believe we have no choice but to make an attempt. Your father will wish to know, even if he was not fond of our aunt."

Fitzwilliam snorted. "That is an understatement, Darcy. But I agree."

Elizabeth stood at the door to the room of the deceased, watching as Mr. Darcy and Colonel Fitzwilliam inspected the body of their aunt. While the wailing of Mr. Collins continued to echo throughout the hall, Elizabeth considered the situation. Something was not right. In fact, something was very wrong.

Did a woman pass in the middle of the night when she had given every indication of health the day before? Elizabeth supposed it was possible that people who appeared healthy passed with great frequency. But the memory of the butler's broken body at the top of the stairs entered her mind, and a chill shot through her. Had that not happened, Elizabeth might not have thought much of the death of an elderly woman. But two deaths in such a short span of time left her suspicious.

When the gentlemen approached her after their inspection, Elizabeth curtseyed. "Please allow me to offer my condolences for your loss, Mr. Darcy, Colonel Fitzwilliam. I know that no words are sufficient."

"Thank you, Miss Elizabeth," replied Colonel Fitzwilliam. Mr. Darcy, however, only looked at her closely, and she fancied she could see his appreciation in his gaze.

"Of course, this is an unfortunate affair, indeed," said the voice of Miss Bingley behind her. Elizabeth had not even known the woman had followed her up the stairs.

"Thank you for your support, Miss Bingley," said Mr. Darcy. "Would you be able to provide the means of dyeing some of Anne's dresses and a few cravats?" He paused and then turned to Colonel Fitzwilliam. "We will need to wait until we can go to town to obtain armbands."

"For the present," replied Colonel Fitzwilliam, "perhaps we can simply tie black cravats around our arms."

Mr. Darcy nodded. Miss Bingley was eager to agree with the request. "Of course, Mr. Darcy. I would be happy to assist. I would honor your aunt with a wreath on the front door, but as you say, we do not have the means of procuring one at present."

"Thank you, Miss Bingley, but that is not necessary."

Miss Bingley curtseyed and departed, seemingly to issue some orders to the staff. Mr. Collins, who had remained forgotten, leaning against the wall, suddenly stepped away, turning wild eyes on Mr. Darcy.

"What is to become of me now?" He wailed his question in a voice which was similar to the howl of a dog. "How am I to continue without Lady Catherine to guide me?"

"Get hold of yourself, man!" snapped Colonel Fitzwilliam. "Lady Catherine was simply a woman. She was not one to venerate from morning until night, despite how she enjoyed surrounding herself with groveling cretins such as you!"

Mr. Collins regarded Colonel Fitzwilliam with astonishment,

which quickly turned to fury. As sycophantic as he was, he might not have done anything—Colonel Fitzwilliam *was* of the nobility, after all. Even so, it was fortunate that Mr. Darcy defused the unpleasantness between the two gentlemen.

"You will continue to manage the parish as you ever have, Mr. Collins. Your appointment is for life until you choose to resign it. Nothing will change for you."

"But it will not be the same," whined Mr. Collins. "Lady Catherine was so wise and so good—how am I ever to cope without her graciously bestowed guidance?"

Colonel Fitzwilliam snorted, but Mr. Darcy ignored him. "It seems to me, sir, your instructions should come from your superiors and, more importantly, from the Bible itself. Lean on the good book when you consider decisions which must be made. Whenever you require the assistance of another opinion, it may, of course, be brought to Rosings."

"But who is the new master of Rosings?"

"I should think it would be obvious, Mr. Collins," said Colonel Fitzwilliam. "Anne is her father's heir and is the legal owner of Rosings. It has been that way for some years now, though Anne did not challenge her mother's management of the estate."

"Of course," mumbled Mr. Collins. Then he shook his head and regarded Mr. Darcy again, the light of fanatical zeal shining in the depths of his eyes. "We will *all* honor Lady Catherine by donning mourning attire. Everyone in residence at Netherfield will show their veneration for her ladyship."

"Mr. Collins," said Elizabeth, feeling it incumbent upon herself to interject, "not only was Lady Catherine in no way connected to the Bennets, but my sisters and I do not have the gowns sufficient to be dyed. Even now, the servants must wash our clothing on a daily basis, as we do not have enough for more than two days."

"Of course, you will mourn her!" cried Mr. Collins. "The degree of kinship does not matter when it comes to such an important personage as Lady Catherine de Bourgh. The servants may continue to wash your things once they are dyed. I absolutely insist."

"It does not offend us if we are the only ones in mourning as is proper, Mr. Collins," said Mr. Darcy. Elizabeth looked at him, grateful for his intervention.

"Nonsense, Mr. Darcy." Mr. Collins bowed so that had he extended his hands, his knuckles would have dragged on the floor. "It is what is right and proper."

"You would not know proper if it picked up a stick and beat you about the head," muttered Colonel Fitzwilliam.

Elizabeth tried to stifle a laugh, and she could see Mr. Darcy in the same straits. Mr. Collins, however, scowled at Colonel Fitzwilliam, before lifting his nose high in the air, a passable imitation of his late patroness.

"I shall speak with Mr. Bennet. I am certain he will see the wisdom of my words. *I* am a parson, after all, and am intimately familiar with the proper behavior in all circumstances. The Bennets will join you in mourning — this I pledge."

Then he turned and made his way down the stairs, likely intent upon finding Mr. Bennet. The three left behind watched his retreating back, Elizabeth with revulsion, the colonel as if he wished to be *holding* the stick that beat Mr. Collins, and Mr. Darcy with annoyance.

"I am sorry, gentlemen," said Elizabeth, curtseying to the two men. "I am sure you must wish for my absence."

"Thank you, Miss Elizabeth," said Mr. Darcy as she turned to leave.

"For what?" asked Elizabeth, curious as to his meaning.

"For your support and understanding. Please know that we will not require you or your family to don mourning clothes."

Elizabeth returned an impish smile on the gentleman. "I thank you, sir. But there is no need to worry. I doubt my father will oblige Mr. Collins in this instance. I rather think he will laugh at my cousin."

Though the situation was what it was, both gentlemen managed to smile in return. Then Elizabeth excused herself, intending to pay a visit to a new friend.

Chapter XI

*B*efore Elizabeth could think of seeing Miss de Bourgh as she wished, she thought it prudent to discover how Mr. Collins's efforts with her father were proceeding. Furthermore, she felt certain the recently bereaved would wish to compose herself before receiving the inevitable visits from the residents. Therefore, Elizabeth made her way down to the sitting-room where she knew Mr. Collins had gone directly after announcing his intentions.

As it turned out, she need not have concerned herself, for her father reacted in exactly the manner Elizabeth might have suspected. She entered the room to the sound of Mr. Collins's droning voice accosting her father. From the expression on various faces, the event of Lady Catherine's passing had shocked them all, though Kitty and Lydia were treating the matter with as little gravity as she might have expected.

"Lady Catherine, you see," stated Mr. Collins in his usually ponderous tone, "was a woman of high stature, both in her influence on all those within reach of her arm, but also in the wisdom, fortitude, generosity, uprightness, knowledge, and condescension toward all, no matter what rank or position in the world."

"I have no doubt of it, sir. Lady Catherine was the most

condescending individual I have ever met in my entire life."

While it was all Elizabeth could do not to choke as she attempted not to laugh at her father's sardonic statement, Mr. Collins returned a beatific smile. He was so silly; he could not imagine anyone harboring different feelings about his patroness.

"Indeed, it is true, Mr. Bennet. She was a veritable jewel, a gift from God on high to us all, and the unhappy event of her passing grievously lessens us. In fact, I dare say we are all afflicted by feelings too delicate to put to words, so tragic is this event, which I would not even have considered possible. Though we are to be pitied, it is for us to throw off this sadness which threatens to render us incapable of any action, no matter how small. I believe it best that we continue to forge our way as best we can. There is little else we can do, and, indeed, I dare say it was what her ladyship would have wished."

"I am certain she is standing amongst the angels even now, Mr. Collins, exhorting us to live our lives, bereft as we are."

Again, Elizabeth stifled a laugh, and so as not to embarrass herself, she looked about the room for something to occupy her while she waited for Mr. Collins to come to the point. It was then that she noticed her youngest sisters were becoming more raucous with their laughter and thought to have a word with them. But as she made her way toward them, another of her sisters spoke before she could.

"Kitty! Lydia!" reprimanded Mary. "A woman has died. Can you not have a little decorum?"

Lydia huffed and said in a snide tone: "Who cares about such a mean old witch? She received what she deserved, in my opinion."

"Regardless of what you think of her, this is unseemly. Death is not a matter to be mocked, no matter who has passed on."

"Mary is correct, Lydia," said Elizabeth when she came close enough to speak in a low voice.

"Surely you did not like her, Lizzy," said Lydia. "She was far meaner toward you than she was the rest of us."

"My personal feelings for Lady Catherine in no way affect the way I act at her passing, Lydia. I will not laugh at anyone who has lost their life. You will offend Mr. Darcy and his relations, and Mr. Bingley will be offended because his guests are. Cease this objectionable behavior!"

"Oh, very well," said a sulky Lydia. "I suppose you must be correct." Then her expression became sly. "I suppose *you* would not wish for Mr. Darcy to be offended."

"Of course not," replied Elizabeth. "And I do not wish for any of Mr. Bingley's relations to be offended either."

"There is no use protesting, Lizzy. We can all see how sweet you are on Mr. Darcy."

Though Elizabeth thought to object, Lydia turned away and began to speak to Kitty in soft tones. As they were not laughing and carrying on, Elizabeth decided to leave it be. If she protested, she knew it would only spur Lydia on, and that was the last thing she wanted at present. So she shared an exasperated smile with Mary and turned her attention back to Mr. Collins. It seemed the parson was wrapping up his argument with Mr. Bennet.

"Therefore, Mr. Bennet, you must see how necessary it is that we support Miss de Bourgh in this difficult time. Indeed, we must all show our veneration for Lady Catherine in any way we can."

"Yes, indeed, Mr. Collins," replied her father, amusement written in every line upon his face. "I have no quarrel with such sentiments."

"Then you will join me in donning mourning in respect for Lady Catherine." Mr. Collins's tone informed Elizabeth he was confident he had made his point.

"Oh, I see no occasion for that."

Mr. Collins's face fell. "But Mr. Bennet!" cried he. "Can you not see how necessary such a gesture is? Her ladyship deserves our respect."

"Respect is one thing, Mr. Collins, and I have no compunction toward offering it. But as we are residents at this estate without the ability to leave, we do not have sufficient clothes to allow my daughters' dresses to be dyed black. Furthermore, we are not connected to Lady Catherine in any way, and as such, donning mourning would be a presumptuous liberty."

"But *I* am connected to Lady Catherine!" was Mr. Collins's shrill protest.

"Then *you* may don mourning if you so choose. In fact, it will not be difficult for you, as you are dressed in black at all times."

Elizabeth snickered even while Mr. Collins colored in fury. Her father, however, was not about to allow his cousin to dictate to them.

"No, Mr. Collins, I cannot see any reason why we would mourn a woman so wholly unconnected to us as Lady Catherine. You may do as you choose, but the Bennets will not follow suit."

As Mr. Collins wound himself up for a lengthy retort, Elizabeth slipped from the room. Her father, it seemed, had everything well in hand. Instead, Elizabeth made her way up the stairs and turned toward Miss de Bourgh's room, knocking on the door quietly when she arrived there.

The maid opened the door, and Elizabeth inquired quietly as to her mistress's situation. The maid spoke with Miss de Bourgh and soon allowed Elizabeth into the room, where Miss de Bourgh was sitting on a chair close to the fire, clearly caught up in introspection.

"I apologize for disturbing you at this time, Miss de Bourgh," said Elizabeth, uncertain how she would be received. "I wished to come and offer my sincere condolences on the occasion of your mother's passing."

"Oh, Elizabeth," said Miss de Bourgh, "did we not agree to call each other by our Christian names?"

"Indeed, we did, Anne," said Elizabeth, relieved her new friend did not consider her actions an impertinence. "I *am* sorry for your loss."

Anne sighed and motioned for Elizabeth to join her. "I thank you for your sentiments. I cannot, however, misunderstand that you are offering them, even given the manner in which my mother treated you, which was, by any reasonable measurement, infamous."

"Whatever your mother said or did," replied Elizabeth, "I cannot help but be sorry for you. I would never wish for the demise of another simply because I disagreed with her."

"That is to your credit. I would not have blamed you had you resented my mother and secretly rejoiced because of her demise." Anne shook her head when Elizabeth made to protest. "Yes, I know you would never have done this. And I would never have expected it of you.

"The fact of the matter is that I am almost . . . confused at my mother's passing. I know not what to feel."

Though heartbroken by the thought of Anne's bewilderment, Elizabeth could readily understand. "I, too, have sometimes shared a difficult relationship with my mother. I think I have some comprehension of what you are feeling."

Anne responded with a wry smile. "I had not considered it, but I suppose that makes a certain sense. Is your mother as difficult as mine?"

"I do not know," replied Elizabeth. "Mother possesses certain beliefs which are in opposition to mine, including a desire to see her daughters wed at any cost to whoever will offer for us. I, however, wish to find a man I can esteem and love, and will not marry if I cannot find such a man."

"That is the direct opposite of my situation," said Anne with a smile. "My mother wished me to be married to *Darcy* at any cost, as I am certain you already know."

"Then I presume she was constantly embarrassing you," said

Elizabeth. "I know my mother was me, though that is mostly from a lack of understanding of how to behave."

"While *my* mother felt she knew the proper way of behaving and mistook the matter entirely!"

The two friends laughed together, relieving a little of the tension and gloom which had built up because of the news of Lady Catherine's death. "Perhaps it is best that we can remember the deceased in such terms as this," said Elizabeth. "It will help you remember her in better times, to remember the good of your mother, rather than those things which caused you grief."

Anne's look became introspective. "I *do* remember better times with my mother." Anne paused and smiled. "She was not always the domineering, insistent woman you have known these past days. Or perhaps I should say she was not always so fearsome, for while she grew ever more impatient and demanding in her later life, she has always been of a forceful personality.

"When my father was alive, we were happy, for my mother, though perhaps she did not love my father, esteemed and respected him. You may not credit it, Elizabeth, but she looked up to him and supported him in whatever way she felt necessary."

"I do not disbelieve you, Anne. I know nothing of your father and had no thoughts or opinions of how your mother might have been earlier in her life."

Anne nodded, still distracted. "It is true. Theirs was a match arranged by their fathers, and it was certainly not a love match. But my father was a good man, who cared for his lands and his family, and my mother esteemed him. But it all changed after my father's death."

She fell silent for a moment, and Elizabeth waited for her to speak again. She sensed that Anne, more than anything, needed someone to simply listen to her, to allow her to unburden her innermost thoughts without interruption or any form of judgment. Elizabeth did not know she was the best person to take on the task, but she was willing to assist her friend in whatever she needed.

"I had a younger brother. Did you know?"

"No, I did not," replied Elizabeth.

"He died about the same time as my father. A fever swept through Kent at that time, and both my father and my younger brother succumbed to it. I managed to fight it off, but my health has not been the same since. When I finally regained what health I could and began to take notice of the world again, my mother had changed. She now worried excessively for me, even as she mourned her husband and younger child. I think that was the beginning of her insistence that Darcy and I marry."

"Because she wished you to be cared for."

"Yes," confirmed Anne. "I am well now, but for several years after the fever, I fell ill again frequently, and I am certain she thought many times that she would lose me to it. I am not robust. I will never be. But I am healthy enough now. But mother took to coddling me as if she wished to avoid any possibility of my falling ill again. Though she has always been a forceful woman, she changed over the years, until she became this woman who attempted to dominate all without any care as to their own opinions. She was . . . difficult to live with at times."

Elizabeth did not quite know what to say. This was a far different picture of Lady Catherine from that she had ever thought to obtain. Perhaps it was for the best that she did not say anything. Anne was remembering the good times, and that was what mattered.

At length, Anne indicated her intention of resting for a time. Elizabeth smiled and wished her a good rest before letting herself from the room. She had been given much on which to think, and she knew it would take some time to sort through her feelings and impressions of the day.

Elizabeth's room was dull. Within the confines of her bedchamber, she had naught but herself and the scene through the window, a dreary landscape which showed her nothing but piled snow, sticklike trees grasping vainly at the sky, and the light of a sun, entirely too weak, even when it could actually be seen through the persistent cloud cover. Even that brought her no joy, for it threatened a resumption of the snow which had fallen unceasingly until the previous night. Even as she had looked out the various windows throughout the day, she had noted periods of snowfall interspersed with times of calm. As the roads were still clogged, there would be no respite from Netherfield soon.

But Elizabeth was also not equal to company—she had little patience for Mr. Bingley's superior sisters, none for the obsequious and whining Mr. Collins, and even the thought of her sisters made her long for her continued solitude. As such, Elizabeth exited her room to once again wander the halls of Netherfield with nothing but her thoughts for company. It was as she was thus engaged that she came upon a conversation she was not meant to hear.

"Well, I for one am happy the old biddy is gone," said a voice. Elizabeth stopped and looked about, noting a door along the hall was open. "She was a hard one to please—that is certain."

"You should not speak that way, Hetty," said a second voice. "If the mistress hears it her anger will be something to behold!"

It seemed Elizabeth had stumbled upon a conversation between two of the maids. Though she did not know the second voice, Hetty had previously worked at the Lucas estate before Mr. Bingley had come to Netherfield.

"Oh, fiddlesticks!" said Hetty. "Miss Bingley hated the grand lady as much as any servant. Why, I heard an argument between them yesterday which would have made the stable boy blush. The language they was using! I thought it might have peeled the paint off the walls, they was shrieking so much!"

"It is no surprise. The way Miss Bingley was always eyeing that Mr. Darcy and instructing the servants to report on his every movement! It is said Lady Catherine wished him to marry her daughter. She would never have stood for such degradation."

"And she was wide of the mark. She should have paid more attention to Miss Lizzy. If there is anyone at Netherfield who is a threat to Lady Catherine's designs, it is Miss Elizabeth. Why, the man almost devours her with his eyes!"

Cheeks flaming, Elizabeth fled in the opposite direction. The supposed attraction Mr. Darcy felt for her, she shunted to the side with little effort. She had seen some of it herself and was not surprised that others had as well, though she *did* object to the characterization of the maids' gossip. This matter of an argument between Lady Catherine and Miss Bingley, however, was something of which she had not known. An awful premonition began growing in her mind. Was Lady Catherine's death natural? Or had there been a more sinister hand in it?

Whether her footsteps took her there of their own accord or she had some intention of moving thither, Elizabeth soon found herself again in the hallway outside the bedrooms the guests were inhabiting at Netherfield. There, standing outside Lady Catherine's room, stood Mr. Darcy. He was wearing a freshly dyed cravat with another tied around his arm as his cousin had indicated, and Elizabeth thought he must just have put them on, as it had not been long since the request for dye had been issued. He was staring at the door to the room, though Elizabeth's understanding was that Lady Catherine's body had been moved to the cellar. He turned when he caught sight of her approaching.

"Miss Elizabeth," said Darcy in greeting. "May I suppose by your dress that Mr. Collins did not succeed in persuading your father?"

"Papa felt no need to comply, as I informed Mr. Collins," replied Miss Elizabeth. "And there are many reasons why we would not."

Mr. Darcy shook his head. "It is nonsensical that he would even attempt to suggest such a thing."

"Mr. Collins has never been known for his sense— at least not as long as I have known him."

A chuckle escaped Darcy's lips, though he was more exasperated with the man than amused. Lady Catherine truly did have a way of gathering the most ridiculous to her like flies to honey.

"I am more interested in your presence here, Mr. Darcy. Is there something amiss?"

"Everything is amiss, I suppose," replied Darcy. He turned his full attention on her. "I could not help but overhear a little of your conversation with Anne earlier." She colored, and Darcy hastened to reassure her. "I thank you for your kindness to my cousin. Fitzwilliam and I have been occupied with the arrangements for my aunt's body, and we don't quite know what to say anyway. You assisted her when you had no reason to do so. For that, I thank you."

"It was nothing, Mr. Darcy," said Miss Elizabeth. "I esteem your cousin very much, though we have only just met. I was happy to provide a listening ear to her."

"Given the way my aunt treated you, it speaks very much to your credit."

Miss Elizabeth turned away, murmuring thanks, though seeming embarrassed by his praise. She was an estimable woman, Darcy decided. Despite her protests, Darcy knew that many women—Miss Caroline Bingley perhaps among them—would not think of offering such comfort when Lady Catherine had behaved as she had. Miss Elizabeth was a rare gem, made all the more precious because she was so genuine, so kind.

Darcy's mind returned to the scene in the hallway when Miss Elizabeth left them. Darcy had watched her in admiration at the resilience she showed and the wit she displayed, even when it was understated as it had been at that moment. When she left, Fitzwilliam had leaned toward him and given him a stern look.

"Darcy, if you do not marry that girl, I think I will. If you have any intelligence at all, you will not allow her to slip through your fingers."

Thinking back on it, Darcy could not help but reflect that his cousin was correct in every particular. She was a rare gem worth much more than the price of everything Darcy owned. He *would* be a fool to allow her to escape.

"I ask you again, sir," her voice returned to draw his attention, "why are you staring at the door to your late aunt's room."

"I do not know," confessed Darcy. "I have been thinking of what has happened, and something about the entire affair bothers me."

Miss Elizabeth hesitated, and then she said: "I have had the same thoughts. I . . . I overheard a conversation only a short time ago. It seems that Lady Catherine and Miss Bingley engaged in a bitter argument only yesterday. I must own that I wondered if Lady Catherine's death was an accident."

Her last words were spoken in a rush as if she attempted to spit them out before she lost her courage. Though Darcy thought the idea of Miss Bingley as a murderer was silly, her thoughts meshed with his seamlessly. Could Lady Catherine's death have been murder?

"I did not know about that argument, Miss Bennet. But Miss Bingley is not the only person who argued with Lady Catherine yesterday. I distinctly remember her quarreling with Mr. Bennet in this very hallway."

Though shocked, Miss Elizabeth quickly recovered, scowled, and rested her hands on her hips, regarding him with no little asperity. "Are you suggesting my father is a murderer, sir?"

She presented an impressive picture. Darcy shook his head. "No, I am not. But I *am* reminding you that you should not jump to a conclusion based on one anecdotal piece of evidence, and one which is not even singular. Other than Miss Bingley and your father, Lady Catherine also argued with *you* and *me*. In fact, Fitzwilliam had every right to be frustrated with her. But I do not suggest that my cousin murdered our aunt, either. Shall we consider ourselves suspects?"

She appeared mollified, for she dropped her hands and nodded, appearing distracted. "If an argument is enough for a person to murder another, you are completely correct, sir. Anyone at Netherfield might have decided to do the deed based on your aunt's behavior."

Darcy grinned. "Though I would like to disagree with your assessment, I cannot. It is unfortunate but true—Lady Catherine often had that effect on others."

"It seems a hopeless business, Mr. Darcy. *Two* people in this house have lost their lives since we were forced to stay here, and all we have are suspicions. I do not even know if *anyone* has been murdered. But it does not seem right to me, especially since your aunt was in good health yesterday."

"And anyone could be a suspect, though I suppose some are more likely than others."

They stood for a few moments, each consumed with their own thoughts. For Darcy, though he thought Miss Elizabeth was focused on the puzzle which was set before them, Darcy found his thoughts slipping to her as much as the subject at hand. She was intelligent enough to solve a mystery, if, indeed, they were confronted by one. But a young lady was held to a certain standard of behavior, and working out the details of such an obscure riddle did not seem to be within the purview of such behavior. Did he dare seek her assistance? In the end, Miss Elizabeth made the decision before Darcy could raise the subject himself.

"Perhaps, sir, we should attempt to discover what truly happened. *If* Lady Catherine was murdered, then there is every possibility there is some danger to the rest of us."

"That is certainly possible," replied Darcy.

"Then shall we investigate? Perhaps there is something in Lady Catherine's room which would shed some light on what happened to her."

A slow grin settled over Darcy's face. "I think, Miss Elizabeth, you have made an excellent suggestion."

CHAPTER XII

The party which gathered together that evening was much subdued, and they were missing two of their number from the previous evening—the unfortunate Lady Catherine and Anne, who had decided it would be best if she remained in her rooms. While Lady Catherine had been a woman who had not been much liked by virtually anyone in residence—even, perhaps, her relations—the fact was that she had died. Whether a person was old or young, thoughts of morality must take precedence at such a moment. Elizabeth could not help but feel a hint of fear. She hoped that she was mistaken in her suspicions, but she feared she was not.

At dinner, the conversation consisted of such banal subjects as to be completely uninteresting. While Elizabeth might have wished for more scintillating subjects to be discussed as a usual rule, tonight, after two evenings of Lady Catherine's harangues, she found dinner to be pleasant. Even Miss Bingley, who could be counted on, in other circumstances, to attempt to draw Mr. Darcy's attention to her, was blessedly silent throughout the meal hour. A glance at Mr. Darcy, confirmed by his returning shrug, told Elizabeth he was thankful to be free of her for the moment.

Elizabeth thought most of those present might prefer to avoid the after dinner sitting-room, but they all trooped there, the gentlemen deciding not to stay behind and partake of port or cigars, or whatever else gentlemen did at such times. For a time in the sitting-room, they were treated to Mrs. Hurst and Miss Bingley sharing their talents on the pianoforte, and Elizabeth was grateful for it. Not only were they talented pianists, but there did not seem to be much appetite for conversation.

After the Bingley sisters left the instrument, Mary, eager as she was to share her talents on every occasion, sat at the instrument after Elizabeth had declined. Miss Bingley used this opportunity for another dig at Elizabeth, though it was halfhearted at best.

"You do not wish to play tonight, Miss Elizabeth?" Then she answered her own question. "Of course, you do not. Perhaps it is best. It is only unfortunate that your sister does not follow your example."

Miss Bingley turned a snide look at Mary. Her sister had chosen a simple piece, and it suited her skill level quite well, allowing her to play it proficiently. Unfortunately, Mary's playing was pedantic, and she used little emotion, as always. But Elizabeth, annoyed as she was by Miss Bingley's ill-tempered attack on Mary, was not about to let the barb pass.

"Mary's playing is pure and free of embellishment, and tonight I find it pleasing. She is ever striving to improve herself, which I find admirable. Would you not agree?"

"Of course," replied Miss Bingley. "It is only unfortunate that she does not find that such things come easily to her. It seems to be a common theme in your family."

"A family of expert musicians, we are not," agreed Elizabeth. "But we all have our strengths and weaknesses. We also know much of our history and have many stories of our forebears, those who built the Bennet name and grew my family's legacy. I am certain you must have similar stories in your own family."

Miss Bingley glared at Elizabeth. "Quite so, Miss Elizabeth." Then she turned and walked away with her sister.

A snort nearby alerted Elizabeth to the fact that her father had heard the exchange. He nodded but did not look at her, intent as he was upon his book. However, from time to time Elizabeth saw his eyes wander away from his page and over the assembled, often stopping to rest upon his two youngest daughters in particular. Elizabeth could not quite make him out—she had never seen him this watchful in a company such as this before.

Soon Miss Bingley, ennui settling over her, called for the card table to be set up, much to Mr. Hurst's pleasure. She entreated Mr. Darcy to play with them, but the gentlemen refused, much to her chagrin. She was caught in a trap of her own making and sat down to a game, Mr. Hurst, Mrs. Hurst and Mr. Bingley making up the rest of the players. As Elizabeth noted that Mr. Darcy held a book which interested her in his hand, she sat next to him on the pretext of discussing it with him, when in reality she wished to ask him about the pact they had made earlier in the day.

"Does any of this seem . . . unusual to you, Mr. Darcy?" asked she after they had spoken of his tome for some moments.

"In what way?"

Elizabeth shook her head. "I cannot quite make it out, sir. Most of the company seems unconcerned about the fact that there have been two deaths at Netherfield in the past three days. Do they not understand how suspicious it all sounds?"

"We have not determined anything yet, Miss Elizabeth," said Mr. Darcy. "It may yet be a tragic coincidence."

"Perhaps. But it strains credulity."

A nod from her companion was followed by a gesture at Colonel Fitzwilliam. "My cousin is certainly not viewing the recent events with sanguinity."

"He seems . . . irritable," ventured Elizabeth.

"He is worried, Miss Elizabeth. He sees what has happened, and he wonders too, though he has no more proof than we. Also, your father has been watching the company closely. This whole situation is unlike anything I have ever before encountered."

Elizabeth turned and regarded him, wondering to what he referred. Mr. Darcy was quick to answer.

"In situations like this, much would be done to prepare for the funeral of the deceased. But as we are trapped at Netherfield at present, all we have done is to ensure Lady Catherine rests in a location which will preserve her body as best we can. This is quite irregular, Miss Elizabeth, as I am certain you understand."

Elizabeth thought for a moment. "What do *you* believe, Mr. Darcy? Do you believe something is happening here which may threaten us all?"

A shaken head was his response. "I am unsure. It does seem suspicious, as you already stated. But there was nothing about the body of Lady Catherine which suggested she met her end due to any violence. I do not believe I saw any marks upon her, and though her bed coverings were haphazardly strewn about, that may be due to nothing more than a restless sleeper, followed by a sudden pain in the heart or other such attacks. Therefore, I must conclude there was no struggle when she passed — or perhaps I should say there was no *visible* struggle."

"Then why are we worried?"

"Because it is unexplained, Miss Bennet. It may be nothing more than coincidence that two people died within days of each other. But it may *not* be a coincidence. I do not think that we are in much danger at present, even if there is one among us who has killed two already. But the longer we are trapped here, the more that danger will rise. It would behoove us all to ensure we are not alone anywhere in this house. Your sisters should stay together, to lessen the chance of harm befalling them.

"The other matter to consider is that *if* there is a killer, why has he killed those two people in particular? What is his motive? It seems odd that two people virtually unknown to each other have met their ends. If they were murdered, what is the connection?"

Elizabeth chewed her lip in thought. "I cannot say. There does not seem to be anything connecting them."

"There must be, even though it is not evident. If there is a killer."

"You are correct, of course," said Elizabeth, still rolling the matter over in her mind.

The sound of giggling then caught her attention, and she looked over to see Kitty and Lydia sitting close to Mr. Wickham. The lieutenant seemed to be relating some anecdote to them, and by their response, they must have found it amusing. Mary had, during Elizabeth's conversation with Mr. Darcy, left the pianoforte and was sitting nearby her younger sisters, regarding them, disapproval evident in her scowl. Since Mary was close by and nothing could happen in a sitting-room, she decided not to reprimand them.

But there was one who was not shy about doing so. "Cousins!" the voice of Mr. Collins cracked like a whip, the first time Elizabeth had ever heard him speak in such a manner. "Cease this carrying on at once! Do you not know my patroness has returned to live among the angels this very day? I must have your respect for her position and authority."

"Of course, we know," said Lydia, sniffing at him with disdain. "Even if we *had* forgotten, you would remind us of it constantly."

The offense felt by Mr. Collins was clear for all to see. But instead of speaking further to Lydia, he focussed on them all. "And what of the rest of you? Playing cards, reading, speaking in a secretive fashion." His sneer at Elizabeth and Mr. Darcy showed him to be mistrustful of their actions. "This is not the way to mourn a woman of Lady Catherine's stature! Why are you not all in mourning garb?"

It was Miss Bingley who responded. "Lady Catherine was not related to us, Mr. Collins. There is no need for us to don widow's reeds as if our husbands had passed."

"We are not offended," said Mr. Darcy, for what seemed like the hundredth time.

Mr. Collins's huff was evidence of his disdain. "Then shall we not at least do *something* to honor the dead? I shall read from the good book if you will all listen."

Though it was clear few wished for such an activity, it seemed a good way to placate the parson. He was correct, after a fashion. This situation was such that it was impossible to do what was normally done in such circumstances, and it seemed best that something be done.

"To that, I can agree," said Mr. Bennet. "Kitty, Lydia, come here. Let us allow Mr. Collins to sermonize to us since he wishes it."

"I believe we shall listen as well," said Mr. Bingley, rising from the card table. His companions huffed, but they rose and followed him without protest.

What followed was such a surprise that Elizabeth would not have expected it. Mr. Collins, it seemed, possessed a voice which was perfectly cadenced for reading from the Bible. Even his choice of material was generally good, for the subjects he spoke on were often those associated with the passing of loved ones.

"*The Lord is my shepherd, I shall not want,*" said he, opening the Bible to Psalms 23. And he continued from there, reading a selection of verses, most of which were quite familiar to Elizabeth. When he concluded his reading about an hour later, the entire room was subdued. The hour was growing late, and Elizabeth wondered if the company would break up soon after.

Before anyone made to leave, Miss Bingley rose to walk about the room. "It is refreshing to walk about after sitting in one attitude," said she by way of explanation. She pulled her sister up to join her. Even Mr. Collins did not object to her slow, measured walk, as he sat with his head bowed, seemingly considering the book which lay open in his lap.

Sensing an opportunity, Elizabeth grasped Jane's hand and pulled her to her feet, moving to join the Bingley sisters. "I hope you do not mind if we join you," said Elizabeth.

For once, Miss Bingley did not protest or otherwise comment. She only nodded and grasped Jane's arm. "Of course, we are happy to have you and dear Jane. Having been away from your home for so many days now, I can imagine you must wish to be back in comfortable surroundings."

"Yes," replied Jane in her usually diffident manner. "I believe I speak for all my family when I say we would prefer to be at home. Not that your hospitality has not been everything lovely."

"Of course, we understand your meaning," replied Mrs. Hurst. "Hopefully, the weather will clear soon, and you can return."

"All your guests will be departing soon after," observed Elizabeth. "We will return to our home, but Mr. Darcy and his family must also bear their aunt to wherever she will be interred."

The introduction of Lady Catherine to the conversation was deliberate, and Elizabeth watched closely to see if the woman made any reaction. She was not disappointed, for Miss Bingley sneered and turned away without saying anything.

"It is such a tragedy," said Mrs. Hurst, seemingly oblivious to her sister's reaction. "I think the family has been quite shaken by what has happened."

"Oh, very shaken, indeed," said Miss Bingley, her tone all that was spiteful.

"It must be a shock to us all," said Elizabeth, ignoring the woman, but attempting to goad her to be more explicit. "I certainly was no friend of Lady Catherine, and she no friend to me. I am excessively sorry for Mr. Darcy and his family, though, for they have lost a venerated member. For the rest of us . . . "

Miss Bingley focused on Elizabeth with more than a little curiosity. "What, Miss Elizabeth?"

Shaking her head, Elizabeth tried to look embarrassed and said: "I am not happy at Lady Catherine's demise. But I am relieved not to be the target of her censure."

Once again Miss Bingley allowed her anger to overcome her. "I am certain *you* are relieved. She was mean and spiteful to us all. Why, do you know she attempted to take me to task for my friendship with Mr. Darcy? That she disapproved of me?"

Gratified she had managed to provoke a response, Elizabeth only said: "No, I was not aware."

"She did!" exclaimed Miss Bingley as if she had suffered some mortal insult. "Nothing was good enough for her. She did not like the room in which she was housed, though we had no word of her coming.

She did not like the meals provided to her, though we did not expect to feed *three* more mouths."

Miss Bingley paused, and she seemed to feel it necessary to exonerate the Bennets, saying: "Of course, I understand circumstances necessitated your stay, dear Jane, and we do not blame you for it. But Lady Catherine! The lady invites herself to stay without even a by your leave, and nothing is good enough for her!"

"That is, indeed, ungracious," allowed Jane, the most she would ever be prevailed on to say negatively about another.

"You have been an exceptional guest," said Miss Bingley. Then she turned to Elizabeth, and though it was easy to see that she did so grudgingly, she continued: "*All* your family has been good guests. But Lady Catherine . . ." The woman growled under her breath, and Elizabeth felt certain she was not even aware she had made such an unladylike sound. "She also accused me of attempting to garner Mr. Darcy's attention to myself! As if I was some unworthy social-climber! How is such a woman to be borne?"

Swallowing the retort that Miss Bingley had been engaged in exactly that, and for more than just Mr. Darcy's stay in Hertfordshire, Elizabeth showed a commiserating smile to Miss Bingley. "I was, if you recall, the recipient of the same accusations."

"That is exactly what I mean!" cried Miss Bingley. She garnered several looks due to her outburst and had the sense to lower her voice when she spoke again. "Our situations are in no way similar and should not be viewed in the same way. I was shocked she possessed the audacity to claim we were engaged in the same behavior."

We were not, thought Elizabeth. It occurred to her that perhaps she should be offended by Miss Bingley's outrage. But she was far too amused by the woman's ridiculous conceit.

"Did you have specific words with Lady Catherine?" asked Elizabeth instead.

"I did! The woman managed to corner me alone yesterday, and she proceeded to speak at *great* length about the inferiority of my connections and the presumption I possessed to think myself high enough that I might aspire to a man of Mr. Darcy's stature in society. It was at least thirty minutes before I could escape the virago! She was in every way horrible! I have never been so angry and insulted in my life!"

Miss Bingley continued to speak at great length on the subject of Lady Catherine. She spoke of her anger that the lady had berated her, how incensed she was to be considered inferior. She regaled them with her disgust at being held to the same standard as Elizabeth herself, though she did not seem to realize how insulting her words were. While Elizabeth tried to give the appearance of interest in her harangue, in reality, she was thinking, considering one statement Miss Bingley had made.

"I have never been so angry and insulted in my life!"

It was clear that Miss Bingley was offended. But had she been insulted enough to consider attempting to end another's life? Could such a thing even be imagined? Or if she *had* managed to murder Lady Catherine, had she done it in a fit of rage in a moment of opportunity?

Such thoughts ran through Elizabeth's mind throughout the rest of the evening, even after she managed to escape from Miss Bingley's fury. There was not much left of it, to be honest, and soon Elizabeth excused herself to return to her room. Of her sisters, only Jane was still in the sitting-room, speaking quietly with Mr. Bingley, and she sensed the evening would end soon for them all.

As she was walking, however, she heard the sound of footsteps, and wondering if someone was following her, she ducked into a side room, which turned out to be the library. Then, careful to remain unseen, she looked through the narrow slot where she held the door open, watching to see who it was. When the man came into sight, it was Mr. Darcy, and he was hurrying as if to catch her.

"Mr. Darcy!" said she in a low voice, swinging the door open a little and beckoning him. He quickly altered his course and joined her in the library, closing the door behind him. While Elizabeth might have preferred the door to remain open to maintain propriety, she knew it was likely for the best. They would not wish to be overheard, considering the likely subject of the coming discussion.

"Miss Bennet," said Mr. Darcy, looking down on her, his expression grave. "I presume you approached Miss Bingley to discover the reason for her disagreement with Lady Catherine?"

"It was not so much a disagreement as your aunt berating Miss Bingley," said Elizabeth with a stifled laugh. "Miss Bingley waxed poetic about it, I assure you. It seemed that most of her outrage was reserved for the fact that Lady Catherine considered her to be on the same level as *I*."

Mr. Darcy did not appear to be amused by Elizabeth's tale. She shook her head and grinned at him. "I apologize, Mr. Darcy. But you must allow me my mirth when presented by such absurdity. Miss Bingley has always spoken down to me. It seems nothing less than poetic justice that she should be given a glimpse of what it was like for me."

His expression softening, Mr. Darcy acknowledged her point. "Perhaps we should focus on the task at hand?"

"Of course. As you are almost certainly already aware, Miss Bingley was subjected to treatment similar to that your aunt directed toward me. The only difference is that Lady Catherine managed to get Miss Bingley alone to vent her displeasure. With me, she was forced to do it in company."

"And what are your thoughts on the matter?"

"I might ask the same as you."

"Yes, I suppose you might." Mr. Darcy regarded her for a long moment. "I am not sure what to think. That Miss Bingley was angry with Lady Catherine is evident. But I cannot see where that implicates her in Lady Catherine's death."

"No, that by itself does not," said Elizabeth. "I dare say that a person who was inclined to take the life of another would have been angry enough to act. I do not know that *Miss Bingley* is such a person."

Mr. Darcy nodded slowly. "Since I did not speak to her, I must trust your judgment."

"But I have made no judgment, Mr. Darcy," replied Elizabeth. "I only said she was angry enough to do it if she were a person who could contemplate taking the life of another. The fact of the matter is that I am not well acquainted with Miss Bingley, so I am not able to judge."

"I do not know her much better."

"But you have been in her company more than I," insisted Elizabeth.

"Much more than I ever wished," muttered Mr. Darcy.

Elizabeth could not help but laugh at his admission. "That is exactly it, Mr. Darcy. You are in a better position to tell me what you think of Miss Bingley's capabilities. Lady Catherine not only attacked her behavior and skills as a hostess, but she attacked Miss Bingley's very respectability and position in society. Do *you* think she is capable of such a response when provoked thus?"

A slow nod was Mr. Darcy's initial response, though he considered Elizabeth's words for a few moments before speaking. "It seems you have understood Miss Bingley quite well, Miss Elizabeth. She is inordinately proud of her education and revels in her place in society, which is largely bought by her acquaintance to me, among a few other ladies who are of a similar mind, but higher connections.

"If she felt that position was threatened, she might, indeed, attempt to defend it." Mr. Darcy's introspection turned to keen focus. "But I have no notion that she would resort to murder to achieve those goals. On the other hand, however, Lady Catherine has not been in society for many years, as she usually prefers to stay at Rosings, her estate. As such, she can have little influence on Miss Bingley's eventual acceptance in society. Lady Catherine has spoken about my 'engagement' to Anne many times over the years, but I have never done anything about it. As such, most in society consider it to be nothing more than a fantasy in Lady Catherine's mind. I doubt Miss Bingley would feel that I am out of reach simply because Lady Catherine blathers on about a spurious engagement."

Elizabeth sighed. "I do not wish to accuse even so objectionable a woman as Miss Bingley of such a heinous crime on so little evidence. I have no love for her, as you are well aware. On the other hand, however, the circumstances do lend some credence to the theory. I know that *I* am not a murderer, and I am certain *you* are not either."

"Are you so completely certain of that, Miss Bennet?" asked Mr. Darcy, a faint sense of amusement about him. "I may be playing along with you in order to throw you off the trail of my nefarious plans."

"Yes, I am quite convinced," said Elizabeth, rolling her eyes. "You have endured your aunt for years, and as you and Anne have jointly determined that you will not marry, there is little reason for you to silence Lady Catherine forever."

"And you have parried Lady Catherine's attacks with such skill that I know you cannot have done it either."

"I thank you for your faith, sir," said Elizabeth. Mr. Darcy grinned at her wry tone and then became serious again.

"It seems to me that we have suspicions but no proof. We do not even have any proof that Lady Catherine did not die of natural means. She may simply have expired in her sleep as the rest of the house assumes."

Elizabeth snorted. "One death may be explained, but two seems like an unusual coincidence to me. The only question is: what are we to do about it?"

"Why, my dear Miss Bennet," said Mr. Darcy, "we investigate."

CHAPTER XIII

While Darcy generally despised disguise of any sort, he decided the next day that disguise would be in order. Though Fitzwilliam and perhaps even Mr. Bennet were suspicious about the turn of events which had led to the deaths of two people at Netherfield, most of the rest of the company did not seem to consider the events to be anything more than coincidence. It would not do to incite panic by speaking of the matter openly. Thus, Darcy and Miss Elizabeth had decided to meet in a covert fashion to conduct their investigation.

"Will you meet me tomorrow morning to inspect Lady Catherine's room?" Darcy had asked the previous evening

"Of course, Mr. Darcy. Indeed," continued she with a laugh, "I consider myself quite the intrepid lady to be involving myself in such matters. Perhaps I should open a shop in London as an investigator? What do you think?"

"Though I have no doubt as to your abilities," replied Darcy, "I suspect you would not receive much business, as few would wish to hire a woman."

"That is, indeed, a drawback." She regarded him with an adorable pout, one which was feigned, but which set his heart pounding at the sight. "It is unfortunate that society's views are so narrow as to discount the abilities of women."

"That sounds suspiciously like the opinion a bluestocking might hold."

She grinned and turned, making her way from the library, her voice floating back to him as she exited the room. "Despise me now, if you dare, for having such heretical opinions."

As it happened, Darcy could not despise her. Moreover, he could not imagine despising her. He was much nearer to infatuation and desire and knew that infatuation could turn to utter love and devotion in the blink of an eye. The force of his initial arguments, that she was not suitable, that she would struggle in the shark-infested waters of London society, that her dowry was less than sufficient, were evaporating like a drop of water on a hot summer day. Thus it was that Darcy was forced to remind himself to focus on their self-appointed task rather than on the increasingly irresistible woman with whom he would undertake it.

Disposing of the other men was no difficult feat. Bingley was content to be in Miss Bennet's company and, thus, had no attention for Darcy or any other. Wickham and Mr. Collins were not even worth mentioning, and even Darcy's cousin removed himself from the equation when Hurst suggested they retire to the billiards room. Miss Bingley might have been a challenge, as the woman was always eager to ingratiate herself to him and had redoubled her efforts since Lady Catherine's death. But Darcy chose the expedient of sequestering himself in Bingley's study, frustrating her design of putting herself in his company. Then, when she was distracted, he simply took himself above stairs to his meeting with Miss Elizabeth.

"Did you have difficulty slipping away from your sisters?" asked Darcy as he checked the hallway for any servants or others watching them. There were none he could see.

"Of course not," was her easy reply. "We Bennet sisters are a disparate group, Mr. Darcy, each with our own interests and preferred activities. I have often been alone in the past few days, either reading what few books I could find from that desert waste Mr. Bingley calls a library or simply thinking as I walk the halls."

Darcy chuckled and pushed the door to Lady Catherine's room open, allowing her to enter, then closing it behind them. "I agree with you concerning Bingley's library. I doubt he reads even one book in a year."

With a distracted look at her, Darcy fell silent, taking in the picture she presented. Miss Elizabeth was diminutive, not necessarily in her height, which he thought was average, but in her figure, which was slender and dainty. Her hands were small and delicate, her face oval, with wisps of hair escaping her elegant coif, and in particular, one lock which hung down the side of her face, refusing to be tamed. Her figure was pleasing, though what it was not was the generous fleshiness which seemed to be in vogue.

"You love to walk, I understand? It must be difficult to be denied one of your pleasures."

"It is, indeed," said Miss Elizabeth, humor lighting her eyes. "At least at Netherfield I have much more room to roam the halls, which I do not at Longbourn. This weather we have had is quite unusual. I do not think I have ever seen snow as has fallen these past days. Even in the dead of winter, it does not snow much. It is more the cold which keeps me indoors."

"Walking is beneficial exercise," said Darcy.

"It is, indeed. And as I am very fond of it, I find it quite enjoyable and convenient." Miss Elizabeth paused, considering some further observation. "I have noticed that some women are a little . . . rounder than I think they should be, and I have often noted that it is due to a sedentary lifestyle. I walk for exercise to keep myself healthy and avoid excess weight."

"Surely you have not had to concern yourself with such," said Darcy. "I could not imagine you becoming the picture you suggest."

Miss Elizabeth smiled. "You have seen my mother, have you not? She was a noted beauty in her youth, but in recent years her figure has rounded."

"Surely that is as much to do with bearing five daughters," said Darcy, not certain they should be speaking of such matters.

"I am certain it must. But as I am much like my mother in figure and form, I feel it prudent to take care in what I eat and obtain the exercise which promotes good health."

"An excellent decision, Miss Elizabeth."

She thanked him with a nod of her head and turned to inspect the room, approaching the bed. Darcy followed her, approval filling his senses at her words. Then he turned his attention firmly to the task at hand.

"Everything seems to be in order," said Miss Elizabeth. "The bed has been made, though I assume the linens were removed and replaced." She looked about with interest. "Have your aunt's personal effects been removed as well?"

"I do not think so," replied Darcy, looking about and approaching the nearest chest of drawers. He opened it and then closed it again, noting there were lady's garments within.

Miss Elizabeth watched him, amused at the reaction at what he found within. "Are you embarrassed at the discovery of what we ladies wear under our dresses?"

"I am familiar with most items," replied Darcy, refusing to give in to her teasing. "I *do* have a younger sister, after all, and I have accompanied her shopping on occasion. But I also do not believe it is proper for me to inspect such things as my late aunt's chemise."

A giggle escaped Miss Elizabeth's lips. "Perhaps not. I shall inspect them to see if there is anything of interest. But first, I believe it would be best to focus on the bed. I did not see the state it was in when your aunt was found. Would you share your memory of what you saw?"

With a frown, Darcy stepped forward, attempting to remember. "Lady Catherine was lying toward the near side of the bed. There were no visible signs of struggle, though the coverlet and sheets were wrapped around her legs. Her head was directly on the mattress, and one of the pillows lay propped up against her side."

"So she might simply have suffered an apoplexy and disturbed the bed in her death throes."

"That is possible," conceded Darcy.

Miss Elizabeth considered the scene he had painted for several moments. "If she *was* murdered, how could it have been done? There were no marks on her neck to indicate strangulation?"

"Nothing of that sort," replied Darcy. "She was not beaten, there was no indication of anything which might have prompted her death. There was not even a glass of water by her bedside for laudanum or the like."

"Did her maid say anything of her requests that night?"

Darcy smiled. "Lady Catherine did not request, Miss Bennet. She demanded." Miss Bennet glared at him, and he chuckled and shook his head. "No. She made no *requests* other than the assistance to disrobe and dress in her night clothes. The maid did as she was bid, saw her situated in her bed, and extinguished the lights as she left. She noted nothing amiss."

A curious look passed over Miss Elizabeth's face. "What is to become of the maid now? I know Anne has her own maid."

"Anne has given her a letter of reference, and she will be free to search for a new position."

An absent nod was Miss Elizabeth's initial response. She turned back to the bed and considered it. "Could she have been suffocated by the use of a pillow over her face?"

"That is an excellent deduction, Miss Elizabeth," replied Darcy, impressed she had come up with a logical explanation. "That would account not only for the lack of any markings on Lady Catherine's body, but also for the position of the pillow as the murderer fled, and the way the bed coverings were twisted about her legs and body."

Miss Elizabeth's rueful smile followed a sigh. "Yes, it does fit. If only there were a motive, we might be able to determine what happened. Other than that of which we have already spoken, did your aunt offend anyone who wished revenge? Did she possess something which another would kill to obtain?"

"Not that I am aware," replied Darcy, shaking his head. "Lady Catherine was a wealthy woman, and Rosings is quite prosperous." Darcy grinned. "Despite her ability to offend with little provocation and her need to manage *everything*, Lady Catherine managed Rosings with an ability her late husband never possessed.

"Even so, the only one who could have profited from Lady Catherine's death was Anne herself. But even then, murdering her was not required. Anne inherited it when she reached the age of one and twenty and could have taken control at any time."

"A jealous lover, perhaps?" asked Miss Elizabeth, directing an arch frown—completely feigned—at him.

"Again," replied Darcy, amused at her actions, "I could have had Rosings myself, had I wished it. I only needed to bow to Lady Catherine's wishes and marry my cousin. My holdings, as they are, occupy my time and keep me busy. The prospect of adding another estate the size of Rosings is onerous. I have never wanted it."

"You will pardon me for saying it," replied Elizabeth, "but I am only attempting to throw out ideas."

Darcy nodded and indicated that she should continue.

"What of your cousin? He, by all accounts, is what the nobility would call a 'poor soldier,' though I have no doubt his father supports him more than adequately. Could he have wished to have his own estate? With Lady Catherine gone, he can now pay court to Anne, and should he succeed, he will obtain his independence."

Far from offended, Darcy was impressed again by the way her mind worked, developing theories and making leaps of intuition based on the available information. "That is an interesting theory, but I do not believe it. Fitzwilliam does own an estate, and while it is not as large as Rosings, he *is* able to settle there whenever he decides to retire. Furthermore, Fitzwilliam, Anne, and I have been close cousins since we were children. I cannot imagine Fitzwilliam sees Anne as a potential wife, even if he possessed the ability to murder our aunt."

"Very well," said Miss Elizabeth, showing him a slight smile. "I apologize and appreciate your understanding. I did not wish to suggest I do not trust your cousin."

"No offense taken."

Miss Elizabeth sighed. "I can think of no other motive which would drive someone to commit murder."

"Nor can I. But Miss Elizabeth, I believe we have spent quite long enough in this room together. I suggest we do whatever searching we can and leave, as it is possible we might be missed."

With a nod, Miss Elizabeth moved to the nearby drawers and opened them one by one, peering inside and pushing the articles to the side to see if anything was hidden underneath. They checked the closet and the vanity to see if anything had been left on its surface. But there was nothing out of order, not that Darcy had expected to find anything.

When Miss Elizabeth completed her search, Darcy approached the door. Opening it, he stepped out into the hall, looking both directions to see if he was being observed. When he saw no one, he beckoned to Miss Elizabeth, closing the door behind her when she stepped through. Then, side by side, they began walking down the hall toward the stairs, speaking softly as they went.

"Do you have any other clever suggestions, Miss Elizabeth?" asked Darcy.

She directed a quick smile at him. "I am not certain about clever, but clever or otherwise, I am afraid I am at a loss."

"As am I."

"Then what do you think?" asked she, focusing a long look at him.

"I do not know," replied Darcy. "But while I would like to attribute it to an elderly woman whose time had come, I cannot. People die all around us, and other than the bereaved families, we take no notice of it, knowing it is the way of life. Sudden deaths happen, even to those who seem otherwise healthy. But in this instance, something is telling me it is all wrong."

Miss Elizabeth nodded, though she appeared distracted. "What was your aunt's age?"

"She did not marry young, for obvious reasons," replied Darcy, eliciting a grin from Miss Elizabeth. "I believe she was already five and twenty when she married. Then she experienced the same difficulties my mother had with bearing a child, losing at least two or three to miscarriage."

"Anne also spoke of a brother who died in infancy."

"Yes, that is true. But that child was born after. Anne would know her mother's exact age, though I do not. But I suspect she was at least thirty when Anne was born, and Anne is now five and twenty, I suspect Lady Catherine was five and fifty, or perhaps even a little older."

"Not old enough that we would not be surprised if she would pass, but old enough that her passing suddenly does not seem odd."

Darcy nodded, but he did not speak. They reached the bottom of the stairs then, and Darcy gestured toward the hall, feeling it would be best for them to join the others for a time. Miss Elizabeth was about to move in that direction when from another hallway, a man emerged and directed a fierce look at them—at Miss Elizabeth in particular. It was Mr. Collins.

"Cousin Elizabeth," said he in his usual pompous tone, one which Darcy had noticed contained more than a hint of superiority when he spoke to his younger cousins, "I fear I must speak to you about this unseemly behavior you have been exhibiting."

Most young ladies might have been offended at Mr. Collins's tone and words, but Miss Elizabeth only lifted an eyebrow. "You have my apologies, Mr. Collins. I did not realize that walking through the halls was a reason for censure."

"Do not attempt to feign misunderstanding, Cousin," said Mr. Collins. "I know what you are about, and I must say that it disgusts me. My honored patroness and Mr. Darcy's revered aunt, Lady Catherine de Bourgh, has not even been laid to rest in her grave and you are already attempting to turn Mr. Darcy's eyes away from his predestined bride. Do you have no shame? Is this what your parents have taught you?"

"Again, Mr. Collins," said Miss Elizabeth, "I have done nothing but walk with Mr. Darcy. Or do you consider a walk a declaration of intent?"

Mr. Collins looked down his nose at Miss Elizabeth, and Darcy felt his hackles rise at the arrogant manner in which he regarded her. "My dear cousin. Have you not heard Lady Catherine state from the moment she entered the house that Mr. Darcy was destined for Miss de Bourgh? Why must you, in defiance of all decency, against the wishes of his whole family, continue on this course? What must be done to stop you?"

"I suggest you cease speaking, Collins," said Darcy, feeling his patience desert him, even if Miss Elizabeth was still watching the ineffectual man with amusement. "I have told you before that my aunt does not direct my life. Your cousin has done nothing wrong."

Mr. Collins turned wide eyes on Mr. Darcy. "Surely, Mr. Darcy, you intend to honor your late aunt's wishes and marry your cousin."

"My intentions are my own, Mr. Collins. I need not explain them to you."

For a long moment, Mr. Collins peered at Darcy. What his conclusions were, Darcy could not say. But in the end, he appeared to realize that no good would come from his continued attempts to push the subject forward.

"Very well, Mr. Darcy," his manner as haughty as Lady Catherine's ever was. "Then I shall not press you on the matter. But as Miss Elizabeth is destined to be my bride, I request, in all friendship and respect, that you keep her at arms' length. It would not do to confuse her or give others the wrong impression."

"What would assist in not giving others the wrong impression would be for you to cease speaking such nonsense."

The sound of another voice prevented Darcy from berating the foolish man, and he turned and noted the approach of Mr. Bennet. The way he glared at Mr. Collins showed that he was not at all amused.

"Mr. Bennet—"

"No, Mr. Collins, you will listen to me," said Mr. Bennet, his impatience oozing out in his tone. "I do not know why you have not understood this yet, but I am not interested in forcing my daughters into marriages they do not want."

The look of utter shock and consternation with which Mr. Collins regarded Mr. Bennet was enough to prompt Darcy's laughter. "But Mr. Bennet! You must see how this is for the best. Your daughters, though they are all that is charming and good, will have very little to call their own when you pass from this world. Surely you wish them to be protected. I can offer that protection."

"Yes, you can offer protection," said Mr. Bennet. "But I will remind you of two things. First, you know nothing of the state of their fortunes, and I suggest you do not attempt to guess it, sir. There are rumors about many things, and it is unfortunate, but rumors are often incorrect. Second, I care deeply for my daughters' happiness. I cannot imagine anything which would make any of them unhappier than to insist they marry a man they do not favor.

"You are, of course, free to attempt to woo any of them. But I will uphold my daughters' right of refusal should they reject your proposal. I am sorry, Cousin, but if you are to have one of them for a wife, you will need to woo them successfully and convince them that you will make them happy."

Mr. Collins looked at Mr. Bennet for a few moments, as if attempting to determine his resolve in this matter. For Darcy, he did not need to look for Mr. Bennet's resolve, for he was convinced the man was telling nothing but the truth. It heartened Darcy, informing him that regardless of Mrs. Bennet's gauche actions and statements, Miss Bennet, for example, would refuse Bingley if she did not wish to marry him, and Mr. Bennet would support her decision. He had not disbelieved Miss Elizabeth when she had informed him as much, but the confirmation was welcome.

While he might have been expected to come to the correct conclusion, Darcy, having been acquainted with Mr. Collins these past days, was not surprised when he did not. For Mr. Collins sniffed in disdain and said:

"I know how it shall be, Mr. Bennet. I know my cousin has no better options. Despite her attempts to attract Mr. Darcy's attention, I know he is destined for Miss de Bourgh. In the end, I am confident that my cousin will see sense. I will have her hand."

With those words, Mr. Collins departed. As they watched him go, Darcy heard Miss Elizabeth mutter: "Your certainty is misplaced, Mr. Collins."

Mr. Bennet laughed at his daughter's statement. "I have no doubt it is, Lizzy. Either way, if you would oblige me, I should like to have a word with Mr. Darcy in private. Can I prevail on you to precede us to the sitting-room?"

While Miss Elizabeth glanced between Darcy and her father, she agreed, curtseyed, and departed. The fondness with which Mr. Bennet regarded her retreating form betrayed his esteem for her. Theirs seemed a profound connection.

"She is my treasure, Mr. Darcy," said Mr. Bennet with an absence of thought. "A man should not have favorites among his children, I know. My daughters are all dear to me, though the youngest are, I will own, trying at times. But Lizzy ... She is a treasure—intelligent, compassionate, strong-willed, beautiful; I cannot summon all the adjectives to attribute to her goodness."

Then Mr. Bennet turned and regarded him. "It seems to me, sir, you are another who has come to appreciate her fine qualities. Am I correct?"

As Darcy had suspected the subject which Mr. Bennet had wished to discuss, he was ready for the question. "I have nothing but admiration for your daughter, Mr. Bennet. I agree with your assessment in every particular."

"I am happy to hear it, sir. I would like to know what you mean to do about it."

It was this question that had consumed Darcy of late, and he was not afraid to confess to it. But when he did not immediately reply, Mr. Bennet continued to speak.

"She is not of your level of society, sir. I know you are intelligent enough to understand this fact. But I am unconcerned about this personally because I have every confidence in Elizabeth's ability to handle herself in any situation. But what you must ask yourself is whether you are able to withstand the naysayers who will disapprove of your choice. Perhaps chief among those are your uncle? I have heard he is an earl?"

"Yes, he is," said Darcy. "But my uncle will not interfere, and he will not risk a schism in the family by disparaging the woman I choose to marry."

Mr. Bennet nodded. "You are also aware that I cannot give her much when she marries?"

"Did you not just inform Mr. Collins that he should not assume that what he has heard of her dowry is the truth?"

Mr. Bennet replied with a laugh. "So you *were* listening. Excellent, sir. I appreciate a man who is not distracted by frivolous nothings." Mr. Bennet's countenance turned serious again. "I have no objections to your interest in my Lizzy, Mr. Darcy, and if you do decide she is the woman to whom you wish to make an offer, I will not object."

"Pending her approval, of course," said Darcy.

"Of course. All I ask is you do not play with her affections. If you wish to pursue her, please proceed. But if you do not, I will ask you to step back. I do not wish her wondering what to expect from you, and I especially do not wish to see her heart engaged when you have no intention of reciprocating."

"In that, I can reassure you, sir. I will own I have not decided to pursue her yet. But I am considering it. She is the most interesting woman I have ever met, and I find myself wanting to know more of her."

Mr. Bennet regarded him, eyes searching before he nodded. "I believe you will do, Mr. Darcy, if that is what you decide. I thank you for indulging a protective father. Lizzy is far too important to me to not inquire after your intentions."

"I understand, sir. I have a sister who is in my care. I would act in the same way."

"Excellent!" said Mr. Bennet. "Now, if you are willing, do you care for a game of chess? I have not had a good game since we came to Netherfield."

"I would, indeed, Mr. Bennet. Lead on.'

Chuckling, Mr. Bennet turned toward the sitting-room where Bingley kept his chessboard. As they walked, he said: "Perhaps you should challenge Lizzy some time. She can best me as much as I can best her."

"That does not tell me much, Mr. Bennet," replied Darcy. "You might not be a strong player."

"You will soon discover it, Mr. Darcy. I will warn you not to underestimate either myself or my daughter."

"I will take your advice to heart, sir," said Darcy.

Inside, however, he was intrigued. Miss Elizabeth played chess? It was not an accomplishment most women could boast. What else might the woman be hiding? Darcy could hardly wait to find out.

CHAPTER XIV

*T*he last day of November was now upon them, and as fickle as the weather had been, coupled with the mood at Netherfield, Darcy decided it would be best to determine the state of the outside world. To that end, he approached the butler, knowing any reports of the roads would find their way to him. His hope that the Bennet's would be allowed to return to their home and that he and Fitzwilliam could leave to see their aunt's body back to Kent, however, were dashed.

"I believe it ought not to be attempted, Mr. Darcy," said the butler. The man fixed him with an apologetic glance, one which bespoke his hesitation—likely he expected a Miss Bingley-like reaction to his news. "Though the snow has ceased falling, it still snows in fits and starts, and the cold and wind complicates the matter. It is uncertain the horses could even navigate the roads, let alone the wheels of a carriage."

"Could a lone rider make his way to Longbourn?" asked Darcy. "If only to gather more clothes for the ladies."

The butler thought on this for a moment. He seemed to sense that Darcy would not react like his mistress and was encouraged to respond with candor. "Again, I think it would be best to refrain at present, Mr. Darcy. Perhaps tomorrow, should the weather improve, we may attempt it. Today it is best to wait."

It was not what Darcy wished to hear, but he knew the man was doing his best and relaying information as accurately as he could. Thus, Darcy thanked him and excused himself, much to the poor man's relief. Darcy judged the unfortunate Mr. Forbes's replacement to be competent, but he was too green for the position. Unfortunately, there was nothing they could do at present, and Darcy was certain a replacement would be the responsibility of the owner, regardless.

"You appear less than happy," said Fitzwilliam as soon as Darcy stepped into the library where Fitzwilliam was leaning back in his chair with his boots on a nearby table, apparently lost in thought. "Has Mr. Collins been spouting his usual nonsense again?"

Darcy scowled. Though Collins had said nothing since the scene in the entrance hall that morning, Darcy was still annoyed. Several times during the remainder of the morning he had caught Collins watching Miss Elizabeth, a hint of possessiveness in his gaze and attitude. Darcy had thought to call the man on his behavior more than once.

But then Darcy remembered the morning, and his feelings softened. Mr. Bennet was an intelligent man, though Darcy judged him to be more than a little eccentric. He had proven a worthy opponent across a chessboard, which Darcy would always think a point in a man's favor. Furthermore, when Darcy had played Miss Elizabeth, he found that Mr. Bennet had not overestimated his daughter's abilities. Darcy had been hard-pressed to emerge victorious.

"You have won this round, Mr. Darcy," said Elizabeth as she toppled her king. "But rest assured that I shall play with my full abilities next time. I *shall* prevail."

And then Mr. Collins had inserted himself yet again when Darcy thought to reply. "Gentlemen, this is unseemly. You are encouraging a young woman to behave in an indelicate manner. Why, my patroness, Lady Catherine de Bourgh, told me only months ago, when suggesting a topic for my weekly sermon at the pulpit, to speak on the delicacy of women. 'A true woman of quality,' said she, 'does not attempt to insert herself in the realms of men. Such unladylike behavior as playing games with men—billiards, chess, and the like— make a woman seem like a bluestocking at best.' Thus, I think it better if Miss Elizabeth should be encouraged away from such activities."

"I care not for your opinion, Mr. Collins," was Mr. Bennet's short reply. "Elizabeth is my daughter, and I shall decide what is appropriate for my progeny."

Darcy, who had been watching the detestable parson, noted his fury. But it disappeared after a moment, and the man shook his head. It was fortunate he decided not to speak further, for neither Darcy nor Mr. Bennet was in a mood to listen to him.

"When he attempted to censure Miss Elizabeth this morning," said Fitzwilliam, bringing Darcy's thoughts back to the present, "I thought for a moment you might beat him to a pulp."

"Had he spoken again, that was a possibility," said Darcy. "But I would have had to reach him before Mr. Bennet did."

Fitzwilliam grinned. "I might have held him down for you. That Lady Catherine found such a specimen is not a surprise, but that he is related to the Bennets is a delicious irony."

"Perhaps it is," said Darcy. "But I did not come here to speak of that." There was no reply—Fitzwilliam regarded him with curiosity, but no apparent surprise. "I assume you possess the same... reservations as I do about two deaths in three days in this house."

"You speak of the possibility of a murderer in our midst?"

"I do," replied Darcy. "I know you will say that coincidences happen, and I would agree with you. But while I have no evidence, nor do I know why, I suspect something more than a simple fall or an apoplexy."

Fitzwilliam sighed and turned to stare moodily out the window. "I will own I had considered it possible. I am not sure what we can do."

"Surely you do not think we should simply wait for the killer to strike again."

"No," said Fitzwilliam, turning back to Darcy. "But I have done a little investigating myself and have not found anything."

Darcy grunted. He had not thought Fitzwilliam, who was a man of action, would sit and wait for another death. For a moment he had sounded passive, frightened. Very little frightened his cousin."

"I have also done a little looking," said Darcy. "I am afraid I have found little myself."

"Then we should pool our resources. Perhaps you have found something I have not."

It turned out that Darcy agreed with his cousin. For the next thirty minutes, they exchanged stories of what they had done and what Darcy had discovered. It turned out that Fitzwilliam had engaged in the same investigations as Darcy, only that he had done so the previous evening. Fitzwilliam had spoken to the servants, asking among them if they had witnessed anything strange in the past few days. But he had come away from those interviews without anything of interest to report.

"It seems there is little enough upon which to base a suspicion of foul play, Darcy," said Fitzwilliam. "Any investigator worth his salt would terminate his inquiries with so little on which to base his suspicions."

"I know," said Darcy. "But something tells me there is something more happening." Darcy paused for a moment, considering whether he should speak of Miss Bennet when he decided his cousin was more adept at such matters as this. "Miss Bennet suspects Miss Bingley."

"She does?" asked Fitzwilliam, his interest suddenly roused. "And why does the intrepid Miss Elizabeth believe that Miss Bingley is depraved enough to murder our aunt?"

"Because Lady Catherine berated Miss Bingley when she discovered the woman's interest in me over the years. Furthermore, Miss Bingley was angry when Lady Catherine informed her that she was not at my level of society."

Fitzwilliam snorted. "If you base an accusation of murder on the ability to offend, then we are all suspects. Lady Catherine has offended everyone in this house multiple times since we were trapped here."

"Perhaps I overstated the matter," said Darcy, feeling it incumbent upon him to defend Miss Elizabeth. "She suggested it as a possibility, one which fit the facts we know. But she is aware of the paucity of evidence. I will say, however, that Miss Bingley was as offended as I have ever seen her. If she thought her position in society, such as it is, was threatened, I have no idea how she would respond."

"And what of the butler?"

Darcy spread his arms out in a gesture of defeat. "That is the problem. There seems to be no connection between them. If Miss Bingley *did* murder Lady Catherine in a fit of anger, then why did she murder the butler? Unless you believe that she was somehow incensed with him too—and there has been no sign of it—then Miss Bingley as the murderer seems problematic at best." Darcy paused. "If I am honest, I do not suspect Miss Bingley. I rather think Wickham is capable of it."

The derision with which Fitzwilliam greeted Darcy's suggestion was pointed, and his cousin did not hold back. "Wickham is a coward, along with all his other faults. But I have no notion he could be considered a suspect. Furthermore, he was not even present the night the butler died."

"Perhaps he was loitering nearby or hiding in the stables? His story of being sent by Colonel Forster has never sat well with me."

"You still have a problem with motive—I know of no reason why

Wickham would kill the butler, of all people. And what could he gain from killing Lady Catherine?"

"Access to Anne?"

"Poor Wickham," mocked Fitzwilliam. "The idea of Lady Catherine as a mother-in-law was enough to drive him to murder."

Darcy only spread his hands. The whole suggestion was thin and did not make a lot of sense—of this, he was well aware. But at this point, there was no further information available to make a judgment.

"Much though I despise Wickham," said Fitzwilliam, "I do not think he is at fault in this instance. It is impossible to link the two deaths together. At this time, based on the information we have available, it seems we have no choice but to conclude it was a tragic accident and the sudden death of an elderly woman. The timing must have been entirely coincidental."

"I know that is the sensible conclusion, Fitzwilliam," said Darcy. "But I hope you will forgive me if I remain watchful."

Fitzwilliam barked a laugh. "You assume I will not? Regardless of what makes sense, I, too, will be watchful.

"But I am much more interested in speaking of Miss Elizabeth." Darcy looked away, not wishing to be teased, which, of course, spurred his cousin on. "I know, from reading between the lines, that Miss Elizabeth accompanied you on your fact-finding mission to Lady Catherine's room. It seems to me you are becoming rather cozy with that young woman."

"Did you not inform me that if I did not claim her that you would?

Fitzwilliam's eyes widened, and he reached over and slapped Darcy on the back. "I did not think you would act so quickly. Good for you, Cousin!"

"I have not proceeded any further than simply attempting to come to know her better. But I believe I am set on my course. She is everything I would ever wish for in a wife."

"I am certain she is. I believe she would be good for you, old man. She is lively enough to draw you from your reticence, and I have no doubt she would keep you busy."

"She would at that. I have already received the talk from Mr. Bennet."

Fitzwilliam guffawed again. "I cannot quite make Mr. Bennet out. He is an intelligent man, but he is also an odd one."

"I know it, Cousin." Darcy paused, turning his thoughts back toward Miss Elizabeth—a more agreeable subject, indeed. "She is also intelligent, and I think I could do much worse than to marry an intelligent woman, even if she has little dowry."

"It is not as if Pemberley is failing. You are well able to withstand the lack of a dowry."

An absent nod was Darcy's response. "The more time I am in her company, the more surety I obtain of the rightness of my course. At first, I thought it was infatuation."

"You have never been infatuated in your life," replied Fitzwilliam, snorting at the very thought. "You are far too rational for infatuation."

"Then I must conclude that my feelings for Miss Bennet are growing and that they extend far deeper than infatuation. It is impossible to court her properly while we are stranded in this house. But once we can leave, and the situation returns to normal—"

"And once the battle axe has been laid to rest."

Darcy nodded, even as he rolled his eyes at Fitzwilliam's words concerning Lady Catherine. "Yes, after *that*, I will make certain she understands my feelings."

"I wish you luck, Cousin. You deserve to be happy with a good woman. Miss Elizabeth might just be the making of you."

"I believe she might," murmured Darcy.

In another part of the house, something of a more serious nature was occurring. Since that morning with Mr. Darcy in Lady Catherine's room, Elizabeth had hardly been able to pull her thoughts from the gentleman, and as she had grown tired of her father's knowing looks, she had decided to walk the halls for a time and think. Even Jane knew something of Elizabeth's growing feelings, at least when she could pull her thoughts away from Mr. Bingley.

There was a situation which brought Elizabeth pleasure. Mr. Bingley's general inattentiveness to the rest of the company when in Jane's presence was the very essence of a man in love. Miss Bingley was clearly displeased with what she was seeing—and Mrs. Hurst was little better—but there was little they could do at present. Elizabeth thought their entreaties to their brother would begin when the Bennets were finally able to depart. By now, however, she thought Mr. Bingley's inclination enough to withstand the machinations of his sisters, and as he would have Mr. Darcy's support, she felt all would end well.

Mr. Darcy! What an intriguing man! Could she love him, marry him, when she had initially discounted him as proud and above his company? Elizabeth was not certain, but she was beginning to think it would be an adventure to discover. It was a circumstance which was not welcome to Miss Bingley. The woman had glared at her all morning after she and Mr. Darcy had returned to the sitting-room, though Elizabeth was grateful she had not said anything.

A giggle caught Elizabeth's attention as she was walking, pulling her up short. She might have thought it was nothing more than a maid flirting with a footman. But she heard it again. She had heard that giggle enough times to know exactly who it was.

"Lydia!" cried Elizabeth, though keeping her voice quiet so she did not attract attention. She pushed the door to a small office open, watching as her sister jumped back from the man with whom she had been flirting. Luckily, it appeared she had not been in his arms.

"Miss Elizabeth!" greeted Mr. Wickham, his tone brimming with ebullience and good cheer. "How fortunate you have come upon us. Your sister was telling me the most amusing story, something about a bonnet and a pool of water?"

Elizabeth glared at the libertine. His manners suggested he did not realize she had caught him in a compromising position with her youngest sister! For her part, Lydia was laughing and looking up at Mr. Wickham, admiration alive in her eyes, though at least she was a proper distance from him now.

"It was ever so amusing, Mr. Wickham," said Lydia. "You see—"

"That is enough, Lydia!" Elizabeth's voice cracked like a whip, and even her senseless sister seemed to understand that Elizabeth was highly displeased. Mr. Wickham, for his part, seemed amused he had provoked a response in her and only watched, hilarity alive on his countenance.

"What do you think you are doing?" demanded Elizabeth, ignoring the officer for the present.

"Just a bit of fun with Mr. Wickham," said Lydia, waving any concerns Elizabeth might have had away as if they were unreasonable. "Mr. Wickham is so amusing and interesting. He has had many experiences in his life, and he was telling me about them."

"It seems to me you were telling *him* stories, not to mention flirting in a manner highly inappropriate."

"Oh, Lizzy! You sound just like Mary. I was only having fun!"

"Nothing inappropriate occurred, Miss Elizabeth," added Mr. Wickham.

Elizabeth rounded on the disgusting man. "My sister, at least, has an excuse, inadequate though it is. I would not expect much more from such a silly, empty-headed girl as she." Lydia let out a squawk of protest, but Elizabeth ignored her. "But *you*, sir, are a man full grown and should know better."

A mournful expression came over him. "If you recall, Miss Elizabeth, I informed you of my unguarded temper. At times it leads me to behave in a manner which is not precisely proper. You have my apologies."

"If I thought your apologies were not worthless in every way, I might accept them."

Mr. Wickham's eyes glittered, though Elizabeth thought it was amusement rather than anger. Lydia, however, was quite seriously displeased.

"Lizzy! How can you say such things to Mr. Wickham?"

"No, Miss Lydia," said Mr. Wickham. "I will not be the reason for strife between sisters. I shall take my leave now."

With a bow, Mr. Wickham quit the room. Elizabeth turned on her stupid sister and hissed: "You stay where you are until I return."

Then she darted from the room in pursuit of Mr. Wickham, calling out to him. He turned and regarded her, a smirk forming. Likely the cad thought he had managed to charm her, as evidenced by what he said when he turned.

"You do not need to apologize to me, Miss Elizabeth. I acknowledge you were correct in every particular."

"I did not come here to apologize, and if you believed for a moment I did, then you are a simpleton."

"Then why did you chase me?"

"To warn you." Mr. Wickham chose amusement at Elizabeth's statement, but by now, she had no more patience for this man. "I *know* what you are, Mr. Wickham. Mr. Darcy has informed me exactly what kind of man you are."

"And you believed him?" Mr. Wickham snorted in disdain. "Why should you not believe my account as easily as you did Darcy's?" Mr. Wickham sauntered toward her, raking her form with his eyes from her head to her toes. "I am much more of a man than he will ever be if that is what you want. Or is it because he possesses riches uncounted?"

"It is because *he* is a gentleman, both in comportment and standing, Mr. Wickham. Your behavior betrays you as the libertine you are."

"You know nothing of me."

"I know far more than I ever wish to know. I suggest you stay away from *all* my sisters, Mr. Wickham. If you think Mr. Darcy will not listen to me when I inform him of your activities and act against you, then you are more of a simpleton than I would ever have imagined."

"That sounds very much like a threat, Miss Elizabeth."

"It most assuredly was. Stay away from my sisters!"

Then with one final imperious glare, Elizabeth turned away and entered the room in which her sister waited. Except that Lydia had come to the door and had watched their confrontation, her mouth hanging wide, eyes open at the scene. Elizabeth took the simple expedient of guiding her wild sister back into the room, closing the door behind her, and then whirling on Lydia once again.

"You ignorant, childish, stupid, thoughtless girl! Were you not told that Mr. Wickham is a bad man and to stay away from him? And yet I find you, alone in a room with him, flirting as if you were nothing more than a woman of the night!"

Lydia gasped. "Lizzy! How dare you say such things to me!"

"I dare because you deserve it! If I had not come upon you when I did, what other foolishness would have ensued? Are you so lost to decency, so stupid that you would throw your life away on a man who will use you and discard you as if you are nothing more than an old pair of boots? What can you be thinking?"

It was the first time Elizabeth had ever spoken to her sister in such a forceful manner, though she had reprimanded Lydia aplenty. The girl was struck speechless, her mouth working, but no words issuing forth.

"What do you think might have happened had it been one of the servants who discovered you?" demanded Elizabeth, deciding not to allow her sister to regain her wits. "Do you even have room for such rational thoughts in your empty head?"

This time Lydia scowled. "What is it to you?"

"It is plenty to me" yelled Elizabeth, causing Lydia to jump at her tone. "You are not so foolish as this, Lydia. You are ungovernable, not completely senseless. You are well aware that what one sister does can affect the others. If you are fallen, we all are fallen. Now, I ask you again, what might have happened had a servant discovered you, a young girl, alone in a room with a man?"

"I suppose I might have been made to marry him," was Lydia's reply.

"Exactly. Papa would have had no choice but to protect the reputations of the rest of his daughters and insist Mr. Wickham marry you. Even then, we would not have escaped without censure. But at least we would have maintained most of our respectability. Do you wish to ruin your sisters' prospects forever?"

"Of course not!" exclaimed Lydia. "It is only . . ."

"What?" asked Elizabeth when her sister's voice trailed off.

Lydia blushed and looked away. When she did not immediately reply, Elizabeth began tapping her foot in impatience. Her sister caught sight of it and sighed, turning back to Elizabeth.

"I have always thought it would be a great joke if I, the youngest, were married before any of my sisters."

"Perhaps you should think of what your life would be should you marry a man such as Mr. Wickham."

Confused, Lydia said: "What do you mean?"

Praying for patience, Elizabeth directed her sister to sit on a nearby chair. "Lydia, sooner or later everyone needs to grow and mature and behave like an adult. I know you are yet fifteen, but as you are already out in society, you *must* consider the ramifications of your actions before you charge into any situation. What do you know of Mr. Wickham?"

"He is a handsome and amiable man," replied Lydia with a frown. "What more could a woman want in a husband?"

"How about a man who has the means to support her and any children they might have?" Lydia's eyes widened. "Do you think Mr. Wickham has any money? My understanding is that he has just joined the militia. Officers are not wealthy men, Lydia, and as Mr. Wickham is the son of old Mr. Darcy's steward, he has no one to support him."

It was clear Lydia was astonished. "But—but he told me he had powerful and wealthy friends."

"Did he *tell* you that, or did he infer it and allow you to make your own conclusions?"

Lydia's frown deepened. "I . . . No . . . I do not know."

"He has misled you, Lydia, and he has done it without telling an overt falsehood. In fact, he is a wastrel, a gamester, and a debtor. He has little of his own and has spent his entire life attempting to extort money from Mr. Darcy."

"He told me Mr. Darcy cheated him!" exclaimed Lydia.

"He lied. Mr. Darcy gave him what he was due—more than he was due. And when he wasted it all, he returned for more. He has left debts in many places, which Mr. Darcy has settled, and even after all that, has betrayed Mr. Darcy most cruelly?"

"How?" asked Lydia, seemingly bewildered.

"I am sorry, Lydia, but I have not been authorized to speak of it. You must trust me."

The mutinous glint which Elizabeth had often seen in her sister's eyes returned. "And why should I trust you? You have your account from Mr. Darcy. What makes him any more believable than Mr.

Wickham?"

"Because he is a man of good character. He has offered the colonel, among others, as corroborating witnesses."

Lydia scoffed. "Colonel Fitzwilliam is Mr. Darcy's cousin. Of course, he will support his cousin!"

"Not if his cousin is not telling the truth—a good man will not allow his principles to be compromised for nothing more than family. Furthermore, Mr. Darcy has also offered to show me Mr. Wickham's debt receipts and has offered the testimony of more than Colonel Fitzwilliam. What did Mr. Wickham offer when he told his tales?"

There was nothing Lydia could say in response, so Elizabeth answered her own question. "I will tell you, as Mr. Wickham also attempted to tell his tales to me. He did not offer any proof. He only flashed his charming smile and expected to be believed on that alone."

"I suppose," said Lydia. She appeared to be thinking about what Elizabeth had said. Considering she had rarely, if ever, stopped to think, Elizabeth thought it must be a good sign."

"Lydia," said she, drawing her sister's attention back to her. "Do not be in such a rush to be married. What does it matter if you are the first?"

"It does not matter. But I thought it would be a great joke."

"Then the joke would be on you. Jane and I have had several years in society, and we have enjoyed the attentiveness of the men, dancing and laughing as we attended events. In many ways, you have much more freedom as an unmarried woman. If you do not have an independent fortune, as we do not, that will change. For now, I urge you to enjoy being a young woman without the cares of a husband and eventually a family. There is no need to rush."

"I suppose there is not," grumbled Lydia.

"Then behave in a manner which will not bring censure on your head. Our situation is too precarious, our prospects too limited to allow for any misbehavior. Do it for yourself, if no one else."

When they left the room a few moments later, Lydia was caught in introspection, which had happened little enough in the past to be noteworthy in this instance. Perhaps she would discount Elizabeth's words in the end. But Elizabeth finally had hope that all would turn out well.

CHAPTER XV

"Well, Darcy," said a detested voice, bringing Darcy from his thoughts of the situation, but more of Miss Elizabeth. "I see you are here, alone, as usual. Does the solitary nature of your existence not become tedious after a time?"

"I have friends enough, Wickham," replied Darcy. He continued to walk, but Wickham only turned to follow him. It seemed the man was eager to provoke him.

"Ah, yes. I believe I know something of your friends." Wickham snorted. "Hangers on such as that Bingley fellow you have inexplicably befriended, or those in society as proud and rude as you, who associate with those they detest because it is expected. What a wonderful circle of friends you possess."

"On the contrary," replied Darcy, not caring in the slightest if Wickham denigrated his friends, "Bingley is one of the best men I have ever met. He is not a hanger on—we are friends due to mutual admiration and complementary tempers."

Wickham snorted. "Very complementary, indeed. Bingley, who is a frivolous man, utterly vacuous, who is best friends with a dour stick in the mud lacking any personality. How you must rejoice in finding each other."

"Was there some reason you wished to insult my friends? Or is this just more of your usual despicable behavior?"

"I only thought you might wish to commiserate about the emptiness of your life," said Wickham with mock concern.

"My life is quite full," said Darcy. Or it would be full once Darcy was able to convince Miss Elizabeth to be his wife. The thought, the first time it had ever appeared, felt so right that Darcy, for a moment, forgot with whom he was speaking, and allowed his thoughts to take wing, imagining how his life would be with her in it.

"How typical," said Wickham, dragging Darcy's thoughts back to his presence. "You high society men are all alike. You comfort yourselves with your piles of money and claim you have everything you would ever need."

"That is rich, coming from you," said Darcy. "For a man who craves wealth above everything else, speaking of a rich man bathing in his wealth is more than a little disingenuous. Of course, it would not matter how much fortune you obtain, for it would slip through your fingers as soon as you laid your hands upon it."

Wickham glared and changed the subject. "Then there is the relative state of our attractions when it comes to women." Wickham released a cruel laugh calculated to rile Darcy's anger. "Or perhaps, I should say, the difference between us. I have no trouble attracting women wherever I go, whereas you scare them. If you had no fortune to augment your nonexistent charms, I doubt you would ever find a woman to look at you twice.

As it was, Darcy was more amused by Wickham's assertions than anything. When they were young, Wickham had been successful in provoking his anger on many occasions using this tactic. But Darcy had changed over the years. Wickham, however, had never seemed to realize this, as he had tried the same thing on the rare occasions they had been in proximity to each other without success.

"You are equally quick in losing the interest of a woman when she discovers what kind of man you are."

Wickham laughed. "You wound me, Darcy. Did you not know that women love a bit of danger about a man? Many have thought they could tame me. Perhaps one day I shall even allow one to succeed."

"Is there some purpose behind this boasting?" asked Darcy. "Your company makes me feel soiled like I require bathing. If all you wish to do is speak of such subjects in an attempt to anger me, you are wasting my time."

"Take Miss Lydia Bennet, for example," said Wickham, ignoring

Darcy's words. "She is a pretty young thing, dumb as a post, of course, but possessing many other qualities a man would find pleasing. As long as he could muzzle her, of course. I could pluck her in an instant, and she would hardly even know I had done it."

"That is quite enough, Wickham," said Darcy, turning a baleful glare on his erstwhile friend. "She is a gentlewoman, regardless of what you think of her. I suggest you keep your distance from all the Bennets."

"She is not much of a challenge, anyway," said Wickham. "Miss Bingley, however, is a different matter altogether. She is, I suppose, handsome in a way, though not what I would call pretty. Her virtues include a handsome dowry, from what I understand, and . . ." Wickham made a great show of thinking about the matter and then shrugging. "I suppose that really is her only virtue. I cannot blame you for avoiding her, though she only wants your wealth and status. That tongue of hers could peel paint off the walls."

As it turned out, Darcy agreed with Wickham's assessment, though not with the man's contemptuous manner. Thus, he only shook his head.

"But a man in my circumstances would do much to obtain a fortune rumored to be twenty thousand pounds. Perhaps I should seduce her, give your insipid friend little choice but to marry her off to me."

"You are welcome to try, Wickham," said Darcy. "As you say, she is fixated on me, and if not on me, then another man of wealth and status in society. She would not give you the time of day. And remember that tongue."

"No, I suppose you are correct." Wickham snorted. "Besides, a man might wish himself dead if he was forced to endure a wife such as Caroline Bingley."

Again, Darcy could not but agree with him. Keeping his temper was not a trial. But then Wickham changed tactics.

"Perhaps, then, I shall simply seduce Miss Elizabeth."

Darcy was not amused, but he settled on glaring at Wickham and saying: "She knows what you are, Wickham. She will not be taken in by your artful stories."

A derisive laugh met Darcy's statement. "If I had a copper for every woman I seduced who knew what I was before I seduced her, I would be wealthier than you."

With a grunt, Darcy turned away. Given how angry he was becoming at the mere mention of Miss Elizabeth's name on Wickham's tongue, it was best that he put some space between them. But

Wickham had other ideas, following closely on his heels, intent on stirring up trouble.

"Come, Darcy, are you that disdainful of the fair Miss Elizabeth Bennet's charms? Given how aligned our taste in women is, I would have thought you eager to be savoring her delights." Wickham let out a raucous laugh. "Oh, of course! It is that stiff-necked Darcy pride holding you back. Or perhaps it is your overweening sense of morality and propriety. You never did know how to enjoy yourself."

"That morality, of which you speak, was also possessed by my *father*, a man you claimed to revere."

Wickham made a guttural sound in his throat. "Your father was useful; I will grant you that. The fact that he believed me instead of you is particularly ironic, do you not think? He was as gullible as anyone I have ever met."

Darcy turned and rounded on Wickham, causing the man to stop sharply, though his sneer never waned. "You never did know when to stay silent, did you, Wickham? By all means, continue to speak—it would be satisfying to plant a facer on you. And for the record, the only reason you are not receiving it now is because I was already aware of what you think of my father."

"Oh, I have nothing but respect for your father." Wickham paused and an ugly smirk cane over his countenance. "I know what holds you back from Miss Elizabeth. You know she prefers me and do not wish to be embarrassed. Good choice, old boy!"

"You always were overly confident," said Darcy. "There is no question of which of us she prefers. If you wish to make a fool of yourself, please proceed. I would find it fascinating and amusing, I assure you."

"I believe I shall!" Wickham's tone was all that was cheerful. "She is a lively thing, is she not? Taming that wild spirit would be highly gratifying. What do you think I would see in her eyes in the moment of ecstasy? I can hardly wait to witness it."

"I suggest you be silent, Wickham," hissed Darcy.

"And if I ruin her, it would be sweet vengeance, indeed. Since you foiled my plans with respect to Georgiana, I will take from you the woman you believe you are coming to love. Poetic—"

Darcy had enough. He grasped Wickham by the shoulders and slammed him against the wall nearby hard enough for his teeth to rattle. At that exact moment, Mrs. Bennet and Miss Kitty rounded a corner and came upon them, their eyes wide with shock.

"Mr. Darcy!" exclaimed the Bennet matron.

Ignoring her, Darcy instead spoke softly to Wickham. "Continue to try me, Wickham—by all means. Though horsewhipping you would give me great pleasure, I do not need to do it. I can simply call in your debts and bury you in the deepest hole I can find. Or perhaps I will leave you to Fitzwilliam."

Fear bloomed in Wickham's eyes—he had always been more than a little afraid of Fitzwilliam. Then Darcy released the disgusting libertine and stalked away. As he walked, he heard Mrs. Bennet making a fuss over Wickham.

"Oh, Mr. Wickham! Are you hurt?"

But Darcy did not hear Wickham's reply, nor did he wish to. If Wickham put one more foot out of line, Darcy would take great pleasure in doing exactly as he had promised. It would have been best if he had done so many years ago.

"Oh, Louisa!" wailed Caroline Bingley. "I know not how I can bear the presence of those awful Bennets much longer! How am I to cope?"

Louisa Hurst, who had been listening to a variation of this complaint since the Bennets had been forced to stay at Netherfield, shook her head, wishing her sister would cease her lamentations. It was giving her a headache and making her irritable.

"And that awful Miss Eliza! That I was compared to the likes of her by Mr. Darcy's odious aunt is more than I can bear! How dare she make such an insinuation!"

"The way I understand it," said Louisa, knowing Caroline would not hear her, "she did not insinuate anything."

True to form, Caroline was ranting and did not hear anything Louisa said. "And Mr. Darcy! He shows more interest in that hussy daily! I thought he was a discerning and sophisticated man, yet he is showing himself to be as fickle and easily led as Charles!"

Louisa was so very tired! She was so tired that she almost wished she was back at Hurst's estate, far from anyone named Bennet. Far from her sister, who had never drained Louisa's patience as she did now. Would that she had never even heard the name Netherfield!

As Caroline continued speaking, carrying on about Mr. Darcy and Miss Elizabeth and the Bennets in general, Louisa allowed her attention to wander, knowing her sister would not notice anyway. At one point, she almost fell asleep! But the sound of Caroline's piercing voice would not have allowed her respite for long, regardless, so it was no loss.

"What can we do, Louisa?' Caroline's voice penetrated the fog building in Louisa's mind. "Charles must not be allowed to propose to Miss Bennet, and we must do something to draw Mr. Darcy away from Miss Eliza."

"I do not believe there is anything you *can* do, Caroline. Mr. Darcy will act as he sees fit. And so will Charles, whether you like it or not."

"Oh!" cried Caroline, her frustration boiling over. "If you are of no use, then I suggest you leave me be. I will handle everything, as I always do."

Caroline stalked to the sideboard in her room where she hefted the decanter of brandy, only to find it empty. She cried out and threw her hands into the air. "Even the servants are now betraying me! Where is that useless maid of mine?"

"Caroline," said Louisa, calling on every well of patience she had ever possessed, "you know I will always stand by you, whatever may be. It is true that Mr. Darcy seems to be getting closer to Miss Elizabeth, the longer we are here. But unless you can persuade Charles to throw the whole family out in the cold, there is no choice but to endure them."

"Then we must concede defeat?" asked Caroline, her tone sulky. "Is that what you are saying?"

"Not necessarily," replied Louisa. "It is true that Mr. Darcy and Charles will act as they see fit. But it is certainly possible we can lead them in the direction we wish them to go. Even Mr. Darcy, who is as determined a man as I have ever met, may act in a way *we* desire if we lead him properly."

A thoughtful Caroline was much more endurable than a petulant Caroline, which Louisa had occasion to witness many times. When her sister stayed silent for several moments, Louisa spoke again.

"The trick, as I see it, is to prevent either from doing something disastrous at present. The Bennets will not be trapped here forever. Ensure they leave Netherfield as soon as possible, distract them both from doing anything we do not wish them to do while the Bennets remain, and once they are gone, we may take steps to detach Miss Bennet and Miss Elizabeth from Charles and Mr. Darcy."

"Perhaps we could insist on returning to town?" suggested Caroline. "Charles mentioned he had a matter of business for which he was required to return. If we close Netherfield and follow him thither, we can distract him from Miss Bennet. And with Mr. Darcy away from this neighborhood, why, I am certain he would forget about Miss Eliza and remember himself. Then if I show him what an excellent match I would be for him, he can hardly resist me!

Despite Caroline's excitement, Louisa was less convinced of the ultimate success of their schemes with respect to Mr. Darcy. The man was immovable as a mountain. Charles, on the other hand, was malleable and easily led, if it was done with subtlety. Louisa knew that Caroline would allow Charles's fascination with Miss Bennet to succeed if it would mean her gaining Mr. Darcy, but Louisa thought it certain it would be far easier to prevent their brother from having his Bennet sister than Mr. Darcy.

But a happy and scheming Caroline was far preferable to a petulant Caroline and much easier on Louisa's nerves. Prudence dictated she support her sister in this and keep her as happy as possible. If Mr. Darcy did propose to Miss Elizabeth, hopefully, they could have Charles engaged to another woman of greater suitability. Caroline could focus on that.

"Very well," said Caroline. "That shall be our plan for now. Thank you, Louisa, for speaking sense. I can see now that all will be well."

"I am happy to hear it," said Louisa. "Now, if you will excuse me, I shall return to my rooms to rest before dinner."

Caroline nodded. As she was leaving, Louisa heard her calling for the maid. As the poor girl stepped into the room, Caroline started berating her. Louisa sighed. At least Caroline would not arrive at dinner soused—had Louisa not redirected her, that eventuality would have been highly possible.

Elizabeth had discovered these past days that Miss Anne de Bourgh was more than she might have ever expected. Though it would be uncharitable to suggest that her mother's death had allowed her to flourish, it was undeniable that the woman Elizabeth knew was much more than the one she had met the first night at Netherfield. And though it might have been improper to discuss the matter openly, on that occasion, Anne did exactly that.

"I am wondering what I should do with myself," confessed Anne as they sat beside the fire in Anne's room. The dress which was draped over her thin form was dyed black as night, which did not at all suit the woman's pale complexion. It made her appear quite ghostly, especially in the evening when the light faded.

"Mother has always controlled every aspect of my life. I find my future liberated, but quite frightening at the same time."

"I suppose you will return to your estate?"

"For the mourning, at the very least," replied Anne. "That would be proper. I should not even know what to do in London, for I have never had a season there."

"Never had a season?" asked Elizabeth with a frown. "Surely a woman of your wealth and standing must have had a season."

"Ah, but you forget," said Anne. "I was to marry my Cousin Darcy. I did not need to be paraded before all the grasping men of society when my future was already secured." Elizabeth could not help but shake her head in disbelief. "It seems your mother was so fixated on this match that she neglected to allow you to live."

"That is true," said Anne. She fell silent for a moment, her gaze far away. "Though I suppose I should not be grateful for such a thing, my mother's death has made my future much brighter. She was a difficult woman, and I will do well enough without her."

The thought that Lady Catherine's death had benefited Anne as much as anyone else crossed Elizabeth's mind. But she did not think this frail creature possessed the will, let alone the strength, to murder her robust mother. Or had she? How much strength did it take to hold a pillow over the head of another?

Elizabeth shook her head, willing such thoughts away. She was seeing murderers behind every door! "I am certain your cousins will assist," said she, in order to dispel the dark thoughts which had gathered.

"I am certain they will," replied Anne. "Darcy's help, in particular, will be welcome. My mother did not have much difficulty in gaining the cooperation of the tenants and servants, but I am not so foolish as to believe I am anything like my mother."

"And marriage?" asked Elizabeth. "Will marriage be in your future now you are not limited in your ability to select a partner?"

"I do not know. I have never thought of it, other than the wish to avoid drawing my mother's attention to the subject of Darcy and her ambitions in that quarter. I suppose I would like to have a husband and children, but I must take care." She laughed ruefully. "My mother always spoke of the unworthy and the fortune hunters of society, and concerning my prospects, that meant everyone other than Darcy. But she was not incorrect, I suppose."

"Not everyone is avaricious or false, Anne," replied Elizabeth.

"I know," replied Anne. "Of those close to me, I suppose it was only my mother who was."

"What do you mean?" asked Elizabeth.

Anne frowned and shook her head. "You heard her, Elizabeth. Her reasons for wishing Darcy and me married had nothing to do with our feelings or any expectation we would make a good marriage. It was entirely because of her selfish desires—the creation of a family with excessive wealth, the possibility of a title for her grandchildren, political power for our family." Anne released a mirthless laugh, all her derision for the woman she had called mother seeming contained in that sound. "The ironic part of this is that *she* has never been in a position to wield political power, and my uncle—who most certainly *does*—does not care for it."

"I understand some disillusionment with your mother, Anne," said Elizabeth. "But I cannot think this is healthy. Perhaps it would be best if you attempted to remember the good times with your mother, rather than agonizing over her faults."

With a shaken head, Anne stood and regarded Elizabeth. "Try as I might, I cannot remember any. I have been a prisoner all my life. And I am struck by the thought that those of us who endured her—myself most of all—have gained because she is now gone."

It was all Elizabeth could do to stifle a gasp, for it seemed like Anne was trying to convince herself of the truth of her statement. It said nothing, of course, for she might simply be justifying her feelings. But it also made Elizabeth wonder concerning the suspicions she possessed about Lady Catherine's death.

"If you will excuse me, Elizabeth, I think I would like to rest now."

"Of course, Anne," replied Elizabeth. She summoned a smile and wished her new friend a good rest. Then she let herself from the room. But she was troubled, for the mystery in which they were all embroiled seemed to have become more complicated, as there were several who fit the description of Lady Catherine's murderer.

"This is astonishing, Cousin. The irony is simply delicious."

Darcy regarded his cousin, feeling grumpy at Fitzwilliam's teasing. "You need not be so gleeful about it."

"As a matter of fact, I believe I do. Had I had my way, Wickham would have been dealt with once and for all last summer when he nearly made off with Georgiana's fortune. Now you wish to do something about him. If we had extracted payment from his hide in the summer, there would be no need to do anything about him now."

Though he may be correct, Darcy did not think his cousin needed to point the matter out in such exhaustive detail. In retrospect, he should have ensured Wickham was not in a position to bedevil him many years ago. The man had no claim to his affection, and his actions after receiving the money from his godfather's will had been enough to sever all pretense of acquaintance.

"I might ask," continued Fitzwilliam, "what has prompted this determination to neutralize Wickham. Has he done something in particular to offend you?"

Darcy hesitated to inform his cousin of his conversation with Wickham, but Fitzwilliam needed to understand what had happened and Wickham's threats. Thus, in a halting manner, he related the tale to Fitzwilliam. As he expected, his cousin's response was part exasperation and part mirth.

"I have never been so certain you are in love as I am now. Wickham knows how to rile you. The fact that you remained calm until he began to speak of Miss Elizabeth has informed him how much she has come to mean to you. That may make her a target, simply due to his desire for revenge."

"I know it," replied Darcy. "I do not fear for Miss Elizabeth, as she knows what he is. But her younger sisters are exactly the kind of girls Wickham preys upon."

"Which would serve his purpose adequately."

"Yes."

"Then what I suggest is to remain watchful and give Wickham enough rope with which to hang himself."

Darcy peered at his cousin, surprised. "And allow him the opportunity to work his wiles on one of the young girls?"

"They are made of sterner stuff than you think, Darcy," said Fitzwilliam, baring his teeth in a grin. "They are silly flirts, but they are not immoral. Besides, their elder sisters watch them like a mother bear watches her cubs. They will protect them if need be. Just keep watch on Wickham. He will do something to hang himself eventually. And then, you may deal with him without waiting for the debt receipts to arrive, allowing Wickham time to escape. He will make a mistake sooner or later, Darcy. Then we may pounce."

Though Darcy did not like it, he had no better ideas himself. There was nothing else to be done at present.

CHAPTER XVI

*D*inner that evening was not to be a lively affair, or at least Elizabeth could not imagine it being so. An ennui had settled over the company, one which Elizabeth thought existed because they were a disparate group of people, and in certain cases, tension ran high between certain of those present.

It was particularly noticeable when Elizabeth entered the sitting-room that evening before dinner. While the youngest Bennets carried on like they usually did and Jane and Mr. Bingley sat together with their heads close together, not everyone was so happy in the others' company. In particular, it seemed most of the room looked upon Mr. Wickham with suspicion. For his part, Mr. Wickham did not seem to care for their opinions if the sardonic sneer with which he favored them all was any indication. No one had much to say to Mr. Collins, though the man himself spoke in a loud voice, seeming to believe everyone was hanging onto his every word.

Anne still kept to her room, though Elizabeth did not know if it was due to mourning or because she did not wish to be in company. Their discussion earlier that day, Elizabeth had attempted to put from her mind. It was true she did not wish to consider the possibility that her new friend had murdered her mother. Something told her, however, that Anne could not have done it.

When Mr. Darcy and Colonel Fitzwilliam entered the room, Elizabeth noted they had their heads close together, discussing something of some import. Mr. Darcy caught sight of Mr. Wickham and scowled—prompting Mr. Wickham's sneer to widen in response—which suggested to Elizabeth she knew the subject of their discussion. Given what had happened with Mr. Wickham and Lydia earlier, Elizabeth was quite as eager as Mr. Darcy to be rid of the militia officer. But when the outburst came, it was from a source Elizabeth might have considered unlikely only a few moments before.

"How dare you glare at Mr. Wickham, sir!" exclaimed Mrs. Bennet when she caught sight of what passed between the two men. "He possesses much more nobility of character and amiable qualities than *you*."

Mr. Darcy eyed Mrs. Bennet. When he spoke, he did so in a conciliatory tone. "I apologize for my behavior earlier today, Mrs. Bennet. But I will only apologize that you witnessed it, not for what I said to Wickham. You do not know what he is; I suggest you do not allow his sibilant whisperings to cloud your judgment of him."

While Mr. Wickham only barked a sardonic laugh, Mrs. Bennet glared at Mr. Darcy, clearly affronted on Mr. Wickham's behalf. "Your apology is no apology at all. You manhandled a guest in this house with such violence as I have never seen. What can you possibly say in your defense?"

"Maggie," said Mr. Bennet, "I suggest you cease this line of conversation. Mr. Darcy is Mr. Bingley's friend, and we are guests in this house. I suspect you do not possess the full story of the history of these two men."

"But you did not see them in the hallway, Mr. Bennet!" cried Mrs. Bennet. "You did not witness him pushing Mr. Wickham against the wall and uttering vile threats."

"If Mr. Darcy uttered threats," interjected Mr. Collins, "then I am certain it was for a good reason. As the nephew of my dearly departed patroness, I am confident in the excellence of his character." Mr. Collins turned and glared at Mr. Wickham. "This . . . *officer* is naught but the son of old Mr. Darcy's steward. I have that from Lady Catherine herself. There is little reason to hold him up as a paragon of virtue."

"There is little reason for anyone to be held up or cast down based on such flimsy evidence, Mr. Collins," said Mr. Bennet. "Be that as it may since we are forced to endure one another's company, I suggest we keep our conversation to acceptable topics to avoid open conflict."

"But Mr. Bennet," whines Mrs. Bennet, "with such a violent man in residence, I do not know that I wish my daughters to be importuned by such as he."

"That is enough, Mrs. Bennet," said Mr. Bennet. At the same time, several other voices rose in support or censure, and for a moment, almost all were speaking, arguing their point of view. Elizabeth rubbed her temples, wondering if the atmosphere in the room could get any worse.

"Enough!" said the voice of one Elizabeth had not expected to hear. Lydia stood when silence ensued, the others all looking at her with shock and wonder.

"I have personal knowledge that Mr. Wickham is not a good man, Mama," said she, turning and glaring at Mr. Wickham. "I have watched you since this argument began, sir, and if my sister's account of you did not inform me of your character, the way you look on us all with contempt confirms it."

"Lizzy told you of Mr. Wickham?" demanded Mrs. Bennet. "What would she know of the matter?" Mrs. Bennet snorted. "Details she has heard from Mr. Darcy, no doubt."

"Your youngest speaks the truth," interjected Colonel Fitzwilliam. "You would do well not to trust Wickham, Madam. He is a snake and a particularly venomous one at that. I, personally, believe he should be in Marshalsea, or perhaps Botany Bay, for the rest of his natural life."

"Since I appear to be the center of this argument," said Mr. Wickham, speaking for the first time, "it falls to me to end it."

Mr. Wickham turned a charming smile on Mrs. Bennet. "I thank you for your spirited defense, Mrs. Bennet—if only there were more like you who were offended by the actions against those who are defenseless. In this instance, I spoke an impertinence to Mr. Darcy, and he reacted, though excessively. I offer Darcy my humble apologies and hope he will accept them in the spirit in which they are intended."

It was clear that Mr. Darcy did not believe Mr. Wickham's sincerity. Indeed, the sneer still twisting the man's lips gave the lie to his supposed penitence. However, Mr. Darcy also clearly understood the need to end the argument and offered a tight nod to his tormentor. Wickham returned it gleefully, seeming to believe he had won a significant point.

"Now that you have so ably defended the defenseless," said Mr. Bennet to his wife, his sarcasm dripping from his tone, "let us put the matter to rest. Come and sit beside me, my dear."

Though reluctant, Mrs. Bennet allowed herself to be led away. Elizabeth watched her, wondering at the matter which had provoked her to speak out. Near the door where they still stood, Mr. Darcy and Colonel Fitzwilliam exchanged a few more words. Mr. Wickham looked out over them all, as if he was a patron at a theater, watching a comedy, and Lydia glared at him, Kitty sitting nearby and following her younger sister's example. At least Lydia seemed to have taken Elizabeth's words to heart. Had she not heard her sister speak, Elizabeth might not have credited the change as being possible.

When Mr. Wickham moved to approach her sisters, Elizabeth mirrored his actions, as did Mary, who seemed to have become more watchful since they had come to Netherfield.

"I am wounded by your words concerning me," his tone all that was insolent. "What have I done to warrant this censure?"

Lydia sniffed at him. "I do not wish to speak with you any longer, sir. If you cannot understand, then you are far more witless than I had ever imagined."

"Ah, cut to the core," said Mr. Wickham, putting a dramatic hand over his heart. "And by a silly girl only just out of the schoolroom, no less."

"Enough, Wickham," said a deep male voice. Mr. Darcy, who had come to stand beside them, glared at his former friend, his demeanor warning. "It is time you left the Bennet sisters strictly alone."

"Though I am unjustly attacked," said Mr. Wickham, "I shall comply."

And with those words, he turned and made his way to his former position. But he still watched them all, a hint of scornful amusement in his countenance.

"You have shown great discernment, Miss Lydia," said Mr. Darcy, showing her a smile. "Mr. Wickham has misled many of greater age and wisdom than you possess."

It was, perhaps, the first time Mr. Darcy had spoken to Lydia and certainly the first time he had spoken in such a kindly manner. Lydia blushed at the praise but soon rediscovered her composure. "It was Lizzy who helped me understand, Mr. Darcy. She should receive your credit."

"But you have still listened to her. It is a good trait, to give your attention to elder siblings and allow their words and wisdom to assist you to gain experience. I commend you."

Again Lydia colored, but this time she only nodded and turned back to Kitty to continue whispering to her. Mr. Darcy turned to

Elizabeth.

"I dare not ask what has brought about this change," said he in a soft voice. "It seems, however, the situation has been rectified and your sisters appropriately warned. Is there anything I should know or anything I can do to assist?"

"As you suggested, Mr. Darcy, the matter has been handled. Given Lydia's currently expressed opinions, I suspect there is little danger on that score any longer."

Mr. Darcy nodded. "Please advise me should anything develop. I will take great pleasure in silencing the libertine as I should have done many years ago."

Before Elizabeth could reply, the shrill voice of her mother interrupted them. "Come, girls—it is nearly time for dinner, and I would prefer to have my daughters near me."

The way Mrs. Bennet regarded Mr. Darcy spoke to her continuing suspicion and revealed her ineffectual desire to keep her daughters from what she considered to be a man lacking in basic goodness. Elizabeth looked heavenward, which prompted a tugging at the corner of Mr. Darcy's mouth. But she said nothing, allowing her mother to direct her sisters away from him. She had not counted on Mr. Darcy's sudden decision to address her mother.

"You take great care of your daughters, Mrs. Bennet," said he. He leaned forward and grasped her hand, bringing it to his lips and kissing it. "I cannot but commend you for it. Your daughters are all that is good and lovely. You should be proud of them."

It was clear from Mrs. Bennet's stupefaction that she did not quite know what to make of Mr. Darcy's praise. Her cheeks became a little rosy, and she stammered her thanks before scurrying away. Elizabeth did not know if it would change her mother's mind concerning the gentleman, but it showed her a little glimpse of a Mr. Darcy who possessed the ability to be charming. Elizabeth grinned at him before allowing her mother to lead her away with her sisters.

They stayed this way, the company divided into little cliques. Mrs. Bennet kept a firm rein on her daughters, insisting they remain nearby, though Elizabeth noted she did not attempt to intrude on Jane and Mr. Bingley. Mr. Wickham stood by himself, watching them all with a sneer, while Mr. Darcy returned to Colonel Fitzwilliam, where they continued to talk in low tones. The two gentlemen ignored Mr. Collins's attempts to attach himself to them, though the way the parson beamed as he stood nearby suggested he had not noticed. As for Mr. and Mrs. Hurst, they had been in the room the entire time but had kept themselves above the fray. Elizabeth did witness, however, a few times when Mrs. Hurst shot a look at her brother in asperity, while Mr. Hurst nursed a brandy in his hand, seeming to wish that he was somewhere else. Only their hostess was not present, which was unusual.

When Miss Bingley appeared in the door, it was with all the pride and fanfare Elizabeth might have expected from the superior woman. She surveyed the room briefly and made her way toward Mr. Darcy, a predatory gleam in her eye.

But all was not well—Elizabeth noted it with a start. For one, Miss Bingley's complexion was a chalky white, far paler than usual, for all that she was of a fair tone of skin. Furthermore, as she walked, she grimaced, and her steps faltered a little, weaving like she was tipsy. When she reached Mr. Darcy, she spoke to him in a loud voice, one which reminded Elizabeth of the braying of a donkey.

"Mr. Darcy! How wonderful it is to see you, sir. I do hope you will escort me in to dinner, for we have not spoken much of late."

It seemed to Elizabeth that Mr. Darcy had also noticed her state, for he gazed at her with no little alarm. "Are you well, Miss Bingley?"

The woman opened her mouth to respond, but there was no opportunity for her to do so. A cry escaped her lips, and she clutched at her midsection as if in great pain. Mr. Darcy's hand flew out to grasp her shoulder, accompanied by a startled: "Miss Bingley!"

Then the woman screamed again. She clutched at her stomach again, before vomiting heavily on the floor. Then with a beseeching look up at Mr. Darcy, her eyes filled with terror, she collapsed in the pool of her own bile and began convulsing.

"Caroline!" screamed Mrs. Hurst, even as her brother shot to his feet and hurried to his sister.

Mr. Darcy and Colonel Fitzwilliam joined him in attempting to assist the stricken woman, each grasping a shoulder, attempting to hold her and prevent injury. Then a foaming froth appeared at Miss Bingley's mouth. She jerked a few more times, shuddered, and then lay still, her head rolling to one side. There was no movement.

Mrs. Hurst screamed her sister's name again and fell to the floor, holding Miss Bingley's head and crying her anguish. Mr. Bingley was calling for his sister, pleading for her to respond. But Elizabeth knew she never would again. The cousins shared a look, their meaning clear for all to see. Miss Bingley was dead.

Mr. Bingley, shocked and numb, was incapacitated. Mrs. Hurst was in no better state. It fell to Mr. Darcy to take control of the situation. He stepped to the door and spoke quickly to someone outside. Elizabeth heard a loud gasp before Mr. Darcy spoke a harsh word and closed the door.

"She was healthy," said Mr. Bingley in a lost voice. "How could this have happened? Is this place cursed?"

"It is no curse," said Colonel Fitzwilliam. "I am sorry to inform you of this, Bingley, but your sister was poisoned."

For an instant, all sound ceased. Even Mrs. Hurst, who was keening over the body of her sister, stopped and stared at the colonel. Then the voices were raised in a great discordance of a dozen voices all attempting to be heard. At its center was Colonel Fitzwilliam. When he had had enough of it, he put his fingers to his lips and a shrieking whistle shocked them all to silence.

"Look at her!" snapped he, gesturing to the fallen woman. "She had pain in her midsection, vomiting, frothing at the mouth, and then she collapsed into convulsions. Furthermore, look at this."

Colonel Fitzwilliam bent over and picked up one limp hand, holding it where they all could see. Under Miss Bingley's nails, white lines had formed.

"This is classic evidence of arsenic poisoning. Given the speed at which she expired, I suspect she was given a massive dose of it."

"But who would have wanted to murder my sister?" asked Mr. Bingley. He looked at Colonel Fitzwilliam with pleading eyes. "She was difficult at times, I will own. But enough for someone to want to kill her?"

"Oh, come, Mr. Bingley," scoffed Lydia. "With her attitude, I would not be surprised if everyone in this house wished to kill her at one time or another."

A cry of rage issued from Mrs. Hurst's mouth, and she struggled to her feet. With fingers extended into claws, she reached out to Lydia, only to be held in check by her husband. Screaming, Mrs. Hurst struggled like a madwoman for several moments until her strength was seemingly spent. She collapsed in her husband's arms, weeping. Elizabeth did not miss the sardonic grin that Mr. Hurst directed at Lydia.

"Be silent, Lydia!" hissed Elizabeth, stepping to the stupid girl and catching her arm up in one hand. "Do not say such disgusting things about one who is just deceased."

"Miss Lydia's outburst *is* uncalled for," said Mr. Bingley, standing and bestowing a sad look on her. "But while her words are true from a certain perspective, and I will own Caroline was difficult, is it enough that anyone would wish to kill her?"

Once again, the voices of many rose up in a discordant rumble of sound, but one voice dominated over the others. "It was Mr. Darcy!" When the others gazed at her in astonishment, Mrs. Bennet colored but would not recant. "I have seen it all! Miss Bingley was determined to become the mistress of Mr. Darcy's estate, and he hated her for it. I have seen the violence of which he is capable! Ask Mr. Wickham! Ask him what form Mr. Darcy's rage takes!"

"You would do well to listen to *nothing* Wickham says, madam," said Colonel Fitzwilliam, offended for his cousin.

For his part, Mr. Darcy spoke to attempt to diffuse the situation. "You are angry and frightened, Mrs. Bennet—I understand this. But though I will not say you are incorrect about Miss Bingley's wishes, I have fended them off for four years now. Why would I choose to act now?"

It was clear Mrs. Bennet had no answer for Mr. Darcy's reasonable assertion. Then another spoke up.

"I was not fond of my sister," said Mr. Hurst, eliciting a gasp from his wife. Mr. Hurst silenced her with a frown. "It is the truth, Louisa. Your sister was a grasping, artful shrew, who made both of our lives miserable whenever she had the chance."

Mr. Hurst turned back to Mrs. Bennet. "But my dislike for my sister-in-law makes me no more a killer than Mr. Darcy. I suggest, Madam, that you take care not to fling about baseless accusations for which you have no proof."

The reproof visibly chastened Mrs. Bennet. At that moment, several footmen entered the room, followed by the butler. The sight of the body on the floor, the ravages of Miss Bingley's passing visible on and around her, caused a pallor to come over the man's features. With the assistance of the footmen, they produced a large blanket, and the body of Miss Bingley was wrapped about and borne away. Mrs. Hurst again let out a keening wail and buried her head in her husband's shoulder. It was odd, given Elizabeth had never seen anything but amusement or languor in Mr. Hurst's manner, but he seemed almost tender with his grieving wife.

"The question, to me at least," said Mr. Bennet, "is who would have had a reason to murder Miss Bingley. While a crime of passion may be the explanation, and someone like Mr. Darcy may, indeed, be under suspicion, I know of nothing recently which may have incensed him to the point where he would be willing to take a life."

Mr. Darcy shook his head. "I have seen little of Miss Bingley in recent days."

"Then was there anyone else with whom Miss Bingley might have argued?"

"Miss Bingley argued with Lady Catherine," said Lydia helpfully."

"Thank you for reminding us of that, Lydia," said Mr. Bennet. "Unfortunately, Lady Catherine is also passed. Unless she set all this in motion before her passing, I highly doubt she returned from the grave to wreak her vengeance."

A flush settled over Lydia's countenance, and she ducked her head. At the same time, Mrs. Hurst sniffled and pulled away from her husband.

"What about Miss Anne de Bourgh? Has she no reason to hate my sister, given the way she argued with Lady Catherine?"

"Unless you have not noticed," said Colonel Fitzwilliam, "Anne's mourning of her mother has been discreet at best. Lady Catherine was not the easiest mother, and Anne is feeling a heady dose of freedom because of Lady Catherine's demise."

"Then is that not a reason for suspicion?" asked Mrs. Hurst, her jaw hardening. "She might have murdered her mother and then my sister."

"I do not think they were connected, my dear," said Mr. Hurst. "While she might have murdered her mother to escape her, I doubt she would have cared if Lady Catherine argued with Caroline."

It was clear Mrs. Hurst was desperate to blame someone— anyone—for her sister's death. The grim set to her countenance suggested mutiny, and as much to silence her as anything else, Elizabeth spoke up.

"I agree with Mr. Hurst. There is no reason to suppose Miss de Bourgh has murdered anyone. But why do you speak of the murder of Lady Catherine, Mrs. Hurst? Does the company not believe she died in her sleep?"

There were several gasps, but it was Mrs. Bennet who turned her thoughts into words. "Perhaps Lady Catherine did not die of an apoplexy! Perhaps she was also murdered! And what of the poor butler? Might his death not have been an accident?"

"My patroness was murdered?" demanded Mr. Collins, the light of zeal alive in his eyes. "If any of you have murdered Lady Catherine, I will pray to ensure the hand of judgment finds you all with the curse of withering death. For the death of such a paragon of virtue, such a woman of insight, goodness, and nobility, must be punished by the highest authority, that of God himself!"

"Murderers *are* under the condemnation of God," said Colonel Fitzwilliam, glaring at Mr. Collins. "Do not suppose that Lady Catherine being a victim makes the punishment any more severe."

"The rest of us are almost happy she is gone," sniffed Lydia. Fortunately, she spoke in a low voice, such that only those closest to her could hear. Elizabeth directed a fierce glare at her sister, who subsided, though not with any grace.

"If there is a murderer in our midst, when will he strike again?"

It was a question none of them could answer, least of all Mrs. Bennet, who had posed it. Indeed, Elizabeth was witness to more than a few suspicious glares from those she accounted to be the sillier of the group. The others—Mr. Bennet, Mr. Darcy, and Colonel Fitzwilliam chief among them—appeared worried.

"I think," said Mr. Bingley, "perhaps it is best we retire for the night. I am sure none of us have the desire to sit at dinner considering . . ." Mr. Bingley stopped, and a lump seemed to form in his throat.

Jane, the compassionate creature she was, laid a hand on his arm, for which Mr. Bingley appeared profoundly grateful. With the support of her approval, Mr. Bingley once again spoke.

"I beg you all to retire to your rooms. I will ask for trays to be provided. If we do have a murderer in this house . . . Well, perhaps it is best if no one is alone."

On the surface of it, Elizabeth agreed with his comments. Unless, of course, one ended up so unfortunate as to be in the sole company of the murderer. Then again, the one who had managed three deaths so far would not be stupid enough to kill the person he was with.

One thing Elizabeth did know: given how Miss Bingley had died, she doubted very much of the cook's excellent dinner would be consumed that night.

CHAPTER XVII

"Fitzwilliam!" hissed Darcy as the rest of the company began to depart from the room.

His cousin turned and regarded him, nodding slightly in understanding. Darcy was grateful for his cousin's support. They were so well acquainted with each other that they possessed the ability to communicate with a glance or a gesture.

A glance at the rest of the party revealed several looks in their direction. But that was not all—it seemed everyone was watching everyone else carefully, understandable since it had now become clear there was a murderer at Netherfield. They were fractured, largely along family lines, the Bennet sisters congregated together closely. Hurst escorted his wife from the room, standing closely—protectively, even—while Bingley vacillated between the two groups. Only Wickham remained aloof, watching the party with what could only be termed as contempt. A glare from Darcy sent the man from the room, though he walked slowly, seemingly unconcerned.

Just before the Bennet sisters left, Darcy caught a glimpse of Miss Elizabeth looking back at him. He knew she wished she could stay with him. Their activities those past two days had informed him she was determined to discover the meaning of the mystery which had beset them all. But she could not disobey her father now, not when the danger of the situation had increased so much.

"You wish to search Miss Bingley's room?" said Fitzwilliam when they were alone.

"I doubt the killer has left any evidence we can use," replied Darcy. "But it must be done, and Bingley is too shocked to do it himself."

"Very well, Cousin. You have my support."

They waited for a few moments for the rest of the group to make their way to their rooms. As they waited, Darcy paced the floor, working the matter over in his mind, attempting to divine the nature of what they faced. But nothing came to mind. The three victims had very little in common, had come from entirely different backgrounds, their only connection being their residence in the house at the same time.

"Sit down, Darcy," said Fitzwilliam after a moment of his pacing. "You are making me dizzy."

"We *must* discover the culprit, Cousin."

"So we must. But wearing a furrow into the floor will not bring us any closer to the answer."

"No. But it helps me think."

"I would appreciate it if you would think more quietly, and preferably in one location."

"Let us go above stairs," said Darcy, too tense to consider sitting at that moment. "The others must be in their rooms by now."

Fitzwilliam acquiesced, but from his introspection, Darcy could see that he too was considering the situation. His frown was such that it was evident he had little more success than Darcy had achieved himself.

There was something not right about this situation. It was as if the killer was murdering random members of the party, though why someone would kill in such a way was beyond his ability to understand. Furthermore, the murders had been accomplished in different ways, meaning there was nothing to connect them or indicate who was responsible.

"None of this makes any sense," muttered Darcy as they walked. "And it all seems to lead back to Wickham."

"What is that?" demanded Fitzwilliam. "Why do you suspect Wickham?"

"I cannot say," confessed Darcy. "But I do. He is the only member of the company with a suspect background who might be depraved enough to kill several people."

"But why those people in particular? What links them together?"

Darcy threw his hands up and stalked on. "I do not know. He might have killed Lady Catherine for blocking his path to Anne, or Miss Bingley for refusing him. He boasted to me that he would attempt to charm Miss Bingley for her dowry."

"And what of the butler? He was murdered before Wickham ever arrived."

Darcy could only acknowledge he had no explanation for the butler's death. What he had told Miss Elizabeth about it now seemed nonsensical. And even if Wickham had loitered about somewhere in the house without being discovered, why would he have killed the butler? Unless the man had discovered him, which was not out of the realm of possibility.

"Do not close your mind and focus on Wickham," said Fitzwilliam as Darcy was thinking. "Your judgment—*my* judgment, for that matter—is clouded when it pertains to Wickham. Though I have little inclination to give him any credit, in this instance, it seems unlikely that he is the murderer. He has never given us any indication he is *that* depraved."

Contenting himself with a grunt, Darcy hurried his steps forward, and soon they had arrived in front of the door to Miss Bingley's bedchamber. Not expecting anyone to be within, Darcy opened the door and was surprised to see light in the room. A maid was moving about the room, straightening Miss Bingley's belongings. An expression of worry and sorrow covered her face.

"Mr. Darcy," said the maid with a squeak, dropping into a hasty curtsey. "May I help you?"

"I apologize," replied Darcy. "I assume you have heard what happened tonight?"

"Yes, sir," replied the maid, her eyes downcast. "I . . . I was shocked. Miss Bingley was good to me, and I will miss her. It is only . . ."

"You fear for your livelihood?" asked Darcy, understanding the source of her concerns.

The maid's eyes widened, and she attempted to stammer an apology. But Darcy interrupted her before she could.

"It is not unnatural in such a situation . . . I am sorry, but I do not know your name?"

"Marie," whispered the young woman.

"You do not need to fear me, Marie," replied Darcy, favoring her with a kindly look. "It is natural to be upset at the loss of your mistress while being concerned for the uncertainty you now face. Speak with the housekeeper tomorrow, and she will relay your concerns to my friend. At the very least, I am certain he will retain you or give you a reference."

The woman hesitated a moment. "I am grateful, to be certain. I should prefer a reference, for if I am to work in another position, it would be a pay cut, and I assist my mother back home in York."

"Understandable," replied Darcy. "Speak with my friend. I am certain you will not be disappointed. Now, we need to look about the room to see if we can uncover what happened. Please stay nearby so we can ask questions if needed."

While the maid curtseyed, she was clearly uncomfortable, as if thinking she might be made to answer questions which did not put her in a good light. Still, she gamely cleared her throat and said: "Perhaps you should start with the glass on the table. Miss Bingley took a drink just before she left for the dining room this evening."

Darcy's eyes followed the maid's pointing hand, and he was shocked to see a bottle of brandy set on the tray with several glasses situated nearby. The bottle appeared to have been newly opened, as there was only a little of the amber liquid missing. A closer inspection revealed that one of the glasses had a trace of brandy still in the bottom.

"Is *this* what Miss Bingley was drinking?" asked Darcy, unable to prevent a hint of incredulous shock from entering his voice.

"It was," replied the maid. "She had a glass just before she left for dinner."

"That is rich, Darcy," said Fitzwilliam, out of the side of his mouth. "Most ladies of quality prefer sherry or some other ladylike drink. Considering what the maid told us, it appears Miss Bingley was raiding her brother's stock of brandy for some time."

"It does explain a few things," said Darcy. Then he turned back to the maid.

"When was this bottle delivered?"

"Late this afternoon," replied the maid. "In fact, Miss Bingley was . . ."

She trailed off, looking uncomfortable. Darcy immediately understood her dilemma.

"You need not fear," said he, regarding her kindly. "We need you to inform us of whatever you know, Marie, for it is vital to solving this mystery. Do not be concerned we will be offended by what you tell us."

"We are more likely to fall to the floor laughing," said Fitzwilliam,

flashing that irrepressible grin. Darcy glared at him—at least he had
spoken quietly, and the maid had not heard him. But it would do no
good to antagonize the help, especially when they required the
information she possessed.

It was fortunate the maid seemed to be a little more at ease. "Miss
Bingley ordered the bottle yesterday afternoon and was quite put out
that it was slow in coming."

"Did she drink brandy often, or did she have some particular
reason for ordering this?"

"She almost always had a glass in the evening," said Marie. "Since
we have come to Netherfield, however, she often drank more, and the
presence of guests had increased the amount she drank." The maid
paused and then said in a hurried voice: "But she never became drunk!
She was always careful to ensure she did not drink much."

"Thank you, Marie," said Darcy, eager to send her off as he sensed
his cousin was about to break out into laughter. "Is there anything else
of note that you can tell us?"

The maid mentioned a few more matters, such as the argument
with Lady Catherine and Miss Bingley's general complaints—which
were about the Bennet family, more often than not. But she had little
else of interest to tell them, and after a moment, Darcy dismissed her.

"Thank you again. We will show ourselves from the rooms. For
now, I think you have earned your rest this evening."

Flashing him a smile, Marie curtseyed and fled from the room,
leaving the two cousins. The moment she left the room, Fitzwilliam
burst into laughter.

"I have often thought Miss Bingley's behavior odd, but the mystery
now seems to have been solved! Surely those times she was a trifle
disguised!"

"Really, Fitzwilliam," said Darcy, shaking his head.

"Come now, Darcy; the woman practically invited derision. Surely
you must own this. Furthermore, I suspect that is the reason why she
was always so late in arising. Obviously, she was keeping company
with Bingley's fine French brandy and drank so much that she was
drunk as a wheelbarrow! She spent the mornings sleeping it off!"

Darcy snorted. The image Fitzwilliam painted was amusing, and
Darcy was certain that it was at least partially the truth. Miss Bingley,
though it was not proper to speak ill of the deceased, had been a
ridiculous woman at times.

"So what do you make of this?" asked Darcy, leaning forward to
inspect the glass. "For Miss Bingley to have consumed that much

poison, the killer must have put a lot into the brandy."

"Not necessarily," said Fitzwilliam, sobering. He hefted the bottle from where it stood and peered into the liquid. "No residue on the bottom. The poison must be dissolved into the liquor."

"What do you think it is?"

"Oh, arsenic. Without a doubt."

"It seems to make sense," allowed Darcy. "As I recall, the Medicis used it frequently when they were prominent in Italy."

Fitzwilliam turned and peered at Darcy. "Do you remember old Lord Winchester?"

"Did he not pass last year?"

"He did. I know you do not care much for society, so you most likely have not heard. It is suspected that his grandson grew tired of waiting and began slowly poisoning him with arsenic. If done carefully, it looks like a natural illness and may cause death in the elderly in only a few months."

"Was he brought before the courts?" asked Darcy, curious. He had not heard any of these rumors.

Fitzwilliam shook his head and turned back to his inspection of the bottle. "There was never any proof."

"The king of poisons or the poison of kings," murmured Darcy. "Colorless, odorless, and tasteless, the symptoms are easily confused with cholera, and as such, it often goes undetected.

"We cannot even be certain that bottle contains the poison," said Fitzwilliam. "Unless you wish to try drinking it to be certain."

"I think I shall stick to port," replied Darcy dryly.

"My brother even joked about using it to deal with my father the last time Father spoke of finding him a woman to marry."

A snort was Darcy's response. The Fitzwilliam brothers had both been close to him all his life, and Blakely, the viscount, was like his brother in essentials. No doubt he would have spoken of the matter in front of the earl, and Darcy suspected the earl would have laughed and jested in return.

"High quantities of arsenic, however," said Fitzwilliam, "can kill very quickly, and in the same manner as we saw Miss Bingley expire."

"Then we should determine where this bottle came from," said Darcy. "And attempt to discover who tampered with it."

Fitzwilliam nodded. "If the killer was smart enough, he would have taken care not to be seen. With such a high concentration of poison, however, I wonder what the possible motive could have been."

"I do not know, Cousin. But this is quickly becoming a serious situation."

When they arrived in the kitchens, they found the housekeeper speaking with the cook. Both women rose in alarm at the sight of the two men invading their demesne, but Darcy spoke quickly to put them at ease.

"Mrs. Nichols, may we have a word with you about something which happened earlier today?"

Though still a little concerned, Mrs. Nichols nodded. The cook stayed silent.

"I understand Miss Bingley ordered a bottle of brandy today. Can you tell me how it was delivered to her rooms?"

Mrs. Nichols frowned. "The brandy was in the cellar, Mr. Darcy, as are all of Mr. Bingley's bottles."

"When was it brought upstairs? And who took it to Miss Bingley's maid?"

"The bottle was brought up soon after Miss Bingley requested it, by one of the footmen, as I recall. At the same time, however, Miss Bingley created a bit of a to do before dinner this evening, requesting a different and more elaborate menu."

"A dinner which went largely uneaten," said the cook.

Darcy sympathized with the woman's hard work going to waste. But there were more important matters to discuss.

"As a result of Miss Bingley's request," continued Mrs. Nichols, "the brandy sat on a counter in the kitchen for some time before Miss Bingley's maid came to take it to her room."

In consideration of the fact they had already spoken to the maid, Darcy said: "Please summon the footman who brought the brandy."

Unfortunately, the footman was of little assistance, for he had fetched the brandy from the cellar as requested, but had then been called away for another task. Though it was possible that either the maid or the footman had used the time when they were alone with the brandy to poison it, he could not see a motive—especially from the footman. The maid, perhaps. But why? If she wished to leave Miss Bingley's service, the opportunity was there, and no master would choose to withhold a reference from a hard-working servant.

"I beg your pardon, sir," said the footman when Darcy dismissed him, "but may I ask what this is all about."

"No, John, you may not!" said Mrs. Nichols. "You may go now."

The footman, chastened, bowed his head and departed. But Darcy could see the look about him, which consisted of worry mixed with a healthy dose of fear. The servants were not blind, neither were they senseless. They knew what had happened in the house the past few days, and they were more than a little frightened.

"I apologize for John's boldness, Mr. Darcy," said Mrs. Nichols. "We are all a little on edge."

"It is quite understandable," said Fitzwilliam. "It is natural that you would be asking questions."

"We do not have any answers at present," added Darcy. "I am certain you are aware that three of the residents have died in recent days, and the situation begins to look suspicious. I do not think that the servants are in danger, but it would be best for everyone to take care."

"If the servants are not in danger, why was Mr. Forbes the first to die, Mr. Darcy?"

That in itself could be deemed an impertinent question, but Darcy did not deny the woman's right to ask it. "I do not know, Mrs. Nichols. We suspect that he might have been the victim of having discovered something he should not, but at this time we do not have answers. Please ensure the staff knows to carry out their tasks quickly and efficiently and stay with others at all other times. In that, I hope we can all remain safe."

"Very well, Mr. Darcy." It was clear that the woman accepted his assurances as the best he could do at present. But she did not even attempt to hide her skepticism.

Soon, Darcy and Fitzwilliam excused themselves, leaving the housekeeper and the cook—who had attempted to remain inconspicuous after her one outburst. The moment they were out of the room, Fitzwilliam turned a questioning look on Darcy.

"What do you think?"

"Either the maid or the footman had the opportunity of adding poison to the bottle. But while the maid might have reason to, the footman did not. It was pure chance the footman brought at all—the task might have fallen to any of the others."

"If the maid did kill Miss Bingley, that still does not account for either Lady Catherine or the butler."

"Which is why we do not appear to be making any progress," said Darcy.

Within a few moments, they entered Bingley's study, and Fitzwilliam poured them each a generous measure of brandy. Darcy took his and gazed at it, wondering if he dared. Fitzwilliam, however, only grinned and tossed it back, grimacing at the way it burned its way down its throat.

"I cannot imagine *every* bottle of brandy in this house is tainted. But if I do expire, give the murderer an extra kick for me, Darcy."

Darcy shook his head at his cousin's manner and sipped his drink, staring moodily at the fireplace, which had long burned down to embers, leaving the room quiet and growing colder by the minute. For an instant, Darcy thought about summoning a footman to build it up again, but he discarded the notion soon after. They would not stay in this room for long, he suspected.

"I do not know what we are to do, Darcy," said Fitzwilliam. He had poured himself another drink when it became evident there was nothing but brandy in the first. "But I will tell you this: if we do not discover the culprit soon or if the killer strikes again, the situation in this house will deteriorate into anarchy."

"It has already begun," replied Darcy.

"Do you wish to speak of possibilities? Perhaps talking through the problem will reveal some information we had overlooked or missed altogether."

"In my mind, there is only one name: Wickham."

Fitzwilliam shook his head. "He *could* explain two of the three deaths. But the third is problematic."

"It is difficult to explain, no matter who you suspect," said Darcy. "Though I cannot fathom the reason for it, I suspect the butler was a crime of opportunity."

"Perhaps," replied Fitzwilliam. "But humor me, Darcy. Can we count out all the Bennet sisters?"

Darcy could not help but laugh. "I cannot think that any of *them* would be a murderer. There is the problem of them even laying their hands on enough arsenic to poison Miss Bingley, to say nothing of the effort required to kill Lady Catherine."

"No, I suppose you are correct, though I must wonder about Miss Lydia."

With a laugh, Darcy shook his head. "I doubt it very much. What of the Bennet parents?"

"If Mr. Bennet killed anyone," said Fitzwilliam, "I would think it would be his foolish cousin. Not only is the man a menace and a born toady, but I understand Mr. Collins is his heir through entailment."

"And Miss Bingley used to crow her expectation that the Bennet sisters had nothing," replied Darcy, thinking quickly. "Mrs. Bennet is too silly, though she too might consider the benefits of being rid of Mr. Collins. But either way, Mr. Collins is not the one who has died."

"Either of the Bennets might have killed Lady Catherine," said

Fitzwilliam. "But Miss Bingley is not so clear. She was an unpleasant woman, certainly, and uniformly unkind to all the Bennets, except for Miss Bennet. But I would not consider being unpleasant to be a reason to take such drastic action against another."

"What of Collins himself?"

Fitzwilliam nearly dropped his drink in his hilarity. "*Mr. Collins?*" managed Fitzwilliam around his laughter. "I was not aware you were such an amusing fellow, Darcy. Can you imagine Collins, of all people, murdering his patroness, the woman he venerates from morning until night on a daily basis?"

"He must be considered, Fitzwilliam."

"The only way Mr. Collins may be considered is if we live in a world of utter silliness." Darcy glared, and Fitzwilliam held out his hands. "I know, Cousin. Mr. Collins would seem like an unlikely suspect to me. What I said of his patroness is the truth. If he perceived that Miss Bingley was somehow disrespecting Lady Catherine, he might take action. But that does not account for the butler."

"Mr. Collins *is* an unlikely suspect, I agree," said Darcy. "That would leave only Mr. and Mrs. Hurst, and Bingley."

"Who are also unlikely, for obvious reasons. But you forgot two others, Darcy." When Darcy turned to regard his cousin, Fitzwilliam grinned. "Why, the two of us. You have so long been pursued by Miss Bingley, the motive is obvious. And Lady Catherine is equally evident."

"And what of you, old boy?" asked Darcy, feeling all the amusement of Fitzwilliam's jests.

"The same reasons as you," replied Fitzwilliam flippantly. "Though my reasons would be to protect you from the harpy and the dragon."

Darcy shook his head. "Though that is an amusing thought, I am afraid we are back to Wickham." When Fitzwilliam made to speak, Darcy cut him off. "I know there are problems with respect to motive, for Wickham. But he is the only one who does not have serious problems attached to the notion of him as the culprit."

"I would never have taken Wickham for a murderer," said Fitzwilliam. "He possesses unpleasant habits aplenty, but to kill someone? I cannot believe it."

"Until we discover something else, I am afraid that is the best explanation we have."

"Then what do we do?" asked Fitzwilliam. "Do you suggest we lock him up?"

Darcy considered the matter for a few moments. "We do not need proof to take steps. But if we agree that Wickham is the most likely suspect, then his logical target is me. Perhaps we can lure him out and catch him in the act."

"You are playing a dangerous game, Darcy."

"Perhaps. But we have no proof, and at present, what we have would never stand up in a court. If we wish to solve this mystery once and for all, we need more to lay at his feet."

"If you simply act against him and throw him in Marshalsea," growled Fitzwilliam, "we would not need this proof."

"But his debt receipts are three days away, and we are snowed in. I think this is the best way."

"Very well." Fitzwilliam drained the last of his glass and stood, bidding Darcy good night. But before he departed, he turned back to Darcy and shot him a devilish grin.

"Just remember, Cousin—if you are wrong about Wickham, the rest of the company may pay the price. For all you know, *I* am the murderer."

Darcy rolled his eyes at his cousin, but Fitzwilliam grinned. "I *am* the only one of us who has ever killed, you know, albeit in battle. I despise Wickham as much as any man alive. Think about that before you convict Wickham without evidence."

And with those chilling words, Fitzwilliam left the room. Darcy sat long into the night, considering all that had happened, and the words which Fitzwilliam glibly flung in his direction as he departed figured prominently in his thoughts.

CHAPTER XVIII

*N*ow that Miss Bingley was dead, Elizabeth did not know where to look or what to think. She had never been certain of the woman's culpability, but she had seemed like the best possible suspect. As Elizabeth was herded from the sitting-room by her father, with her sisters closely in tow, Elizabeth noted two things. Mr. Darcy had stopped Colonel Fitzwilliam with a glance, making it clear he and his cousin intended to investigate further. Elizabeth wished she was able to attend him.

The second was how Mr. Wickham was watching them all. His ever-present sneer was firmly affixed to his face and only became wider when Mr. Darcy glared at him. Could Mr. Wickham be the one as Mr. Darcy had averred? As he began to move, provoked by Mr. Darcy's glare, his gaze roved over the gathered Bennet sisters, leaving Elizabeth feeling breathless and troubled. For the first time, Elizabeth began to think of Mr. Wickham as possibly more than a charming rogue, and as a man who may contemplate murder to achieve his ends. Then he was gone, and the Bennets left the room too, following the quick pace of his boots striking the tiles as they faded off into the distance.

"It seems we must band together to protect ourselves, Mr. Bennet."

Startled by the voice, Elizabeth noted the presence of Mr. Collins. He was watching them all carefully, but the way his eyes roamed up and down the hall through which they walked as if he expected ten murderers to jump out and attack them, almost brought Elizabeth to laughter.

"I have no notion of who has been committing these iniquitous sins," continued Mr. Collins when Mr. Bennet looked at him, mirth brimming in his own eyes. "But when I discover it, I shall call down the judgment of the heavens upon the one responsible. They have deprived the world of a veritable angel from heaven, a woman of such high nobility and character that we all must be less because of her absence from our lives!"

Such was the fanatical zeal in Mr. Collins's voice when he spoke of his patroness, Elizabeth wondered at this man being a clergyman. Should the clergy not worship God instead of a woman?

"Her death is of no more importance to God than that of the butler or Miss Bingley, Cousin," replied Mr. Bennet. Though Elizabeth knew her father to be laughing at his cousin, she could also hear the tension in his voice, understood the worry which had settled over him.

"God does consider us all to be equal, yes," replied Mr. Collins, proving that he had some little knowledge of the religion he was sworn to promote. "But for us mere mortals, the loss of such a woman of virtue, goodness, and talent must be greater than the mere daughter of a tradesman."

"Stop speaking of her as if she were a God herself!" Mrs. Bennet's shrill voice interrupted their conversation, and Mr. Collins turned to regard Mrs. Bennet, astonished beyond all measure. "She was a mean, vicious, virago, who attacked my Lizzy and anyone who did not agree with her every word. Do not attempt to tell us what a wonderful woman that shrew was!"

"How dare you!" spat Mr. Collins in return. "Lady Catherine possessed every right to speak as she did!"

"You are a fool, Mr. Collins, the same as your father. I wish you had never come to Hertfordshire!"

Mr. Collins turned an angry glare on Mr. Bennet. "Will you allow your wife to speak to me in such a manner?"

"I happen to agree with her."

Elizabeth had little doubt Mr. Collins understood the double meaning of Mr. Bennet's words. He raked his angry eyes over Mrs. Bennet once again before doing the same to Mr. Bennet.

"Your family should not expect charity from me when you are

dead, Mr. Bennet." He turned to look at Elizabeth. "I shall still be generous and marry your second daughter, but the rest of your family will be required to shift for themselves."

"You may take your wooing, such as it is, elsewhere," said Elizabeth. "If you think I would marry a man who would condemn my sisters and mother to poverty, you have sorely mistaken my character."

"I know how it shall be," said Mr. Collins, waving her words away like he was trying to put out a fire. Then he turned and stormed away.

"Good riddance," muttered Mr. Bennet. "He is as odious as his father, only his father was rough and stupid, while he is sycophantic and stupid." Mr. Bennet's eyes again found his family. "Come, let us get you all settled for the night."

It seemed like Mr. Bennet had a different idea of what that would look like for the Bennet sisters. When Lydia and Kitty attempted to go to their own rooms, Mr. Bennet called them back with a sharp word, leading them instead to the rooms he and Mrs. Bennet had occupied. As he led them into the room, he crossed to the bell pull and gave a tug, and then turned to face them.

"I do not wish any of you girls to be alone any longer," said he. "You will all sleep in your mother's room, and your mother will sleep with me."

"Sleep in Mama's room?" asked Lydia, perplexed.

"Yes. I will have some cots delivered here, and whoever cannot sleep in the bed must sleep on the cots. It seems Lady Catherine was already murdered in her sleep—I will not risk the same thing happening to one of you."

The chill which moved down Elizabeth's spine was mirrored in her sisters, Elizabeth was certain. Soon they had, in groups, gone to their rooms to retrieve their sleep garments, Elizabeth with Kitty and Lydia, while Mary and Jane went together. When they returned, two additional cots had been made up near the end of the bed. Mrs. Bennet, appearing quite astonished, had already moved her things into her husband's room. Elizabeth thought her mother had a right to be astonished—she did not think her parents had slept in the same bed in the past ten years.

They quickly decided that Elizabeth would sleep on one of the cots, but the other one was subject to debate. When it was suggested Jane, as the eldest sister, should take the other one, Kitty protested.

"But I do not wish to sleep with Lydia! She is restless, and kicks when there is anyone else in the bed."

"Then Lydia should take the other cot," said Mrs. Bennet. "Now, Liddy, dear," soothed she when Lydia—predictably—protested, "you are also the stoutest and tallest, and would take up the most room in the bed, which shall already be cramped. The cot is small, but you shall have it to yourself."

Though she was not happy, Lydia relented. But her complaints were not at an end. "I am so hungry, Mama!"

"Then it is fortunate I have thought of that," said Mr. Bennet.

At that moment, the door opened, and a pair of maids brought several trays into the room. It was not much—some bread, cheese, cold meats and two flagons of water for them to drink. But it seemed like a veritable feast to Elizabeth, who was also experiencing the pangs of hunger.

"But what of supper?" whined Lydia. "Surely a meal was prepared for us."

"Lydia," said Jane as the most patient of them all, "a woman was poisoned tonight. No, it was not the dinner we were to eat. But do you wish to take the chance?"

A pale Lydia shook her head—clearly, she had not thought that far in advance. The family gathered around the table, and they divided the food between them. They ate, though largely in silence, with only a few words spoken between them, along with a few softly spoken words and Kitty and Lydia's incessant whispering. When they had finished eating, the servants were called to clear the trays, and the family sat for some time together, speaking. There was little to do, so they eventually retired early.

"I shall leave the adjoining door ajar," said Mr. Bennet, when they began to prepare. "Should anything at all happen during the night, wake me. As soon as we are able, we shall depart for Longbourn."

While Elizabeth thought she was fatigued, when she lay down on her cot, she found she could do little to fall asleep. The cot was, surprisingly, not at all uncomfortable, and she had sufficient blankets to keep her warm. No, her insomnia was brought about by the thoughts flying through her mind, and there was little she could do to quiet them.

When she heard the clock strike eleven, Elizabeth gave it up for a lost cause and rose from her cot. Though the room was dark, she could see the profiles of her sisters in their beds and noted they all appeared to be asleep. Likewise, through the door to her parents' room, there was no sound, leading her to believe that her parents were also sleeping. Elizabeth considered the situation for a moment and then, though she knew it might be foolishness, she rose, wrapped her robe around her shoulders, put on her slippers, and slipped from the room.

The butler still had not snuffed out the lanterns in the house, and Elizabeth had enough light to see. She made her way to the stairs and then down, and when she arrived in the entrance hall, she considered her options and chose the direct route to the kitchens. About her as she moved, the shadows in the halls, caused by the light shining down from the periodic lanterns, seemed to combine with the danger of the situation, lending a slightly sinister and ghoulish cast to the hall. But she persisted, pushing such fanciful thoughts from her mind.

"Miss Elizabeth!" cried the housekeeper when she stepped into the kitchen. The woman hurried to her and pulled her into the room, scolding her as she did so. "Why are you walking the halls in such a state as this? It is dangerous for you to be up and about by yourself!"

"I apologize, Mrs. Nichols," said Elizabeth, "but I could not sleep. This situation is causing such a great perturbance of mind that I cannot rest until I learn all that I can."

Mrs. Nichols clucked and shared a glance with the cook. "That young man, Mr. Darcy, was here earlier for the same purpose. He has, however, retired to his bedchamber as you ought."

"Please, Mrs. Nichols! I wish to solve this mystery and will lie awake all night if I do not at least speak of it."

The housekeeper sighed. "Though we have not been well acquainted, Miss Elizabeth, Mrs. Hill has told me much of you over the years. I can see how she was entirely correct."

Elizabeth looked down, embarrassed by Mrs. Nichols's words. The woman chuckled with amusement. "Do not take that the wrong way, Miss Elizabeth. Mrs. Hill is extremely fond of you—of all you Bennet girls, though she does complain your youngest sisters can be a handful."

"She is entirely correct," replied Elizabeth.

"Very well. I do not know if it is right to allow you to stay, but I will allow it for the present. But you will need to go above stairs soon, lest your father worry for you."

Elizabeth refrained from informing the woman that her father was asleep. Instead, she allowed the women to lead her to a nearby table and accepted a cup of tea and a few biscuits. Then she turned to the matter at hand. "Has Mr. Darcy discovered something?"

"He has," said Mrs. Nichols, though looking ill at ease. "Something Miss Bingley drank was tainted."

They delved into the matter, Mrs. Nichols informing her of the gentlemen's visit to Miss Bingley's rooms, their discovery of the bottle of liquor they suspect had been poisoned, and the questioning of the footman. Elizabeth listened intently, asking questions to clarify at times. But the fear was growing within her. It did not seem like they were any further toward solving the mystery now than they had been before Miss Bingley's death.

"I have also done a little research into what happened to Miss Bingley myself," added Mrs. Nichols when she had explained everything.

"And what have you discovered?" asked Elizabeth eagerly.

"Relatively little, unfortunately," replied the housekeeper. "John brought the liquor up from the cellar, but we were distracted by other instructions which had come from Miss Bingley, and it had sat there for some time unattended."

"You think the poison was added at that time?"

"That seems to be the only explanation," said Mrs. Nichols.

"But surely there were others present," protested Elizabeth. "How could someone have poisoned it with so many people coming and going?"

"The tray was placed on the table by the door," said Mrs. Nichols, pointed to another table across the room. "As you can see, it is small and out of the way, not within sight of the main part of the kitchens."

Elizabeth nodded—it was possible that someone might have been able to tamper with it without being discovered if it had sat in such a location.

"Furthermore," interjected the cook, "one of the scullery maids reported having seen someone when we questioned them."

"Who was it?" asked Elizabeth.

Mrs. Nichols shook her head. "Unfortunately, the girl does not know. She thought it might have been a man, but she only saw him— if, indeed, it was a man—for an instant. She did not think anything of it and returned to her task at the time. But it seems likely whoever she saw was the likely culprit."

There was little useful information in the maid's account, and Elizabeth shook her head, feeling all the despair of having an answer so close, yet so far out of reach. "Then the mystery remains."

"It does, child," said Mrs. Nichols. "The best thing you can do now is to protect yourself. The staff has been instructed to always be with someone else to avoid giving this person an opportunity or coming upon them alone. I suggest you do the same."

The advice was given with a significant look, the voice firm and unyielding. Elizabeth understood the message and nodded, knowing it was good advice.

"I shall certainly do so. Thank you, Mrs. Nichols, for humoring my curiosity. I shall return to my rooms directly."

"Not alone, you shall not," said the cook. "We will escort you and then return here ourselves."

Grateful for the company, Elizabeth acquiesced and made her way back to her room with their company. Soon she had slipped back into the room where her sisters were slumbering and settled into her cot. Though the mystery continued to plague her, Elizabeth's mind quieted long before she might have thought, and she slept.

When Elizabeth woke the following morning, the same thoughts crowding her mind, she immediately thought to dress for the day and find Mr. Darcy. While the night passed peacefully, she had awoken on one occasion, her heart pounding at some night phantasm she could not even remember. Shaking off the last vestiges of sleep, Elizabeth rose and dressed quickly, and then slipped from the room quickly.

She accomplished the short walk to the breakfast room quickly and without incident, and when she stepped in, she was unsurprised to see Mr. Darcy there. He rose upon her entrance, his countenance lighting up at spying her. Elizabeth felt her cheeks turn rosy, and she regarded him shyly, her gaze finding the floor in her unexpected abashment.

"I was not certain anyone would take breakfast here, Miss Elizabeth," said Mr. Darcy, holding a chair out for her.

Elizabeth allowed him to seat her and turned a questioning gaze on him. "I suspected the same. But I thought you would come here. Do you think we can trust the food?"

Mr. Darcy grinned and set about fixing a plate for her. "Mrs. Nichols assured me this morning of the quality and untainted nature of the meal. They have watched everything carefully. Most of the food here, she suspects, will be returned to the kitchens later, as she believes most of the residents will order trays in their rooms."

"I suppose that is not surprising," murmured Elizabeth. Mr. Darcy set the tray before her, and she grasped her fork in one hand, inhaling the scent of the eggs and sausage, realizing at that moment she was very hungry. "Will they not be fearful of the food when it is delivered?"

Taking his seat again, Mr. Darcy shrugged. "I suppose the possibility of a repeat exists. But I doubt the killer will attempt the same thing again."

Raising the fork to her mouth, Elizabeth chewed, savoring the exquisite flavor of the cook's eggs. "That is the question, sir. Do we even know the killer will strike again?"

"It is impossible to predict. So far there does not seem to be any reason to what has occurred here. I am at a loss to explain it."

Mr. Darcy began an explanation of what he and his cousin discussed the previous evening and what they learned from the kitchens. Elizabeth reciprocated by explaining her own late-night visit to the kitchens and the tidbit she had learned herself. Mr. Darcy admonished her for taking such a risk, but he did not dwell on her foolishness. For that Elizabeth was grateful.

"You trust your cousin, do you not, Mr. Darcy?" asked Elizabeth, when he had explained his cousin's final words the previous evening.

A grimace settled over Mr. Darcy's countenance, but he nodded. "I do. He is correct that he is the only one who has actually killed. But that was done in battle, in defense of his comrades, himself, and England. Furthermore, Fitzwilliam loves to confound me, though I must question his judgment and his very sanity for being flippant at a time like this."

"Then what are we left with?" asked Elizabeth.

"A set of clues which lead to no obvious conclusions," replied Mr. Darcy. "It seems, however, that Miss Bingley was not responsible for the first two deaths. Unless, of course, she poisoned herself."

Elizabeth snorted, feeling a sort of detached amusement. "I suppose it would serve her right if she did. But you forget one possibility, Mr. Darcy."

When Mr. Darcy looked at her askance, Elizabeth said: "It is possible there is more than one murderer."

The shudder which ran through Mr. Darcy's frame was unmistakable. It was also amusing, even given the fact that nothing about this situation should be amusing.

"Do not even suggest such a thing, Miss Bennet. Not even in jest."

"I suppose you are correct," said Elizabeth. "You have my apologies for attempting such an inappropriate joke."

Mr. Darcy shook his head. "You are quite different from most young ladies I have ever met. I find the difference quite intriguing, I assure you."

Once again Elizabeth felt the heat of her cheeks rise. She covered her embarrassment—and the thrill she felt at his words—by attending to her breakfast again. Mr. Darcy, for his part, fell silent, pensively considering what they had discussed.

"But I cannot help it, but my mind continues to turn to the one person here who is capable of depraved behavior."

"I assume you mean Mr. Wickham?"

"I do," said Mr. Darcy.

"And have you ever suspected Mr. Wickham of such heinous crimes in the past?"

"I will own I have not," replied Mr. Darcy. "But I have also kept him at arms' distance these past years, and I know not what he has become. I know he was willing to overthrow every memory of my father and attempt to abscond with my sister's fortune. But is he capable of so much more?" Mr. Darcy paused his gaze heavy with thought. "I do not know. But I fear very much that he is capable of it."

"Is there any evidence to support your theory?"

"Nothing specific. Wickham openly bragged to me of how he would attempt to seduce Miss Bingley for her dowry."

"But that is no reason to kill her!" protested Elizabeth. "Quite the opposite, if he wished to have her fortune. Her death puts it forever beyond his reach."

"Unless he killed her in a fit of rage," replied Mr. Darcy. "I am aware of Miss Bingley's ways, and I am convinced she would give him no hint of attention and would, in fact, respond with derision, should he have attempted to charm her."

"A man who kills in a fit of rage does not do so by such subtle means as poison."

Mr. Darcy had nothing to say to that, for he nodded and fell silent. After a moment, Elizabeth asked another question.

"What of Lady Catherine? Why would Wickham murder her?"

"To remove an obstacle preventing him from approaching Anne? Lady Catherine would have thwarted any hint of his wooing to her. He might have thought her removal necessary."

"And yet he has paid little attention to Anne. In fact, why would he attempt to charm Miss Bingley when Anne's fortune—consisting of an estate—would be so much greater a prize?"

"Anne has also sequestered herself in her rooms since her mother's death," said Mr. Darcy. "He may have decided Miss Bingley was the easier target."

"That is possible," allowed Elizabeth. "But it seems to me we have nothing more than supposition and conjecture. There is not a shred of hard evidence to convict Mr. Wickham. Why, given the knowledge we possess, the murderer is equally likely to be my sister Lydia, or even Mr. Collins!"

Mr. Darcy chuckled. "I suppose you are correct."

They sat in silence for some few moments. Elizabeth ate her breakfast, but much of it was mechanical, as she did not note either the taste of what she was eating, or even pay attention to what she was eating. Thoughts of the conundrum under which they were trapped gnawed at her mind. She puzzled at the information they possessed, attempting to sort it in a manner in which it would all settle into place. But it remained elusive, and Elizabeth very much suspected some vital pieces were missing.

"What do we do from here?" asked she after considering it for perhaps ten minutes.

Though he had been lost in his own thoughts, Mr. Darcy responded immediately. "It seems there is nothing to do but continue to try to find more information. There may be something we have missed.

"Of more immediate concern, however, I suspect the weather is about to turn. If possible, I should like to send you and your family back to Longbourn for your protection."

"But if we are allowed to leave the house, it becomes more likely the criminal will escape judgment," protested Elizabeth.

"Perhaps," said Mr. Darcy. "But I think it is more important at present to ensure your safety and that of your sisters."

Elizabeth nodded, though slowly. "Until that eventuality, we should gather as much information as we can."

"We should," agreed Mr. Darcy. "I think we must do whatever we can to unravel this puzzle as quickly as possible. It seems likely it is only a matter of time before our killer strikes yet again."

Those words chilled Elizabeth to her very core. But she could not say Mr. Darcy was incorrect.

Chapter XIX

While there were a few who did not appear, the majority of the residents of Netherfield eventually did descend, if only for a short time. It was not until luncheon, however, confirming Darcy's suspicion about the likelihood of many of them requesting breakfast in their rooms. Or perhaps they had not eaten at all — Darcy could not claim to know them all well enough to predict their early morning habits.

When they gathered for luncheon, however, only the most obtuse would not notice the atmosphere of sorrow, confusion, and, above all, a pervasive fear which hung over them like a cloud. Suspicion too was part of the makeup of the group, and it seemed to Darcy like everyone in the company watched the others closely, as if one would rise in the middle of the meal to slay the rest where they sat.

Miss Elizabeth, as they were eating, caught Darcy's eye and she smiled, and Darcy felt some of his cares fall away. It was silly, given the circumstance, but he felt it nonetheless. As Darcy ate, he considered what he had just been thinking. The Bennets, rather than eye each other with suspicion, were a tight-knit group, gathered together for their mutual protection. Likewise, no glares or glances passed between Darcy and his cousin, who was eating with seeming unconcern.

Bingley, of course, did not have a suspicious bone in his body, and he appeared to be wallowing in his grief. Hurst looked thoughtful, though his wife was not present, having sequestered herself in her room, refusing to emerge. Darcy's eyes roamed a little further down the table, and he noted the ineffectual presence of Mr. Collins, the man watching everyone else, an almost comical suspicion evident as he peered up and down the table. And then there was Wickham . . .

"I say," said the detested man at that moment, "I have never been in company with such dour people in all my life! Perhaps we should retire to the sitting-room and play a game."

Several of those present glared at Wickham, while he only grinned back at them, seeming determined to wring every bit of enjoyment he could from the situation. Darcy had always known the man was a snake, but he was proving himself worse than Darcy had ever imagined.

"In case you were not aware, Mr. Wickham," said Bingley, in the most disgusted tone Darcy had ever heard his friend use, "there have been several occurrences these last days which render frivolity impossible."

"I dare say we have hit a spot of trouble," said Wickham, still fixing them all with his insufferable grin. "But we must strive to keep our spirits up, to look forward to better times. I believe that is what our dearly departed would have wished."

"Since you did not know any of the dearly departed," said Bingley, "I suggest you do not speak as if you did."

"Oh, very well. But nothing will improve if you all insist on these long faces and dreary attitudes."

"You might wish to be silent, Wickham," said Fitzwilliam. "I believe you are in great danger of losing some of your fine, white teeth. Or perhaps Bingley will simply throw you out into the cold and rain."

Wickham smirked and raised his glass but did not say anything more. The rain was another development, though Darcy could not say that it was an improvement. The temperature had increased a little, and now, instead of the snow, it was raining, a fine, misty drizzle which would undoubtedly soak a person within minutes. As the ground was still frozen with ice and snow, the rain tended to freeze when it fell, creating an even more difficult situation for a team of horses or a carriage.

"I, for one, believe you *should* throw Mr. Wickham from the house."

Darcy could not help but start in surprise to hear Miss Lydia Bennet speak. It appeared several others were in the same straits, though Wickham regarded the girl with a smile that was a little more forced than it had been only a few minutes before.

"That is just what I would have expected from you," said Wickham. "From you all, in fact." He shook his head and looked down at his breakfast mournfully. "*I* am naught but a lowly soldier, one who has been betrayed in every possible way and forced to make my way in the world alone."

The scoffing sound Miss Elizabeth made summed up neatly the response to Wickham's words. The man himself looked back at them all, seeming aggrieved, but Darcy, who knew him well, knew his anger was mounting. It was, he thought, primarily because Wickham's lies had not been believed in this instance. That had been a rare occurrence in the past.

"He is a danger to us all," persisted Miss Lydia. "I would not be surprised if he killed those people."

It seemed there was one present who agreed with Darcy, though he could not fathom how she had come to that conclusion. Wickham, however, only rolled his eyes and shook his head.

"I am sure one as young as you, Miss Lydia, must see dangers lurking around every corner. I have never claimed to be a perfect man, but I am no murderer."

"I think there is a more likely explanation for what has happened," said Mrs. Bennet, eying Darcy with distaste.

"Yes, Darcy," said Wickham with an unpleasant grin. "Where were you when Miss Bingley swallowed her final drink?"

"That is enough," said Bingley. Once again, he was harsh, his glare at Wickham dark and severe. "Darcy is my greatest friend, and I will not hear one word against him. I would trust him with my very life. I suggest, Mr. Wickham, that you do not try my patience. I do not know that you have done anything wrong, but your behavior is insolent, and I will not tolerate it."

"I can see my company is not wanted," said Wickham, pushing his chair back and rising. "I will burden you with it no longer."

"That is perhaps the most intelligent decision you have ever made, Wickham," said Fitzwilliam as Wickham left the room. Wickham did not deign to answer, though Darcy was certain he had heard every word.

The rest of the meal passed in silence. Darcy noticed that the appetites of the company appeared lacking, as most did not eat as much as he had seen them consume before. Mrs. Bennet continued to watch him with distaste, but Darcy ignored her. The rest of them seemed content to tend to their own thoughts.

"Girls," said Mr. Bennet when they had finished, "let us return above stairs. I want you to all stay together."

As the Bennet women rose, Fitzwilliam nodded at Mr. Bennet in approval. "That is likely for the best."

At the same time, Darcy stood and approached Mr. Bennet, speaking in a low voice. "Will you not join my cousin and me in Bingley's study? I believe we must have some conversation about the situation."

Mr. Bennet's eyes searched Darcy's, and he nodded after a moment. "Allow me to see my wife and daughters settled, and I will join you."

"I will accompany you above stairs and walk to Bingley's study with you. None of us should be alone at present."

A nod was Mr. Bennet's response, and soon he was herding his family from the room. Darcy turned and nodded to Fitzwilliam, watching as he approached Bingley and Hurst for the same reason. Then Darcy followed the Bennets from the room.

When the ladies were settled, the two men walked down and entered the study, noting the other three had all gathered. Bingley was poking listlessly at the flames in the grate, while Hurst sat nearby, nursing a glass of port in his hand. Fitzwilliam was looking out the window at the front drive of Netherfield. Darcy was certain he did not like what he was seeing.

"Now we are all here, we should discuss the general situation in which we find ourselves."

Mr. Bennet's eyebrow rose at Darcy's declaration. "I understand why you would not wish Wickham to be here, and I will not gainsay you. My cousin, however, is also not present. Though I do not think much of him in general, should we not call him to attend?"

"Do you truly think Mr. Collins would be of any assistance?" asked Darcy. "Or will he simply blather on about the mortal sin of murdering my aunt and calling for justice against the perpetrator?"

"I suppose you must be correct," said Mr. Bennet. "Though I suspected a man very like his father when he came, I was proved only half correct. He is as odious and stupid as his father, but I suppose Mr. Thaddeus Collins beat the roughness out of him and made him into the servile creature we all now see before us."

There were several snorts in response to Mr. Bennet's words. Bingley appeared not to hear, as he was still poking at the fire. Fitzwilliam was grinning openly, and Hurst was shaking his head, taking a sip of his port.

"Very well, Mr. Darcy," said Mr. Bennet. "You have called us here. What do you wish to discuss?"

"We must speak of our situation. Fitzwilliam and I," Darcy deemed it prudent to avoid informing Miss Bennet's father of her contribution, "have been investigating, and we have discovered a few facts about Miss Bingley's death. There is little enough to go on, which is why we would appreciate any input you might have."

"Yes, Darcy," said Bingley, his interest suddenly excited. "Let us hear what you have discovered."

The light of intensity shone in Bingley's eyes, such as Darcy had never seen before—or at least Darcy had not seen it at any time Bingley was not contemplating his latest angel. Though Darcy was certain Bingley had not even liked his sister much at times, it seemed Bingley burned with the need for justice. Or vengeance. Darcy could not quite determine which it was.

Shaking himself free of extraneous thoughts, Darcy launched into his explanation. He informed them of their suspicions regarding the tainted brandy, what they had learned from the housekeeper, as well as the fruits of Miss Elizabeth's investigations from the previous night. Of Lady Catherine's death, there was little but suspicion, as was the case with the butler. But Darcy explained what he knew, informed them of his suspicions regarding each of those present in the house— not excepting those in the room. When he ceased speaking, silence fell over the room.

"You have my apologies, my friend," said Bingley. Darcy could hear the mournful quality in his voice, so unusual for his close friend "You have taken it upon yourself to look into these matters when rightfully that duty should have fallen to me as the master of this estate."

"Do not concern yourself for such things, Bingley. You lost your sister only yesterday—it is understandable that you would be distracted."

"And did you not lose your aunt?"

"An aunt who was only tolerated," interjected Fitzwilliam.

"How many times did I only tolerate my sister?" asked Bingley. "You should be well acquainted with that state, Darcy, for I know you endured her for nothing more than the sake of our friendship."

"Gentlemen," said Mr. Bennet, "perhaps we should move the conversation along. A situation such as this is so far beyond the purview the owner of an estate would be expected to manage as to be absurd. Mr. Bingley was distracted, so Mr. Darcy stepped in with the help of his cousin. There is no need to praise or censure."

The sigh which Bingley released was forceful and full of exasperation. "I suppose you are correct, Mr. Bennet." Bingley eyed them all with curiosity. "What do you all think of this information Darcy has given us?"

"It tells us little more than we knew," came Hurst's rumbling voice. "We might not even have considered Lady Catherine's death as suspicious, had not Caroline died in the fashion she did."

"How is Louisa coping?"

Hurst's responding sigh was more sorrowful than Bingley's. "Not well, I am afraid. Caroline tried even Louisa's nerves at times, though they *were* close. She feels that she is somehow to blame for Caroline's death."

"But that is absurd!" exclaimed Bingley. "Louisa could no more have prevented it than she could have stopped the moon in its course."

"That may be so. But we rarely think of such things when we are grieving. Caroline . . . Let us say her drinking of your brandy had become a problem these past months, especially since we came to Hertfordshire. She feels she should have done more to curb her sister's habit, and that if she had, Caroline might still be alive."

"Of course, she could not have," said Mr. Bennet. "The inevitable would simply have been delayed unless your sister had eschewed it altogether. Then it would have been one of us who drank it."

It was a sobering thought. Mrs. Hurst would eventually recover, Darcy thought. But the manner in which her sister had died would almost certainly stay with her for the rest of her life.

"Personally, I suspect Wickham," said Darcy.

All eyes focused on him. "What is your reasoning?" asked Mr. Bennet.

"He is the only one of us who does not have a reason *not* to kill at least one of the victims—everyone else has some connection to one of the deceased."

"I am not attempting to blame one of my family," said Mr. Bennet, "but none of us have a connection to any of the deceased."

"Could any of them have procured arsenic in sufficient quantities as to kill Miss Bingley with such swiftness?" asked Darcy.

"As I said, I do not think any of my children could have done it. But it seems to me, Mr. Darcy, that you have fixed on Mr. Wickham as the killer."

Fitzwilliam snorted. "Aye, Mr. Bennet. I have told him that myself."

"There is also the matter of his openly bragging to me he would seduce Miss Bingley for her fortune. And before you say that is not a reason to kill her, what if his attempts at charming her failed?"

Mr. Bennet held his eyes, his gaze even. "I understand you have a history with Mr. Wickham. Are you allowing that history to affect your judgment of the man?"

"I *do* have a history with him," confessed Darcy. "But I believe I am as rational a man as any when it comes to Wickham." Darcy gave a lazy wave at his cousin. "I would say that Fitzwilliam is much more apt to become irrational when confronted by his iniquities."

"That is the truth!" said Fitzwilliam with a snort. "It is also what is so curious about this situation. When did *I* become the rational one between us?"

Darcy shrugged, and Fitzwilliam waggled his eyebrows. Mr. Bennet shook his head at them.

"I knew nothing of any of you before you came here. But I would assert that fixing on Mr. Wickham as the killer and ignoring any other possibilities is foolish. It might be anyone present who is responsible — it could be anyone in this very room."

"I would never kill my own sister!" cried Bingley.

"With all due respect, Mr. Bingley, people killing family members is not unknown. I do not say this to accuse you. I am merely pointing out a fact."

"He is correct," said Hurst. "There were times when we, both of us, would have rejoiced had we known Caroline would not vex us again."

"I never wished her dead."

"Nor did I," replied Hurst. "But you cannot deny how much your sister annoyed you, Bingley. She was enough to drive us both to Bedlam, and not only for her pursuit of Darcy."

Bingley threw up his hands and turned away. Darcy knew his friend, and the closest adjective he could state which described his friend's behavior was sulky.

"I never meant this to become such a discussion," said Mr. Bennet. "I merely wished to point out that the information we possess has not eliminated anyone as a suspect, though I will grant that Mrs. Hurst and Miss de Bourgh appear to be innocent."

"The question then becomes what we do about it."

No one had an answer for Fitzwilliam's question. At least, no one could say anything more about who had committed the murders. For Darcy's part, he was more interested in removing the ladies — one lady in particular — from harm's way.

"What of the weather?" The rain does not appear any more promising than did the snow. Bingley, have you heard from your groundskeepers concerning the state of the roads?"

Bingley roused himself, grimaced, and said: "Nothing any of us would wish to hear. The rain has done nothing yet except to make the roads even worse. One of the men believes that the weather will turn significantly warming tomorrow, but that carries its own challenges. The bridge down by the end of the property is known to be submerged when there is excessive rain or melting of snow. That would prevent us from leaving via the main road, as it would be too dangerous. There are a number of other tracks, but they are too small for a carriage."

"If this continues," said Mr. Bennet, "I may just chance it. I would wager Elizabeth would be able to guide us home by lesser used tracks."

"The problem remains of the deepness of the snow," said Bingley. "I would not recommend trying to walk until several days of melting has passed."

"Under normal circumstances, you may be correct. But given what has happened here, I am not certain. It would be better to be in our home and safe, even if we became wet and bedraggled on the way."

"If you were able to arrive safely," said Bingley.

His concern was clear for all to see and fixed squarely on the person of Miss Bennet. Darcy did not blame his friend at all, for he felt the same for Miss Elizabeth.

"It is clear that it is impossible for you to contemplate such a step at present," said Fitzwilliam. "It is best that we remain watchful, stay together, and do not allow our killer to come upon any of us alone."

"Agreed," said Mr. Bennet. "But I reserve the right to do whatever necessary to protect my family."

The gentlemen talked for a few more moments, but nothing more of substance was said. As they spoke, Darcy said little, instead watching Mr. Bennet, wondering at what he knew of the man. Darcy had always thought he was an indolent man. But if he was, that trait seemed to have fallen away, leaving him intent upon protecting his family. For that, Darcy could only applaud him. But was he truly foolhardy enough to try a three-mile journey on foot with six women? Surely they would be safe enough should they do as he had said: ensure they were never alone.

As Darcy was engaged in his ruminations, he was not paying attention to the conversation. As such, he was surprised when the others rose to depart. Fitzwilliam shook his head when he noticed

Darcy's sudden look of surprise, but he did not say anything. He simply followed Hurst and Bingley from the room, leaving Darcy in the company of Mr. Bennet.

"I am grateful the others have left with such alacrity," said Mr. Bennet before Darcy could react. "I wished to speak with you for a moment before I return to my family."

"Yes, Mr. Bennet?" asked Darcy, wondering what the man could have to say, in light of how he had already asked after Darcy's intentions toward Elizabeth.

"It seems to me that my second daughter is becoming involved in this mystery, Mr. Darcy. I wish to know your role in encouraging her."

"You believe *I* have encouraged her in this?" asked Darcy with surprise.

"Perhaps 'encouraged' is a strong word, given the situation. Let us say you have not 'discouraged' her." Mr. Bennet chuckled. "I know my daughter, Mr. Darcy. I am aware of how headstrong she is, how she would find a puzzle of this nature irresistible, how she would wish to discover the truth of the matter for herself. I know you disappeared with her for some time a few days ago, and while I do not know what you were doing during the time you spent together, I suspect I know the answer. I have also been witness to the secretive conversations which have been passing between you. And I witnessed my daughter's thirst for information last night myself."

Darcy felt his eyebrows rise above the fringe of hair which hung over his forehead. "You know of Miss Elizabeth's adventure last night?"

"She is not able to hide from me nearly so well as she believes," replied Mr. Bennet with a chuckle. "Sleep had not found me when she rose and slipped from the room last night; the door between the two rooms was ajar, and I noticed movement in the adjacent room. I followed her down to the kitchens, partially to ensure her safety and partially because I wished to discover what she was doing. When she was finally persuaded to return, I again followed at a distance, entering my room once Elizabeth had lain down to sleep. I do not think she noticed me at all."

"No, I would say she did not," replied Darcy, a new measure of respect for this man's abilities growing within him. "I apologize, Mr. Bennet. I knew of her late-night adventure, but I did not inform you of it."

"There is no need to apologize," replied Mr. Bennet with a wave of his hand. "Elizabeth was at fault, after all. What I wished to speak to you about was the amount of involvement Elizabeth has in this matter. As I said, I understand her intelligence and curiosity will drive her to attempt to solve the mystery, and I am certain it will be almost impossible to stop her. But I wish to ensure that you are not putting her to unnecessary risk should you find yourself together. We do not know what evil our tormentor has in store for us, and I would not have her caught in a situation in which she will find herself in mortal danger."

"Nor do I," Darcy was quick to say. "Miss Elizabeth's safety is my paramount concern."

"Thank you, Mr. Darcy. Please, if you cannot prevent her from putting herself in danger, inform me at once. She will not like it, but I will keep her near me and limit her movements if necessary. I would rather she be safe and resent me than in peril due to her headstrong nature."

"I cannot agree more, sir," said Darcy.

"Excellent!" Mr. Bennet paused, and Darcy felt his appraising eyes on his person. "I will declare, Mr. Darcy, that I believe you are well-matched with my daughter. Though I will be sorry to lose her to a man who lives in Derbyshire, I suspect she will be happy with you, should you choose to pursue her."

"That is my intention, Mr. Bennet. I would like nothing more than to persuade your daughter that I require her presence in my life forever. If I can make her happy, I will be guaranteeing *my* happiness."

"I dare say you will." Mr. Bennet grinned. "But do not suppose she will follow your lead in everything, play the role of the obedient wife. She will challenge you, will disagree with you when she thinks she is correct."

"Intellectual stimulation is one of the main reasons I find her irresistible, Mr. Bennet. I have had enough of simpering young ladies agreeing with everything I say for a lifetime."

"Well, you will certainly not find that with my Lizzy! Now, if you will excuse me, I should like to reaffirm my family's safety."

"Of course," replied Darcy. For his part, he was eager to confirm it himself, and if he could, to induce the Bennets to descend to the sitting-room before dinner. Perhaps the situation demanded a sober frame of mind, but Darcy thought taking their mind from recent events would do them all some good.

They departed from the room, making their way down the main hallway toward the entrance hall. As they walked, a few banal comments passed between them about matters of no great import. This man was far more interesting than Darcy had originally thought, and he was becoming certain that Mr. Bennet would make an excellent father-in-law.

They stepped from the hallway and into the larger entrance hall, and Darcy turned to Mr. Bennet to make an observation.

A shot rang out.

CHAPTER XX

The crack of the pistol echoed in the entrance hall and was accompanied by a loud thud as the ball impacted the wall behind Darcy and Mr. Bennet. Both men instinctively ducked at the sound. Though the cover provided by the nearby stairs was dubious at best, both men hunkered down behind it. And that was when Darcy heard hurried footsteps fading in the distance.

"Wickham!" roared Darcy.

He set off in pursuit, calling for the servants as he ran. Two footmen appeared from a room to the side, and Darcy pointed imperiously at them.

"Search down this hall. I want Wickham brought to me at once!"

The footmen immediately set about their task. Darcy was not idle. He stalked down the halls, inspecting each room as he went. They were all empty of the scoundrel, though there were maids in certain areas of the house. But when questioned, they denied seeing anyone running through the halls.

By this time the entire staff had been alerted, and mayhem reigned. The butler showed his inexperience by scurrying this way and that himself, rather than directing his staff, but by this time Darcy knew they would not find Wickham in this part of the house. Somehow, he managed to escape the immediate vicinity. Then Fitzwilliam arrived.

"I am told someone shot a pistol."

"It was Wickham," growled Darcy. "It seems he has decided to take a direct method of eliminating me, rather than the underhanded means he has used thus far. True to form, however, he missed."

"Far be it for me to contradict you, Mr. Darcy," said Mr. Bennet, "but I did not see anyone before the shot was fired. The shooter may just as easily have been aiming at *me*."

"That is nonsensical," said Darcy. "The most likely culprit is Wickham, and he would not have been aiming at you, sir. Why would he do so?"

"I am afraid I have no answer for you. But this seems suspiciously like a leap to a conclusion when not all the facts are known."

"What facts?" asked a new voice. Wickham sauntered into the room, his usual insouciance on display for all to see. Behind him, Bingley and Collins were following, expressions of intense interest on their countenances.

"Do not play stupid, Wickham," spat Darcy. "I know it was you."

"A great many things are me, Darcy. In this particular instance, I do not know of what you are accusing me. Perhaps you should be explicit."

A low growl issued forth from Darcy's mouth, and he stepped toward Wickham. Fitzwilliam, however, seeing his intent, stepped between them, holding Darcy back from the libertine. Wickham, for his part, never allowed his sneer to fade. He regarded Darcy, contempt etched in the lines on his face, his eyes as hard as agates.

"I know it was you, Wickham. I know you shot at me. I will have your hide for all you have done."

"Someone shot at you?" Wickham snorted. "It is a great pity they missed. Your arrogance could use pricking."

Fitzwilliam tensed and would not allow Darcy to attack Wickham and give him the beating he richly deserved. But he turned on Wickham and with a scowl which made the man pale, said: "I suggest you rein in your glib tongue, Wickham. It would take little to provoke me to allow my cousin to tear a few strips from your hide. I might even join him."

Wickham sneered. "I know not who shot at you, Darcy. But I can assure you that if it had been me, you would be lying dead."

A guttural growl of disdain informed Wickham of what Darcy thought of his assertion. "The fact that you missed strengthens my assertion it was you. You consider yourself an excellent marksman, but

I well know you can only hit a stationary target. When the target is moving, you have not a hope of hitting it. You never were any good at hunting."

A scowl replaced Wickham's sneer, but he did not respond. Fitzwilliam turned to Darcy and at his tight nod, released him. Wickham turned to go, but Fitzwilliam's voice arrested his departure.

"Not so fast, Wickham." He focused on Mr. Collins and Bingley. "Were either of you with Wickham just now?"

"I am sorry, Fitzwilliam," said Bingley with a shake of his head. "I had stepped out the side entrance to inspect the state of the grounds and the front drive. I only learned of this when I returned into the house."

"And you, sir?" asked Fitzwilliam of Mr. Collins.

"I assure you, Colonel Fitzwilliam," said Mr. Collins with a sniff of contempt for Wickham, "I have no desire to associate with this man. I was engaged in the act of speaking with God, attempting to determine the proper way to proceed, given the complexity of this situation. Our Lord cannot be pleased with us, and it is on my mind to call down judgment on the perpetrator, exposing him with the wrath of the almighty God for daring to raise his hand—"

"Were you with Wickham?" repeated Fitzwilliam. "I have no need of your rambling, Mr. Collins. I wish to know if you can exonerate this cur from firing at Darcy."

Mr. Collins's jaw tightened, and he glared at Fitzwilliam. But he did not refuse to speak, saying, a moment later: "No, Colonel, I cannot. As I said, I was alone."

"Then we cannot prove that it was Wickham who fired the weapon." Fitzwilliam turned to Darcy. "Then again, we cannot prove it was not any of them."

"I would not fire at Darcy!" cried Bingley, at the same time as Collins said: "I am a servant of the Lord! I have fired no weapon!"

"I did not say either of you did it," said Fitzwilliam mildly. "I merely said you could not be ruled out." Fitzwilliam frowned and looked at Bingley. "Though I suppose Bennet was with Darcy at the time, and it could not have been him either."

"Thank you for your faith, Colonel," was Mr. Bennet's sardonic reply.

"I think we should confine Wickham," said Darcy.

"You may if you wish," said Wickham. "I invite you to do it, Darcy, if you wish to prove a point. But I warn you if you do: you will be forced to exonerate me the next time something happens, knowing that I could not have done it."

Darcy almost started at Wickham's words. He had never known the man to be anything other than glib—Wickham had never shown any other face to Darcy since they were fifteen years of age, as Darcy had already learned of his friend's true character by that time. A glance at Fitzwilliam showed that his cousin saw it too; Wickham was entirely sincere, though Darcy could readily acknowledge it may be nothing more than Wickham acting the innocent, as he was so proficient at doing.

"Well, Darcy," said Bingley. "Shall I give the order to lock Wickham in the cellars?"

While Darcy watched him, Wickham continued to look at him, apparently quite serious for the first time Darcy could remember. Few had been the occasions in which Darcy had felt indecisive, but this was surely one of them.

"Perhaps, then," said Wickham, "you should include me in whatever information you have about our killer. It is possible I might have seen something you have not."

Then Wickham turned and sauntered away, unconcern written in his gait, his posture, his very being. Darcy swore to himself—even if the killer did not turn out to be Wickham, he was correct in pointing out that something occurring while Wickham was incarcerated would clear him if nothing else.

"If you will excuse me, gentlemen," said Mr. Bennet with a bow. "I believe I should like to go check on my family. They have been alone long enough."

With those words Mr. Bennet stepped away, leaving Darcy, Fitzwilliam, and Bingley standing together in the entrance hall. Bingley gave the signal, and the assembled footmen also dispersed, leaving the three men alone. When they had gone, Fitzwilliam turned to Darcy.

"What do you think? We can still have him taken by the footmen and locked away."

With a scowl, Darcy turned away. "I almost thought he was telling the truth, which is notable, as it has been many years since I trusted anything coming out of his mouth to be anything but lies."

"Agreed," said Fitzwilliam with a snort.

"Then we watch him and remain vigilant," said Bingley. "If he is lying, sooner or later he will make a mistake."

They agreed and soon broke up. Darcy watched his cousin and his friend leave, thinking about what had happened. He was less certain than he had been earlier that Wickham was guilty, but the thought of what his former friend had become would not leave him. He feared that their next indication of something wrong would come soon and that they would regret not neutralizing Wickham when they had the chance.

"Mama! I am so bored! Can we not leave this room for a time?"

"I know, Liddy, my dear," said Mrs. Bennet. "But your father has insisted we stay in this room together. I would not wish for something to happen to you because you disobeyed and put yourself within reach of that odious Mr. Darcy. I am sure he is behind everything! How I wish we could depart!"

As it felt like it was at least the hundredth time Mrs. Bennet had said something to the effect that she believed Mr. Darcy to be the source of their troubles, Elizabeth could not quite stifle a sigh. Her mother, unfortunately, did not miss it."

"There is no need to sigh like that, Miss Lizzy," said Mrs. Bennet. "Though he has become your favorite—and I am unable to fathom why you would favor such a dour man—I am certain in the end it will be proven that it is Mr. Darcy who will go to the gallows for the murders we have seen."

"And why do you say that, Mama?" asked Elizabeth, a hint of an edge in her voice. "Why would you suspect Mr. Darcy in particular?"

"Because he is a violent sort of man. You did not see him with Mr. Wickham. I have never seen such brutality from a man in all my life, and to assault such an amiable man as Mr. Wickham! I do not trust him! You will all stay away from him!"

"Oh, Mama!" exclaimed Lydia. "I am sure Mr. Wickham got nothing more than he deserved!"

While Elizabeth was grateful her younger sister had taken her words concerning Mr. Wickham to heart, Elizabeth could see that her mother was not in the mood to be scolded by her daughter. Mrs. Bennet had never been able to see past a man's appearance to discover that which lay beneath.

"I am sure Mr. Darcy has portrayed himself in such a matter to you, Liddy. But I quite detest the man, and I am sure he is the reason for our woes."

Elizabeth caught Lydia's eye and shook her head, indicating that she should hold her tongue. Lydia did, but not without a huff of annoyance.

"I believe it is quite wrong to pronounce judgment on a man when we have no proof of wrongdoing," said Mary in her usually pompous tone. "'Judge not, that ye be not judged,' saith the Lord. It is a commandment we would all be well served to obey."

Her mother opened her mouth, no doubt to deliver a stinging retort, when the crack of a gun rent the air, the noise of it making it seem like it was quite nearby. The Bennet ladies instinctively flinched as one. Elizabeth soon realized there was no danger to them at present and went to the window to look out.

"Oh, Lizzy!" cried Mrs. Bennet. "Come away from the window! You make yourself a handsome target standing there in all that state."

"There is no one outside that I can see," said Elizabeth. But she moved away from the window as her mother had commanded, returning to her chair. When she sat again, she did not miss how Lydia, who had been sitting beside her, pushed herself until she was in close contact with Elizabeth.

"I am afraid, Lizzy," said Lydia, her eyes wide, darting this way and that.

"I do not know what it was," said Elizabeth. "But it does not seem to have been aimed at us."

The Bennet ladies sat for some time, listening to any little sound which would announce the approach of danger, but nothing came. There was no sound — it was as if there was no one else within the house. But they were accompanied by the soft sound of her mother's fearful sobs, and the way she mumbled: "God help us all! Whatever are we to do?"

It was perhaps fifteen minutes later when the door opened, startling them all. It was soon revealed to be their father, who stepped into the room and closed the door behind him. He was immediately inundated with loudly spoken questions and demands to know what was happening.

"One at a time!" exclaimed Mr. Bennet as his family all crowded around him. "If you will all return to your seats, I shall inform you of what I know."

Elizabeth and her sisters did as they were bid, albeit reluctantly, and Mr. Bennet joined them, though not without first pouring himself a finger of the port wine on the table. Elizabeth was amused to note that Lydia, with whom she had never been close, now insisted on staying close to Elizabeth's side.

"I assume you hear the gunshot?" said Mr. Bennet after he had gathered his thoughts. "Unfortunately, we do not know who fired it. But none of us are injured, though I was walking with Mr. Darcy at the time.

"Mr. Darcy?" gasped Mrs. Bennet. "But . . . But . . . Why would someone be shooting at Mr. Darcy?"

"Perhaps to kill him?" asked Mr. Bennet with an arch of his eyebrow. "After all, it seems that has been in vogue of late, has it not?"

"Or maybe someone wished to stop him before he could kill another," snapped Mrs. Bennet.

"If we had any proof that Mr. Darcy had killed," said Mr. Bennet with a pointed look at his wife, "we would have locked him away so he could not kill another. The notion that someone was trying to kill him before he kills is rather silly, do you not agree?"

"So we still do not know," said Elizabeth with a sigh.

"Well," said Mr. Bennet in a conversational tone, "Mr. Darcy is rather adamant in his belief that Mr. Wickham is the culprit."

Mrs. Bennet snorted. "Of course, that man would blame Mr. Wickham. It is my understanding that Mr. Wickham's current state of poverty is at Mr. Darcy's instigation. It seems he will stop at nothing to ensure Mr. Wickham's life is ruined."

"It seems to me it is exactly the opposite," replied Elizabeth. Lydia nodded vigorously in support.

"You two may look on Mr. Darcy with admiration if you like," said Mrs. Bennet. "When all is said and done, I hope we survive the man's depredations."

"It is nonsensical to say such things, Mrs. Bennet," said Mr. Bennet. "After all, Darcy was with me, and it seems whoever pulled the trigger was aiming at us. Unless you are somehow convinced that Mr. Darcy has the ability to be two places at once."

Mrs. Bennet had no answer for her husband's words, and for once, she chose to remain silent. Mr. Bennet nodded and turned his attention back to them all.

"I do not know who has been doing these things, girls. But I wish to keep all of you as safe as possible. Remember what I have told you — always stay with one of your sisters at the very least. We shall go down to dinner together — I believe it will be safe enough to do so. But I do not wish for any of you to be alone at any time."

"Yes, Papa," they all chorused, to their father's approval.

The rest of the afternoon passed in much the same fashion as the morning. The Bennet sisters attempted to stay busy, but it was difficult, given their position in the family's rooms. Elizabeth, of course, had her books with her, but it was difficult to read, with sisters' — and mother's — continued complaints interrupting her. Kitty and Lydia tried to lead them through some games, and for a while, they were able to stave off the boredom by playing charades, and they even had a deck of cards delivered to them by the servants.

But there was not a person among them who was not relieved to finally quit the room when the call for dinner arrived, even knowing the dangers which might await them. As one they made their way down to the sitting-room, and there Elizabeth noted the presence of all those who she had become accustomed to seeing. The only members of the party who were not present were Mrs. Hurst and Anne, not that Elizabeth had expected them to leave their rooms.

However, on this day, the dynamic seemed to change a little. There were still suspicious looks aplenty between the company, Mr. Wickham stayed aloof, watching them all with dark amusement, and certain tensions between the members of the company. It seemed, however, that a certain one among them had decided to forgo what he likely thought was his understated wooing and turned quite blatant.

"Cousin Elizabeth," said Mr. Collins as soon as she had entered the room. He stepped toward her and bowed low, extending his arm for her to take. "How happy I am you—and your wonderful family, of course—have decided to attend us for dinner. I would be happy if you would sit with me before dinner so that we may become better acquainted."

"Remember what I told you, Collins," said Mr. Bennet, softly, but with a significant look at his cousin.

Whether she did not hear him or simply ignored him in her zeal to have one of her daughters married, Mrs. Bennet was not shy about pushing Elizabeth toward the loathsome parson. "Of course, you must go sit with Mr. Collins, Lizzy!" Then she lowered voice and spoke softly—meaning the entire room could hear every word: "Give all your attention to Mr. Collins, Lizzy. The more you encourage him, the more attentive he will be to you."

Elizabeth had no desire to be in the same county as Mr. Collins. But she knew there was little chance of escaping him, so she allowed him to lead her away to a settee, though she refused to take his arm. Mr. Collins seemed to accept this without any indication of offense. In fact, he beamed at her, as if she had just declared her undying love for him. The very thought made her want to gag.

"How lovely this is!" said Mr. Collins as soon as they were seated. "I am sure I anticipate many more evenings spent in such a manner. I am happy to inform you that Lady Catherine, in her infinite wisdom and boundless understanding, was instrumental in ensuring the parsonage, which is my home, has received the best care and attention for which one could ask. Her ladyship suggested many of the improvements in my home, and I am certain you will be amazed by her thoughtful devotion to ensuring the comfort of my future wife."

Elizabeth gazed at the man in astonishment. "Mr. Collins," said she, catching Mr. Darcy's glare out of the corner of her eye, "I do not believe this is an appropriate subject. Your patroness has only been deceased these past few days, and there are members of her family present!"

"I assure you that I am acquainted with all the customs, my dear Cousin." The man waved her words away, ineffectual to the last. "In speaking of Mr. Darcy's aunt in such a fashion, I am showing my respect and veneration for her. I am sure these fine gentlemen cannot be offended by the praise I so liberally bestow upon her."

"There you would be incorrect," Colonel Fitzwilliam's muttered words made their way to Elizabeth's ears. For his part, Mr. Darcy continued to glare, though it did not do any good, as Mr. Collins was too caught up in what he was saying.

And so he continued to speak, his mind moving from subject to subject without any thought, or seeming connection. While, as ever, Lady Catherine was foremost in his thoughts, he was focused primarily on assuring her of how charming she would find his home, and how fortunate she was to have gained his notice. Within moments, Elizabeth was desperate to escape, even if she must hit him over the head with a candlestick to do so.

When they were called to dinner, she jumped up, eager to be out of his presence. It was fortunate, indeed, that while her predicament had amused her father, he was willing to bring about an end to her torment.

"I shall escort Elizabeth to dinner, Mr. Collins," said Mr. Bennet when Elizabeth directed a pleading look at him. "I believe you have had enough of her time."

"Of course, Cousin!" exclaimed Mr. Collins, though there was something in his manner which suggested annoyance. "How charming you are together! All your daughters are charming! I am quite enraptured!"

"And we would all be grateful if you would keep your raptures to yourself," muttered Elizabeth. Her father heard her comment and grinned, and Elizabeth heard a snort from behind which suggested someone else had also overheard. As for Mr. Collins, he continued to speak in his blathering tone. Elizabeth almost wished the man would propose so she could inform him of her unwillingness to become his wife.

For the rest of the evening, Elizabeth spent her time avoiding Mr. Collins. It was not difficult to do when they were at dinner, though much more difficult when they returned to the sitting-room. It was fortunate for Elizabeth's sanity that they did not linger long.

When Mr. Bennet rose and beckoned his daughters to depart, Elizabeth noted that Mr. Collins rose with alacrity to offer her his arm. But Mr. Darcy also rose, and he reached her first.

"Miss Elizabeth, might I escort you above stairs? I believe it is time that I retired as well."

While Elizabeth noticed her father nodding at Mr. Darcy, she did not fail to recognize Mr. Collins's scowl at Mr. Darcy. "I believe, Mr. Darcy," said he in a frosty tone, "that the right of escorting my cousin belongs to me."

"Of course, I am happy to walk with you, Mr. Darcy," said Elizabeth, accepting Mr. Darcy's offered arm.

Mr. Collins's scowl deepened. But he was soon interrupted by her father, who was shooing Elizabeth's sisters from the room, Mrs. Bennet leading them. Elizabeth also saw her mother's pointed look at her, but she took great pleasure in ignoring.

"I think it might be best, Collins," said her father, as Elizabeth began to walk from the room with Mr. Darcy, "if you keep your distance from Elizabeth. She does not favor you, and as I have already told you, I have no interest in forcing any of my daughters to accept offers against their inclinations."

"But, Mr. Bennet!" exclaimed Mr. Collins.

But her father was firm. "No, Mr. Collins. I have already informed you of my feelings. I will not speak on the subject again."

"I am glad your father is speaking with Mr. Collins," said Mr. Darcy quietly. "I am afraid I have difficulty tolerating the man."

"*You* are not the focus of his attempts at wooing," whispered Elizabeth back.

"No, Miss Elizabeth," said Mr. Darcy. "And I hope I never am."

Elizabeth could not help the giggle which escaped her lips. But then she remembered what had happened that afternoon, and she felt her mirth depart. "You *are* well, are you not, Mr. Darcy? You were not injured?"

A shake of his head was Mr. Darcy's response. "I was not injured. Fortunately, the shot missed."

"Do you have any notion of who might have done it?"

"I still suspect Wickham. But I cannot be certain."

"I hope we discover it soon. This situation is wearing on us all."

Elizabeth was distracted at that moment by the departure of Mr. Collins. He was glaring at her, apparently injured that she had not accepted his offer to escort her. Her sisters had already departed with their mother, and only Mr. Hurst and Mr. Bingley were left, speaking together in soft tones. With Mr. Collins's departure, Mr. Bennet returned to Elizabeth's side.

"If you wish to escort my daughter, I have no objection, sir," said Mr. Bennet. "But I expect her returned to me quickly."

"Of course, sir. We shall make our way there directly."

Mr. Bennet nodded and exited through the door, leaving Elizabeth with Mr. Darcy. She was surprised that he had allowed it, but she supposed Mr. Darcy had gained his trust. Elizabeth felt a warmth well up within her at the thought—Mr. Darcy had *her* trust, too.

CHAPTER XXI

"*D*o you wish to go above stairs immediately, Miss Bennet?" asked Mr. Darcy.

Interrupted from her contemplation of her father's departure, Elizabeth turned and smiled at her companion. "Is that not what Papa instructed?"

"I believe a few moments' delay will not do any harm."

Elizabeth laughed. "I am certain it will not, sir, though my father might lose somewhat of the trust he has shown in you."

"We would not wish for that to happen, now, would we?"

"We have not had the opportunity to speak today," said Elizabeth. "Mr. Collins's actions prevented it. Have you discovered anything more we did not already know?"

"No," replied Mr. Darcy with a grimace. "The situation is the same as it was before today's events. I was with your father when the shot was taken—shortly before that, we were together with Bingley, Hurst, and Fitzwilliam."

"Mr. Wickham and Mr. Collins were not there?" asked Elizabeth with a frown.

"They were not." Mr. Darcy paused and shrugged. "We were discussing the situation, including the state of the roads and the possibility of you and your family departing for Longbourn. I did not believe either Collins or Wickham would have much to add to that discussion."

Elizabeth nodded slowly, distracted again by her thoughts. "I can see where it would be beneficial for you to be as little in Mr. Wickham's company as possible, and I cannot imagine Mr. Collins being of much use in *any* conversation of substance."

"My thoughts exactly."

Round and round Elizabeth's thoughts went, but she could not make heads nor tails of what she was hearing. She knew Mr. Darcy suspected Mr. Wickham but was it possible that there was another explanation?"

"How long after the other gentlemen left were you shot at?" asked Elizabeth.

"As little as five minutes, perhaps," replied Mr. Darcy.

"Enough time for any of the gentlemen to have retrieved a weapon," murmured Elizabeth. "To say nothing of Mr. Wickham and Mr. Collins, who were not even present. Or any of the women in residence."

"Are you offering yourself or your sisters as suspects?" asked Mr. Darcy, his countenance alight with amusement.

"I believe I can account for my mother and sisters during that time," replied Elizabeth. "Unless you suspect the Bennets of plotting together to slay everyone in residence."

"Have you a motive?"

"Did you not know?" asked Elizabeth, fixing him with a saucy look. "We Bennets are known for our shifty behavior and utter lack of anything resembling morals." Mr. Darcy guffawed, drawing the attention of Mr. Hurst and Mr. Bingley. But Elizabeth became serious again. "But Miss de Bourgh and Mrs. Hurst were not accounted for at that time unless their maids or someone else could vouch for them."

"That is true," replied Mr. Darcy. "But I do not suspect either. They were intimately connected to both Lady Catherine and Miss Bingley, and while both were unpleasant women, I have never witnessed anything but true affection from either for their relation."

"Perhaps. But we should not discount it. Given these facts, our pool of suspects has shrunk to Mr. Bingley, Mr. and Mrs. Hurst, Miss de Bourgh, Mr. Wickham, Mr. Collins, and Colonel Fitzwilliam."

"And many of those I would eliminate from the list just because of what I know of them."

"I understand, Mr. Darcy," said Elizabeth, filled with compassion for this man. All her family had been eliminated from suspicion, whereas his close friend and two of his relations were on the list. But just because Mr. Darcy knew those involved did not mean they were innocent.

"I do not wish to cast aspersions, sir. But there are times when we do not know a person as well as we might have thought. Vices, evil tendencies, anger, hate, or rage—these can all be hidden if the one hiding them possesses enough control. Mr. Wickham might have fooled me, for example, had the circumstances between you and I been different."

The gaze Mr. Darcy bestowed on Elizabeth caused a shiver to run up her spine. "I find it difficult to believe that Miss Elizabeth. You are among the most intelligent, discerning young ladies of my acquaintance. At the top of that list, actually. Even had you despised me, I do not believe Wickham could have deceived you for more than five minutes."

"We shall never know. Regardless, the situation is what it is. I do not know what to think. I only know that we should not eliminate anyone of whom we are not certain, regardless of our fondness for them."

"Agreed."

Silence fell between them, but for the low murmur of Mr. Hurst and Mr. Bingley's continued conversation. The thoughts continued to flow through Elizabeth's mind, but she could not organize them no matter how hard she tried. Of one thing Elizabeth was becoming certain: there was something they were missing. She did not know what it was, but she wondered if it would unravel the entire mystery.

A moment later, Elizabeth put aside her ruminations and looked back up at her companion again. Mr. Darcy was watching her, and his expression informed her it was with more than mere interest. Elizabeth felt a warmth seep through her, like the feeling of a hot bath on a cold winter night, or the glow of the sun's rays on her upturned face. How was this man able to evoke such exquisite feelings in her? And how had it all come about, considering her ambivalent opinion of him only a few days prior?

"I enjoy watching you think, Miss Elizabeth," said he, his voice soft, the depth of it speaking to his well of emotion. "I can almost see the greatness of your thoughts passing through the open windows of your eyes. They are made all that much finer and more beautiful by your intelligence and insight. What man could possibly resist you?"

Hearing such a man speak such exquisite words about her caused the breath to still in Elizabeth's body. She ducked her head, unaccustomed to the shyness which had come over her, knowing her cheeks were likely redder than the rosebushes at Longbourn.

"I am not a man given to flowery speeches or poetic gestures, Miss Elizabeth. But I speak from the heart. I have never been intrigued, captivated, and lost all at once, and it is all due to your incandescence.

"I have . . ." He paused and considered his words. "It seems to me that you are not averse to my presence. Dare I hope that is so?"

"You may," replied Elizabeth softly. Then she forced her head up to meet his gaze and shot him a grin. "I think, however, you may be mistaken about not being a poet, sir. It seems to me your words were lyrical, indeed."

"Then, Miss Elizabeth," said Mr. Darcy, reaching down and cradling one of her hands in his, "might I request the honor and privilege of calling on you when you are finally able to leave this place?"

"Yes, you may."

"Bravo!" said another voice, startling her.

Mr. Hurst and Mr. Bingley had ended their discussion and risen to their feet. It was Mr. Hurst who had spoken, though Mr. Bingley was watching them with approval, though a hint of melancholy.

"It seems, Darcy," said Mr. Hurst, "Lady Catherine may have had something to concern herself over, after all."

"I, for one, never doubted it," said Mr. Bingley. He clapped his friend on the back. "We will depart now. If you would like some advice, however, I would suggest you do not linger much longer. I believe you are already past the point Mr. Bennet indicated when he informed you of his expectation that his daughter would be returned to him 'directly.'"

With a laugh and a nod, Mr. Bingley departed, with a serious-looking Mr. Hurst following closely behind. It was strange, Elizabeth thought, but she did not feel quite so bashful at their teasing as she had when Mr. Darcy had declared his intentions. When she turned to him, he was watching her, a question written upon his countenance. Elizabeth thought she understood.

"I am quite content to allow Mr. Bingley his fun, Mr. Darcy. But perhaps we should wait until we are able to depart from this estate to proceed any further. It would not be proper, consider we are living under the same roof at present."

"That is correct," said Mr. Darcy. "I will call the very day I am able after I have completed my responsibilities to my family."

Thrilled that he wished to proceed in an expeditious manner, Elizabeth nodded and took his proffered arm. The hall outside the sitting-room was already devoid of Mr. Hurst and Mr. Bingley, as they had quite obviously made their way above stairs quickly. All was silent. Had Elizabeth not had this tall, imposing man as an escort, she might have found it more than a little frightening.

Mr. Darcy led them forward quickly, understanding that he was likely testing Mr. Bennet's forbearance as it was. Their footsteps echoed through the long hall as they walked, and Elizabeth looked about, the shadows cast by the few lights which remained on playing tricks on her mind, inducing her to see things which were not there.

Then they heard voices. Mr. Darcy, who heard them first, stopped suddenly, bringing Elizabeth to a halt while motioning for silence. There were a number of open doors along the hall, but Elizabeth was certain the voices were coming from a door a little further along, a supposition which was borne out by the fact that there was a faint light flickering through the door, which was open just a crack. Though she could not make out any words, it seemed like an argument, for the voices were raised and the tone angry.

Using soft steps, taking care that his shoes did not click against the tiles and give them away, Mr. Darcy led her forward. As they approached, Elizabeth realized this was the door to the library, for she could see one of the bookcases—woefully understocked with books, though the narrow gap. As they drew near, they heard a voice speaking, and this time clearly.

"I know you are in a position to be generous. I shall await your response."

Mr. Darcy turned a determined glance at Elizabeth and stepped to the door, pushing it open. As the room opened to their view, they noted that no one was on the side revealed by the open door. Mr. Darcy rushed in, letting Elizabeth's hand fall, and Elizabeth hurried in after him.

On the far side of the room, a lone man whirled upon their entrance, and then straightened, throwing them a sardonic sneer. It was Mr. Wickham.

"With whom were you speaking, Wickham?" demanded Mr. Darcy. He did not wait for a response, rather exiting through the nearby door into the room beyond. He did not stay long before he returned, his suspicious eyes falling on Mr. Wickham. The militia officer did not seem to be affected by Mr. Darcy's presence.

"Good evening to you too, Darcy," said the man, insolence in his tone and manner. "Of course, I would expect you to rush in and make demands without waiting for a response."

"Spare me your glib tongue, Wickham," snarled Mr. Darcy. "I have not the time nor the inclination for it. It sounded suspiciously like you were attempting your usual tricks, though blackmail is a new low, even for you."

A grunted laugh was Mr. Wickham's response. "My business is my own, Darcy. It has nothing to do with you."

"I believe it does," replied Mr. Darcy. He stepped up to Mr. Wickham, his merciless gaze bearing down on the other man. Though Elizabeth had thought Mr. Wickham a tall man, Mr. Darcy stood at least three inches taller, and he did not scruple to use his height to intimidate.

"Of course, you do," said Mr. Wickham, apparently not intimidated in the least. "The great Fitzwilliam Darcy, the master of Pemberley, possessor of the most inscrutable mask in all of England, and the appointed protector of all about him." Wickham snorted in disdain. "My business is my own, Darcy. If you believe I have done something wrong, I suggest you lock me in my room, as you suggested to your cousin. He, at least, has a little more objectivity than you possess. But I warn you—when you are proven wrong about me, you will be left with naught but another body on your hands."

"What do you mean?" challenged Mr. Darcy.

"Merely that I have harmed no one," said Mr. Wickham. "I know you suspect me. But you are not nearly so intelligent as you believe." Mr. Wickham sneered. "Poor Darcy," mocked he. "You are so focused on me; you neglect to consider other options. I am not your quarry."

"If you know something, you will tell me, Wickham. Or I swear I shall break you!"

"Do you see what manner of man this is, Miss Elizabeth?" asked Mr. Wickham.

He deftly stepped back from Mr. Darcy and sauntered toward her, though she noted that he kept a wary eye on Mr. Darcy. For his part, Mr. Darcy was not about to allow the man to escape so easily, as he reached out and grabbed Mr. Wickham's arm. Mr. Wickham only shook him off.

"High handed, is he not?" Mr. Wickham threw a contemptuous glare back at Mr. Darcy. "This is only one of his many faults. Do you know that he is widely considered to be a man of arrogance and conceit, one who looks meanly on all others, even those of his supposed station in life?"

"You may say what you like, Mr. Wickham," said Elizabeth, standing her ground, "but I have no doubt who is the better man between you."

"What a laugh." The full force of Mr. Wickham's sneer was turned on Elizabeth herself. But he did not intimidate her. "I have often seen young ladies attempt to attach themselves to Darcy and others who possess the same wealth. Just like all the others, I am afraid you will be disappointed."

"That is enough, Wickham!" commanded Mr. Darcy.

Elizabeth glanced at him and knew there would be greater unpleasantness if this continued much longer. She was certain that Mr. Wickham was also aware of this, though one might have been excused for misinterpreting it due to the man's continued goading.

"Darcy *does* possess the wealth, Miss Elizabeth. But he is not half the man I am."

He stepped close and peered down at her, running his tongue over his lips in what was intended to be a seductive action. Elizabeth felt nothing but repulsion.

"If you give me half a chance, I will show you the difference between us."

Mr. Darcy snarled at Mr. Wickham, and Elizabeth knew he was on the edge of attacking the libertine. She stepped around Mr. Wickham deftly and stepped to Mr. Darcy's side, placing a hand on his arm, a gesture she intended to be both possessive and pointed.

"There is nothing you can say which would induce my belief, Mr. Wickham," said Elizabeth. She looked him up and down. "All I can see is a man who has been grasping all his life, who has thrown away the advantages with which he was gifted time and time again."

A laugh—forced, Elizabeth thought—burst from Mr. Wickham's mouth, and he shook his head. "It seems wealth has won again. A great pity it is."

Mr. Wickham turned to Mr. Darcy and saluted him with a mocking bow. "I commend you, sir, for winning the loyalty of the fair Miss Elizabeth. I hope you enjoy her. And I hope you will not be hurt in the process, my lady."

Then Mr. Wickham exited the room, though with unhurried steps, which he intended to signal his utter lack of fear for anything they could do. Elizabeth felt Mr. Darcy's muscles bunch beneath her hand, indicating his intention of following Mr. Wickham from the room.

"It is, perhaps, best to simply allow him to leave at present, Mr. Darcy."

Mr. Darcy looked down at her, and his expression softened. He relaxed, but Elizabeth was certain she had only postponed the inevitable.

"Though it is against my inclination, I believe you are correct. And Bingley was also correct—I believe your father will come looking for us if I do not return you to him." He gestured toward the door. "I can deal with Wickham later."

His final words stayed with Elizabeth as they made their way from the room. The corridor once again was as empty as it was the last time they walked within it, but Elizabeth saw none of it. Instead, she pondered the meaning of what they had overheard. She also thought of Mr. Darcy's meaning.

"It is apparent to me you are deep in thought, Miss Elizabeth," said he, drawing Elizabeth from her deliberations.

"I suppose it is evident," said Elizabeth, smiling up at him.

"Even more so as you were chewing on your lower lip."

The intensity with which he said this took her aback. "I had not even been aware I was doing it," said she, a little breathlessly.

"It is one of those mannerisms I find irresistible about you, Miss Elizabeth. But I am wondering what you were thinking."

Elizabeth sighed. "I hardly know. I suppose I was attempting to divine the meaning of what we heard." Elizabeth peered up at him, uncertain she should ask the question she wished to ask. "Do you mean to extract the information from him tomorrow?"

"I believe we must," said Mr. Darcy. "I know not what he was doing, but it is clear it was nothing good. We have enough problems at present without dealing with more of Wickham's schemes."

"Of what schemes are you speaking, sir?"

Elizabeth and Mr. Darcy looked up as one to see her father descending the stairs toward them. Though Elizabeth thought her father was not displeased, she knew he would demand an explanation for their tardiness. Mr. Darcy did not hesitate to give one.

"That is interesting," said Mr. Bennet when the matter had been explained to him. "Given your account of Mr. Wickham, I wonder what he is planning."

"I am concerned as well. I shall roust Fitzwilliam from his bed tomorrow morning, and we will ensure we obtain answers from Wickham. If nothing else, I hold enough of his debts to see him in prison for a long time. If he decides he does not wish to be forthcoming, I can use that against him."

Mr. Bennet nodded slowly. "That is for the best, sir. Can he be persuaded to resign his commission and leave the community? An unscrupulous man such as he can do much damage to the shopkeepers."

"Fitzwilliam will take great pleasure in it, Mr. Bennet. I suspect Mr. Wickham will have a choice in his near future—he either resigns his commission or finds himself transferred to the front lines in Spain."

The two men shared devilish grins, and Elizabeth could only laugh at it while being thrilled her father and the man she had come to esteem seemed so easy in each other's company. It boded well for the future.

"I shall leave it in your capable hands, Mr. Darcy," said Mr. Bennet. "For now, I believe it is best to return my daughter to her sisters and mother. There will be more time to come to know each other on the morrow."

"Of course, Mr. Bennet." He smiled at Elizabeth. "I will be happy to cede your daughter to your care."

Then Mr. Darcy bowed and, capturing Elizabeth's hand, bestowed a lingering kiss on it. Elizabeth felt the heat rise in her cheeks again, a fact which her father could not help but notice.

"Good night, Mr. Darcy," said Elizabeth before allowing her father to lead her away.

They climbed the stairs, Mr. Darcy following behind, and when they reached their room, her father paused in front of the door. A quick look down the hall revealed that Mr. Darcy had already entered his room, leaving father and daughter alone in the hallway.

"It appears you have made a significant conquest, my dear," said Mr. Bennet.

His manner, while teasing, as usual, was a little wistful. Elizabeth immediately understood—she, who had always been his favorite, had attracted a wealthy man, but more importantly, a man who lived some distance away. She would not be settled close to him, and though she knew he had always wished for that, he would not stand in the way of her happiness.

"I esteem Mr. Darcy very much," said Elizabeth. "But I would not call it a conquest, Papa. He would like to call on me. But there is a long way to go before that turns into anything more."

"There is little doubt it will, my beloved child," said Mr. Bennet, bestowing a kiss on her forehead. "The way he regards you tells me everything I need to know. He is a man who will treat you like the jewel you are, and for that, I could not be happier."

"I hope so, Papa," said Elizabeth in a voice barely audible.

"Just take care to remain unobtrusive when in your mother's presence." Mr. Bennet chuckled. "Your mother seems to be convinced that Mr. Darcy is the one to blame for everything that has happened here. I expect that once we leave and Mr. Darcy comes to call on you, she will be won over by reports of his income and position in society. Until then, however, prudence would be advisable."

"Perhaps it is," said Elizabeth, exasperated at her mother all over again.

As her father turned to open the door, Elizabeth followed him into the room, hearing the welcoming voices of her sisters. While she knew she would be the target of their teasing jests, Elizabeth knew she should treasure these times. For if her father was at all correct, she would soon be leaving her father's home to be mistress of her own. The thought of leaving her family was a little daunting, as she knew most young women would feel at the prospect. But it was also exciting. Especially when she would be moving to the home of a man she could love without reservation.

CHAPTER XXII

*A*fter the event, Darcy was relieved he had rousted Fitzwilliam from his bed, not that it had been easy. For all that Fitzwilliam was accustomed to rising early due to his position in the army, Darcy had never known a man who was able to sleep quite like Fitzwilliam was. When Darcy entered his room that morning, throwing open the drapes to the grey of the predawn world outside, his cousin leaned on one arm and fixed Darcy with an unpleasant glare.

"I hope there is a good reason for disturbing my repose, Cousin. Otherwise, I shall be rather put out with you."

For his part, Darcy was not in the most congenial mood, for he had slept ill the night before. His mind had been full of thoughts of George Wickham, continually running over the few short words he had overheard the previous evening. While he had not thought it the previous evening, now he wondered if Wickham had been speaking to the murderer. Discovering the truth and then threatening to expose the killer unless compensated was something Darcy could well imagine Wickham doing.

"There is," replied Darcy shortly. "Get up. You and I are off to greet our good friend Wickham and force some information from his worthless hide."

"I like it," said Fitzwilliam, throwing aside the covers. Darcy had known any mention of Wickham, especially if he implied violence, would capture his cousin's interest. "I *am* curious, however, as to the reason for this sudden change of heart."

"Get dressed, and I shall tell you."

Darcy did so as Fitzwilliam pulled on his clothes, grumbling about the lack of his batman, who was still in London. He asked a few questions as the account became more interesting, which Darcy answered as much as he could. In the end, his cousin was not hesitant to voice his disgust, both with Wickham, but also with Darcy.

"I should have known. Even if he is not capable of murder himself, it should have been clear to us all that Wickham is capable of anything which will be of benefit to himself." Fitzwilliam turned a displeased scowl on Darcy. "We should have taken Wickham in hand many months ago, Darcy. You know this. Had he been neutralized from the beginning, you would not have spent good money to pay his debts, and he would not have importuned Georgiana."

"You may be correct," said Darcy, not ruffled in the slightest. "But we might have remained ignorant about the identity of the true murderer. I suspect Wickham at least knows or has discovered something. I mean to obtain that information."

Fitzwilliam grunted. "I hope so. I will promise you that if he knows something, he will part with it. It will go very ill with him if he does not."

It was this implacable side of Fitzwilliam's character which sometimes caused Darcy apprehension. Fitzwilliam had held many roles in the army, and Darcy knew his cousin had been called on to perform some truly unpleasant tasks in addition to having fought in battle. Darcy did not know the extent of it, and he would never ask his cousin to be explicit. But he knew Fitzwilliam was capable of extracting information from Wickham by whatever means.

"After you, Cousin," said Fitzwilliam when he was ready to depart.

The fact that Wickham's room was situated at the end of the hall, separated from the rest of the company as an unwanted guest, Darcy now counted as a blessing. It was far enough away from the other inhabited rooms and the hour was so early that any noise Wickham made would not be easily overheard.

Except Wickham was not there. When they entered, Darcy noticed the bed was made and had not been slept in, the curtains still wide open to the outside world. There were not even any possessions in evidence to suggest the room was even in use.

"Perhaps he has decided it would be best to flee," said Fitzwilliam. "It would not be the first time."

"Or it is possible he is meeting with the other person we overheard last night," said Darcy. "We should check the rooms below stairs, particularly the library."

Fitzwilliam gestured for Darcy to lead the way, which he did. They made their way to the library in silence, taking the stairs swiftly, Darcy eager to discover the information he was certain Wickham held, while he thought Fitzwilliam was more interesting in extracting retribution from the other man's hide. It was in the library where they made the gruesome discovery.

"Wickham!" gasped Darcy as he entered the room and took in the sight which was spread out before them.

Wickham—for it was immediately evident that was the identity of the body—was lying in a pool of his own blood, much of it already beginning to congeal. Beside him on the floor lay a broken candlestick, the heavy type a butler would use to provide light in the darkness as he walked through a house. It had been used on the unfortunate bounder, as the wounds on the back of his head, from which the blood had flowed, clearly announced.

"I suppose there lies our proof that Wickham was not the murderer," said Fitzwilliam. Darcy turned to his cousin in wonder—Fitzwilliam's voice had displayed no emotion, rather a clinical detachment Darcy had never heard before.

His cousin only shrugged. "You did not like him any more than I did, Darcy. There is no point in pretending otherwise. If I am honest with you, the only thing I feel at his death is relief. He was a millstone about your neck and worse."

"I know," replied Darcy softly. "But I cannot help but mourn for what he could have been."

"By all means, do so," said Fitzwilliam, stepping closer to the body to inspect it. "But do not mourn the man he became. He was *not* a good man. You know this better than anyone alive."

Darcy followed Fitzwilliam as he stepped to the body and crouched down. "The candlestick was used to kill him," said Fitzwilliam as he looked Wickham over. "He was struck several times, as if in great anger.

"Look here," said he, pointing to the wounds on Wickham's head. "He was struck at least five times that I can see and with great force. I suspect the killer only stopped when his weapon became unusable."

Fitzwilliam rose and looked about. "It seems he was sitting in this chair," continued he, looking over the furniture in question. "There is blood spattered on the top and behind, likely from when the killer struck him the first time. I suspect that he fell asleep in the chair and his enemy came on him unaware. Then after he fell to the floor after the first strike, the killer continued to beat him."

"I am impressed you are able to deduce this much," said Darcy. "I might not have put all these clues together."

"I have had occasion to investigate certain crimes in the past," said Fitzwilliam with a shrug. "I am not an expert, but the signs are obvious enough that they are easy to see."

"There is nothing here that indicates who might have killed him," said Darcy, sighing with resignation.

"No," said Fitzwilliam. "But the force with which the killer struck Wickham over and over suggests that our killer was almost certainly spattered with his blood. We may successfully discover him from that evidence."

"If he has not managed to wash it from the affected garments," muttered Darcy.

Fitzwilliam nodded in distraction. He turned and looked around the room. Darcy waited for him to speak, knowing his cousin was deeply immersed in his thoughts.

"If my theory about Wickham falling asleep is correct, it was the last mistake he ever made. It is the only thing that makes sense. Otherwise, he would not have been taken unaware."

"Could he not have left the door open?" asked Darcy.

"He might have," said Fitzwilliam. "But this chair is situated away from both doors, commanding a view of them both. If he had been awake and alert, he would not have been caught."

Darcy nodded. He allowed Fitzwilliam to search the room more thoroughly, but there was nothing else to be found. While he watched his cousin, Darcy was at a loss. They had been so close to uncovering the person who had done this. If only he had acted on his suspicions the previous evening!

"There is nothing else to be found at present," said Fitzwilliam, breaking Darcy's thoughts a few moments later. "We should call the butler in to take care of the body and remove this rug." Fitzwilliam kicked at it. "The stain will not be removed."

A growl escaped Darcy's lips. "We were so close!" He began to pace the room, feeling the restless energy built up within his frame. "Had I only acted last night, we might, even now, have the killer in our grasp."

"That is possible," said Fitzwilliam with a shrug. "But it is also possible Wickham would have refused to give him up."

"What of your conviction you would have pulled the name from his unwilling lips?" asked Darcy with a snort.

A lazy shrug was Fitzwilliam's response. "Wickham was unpredictable at times. He may have withheld the information until the time it would have benefited him the most to release it. He might have hoped to barter it for money."

"Aye, that is something he would have done." Darcy scowled at the body. "I know he was worthless, Fitzwilliam. But his passing has affected me, though I cannot explain it." He shook his head. "It is as if my last link to my father is now gone."

"He has not been such a link for many years," said Fitzwilliam, directing a pointed look at Darcy. "If you wish for a link to your father, consider your dear sister, not a man who squandered every opportunity he ever had."

"You are correct, of course." Darcy released an explosive sigh. "It is all such a waste, and we are no closer to the identity of our tormentor."

"We will be, Darcy." Fitzwilliam turned and glanced around again, introspection settling over him. "There is something off, something I am missing. I am certain of it. If I think on it, I am certain it will come to me."

"I will call the butler and go speak with Bingley," said Darcy, prompting a distracted nod from his cousin.

The butler's eyes were filled with fear when Darcy told him of the situation. He was instructed to gather a pair of footmen and go to the library, to which he agreed readily enough. Darcy did not even bother to ask the man to keep the situation quiet—the footmen would speak of it, and the servants would know of it before breakfast, Darcy was certain. At least none of the maids had come upon the gruesome sight, unlike Mr. Forbes's discovery.

Bingley was distressed, of course, as Darcy might have predicted. He insisted on viewing the body himself, though Darcy told him it was not necessary. They arrived back at the library when the footmen were removing Wickham, and Bingley, appearing white as a sheet, watched them as they bore it away, the same as the other three bodies.

"Whatever shall we do?" moaned Bingley when the three gentlemen were alone in the room. "I cannot even begin to fathom what has happened here. I curse the day I ever heard of this estate!"

"I understand your feelings," said Darcy. Unhappy though the events were, he personally would never curse anything which led him to Miss Elizabeth. "But this time it appears Wickham attempted to swindle the wrong person and paid for it with his life."

"What do you mean?" demanded Bingley.

Darcy explained what had happened the previous evening, Bingley listening intently. He expressed dismay that they had lost the opportunity to learn the identity of the killer, but nothing of censure toward Darcy escaped his lips. Before Darcy could complete his narration, however, a pair of ladies appeared at the door, looking in with curiosity.

"Do not enter, ladies," said Fitzwilliam, stepping toward them before Darcy could move. A quick glance revealed the bloodstains on the tiles were still present from where they had seeped through the rug on which Wickham had lain.

"What has happened?" gasped Miss Bennet.

"Has there been another incident?" added Miss Elizabeth.

"I am afraid there has," said Fitzwilliam. He escorted the sisters from the room, Darcy and Bingley rising to follow them. "It appears Mr. Wickham is no longer with us."

A stifled gasp was Miss Bennet's response, though Miss Elizabeth appeared to take the news with stoic gravity. Tears appeared in Miss Bennet's eyes, and she began to weep, more for the situation than any sorrow over Wickham's death, Darcy thought. Bingley, it appeared, could not endure her tears, for he stepped forward, offering his handkerchief. It was all he could do, under the circumstances.

"Do not cry, Miss Bennet," said he. He stepped close, grasping one of her hands between his own. "It shall all be well in the end. You will see."

They stood close together, Bingley offering comfort while Miss Bennet wiped at her eyes and nodded at his words. Fitzwilliam had slipped back into the room, Darcy thought to ensure the floor was cleaned. Miss Elizabeth, who had been watching her sister, sidled up to Darcy.

"Mr. Wickham, was it?" When Darcy nodded, she spoke only one more word: "How?"

Careful to avoid injuring her delicate sensibilities, Darcy informed her of what they had discovered, though keeping as much of the details from her as he could manage. Miss Elizabeth listened with grave attention, her brow furrowed in deep thought. It was incongruous to the situation they now faced, but he found even this mannerism of hers nigh irresistible, unable to keep the admiration from welling up within him.

"I can scarce believe we have lost yet *another*," said Miss Elizabeth at length.

"I will own I am at a loss, Miss Elizabeth," replied Darcy. "Wickham seemed the one whom the facts fit, though I will own the evidence was not perfect. Now we are back at the beginning, and I do not know what to think."

"It all seems to return to whoever was in the room with Mr. Wickham last night," said Miss Elizabeth.

"I do not suppose you recognized the voice?" said Mr. Darcy, with a half-hearted attempt at seriousness.

"The second voice was quiet, almost inaudible." Miss Elizabeth sighed and shook her head. "There is no hope from that perspective."

"Then we shall have to continue as we were," said Darcy. "Stay with your sisters, Miss Elizabeth. I cannot help but think that Netherfield has become extremely dangerous for us all."

Mr. Darcy's ominous words stayed with Elizabeth for the rest of the day. Though it was possible Mr. Darcy had meant to keep Mr. Wickham's death a secret from all but the gentlemen, and she could understand his reasons, it was not to be. When she and Jane returned to the family rooms, the matter was quickly pulled from them by their mother.

"That is the end," said her father, looking out over all his progeny. "You will all stay in these rooms until we are to depart for Longbourn. No exceptions."

It was clear to Elizabeth that her father was speaking more to her than her sisters, and she agreed to his stipulation. Even Lydia and Kitty, tired of being confined as they were, gave no objections to their father's command.

Several times through the day, either Mr. Darcy or Colonel Fitzwilliam came to the door and spoke with her father in low tones. Mr. Bennet even left with them a time or two, though he always returned swiftly. Of what they were speaking, Elizabeth could not determine, and her father declined to be explicit. On one occasion, however, Elizabeth was able to induce him to inform her of the content of his discussions.

"I assume you have looked out the window, Lizzy," said he, his own eyes finding the panes of glass separating them from the outside.

"It has begun to rain in earnest," replied Elizabeth.

"It has, indeed. Unfortunately, rather than making the situation better, it is making it much worse. The flooding concerns concerning the bridge have been realized—the water is flowing over the top of it, and it will be a miracle if it is not washed away."

"But surely it will return to normal quickly," said Elizabeth.

"I have reason to believe it will," replied her father. "It will, however, confine us to Netherfield until at least tomorrow, and likely until the day after. The tenants are also suffering it seems, particularly those down by the river. It will take significant effort to return things to what they were before, and I can only guess the state of Longbourn's lands."

"We shall weather it, Papa," said Elizabeth. "This is not the first time Mother Nature has played havoc with our lives."

Her father responded with a grin, though it did not take anything away from his worried countenance. "You have always been the most resilient of your sisters, Lizzy. I am happy and privileged to be your father. But more than this, I am eager to leave this estate behind and return to our home, where I can see to the safety of you, your mother, and your sisters myself." Mr. Bennet paused, and his eyes were unfocused for a moment. "I think I shall insist on Mr. Collins's return to his parish as soon as may be arranged. It would be better if we did not host anyone at present."

While Elizabeth would not wish for one gentleman caller, in particular, to be turned away from Longbourn's door—and knew Jane felt the same way about *her* caller—she knew her father spoke nothing but sense. As such, she agreed with his assessment.

"The other issue," said Mr. Bennet, returning to his serious demeanor, "is that the servants have begun to abandon the estate."

"I suppose we should have anticipated that," said Elizabeth. "How bad has it become?"

"Thus far only a footman," said Mr. Bennet. "I do not know what the chances are of his reaching his destination safely, but he announced his intention to depart to another, and left the house."

Elizabeth gasped. "Could he be the one responsible?"

"It does not seem likely," replied her father with a shaken head. "I have been speaking with Mr. Darcy today, and we are almost assured that the murderer in one of us."

With that pronouncement, Mr. Bennet moved away and left Elizabeth to her sisters. She could not fault their conclusions—she had always suspected someone of the company herself. Their number was diminishing, however, and soon it would not be possible to continue to take lives and not be discovered.

They continued in this way throughout the entire day. The Bennet sisters were kept in their room by the command of their father, who was intent upon seeing them all protected. They largely split into two groups. Kitty, Lydia, and Mrs. Bennet, from what Elizabeth could determine, occupied themselves by speaking this piece of gossip or that, ruminating about the officers they had not seen since the night of the ball, interspersed with complaints of ennui and the wish they could leave Netherfield. Elizabeth largely sat with Mary and Jane, and while Mary's society was made irksome by her frequently stated desire to go to the music room for the pianoforte, the three young ladies did well enough together.

Only once was their solitude challenged. Not long after Elizabeth's discussion with her father, there was a knock on the door. Mr. Bennet motioned to his daughters to stand clear, and he went and opened it himself. The identity of the person on the other side was immediately evident by the loud voice and grand pronouncements, though Mr. Bennet kept the door in a position which did not allow Elizabeth to see the parson. It also soon devolved into an argument.

"Ah, my dear cousin!" said Mr. Collins. "I can see you are keeping your lovely and amiable daughters sequestered away in your rooms. Good for you! As we are all members of the same family, I know you will wish to allow me entrance, particularly when I have not seen your fair daughter Elizabeth since yesterday. I am quite certain she is pining for my presence."

Elizabeth felt like gagging at the notion she would wish to see Mr. Collins, but her father, fortunately, was not amused by the parson's silliness. "These are bedchambers, Mr. Collins," said he. "Regardless of the situation, it would not be proper for you to be within them. I am certain Elizabeth can manage without your presence."

"But, Cousin! I am alone, and given what has happened, I am convinced we shall all have a greater chance at safety should we stay together. I am confident that as I am a man of the family—the next head of the family when you should go to your reward—that there is no impropriety."

"There you would be wrong, Collins," was Mr. Bennet's testy reply. "I have already informed you of the impropriety of your request, and I have told you numerous times that my daughters are free to marry whomever they choose. I would ask you to cease speaking of Elizabeth as if she is your betrothed. I have it on very good authority she will refuse you, should you possess the poor judgment to offer for her."

And with those final words, Mr. Bennet closed the door, quietly, but firmly. If Elizabeth thought that was the end of the matter, she would have been sorely mistaken.

"But, Mr. Bennet!" wailed her mother. "Our daughters must marry! This talk of Elizabeth waiting is all nonsense. Mr. Collins's offer is before her; she must accept it!"

"Mrs. Bennet," said Mr. Bennet, his tone one which he rarely used with any of them, but one which they all knew was not to be questioned. "Please recall that it is *I* who have the responsibility of agreeing to suitors' requests for our daughters. If Elizabeth were forced into marriage with Mr. Collins, she would be miserable."

Her mother seemed about to object again, but Mr. Bennet's countenance softened, and he approached her, smiling at her. "All is not as bleak as you think, my dear. I suspect you will be pleased with the man Lizzy eventually marries. Indeed, I cannot think of how you could possibly object."

Then with a wink, Mr. Bennet moved away. Elizabeth felt herself the focus of Mrs. Bennet's curious glances, and she thought more than once her mother would speak to work on her to accept Mr. Collins, but in the end, she allowed the matter to rest and remained silent.

And so it continued. The Bennets requested their dinners in the room, and after dinner, there was naught to do but go to bed. Elizabeth did not think she was fatigued, but she soon fell into a slumber.

When she woke, the darkness of the room attested to the lateness of the hour, and she tried to once again drift off to sleep. But as she tried, her mind remained awake, becoming more alert by the moment. Something was bothering her, something Mr. Collins had said earlier. And regardless of her father's edict, she could not rest until she learned the truth of the matter.

Thus, Elizabeth silently rose and donned her robe, and slipped out the door.

CHAPTER XXIII

"*U*nfortunately, Darcy," said Fitzwilliam, "I cannot make heads nor tails of this. There *must* be something linking the four victims together, but if there is, it is eluding me."

Darcy nodded, rose, and went to the fireplace, sticking the poker in and pushing the coals about, sending sparks shooting up into the chimney. They had made their way to his room after dinner, not that dinner had been much of an affair at all. They had seen no one else, except for Bingley for a few short moments, and Mr. Collins, who carried on with his pompous nothings until Darcy told him in no uncertain terms that he did not wish to speak with a sycophant. The rest of the company had remained in their rooms, requesting dinner there, and even the servants were paired up when delivering the meals.

"I was convinced it was Wickham," said Darcy at length.

"I know you were, Cousin. And I can understand your suspicions, given your history with him." Though Darcy was turned with his back to his cousin, he heard Fitzwilliam sigh and shift in his chair. "I have little desire to exonerate Wickham in *anything*. But I will say that he has never struck me as a killer—a bounder, a debtor, a seducer, and perhaps every other vice known to man, yes. But a killer? I never thought he had the stomach for it."

Darcy sighed. "When I was shot at, it seemed so obvious." Turning, Darcy looked at his cousin. "Who else would have wished to kill me in such a manner?"

"I think you are missing something here, Cousin." Fitzwilliam leaned forward, his eyes fixed upon Darcy. "You were not the only one present when the shot was fired."

He had not thought of that. "You suspect the shooter was aiming for Mr. Bennet?"

"I am only suggesting it is possible. That is part of the reason you were so fixed on Wickham—the idea that it *must* have been you who was the target. What if that were not the case?"

"Then it seems we must consider who might have wished to kill Mr. Bennet. There is one obvious suspect, but considering what I know of *him*, I can hardly think he would have been responsible."

Fitzwilliam barked a laugh. "It does seem ridiculous, does it not? To think an ineffectual bootlicker such as Collins might have attempted to shoot Mr. Bennet sounds like something out of a novel. I am not even certain the man knows what end of a pistol to fire."

A chuckle escaped Darcy's lips, and he was forced to agree that his cousin was entirely correct. "But I suppose we should not eliminate him, regardless of how stupid he presents himself to be."

"The important consideration, then, is whether Mr. Bennet might have anything in common with any of the others."

Darcy paused and considered the matter. "Mr. Bennet having something in common with Lady Catherine? I cannot think of what if there is something. And Miss Bingley?" Darcy snorted. "I would think that Miss Bingley would have more in common with Lady Catherine, rather than Mr. Bennet. And the butler is nothing like any of the others."

"Except, perhaps, his looks."

Curious, Darcy turned to regard Fitzwilliam, noting his distracted air. "What do you mean? Mr. Bennet looks nothing like Mr. Forbes."

"From the front, no," replied Fitzwilliam. "But one could easily be mistaken for the other from behind if you do not take into account the slight difference in height and that of dress."

"Are you suggesting that Mr. Forbes was murdered because he was mistaken for Mr. Bennet?"

Fitzwilliam did not immediately respond, and when he did, he spoke slowly. "I do not know I am suggesting anything, Darcy. Now that I think of it, however, it strikes me that Mr. Forbes was a man of approximately Mr. Bennet's age, I believe, and they both have a similar look from behind. In a darkened hall, it is quite possible one who wished Mr. Bennet harm might have mistaken the butler for him."

"Very well," said Darcy, frowning in thought. "If we assume that, it seems that Mr. Collins is the most likely suspect. The problem, however, lies with the fact that Mr. Collins would never have killed Lady Catherine."

"Could there have been some sort of chain of murders, one leading to the next?"

"I do not know how that could be," replied Darcy. "If I understand what you are attempting to say, that would mean Lady Catherine killed the butler, was in turned killed by Miss Bingley, who was slain by Wickham and then he by someone else. Beyond the fact that Lady Catherine would have no reason to kill Mr. Forbes, I cannot imagine anyone would have been motivated to vengeance for his sake, lest of all Miss Bingley."

"I do not necessarily mean that the killings were vengeance motivated, one after the other. I only wondered if there could have been a chain of events which led to each one."

"If there is, then I do not believe either of us is intelligent enough to decipher it."

They fell silent for a time after, Darcy stalking the room, his mind a whirl, trying to solve the riddle. It appeared that Fitzwilliam slept, for his eyes were closed and he made not a move. Darcy, however, was filled with restless energy, felt it rolling off him in great waves. He was incapable of sitting still and would be able to sleep not a wink, even should he attempt it.

"It seems to me, Darcy," said Fitzwilliam, his eyes cracking open and following Darcy's movement about the room, "it all comes back to what you and Miss Bennet overheard last night. Wickham was speaking about blackmailing someone, and I can imagine no other reason he would attempt to do such a thing unless he had deciphered the riddle."

Darcy stopped and turned to consider his cousin. "He *was* insufferably smug, more so than he usually was. He seemed to think he knew something I did not."

"We have returned to not wishing to attribute anything good to George Wickham. But much as I detested him, he was not unintelligent. It is quite possible he discovered the truth."

"And it would be just like him to keep the knowledge to himself for his own gain," growled Darcy.

With a sudden motion, Fitzwilliam rose to his feet. "Come, Darcy.

I wish to check the library again. I have had a sudden thought."

Then, without speaking another word, Fitzwilliam strode from the room.

Elizabeth knew she had made a tactical error the moment she walked into the kitchen. Her only thought had been the questions she had wished to ask the housekeeper, and she had not taken any thought for how the woman would react to seeing her wandering the house alone again.

"Miss Elizabeth!" exclaimed Mrs. Nichols when she entered. "Why are you here again, and at such an hour?"

She felt like a young girl, caught stealing cookies from the kitchens at Longbourn. Though her courage was equal to the task of withstanding the anger of Netherfield's housekeeper, she had no desire to justify her actions. Thus, she said the first words which came to her mind.

"I came with my father. He is in the library and is awaiting my return."

Mrs. Nichols was openly skeptical of Elizabeth's explanation, but Elizabeth did not allow her any time to consider it. "I had another question if you do not mind."

"Of course," said Mrs. Nichols. Her tone was more conciliatory, as she seemed to remember that she was speaking with a guest and a gentlewoman. "How can I help you?"

"I wished to know of the brandy which was sent up to Miss Bingley's room. Is there anything else you can think of which might shed some light on it? Brandy, for example, is a man's drink—I am surprised Miss Bingley had it in her room, rather than sherry."

"I remember thinking the same," said Mrs. Nichols. "But Miss Bingley drank more brandy than even her brother, given the number of times we were called upon to replenish what she kept in her room."

"Is it possible someone might have thought the brandy was intended for a man?"

"Of course, it is possible," said Mrs. Nichols. "Were you thinking of anyone in particular?"

"No," confessed Elizabeth. "It just struck me as odd that someone would have known to poison that particular bottle of brandy when a woman would usually choose other, milder liquors."

"I suppose," muttered Mrs. Nichols. "But I assure you that the servants have not gossiped. I do not know of any way any of the other guests would have learned of Miss Bingley's predilection."

"Then they could not have known to poison the brandy unless one of the servants had been induced to share who had requested it."

"I have questioned all the servants myself, Miss Bennet. None of them reported anything unusual from any of the guests."

Elizabeth bit her lip in frustration. She was certain the answer was just beyond her grasp, could almost feel her fingers brushing up against it, sending it fluttering just a little further out of reach. She was so close — she could feel it!

"Could someone have been trying to poison Mr. Bingley?" asked she, more to herself than the housekeeper. "Or Mr. Darcy or Colonel Fitzwilliam? If it had been port wine, I might almost have thought it was intended for my father."

"Port wine, did you say?" asked Mrs. Nichols.

A glance up confirmed what Elizabeth had heard in the woman's voice. She appeared almost spooked at whatever Elizabeth had said, though Elizabeth could not hope to fathom the meaning of her reaction.

"Yes," said Elizabeth. "My father's predilection for port is well-known among his friends and family — he rarely has anything else in his study."

Eyes wide, Mrs. Nichols swallowed thickly. "I have just recalled, Miss Bennet, that there was also a request that day for a bottle of port wine to be taken to your father's room. In fact, I believe the port and the brandy sat together for a little time before Miss Bingley's brandy was taken above stairs. The port was not delivered until later in the day."

A chill raced through Elizabeth's veins, though she attempted to contain her shock and fear. She thought she did a credible job of hiding her reaction to the housekeeper's words, as the woman did nothing more than look at her in shock. When she felt she had mastered herself enough, Elizabeth attempted to speak again.

"The port and brandy sat together?"

"Yes. I did not remember it until this moment, as we had all focused on the brandy."

"Then it is possible that whoever poisoned the brandy, thought it was destined for my father's room. Not expecting a woman to be requesting brandy, he might have made an assumption and been tragically wrong."

"That is possible. But who would wish to kill your father?"

In fact, Elizabeth thought she knew quite well who would wish to murder her father. But another thought entered her mind, and she gave voice to it before even taking a moment to consider it.

"Mrs. Nichols, another question: are you aware of Lady Catherine's insistent demands for a better room?"

An expression of disgust from the housekeeper told Elizabeth she was well acquainted with it. "The woman sought me out herself no less than thrice. She argued with Miss Bingley too, on several occasions, from what I understand."

"Do you know with whom she wished to exchange rooms?"

"She required a change of rooms for both her and her daughter, with an adjoining door between them," replied Mrs. Nichols.

"I believe she had words with your father. As you know, Mr. and Mrs. Bennet were assigned adjoining rooms."

Elizabeth was well aware of it, for had she not spent the last two days complete trapped in that room with her sisters, hoping they survived long enough to return home? Her mind flashed back to the argument she had witnessed between her father and Lady Catherine, and she distinctly remembered Mr. Collins watching them as well. The implications were stunning. Not only had *two* bottles of liquor been prepared to be taken above stairs, but might Mr. Collins not have assumed his great patroness would carry the day, ousting her parents from their rooms? Then, logically, they would have been installed in Lady Catherine's room. And Lady Catherine was murdered overnight.

"I . . . I must go," stammered Elizabeth, turning and making for the door without seeing where she was going.

"Miss Elizabeth!" exclaimed Mrs. Nichols. "Should I not escort you?"

By this time, Elizabeth was running, heedless of whatever was said by the housekeeper. In the recesses of her mind, she could see images of a vengeful Mr. Collins entering her parents' bedchamber even now, his despicable actions leaving her and her sisters orphans. The need to return to her family was nigh overwhelming. Elizabeth ran.

The library was dark and cold, the fire having burnt down in the grate. The candle Darcy had had the presence of mind to take from his room provided scant light, its flickering casting shadows on the walls, undulating like some tortured ghosts. The room was deserted and quiet, though a wind had sprung up, howling outside, some ominous music wailing in tune with the beating of Darcy's heart.

"What do you hope to find?" asked Darcy of Fitzwilliam as his cousin began to look about the room.

"A passage in the walls, perhaps," said Fitzwilliam, his distraction causing him to murmur lowly. Darcy was forced to strain to hear him. "Light some of these candles," said Fitzwilliam, gesturing about the room to the candles in the sconces. "We will need some light to find what we are looking for."

Darcy did as he was bid and spoke at the same time. "Do you truly think there are passages in the walls?"

"It is possible," said Fitzwilliam absently. "Snowlock has them, as I am certain you remember. Some houses are positively rife with them."

Nodding, Darcy continued to light candles, and in a few moments, enough were shining on the room as to give them some light by which they could see. Then Darcy turned back to his cousin, who was surveying the room and speaking in a soft tone.

"Not on the outside wall. The inner wall, too, has not enough room to hide a passage." Fitzwilliam strode to the door on the side of the room and peered through it, nodding to himself as he did so. "This wall is also too narrow to accommodate a passage. Thus, if there is one, it could only be in this wall."

He spoke his last words pointing to the wall near where they had found Wickham. In that particular wall, the large fireplace was set and flanking it were two bookshelves, each taller than Darcy and almost as wide as he could spread his arms. Most of Bingley's small collection were resting on the shelves on the inner wall, leaving these cases almost bare.

"That would make sense, of course," said Fitzwilliam, speaking with what Darcy thought was an absence of mind. "It has bothered me since we found Wickham that he might have been taken unaware, even if he had fallen asleep. If the murderer was able to come upon him from behind, that would better explain it."

"There does not appear to be any break in the wallpaper," said Darcy, running his hands over the far side of the wall away from the fireplace. "Except for the obvious seams between the sheets. That would leave the bookcases."

Fitzwilliam nodded, though he had been inspecting a section near the outer wall. "Then the bookcases it is."

"This room is a disgrace," muttered Darcy. He began to run his hands along the sides of the bookshelf, searching for anything out of the ordinary. His cousin was doing the same with the other one.

"I assume you mean the lack of books here?" Fitzwilliam shook his head and chuckled. "Not everyone is as intent upon reading every book in the world as you are, Darcy."

"I am *not* intent upon reading every book," said Darcy, teasing his cousin with his lofty tone. "Only the good ones."

Fitzwilliam barked a laugh. "I fear there are far too many of those for you to read them all in one lifetime."

"You may be correct," said Darcy, far from perturbed. "But I shall do my best, regardless."

They did not speak for several moments, each concentrating on their task. The wood was cool to the touch and smooth, and as Darcy continued to search, he caught a hint of the scent of the polish which caused the wood to gleam. The grains were clear of dirt and other substances, free of dust, which prompted Darcy's approval—the housekeeper knew her business and took care to ensure that even unused pieces of furniture were cleaned regularly.

"Darcy. I think I have found something."

Darcy glanced at his cousin, to see him working at a section of the bookcase near the floor. Leaving his bookshelf, Darcy stepped forward, only to hear the click of a latch being released and see the shelf swing out an inch or two. There was naught but darkness beyond.

"It is hidden in the wood of the bottom shelf," explained Fitzwilliam.

He pulled the bookcase forward, and it swung on silent hinges, leaving a narrow corridor, shadowed and dusty. As Darcy grasped the candle in its holder, he noted that there were tracks in the dust— several tracks, both leading to and from the library. He quickly pointed them out to his cousin.

"The hinges are hidden well, too," said Fitzwilliam, gesturing to where they were situated behind the edge of the bookcase. "And they have been oiled recently, as they made no sound."

Fitzwilliam stooped and ran a finger along the lower hinge, his finger coming away with a line of dark liquid clinging to it. Darcy raised the candle, inspecting the walls and ceiling of the passage.

"I suspect cobwebs have been cleaned away too," said Darcy.

"Well, then," said Fitzwilliam turning a grin on Darcy. "Shall we?"

Nodding, Darcy stepped in, leading the way with his candle. It was not the first time he had walked such eerie steps. But he could not help the shudder which passed through him.

While Elizabeth had fled the kitchen, certain her father was about to be murdered in his bed, sanity soon set in, and she stopped to take stock of her situation. She still had no proof that Mr. Collins, of all people, was behind the recent deaths, and even if he was, if he had been able to murder her father in his bed, he would already have done so. For the moment, at least, Elizabeth thought her father was safe.

Of more immediate concern was her situation. The housekeeper had not followed through the halls, suggesting she had believed Elizabeth's lie concerning her father's presence in the library. Or been too shocked by Elizabeth's sudden departure to pursue her. But alone as she was in the house late at night, she knew it would be best to return to the kitchen, confess, and request an escort back to her room. But while she knew her father was likely safe, she was loath to allow even one minute's delay in returning to their rooms.

A look down the long hall in both directions informed Elizabeth that there was no one present, though she could not discount the possibility of one of the rooms being occupied. All was silent and still as the grave. A moment's more thought, and Elizabeth decided to return to her rooms on her own. That was when she saw the light.

It was ahead of her, and near the end of the hallway where the entrance hall was situated, and given it was on the left side toward the back of the house, Elizabeth knew it was the library. Given what had happened in the library only the previous night, Elizabeth was loath to be in the room alone. But her path back to her family's quarters led past that open door, and she was unwilling to be further delayed.

On light steps, determined not to alert whoever was in the room of her presence, Elizabeth crept forward. The soft sounds of her slipper-clad feet barely reached her ears, but sounding as loud as the thudding of her heart in her breast, both filling her ears so much she thought it a wonder it was not heard all the way to Meryton. Elizabeth clutched her dressing gown around her form, feeling the cold clamminess of her hands, her eyes peering this way and that in the gloom. But nothing moved, nothing stirred, and the closer she came to the open door, the more she could see from the light spilling out into the corridor.

After a brief hesitation, Elizabeth eased her way around the door frame, risking a glance inside the room which was lit by, perhaps, half the candles in the sconces. Other than the burning wicks, there did not seem to be anything at all in the room out of the ordinary. Frowning, her curiosity getting the better of her, Elizabeth crept forward a little further, her eyes darting this way and that, keeping to the balls of her feet, poised to flee at the first sign of hostility. But nothing greeted her questing gaze. The room was deserted.

And then she saw it. On the right side of the room stood two bookcases, one on either side of the massive fireplace which provided heat to the room. One of the bookcases, however, had swung aside, leaving the gaping maw of an opening visible behind it. It was a passage, narrow and completely hidden by the shelf when closed, but only just tall enough for Colonel Fitzwilliam to walk through without hitting his head on the ceiling.

Elizabeth stopped and frowned at what she was seeing, her mind whirling with possibilities. Whoever had opened it had neglected to close it, though whether that was due to forgetfulness or the knowledge that a swift retreat might be necessary, she could not say. But the existence of passages in the walls, of which Elizabeth had heard before, particularly in the novels Lydia and Kitty so enjoyed, would potentially provide unseen entrance into many rooms in the house. The implications were staggering.

In Elizabeth's defense, she knew it was best to depart, to leave the discovery and inform her father, who could rouse Mr. Darcy and Colonel Fitzwilliam to investigate. As she considered the opening before her, however, Elizabeth drifted forward, fascinated by what she was seeing. And as she was only a few steps away, she thought it would do no harm to look inside quickly and see if there was anything to be seen.

There was not. The inside of the passage was dusty, as she might have thought, but with footsteps both leading away and toward the library. There was no light emanating from within, for which Elizabeth was grateful, for it suggested there was no one approaching. As she did not fancy setting off down the passage herself, she turned to leave.

"Well, well, I must own that you have been clever. Unfortunately for you, too clever by half."

CHAPTER XXIV

*H*ad Darcy been a man who feared small, enclosed spaces, he might have found himself nervous in the passage he traversed with Fitzwilliam. His cousin would have it worse, as he was taller and wider than Darcy, a truly large man. It was, indeed, narrow, jagged edges of the rock of the walls protruding, to scratch and tear his clothing if he did not take care. It was also colder than the rooms of the house, a fact he attributed to the lack of a heat source, though he suspected the area behind the fireplace did receive some heat when it was lit.

When they entered in, they noted that the passage did not go far to the right, as it would intersect there with the inner wall of the hall beyond. Darcy considered the layout of the house, and he determined that the entrance hall was on the other side of the passage. The realization caused him to curse, given what had happened there only days before.

"What is it, Cousin?" asked Fitzwilliam. He glanced back at Darcy, his gaze filled with curiosity.

"I suspect this passage was used only two days ago," replied Darcy, still muttering to himself. "When Mr. Bennet and I were shot at, the culprit disappeared, and we could not even find any hint of him fleeing."

"Then it was an audacious attempt," said Fitzwilliam. "Whoever it was, he could not have lain in wait for you long, for if he had, he might have been discovered."

"He may have simply taken an opportunity which presented itself."

"Perhaps." Fitzwilliam shook his head and turned back toward the passage which yawned in front of them. "I do not dispute that this was likely the malefactor's escape method. I am only stating that whoever it is, he must have a deep well of nerve."

Darcy did nothing more than grunt. The other side of the corridor ended, turning to the left, while a set of stairs led up and to the right, ascending up into the gloom. Fitzwilliam turned and eyed Darcy, a question in his gaze. Darcy shrugged, and they made their way toward the stairs. As they approached, Darcy noted they were wood, dusty, and he eyed them dubiously, uncertain if they would bear the weight of two grown men the size of himself and Fitzwilliam.

"Come, Darcy," said Fitzwilliam, laughing as he looked back. "What is life without the spice of the unknown?"

"The unknown is all well and good," replied Darcy. "But I prefer not to discover that the stairs cannot hold us when we are halfway to the upper floor."

Fitzwilliam laughed in his usually nonchalant manner. "If we hesitate now, the mystery will go unsolved."

With a quick and determined step, Fitzwilliam approached the stairs and climbed a few experimental steps. Darcy noted the creaking and groaning of the stairs under his cousin's weight, but they seemed to be sturdier than they looked. But then Darcy's eyes fell on something gleaming in the light of the candle he held.

"Hold, Fitzwilliam," said Darcy. He took no note of his cousin, who turned and looked at him askance, and stepped down, reaching through the gap in between the stairs, grasping the item which lay just within reach of his outstretched fingers. It was a pistol.

Fitzwilliam let out a low whistle as he noticed what Darcy held, and he stepped down beside him to inspect it more closely. Darcy offered it up to him, knowing his cousin was more knowledgeable about such things.

"A smoothbore pistol, it seems," said Fitzwilliam, taking it from Darcy and turning it this way and that. "Not a newer pistol with rifling, but not ancient either. It seems like whoever used it did not wish to be discovered with it and, so, dropped it in a location where he thought it would remain hidden."

"Or if it *was* discovered, it would have no immediate connection to him." Darcy paused and considered. "The possession of this weapon seems to suggest our murderer came here with the intent to commit murder."

A nod was Fitzwilliam's response. "That is certainly possible, though not evidence, of course. But we still do not know who—the one intending to commit murder—nor do we know why."

"But we do know how he has been able to make his way through certain parts of the house without being seen."

"To that end," said Fitzwilliam, looking about in interest, "perhaps we should explore this level first."

Darcy agreed, and they set off, eschewing the stairs up for the time being. The corridor which now ran along the outer wall, descended a few steps until Darcy thought they were passing below the library windows along the back of the house. It ran the entire length of the house, with several branches back toward the middle, no doubt leading to doors such as the one through which they had just passed. The tracks in the dust were fewer in this part of the passage, but near the end, they discovered another answer to their long-held questions.

"I suspect this door leads to the corridor outside the kitchens," said Fitzwilliam, pausing in front of what appeared to be a door back to the main part of the house.

"Which suggests it was the means by which the killer reached the brandy Miss Bingley drank," replied Darcy.

"And the door shows signs of recent use."

They inspected the area for a few moments before they backtracked again to the stairs and took themselves to the upper floor of the house. There they found a long passage which seemed to go the entire length of the house. Netherfield was not truly large enough to have separate family and guest wings, but Miss Bingley had placed the newer arrivals—the Bennets and Lady Catherine and her daughter—on the opposite side of the stairs from where her brother inhabited the master's suite, and she and her sister also had apartments. It was strange, but Fitzwilliam had also been housed next to Darcy himself, though whether that presaged some intention on the lady's part to pursue him should Darcy prove impossible, Darcy could not say.

"The steps toward the master's chambers are fewer," said Fitzwilliam, pointing out the thick layer of dust which had been little disturbed.

"And more toward where Lady Catherine had her rooms," replied

Darcy, looking in the other direction.

Without speaking, they first went in the direction of Bingley's chambers. As the corridor was situated along the back of the house, he knew Bingley's suite, as well as that which had been occupied by Miss Bingley, had been on the back of the house, overlooking the gardens. Darcy pointed this out to Fitzwilliam as they walked and inspected.

"Then on the other side," said Fitzwilliam, "would be Mr. and Mrs. Bennet's suite, that of Lady Catherine, Anne, and then Mr. Collins, if I am not mistaken."

"And the Bennet sisters on the other side," replied Darcy. "Mr. and Mrs. Hurst are on the opposite side of the house close to Miss Bingley's chambers, and you are nearby them."

"There will be a similar passage on the front side of the house. And entrances from the first floor to the upper levels."

"Which means there is likely a similar hall running perpendicular to these long corridors on the opposite side of the house from the library."

"Well, there does not seem to be much to be seen here," said Fitzwilliam. "Though there *are* footsteps, it seems our ghost was only familiarizing himself with the layout of the house." Fitzwilliam bent forward and examined a door which stood in front of them, Miss Bingley's unless Darcy was incorrect. "This door does not appear to have been opened in many years."

"Then let us backtrack to the other side of the house."

They made their way back according to Darcy's suggestion. A little past the stairs they had climbed, they found an identical set leading down, confirming their suspicion that they were connected to passages on the lower level on the south side of the house. Beyond that, however, was where it became interesting.

"Mr. Bennet's door appears to be jammed," said Fitzwilliam, pointing to the rust on the hinges, so thick that Darcy thought them to be immovable. "And the tracks outside Mr. Bennet's door are thick." Then Fitzwilliam gestured to damage to the door itself. "It appears whoever did this lost his temper on at least one occasion, for there are some chips in the mortar in the back, where someone struck the door repeatedly."

Darcy frowned. "Is this not *Mrs.* Bennet's door? I am certain her room is closer to the stairs than Mr. Bennet is."

"Ah, but look at the distance we have traversed from the stairs," said Fitzwilliam, his gaze back down the corridor drawing Darcy's own eyes. "I suspect that as the rooms are joined, there is no door to

Mrs. Bennet's bedchamber."

Comprehension filled Darcy's mind. "Then the next chamber should be Lady Catherine's."

A grim nod was Fitzwilliam's reply. He continued, and they soon stood in front of the door to Lady Catherine's room. The dust and cobwebs had been disturbed, indicating someone had used it.

"I think we have discovered the killer's means of entrance," said Fitzwilliam. "And if you look at the tracks, they continue to be heavy from here toward the southern end of the house."

Darcy nodded, feeling rather bleak himself. He pushed past Fitzwilliam and continued to follow the tracks, certain he knew what he would find. His supposition turned out to be correct.

"Most of the tracks come from this room, Fitzwilliam," said he quietly. "There are a few which continue toward Wickham's room, but the majority lead to this room."

"Mr. Collins?" queried Fitzwilliam with disgust. "Of all those in residence, I would have expected him to be our killer the least. The man is obsequious and seems to be afraid of his own shadow."

"Anyone can wear a mask before the world," said Darcy, thinking of his own situation. "Do we enter and confront him in his room?"

"No," replied Fitzwilliam. "Let us go down below. I would prefer to have a few sturdy footmen at my back when we challenge him."

Darcy allowed that his cousin's plan was prudent, and they made their way back toward the stairs.

The sound of a voice behind her startled Elizabeth, and she whirled about, her heart pounding loudly in her ears. Every fear she had harbored of being caught in the house with no one else about rushed into her mind, and along with the beating of her heart, she could hear the rush of air, as if she was caught in a gale. There, near the door through which she had entered, stood a man, watching her, a sneering sort of smirk directed at her.

It was Mr. Collins. The last man she wished to corner her in that room.

"My dear, Cousin," said he, in what she was certain was a mocking tone, "why are you wandering the halls late at night with no escort? If I was not already certain of your character, I might have thought it was *you* who was bedeviling us these past days."

"I could not sleep and thought to obtain some tea from the kitchens," said Elizabeth. She shifted slightly to the side, putting a chair between herself and Mr. Collins, a motion he did not seem to notice. "As I was returning to my rooms, I saw a light and thought to investigate."

Mr. Collins's eyes glittered as he watched her, his eyes darting between Elizabeth and the open door of the passage. He strolled a little further into the room, his movements casual and unthreatening. With Elizabeth's epiphany, everything this man did was now suspect, and she did not believe his nonchalance for a moment. The most disturbing thing about him, however, was his behavior. It was not the Mr. Collins she knew and detested. There was nothing of servility about him; his continual bowing was absent, and even his condescending tone when speaking was lacking. He was cold, his ice-like eyes watching her with amusement, disdain shining in their depths.

"It seems you have discovered something, indeed," said Mr. Collins, gesturing toward the passage. "I had no notion you would make such a discovery, or that you even suspected there were passages in the walls. Tell me, Cousin: how did you work it out?"

At once Elizabeth realized Mr. Collins thought *she* had opened the door, which meant that someone else *had*. If he had opened it and left it open himself, why would he think that she had? Hope surged in Elizabeth's breast. Someone was investigating those passages even now! If she could stall him long enough, maybe help would come to her.

"It truly was not difficult," said Elizabeth. Now that she thought on the matter, she wondered why she had not considered the possibility before. "Whoever had access to Lady Catherine must have been able to move unseen. Furthermore, when the killer shot at my father and Mr. Darcy, he could not be located—they did not even manage to catch sight of him."

A sage nod was Mr. Collins's response, and Elizabeth was again struck by how different he was acting from what she was accustomed. "How perspicacious of you, my dear cousin. It is, unfortunately, a miscalculation. Your father should not have educated you in the manner in which he did, a mistake for which you shall pay dearly. But do not worry, Cousin Elizabeth, for he will soon be joining you."

"You *have* been trying to murder him!!" accused Elizabeth.

"Murder is not a nice word at all, Cousin," said Mr. Collins, his tone chiding. "I have merely attempted to take what is my own."

"Your own?" demanded Elizabeth. She warily watched the man for any movement. For now, however, he seemed to content to exchange words with her. "What could my father possibly have that you would wish to own so much that you would kill him over it?"

"Why, Longbourn, of course!" said Mr. Collins, as if it were the most obvious thing in the world. "I have lived in squalor long enough. It is time for me to take my rightful place among the elite of society."

"You are delusional! Not only have you killed *four* others instead of my father, but Longbourn is not rightfully yours. And now it will *never* be yours!"

"Oh, I assure you, it will."

"Do you not think it will be suspicious if my father suddenly dies? Especially given the events of the past few days?"

Mr. Collins laughed, a cruel, harsh sound which grated on Elizabeth's ears. "Who would suspect me?" asked Mr. Collins rhetorically. "I am the lowly parson, the toadying twit who cannot speak without praising those of a higher sphere. I assure you, Cousin Elizabeth, that once I have closed the door to the passage, no one will ever suspect me. Of course, you will predecease your father. I am certain I can make it appear to be an accident."

"I doubt it," replied Elizabeth, a fierce will to fight and live welling up within her. "Do you think I shall make it easy for you?"

"It matters not what you do, Cousin. I am far larger and stronger. I shall do what I must."

When he began to move toward her, Elizabeth ducked to the side, putting a sofa between her and Mr. Collins. He laughed at her efforts to elude him but Elizabeth, still thinking of the open door, grasped at anything to stall him for a few more precious moments.

"I must own that I am shocked to learn that you killed Lady Catherine." Elizabeth smiled thinly at him. "The way you venerated and praised her to the heavens, I would have thought you incapable of it."

A shadow crossed Mr. Collins's face. "Lady Catherine was not mean to die," was his short reply.

"Then why did you kill her?"

"It was supposed to be my cousin. I heard him arguing with Lady Catherine, laying claim to the room he and his ridiculous wife were using. Naturally, I assumed that she would carry her point as she always does."

"So you killed her, thinking that she was my father?" asked Elizabeth, incredulous hilarity in her tone catching his attention. "You did not even think to confirm who your target was? And did you not see the difference between a lady and a gentleman when she lay sleeping before you?"

"The room was dark!" said Mr. Collins, his tone defensive.

"In other words, no," replied Elizabeth in a scornful tone. "Can I assume that Miss Bingley and the butler were also a case of you missing your mark?"

"The butler looked like your father from behind in the dark," said Mr. Collins. "And how was I to know that Miss Bingley drank a man's drink?"

"Again, you assumed," replied Elizabeth, fixing the man with a glare of disdain. "Had you murdered my father, you would have brought sorrow on his family, but at least it would have spared the rest of the company. Can I assume Mr. Wickham was also an error?"

"No," was Mr. Collins's short reply. "The man had the temerity to attempt to extort money from me in exchange for his silence. He soon learned that I am not to be trifled with."

"Oh, indeed you are," replied Elizabeth. She glared at him with no little contempt. "You must be the most inept marksman in the history of the world, sir. You caught Mr. Wickham because he was overconfident, and I can only assume that was your failing as well. Even now you have killed four, and yet your true mark is still alive and well."

Mr. Collins's eyes glittered with anger and hate. But when he spoke, it was with the same conversational tone he had used to this point.

"It truly is a shame, Elizabeth. I had intended you to be my wife when I become the master of Longbourn."

"And you think I would marry the man who murdered my beloved father?"

"You would never know. You would have lived your life in ignorance and been happy."

"I could never be happy with *you*,' spat Elizabeth. "Even if you were not a murderer, you are a disgusting, loathsome man. I had not known you for five minutes before I knew I would die rather than marry you."

"Then you shall have your wish." Mr. Collins grinned. "I shall take your eldest sister to wife. She is much more beautiful and compliant than you."

"She will marry Mr. Bingley."

"Oh, I think not. If the gentleman persists, why, I may deal with him too."

"You disgusting worm!"

In a flash, Mr. Collins lunged for her, and Elizabeth slipped nimbly to the side. He overturned with the sofa, going over it in a heap, but for a man as large as he, he proved to be agile, as he immediately shot to his feet. Elizabeth was already moving, past the open door and around the chair toward the fireplace with Mr. Collins almost on her heels.

Desperate for something with which to defend herself, Elizabeth spied the fireplace poker in its stand, and she grasped the handle as she felt the tug on her dress. The tug became a hard heave. Elizabeth stumbled. With the poker in hand, Elizabeth turned and with a cry brought it down with all the strength she could muster.

It was the sound of voices which drew Darcy up short. The stifled oath from his companion as he attempted to avoid him drew Darcy's attention, and he held up a hand for silence.

"What is it?"

"There are voices in the library," said Darcy, whispering.

They crept forward, careful to avoid making any sound. As they came closer, Darcy could hear the high tones of a woman, and the voice deeper of a man, but he was still unable to make out who it was.

Then the sound of a crash of falling furniture reached Darcy's ears, with the tapping of light feet fleeing in panic. With a roar, Darcy surged forward, darting the rest of the way down the corridor, Fitzwilliam on his heels. He gained the door and dashed into the room, just in time to see a man clutch at Miss Elizabeth's nightgown. She screamed in defiance and brought a fireplace poker down on his head. Mr. Collins dropped to the floor and lay still.

"Miss Elizabeth!" exclaimed Darcy, dashing forward.

Her wild eyes rose and met his, and she raised the poker in a defensive gesture. And then she seemed to realize who he was, and she slumped, the poker falling from her limp hand. Darcy reached out and caught her as she was sinking to the floor, cradling her to his breast. She sobbed once, twice, and then let out a shuddering breath before falling quiet. It was highly improper for her to be in his arms like she was, but she did not protest. Darcy never wished to let go.

The sound of movement nearby caught Darcy's attention, and he looked up, pulling Miss Elizabeth to the side, a more protective position. But Mr. Collins had not moved—it was Fitzwilliam.

"It seems you are seeing to Miss Elizabeth's comfort," said Fitzwilliam, his wry tone understated, given the events of the past few moments. "Watch him. I will return with the butler, a couple of lads, and some good, stout rope."

Darcy replied with a curt nod. Then Fitzwilliam departed, leaving

Darcy watching Mr. Collins while supporting the precious bundle on his lap. Within a few moments, Miss Elizabeth began to stir, and she pulled away from him, looking into his eyes.

"You were exploring the passages?" asked she.

"Yes," replied Darcy. "Fitzwilliam suspected their existence, given Wickham's death. We found them not more than fifteen minutes ago. How did you learn of them?"

"I came across the room only a few moments after you left. I had gone to the kitchens to speak with the housekeeper?"

"Late at night and alone?" asked Darcy, his tone chiding. "Did you not quench your thirst for adventure the last time you attempted such a thing?"

Though her cheeks bloomed, Miss Elizabeth was not intimidated. "Perhaps you are correct. But I learned that not only had my father also requested spirits to be delivered to his room the night Miss Bingley was poisoned, but he had argued with Lady Catherine over her demand he give up his room to her."

Those were facts Darcy had not known. He was impressed that this woman had managed to piece so much of the mystery together.

"We found steps in the passageways," replied he. "Most could be seen leading to and from Mr. Collins's room. In particular, he attempted to get into your father's room from the passage but was unable because the door was stuck."

Miss Elizabeth shuddered. "Then my father survived by the purest chance, and others have suffered in our stead." She turned her eyes to where the form of Mr. Collins was still prone on the floor. "He confessed to it all."

"How so?" asked Darcy.

With a sigh, Darcy listened as Miss Elizabeth recounted her conversation with Mr. Collins, and Darcy marveled over again. This woman was fashioned with uncommon mettle. Not only had she kept the man who was intent on killing her speaking to learn his secrets, but she had successfully defended herself when the man had made the attempt. What a marvelous woman she was!

"He shall never harm another, Miss Elizabeth," said Darcy. "You have discovered the secret and have rendered a horrible man helpless to avoid meeting his destiny. Do not concern yourself with your father's fortunate survival for he is safe. I am glad of it."

They heard the sound of others approaching. Seeming to realize the compromising position they were in, Miss Elizabeth stood and straightened her nightgown. Darcy also rose, though feeling bereft of her presence. Fitzwilliam entered the room, followed by the butler and two large footmen. In a trice, they had Mr. Collins bound hand and foot, and Fitzwilliam deposited him, none too gently, into the chair which had been found by the body of the unfortunate Wickham.

"Now," said Fitzwilliam, glaring at a moaning Mr. Collins. "Perhaps we shall obtain some answers."

Chapter XXV

The situation at Netherfield Park improved the following morning, though it could not be said that all was well. The terror of the previous days could not be undone, even with the capture of the murderer who had taken so many of them. But the mood was not quite so oppressive, a matter which was reflected in the weather. Though the clouds still hung low and sullen over the estate, the constant rain and snow had ceased, and the air held a hint of warmth in it which had been absent since several days before the ball.

The ball was a time which, it seemed to those in residence, had been a lifetime before! It was the last truly happy time many of them could remember. There were some among their number who were more resilient, having discovered thoughts and feelings which would blossom over the coming months and years. Still, there was not one among them who had not lost one of their number. Even the Bennets, who had emerged unscathed in their immediate family, understood they were to lose Mr. Collins. And while he was now roundly despised and had not been known to them before his coming in the days before the ball, he was still, in some undefinable way, family. His days were numbered on the face of the land.

Elizabeth felt so very tired, and it was not all due to having been awake most of the night. Mr. Darcy had personally delivered her to her family's rooms early that morning before he and Colonel Fitzwilliam interrogated Mr. Collins, and her father had not been happy to see her. Or perhaps it was correct he was grateful she had returned to him, while his annoyance for her disobedience and the danger in which she had put herself was made known to her without a hint of a doubt.

"It seems I might have been remiss in my indulgence of you, Lizzy," said he, as he pushed her away from his embrace, his eyes suspiciously bright. Mr. Darcy had already gone, and Mr. Bennet, in his realization she had been at great risk, had crushed her to his breast, leaving her feeling cherished and bruised at the same time.

"You have always been the most intelligent and the most level-headed of my daughters, Lizzy. But in this instance, I must wonder at your impetuosity."

"I am sorry, Papa," replied Elizabeth. "It appears I have been headstrong."

Mr. Bennet's raised eyebrow told Elizabeth exactly what he thought of her admission, and it prompted her to laugh. Soon, her father joined her, though his laughter was tinged with a hint of hysteria.

"Please, Elizabeth," said Mr. Bennet after their emotion had run its course, "exercise better judgment in the future. My old heart is not prepared to be shocked like I was when you returned."

"I promise, I shall," replied Elizabeth, favoring him with a wan smile. "Should I ever have occasion to be trapped in a house with a murderer, I shall lock the door and refuse to show myself."

Mr. Bennet barked a laugh. "I am happy to hear it, Lizzy."

So saying, Mr. Bennet led her back into the room where her mother and sisters were still sleeping and saw her settled on her cot. Then he returned to his bed for the remainder of the night. Quiet reigned over them once again. But while Elizabeth was in her bed, it did not follow that she spent a restful night. The attack she had fought off still preyed on her mind, and she knew it would continue to haunt her dreams, to say nothing of the horror of the experiences they had all endured. Indeed, it would be many months before the scars were healed enough for any of them to return to themselves.

The following morning, Mr. Darcy and Colonel Fitzwilliam roused them all from their rooms, promising they were safe and requested their attendance in the sitting-room to explain what they had found. It turned out it was little less than a demand, for even Miss de Bourgh and Mrs. Hurst, both of whom had not emerged from their chambers in days, were persuaded to join them. It was the first time they had all been together since Lady Catherine had been taken from them.

As she sat in that room with the rest of the company, Elizabeth attempted to assess the mood of those around her. They were all solemn, even her youngest sisters being affected by all that had happened. Miss de Bourgh was contemplative, Mrs. Hurst dull and uncaring, Mrs. Bennet relieved, and the gentlemen a mix of relieved and angry.

"You have discovered who is behind these events?" asked Mr. Hurst when they were all present.

Mrs. Hurst, who had seemed unaware of what was happening around her, looked up at the two gentlemen, the light of zeal in her eyes. "You have? Tell me at once!"

"Louisa," said Mr. Hurst, his tone soothing, "let us listen to them, shall we?"

"Tell me at once!" demanded Louisa. "Where is he?"

"I will not allow you to see him, Louisa," said Mr. Hurst. Her unwilling eyes found her husband, and he locked his gaze with hers. "Put aside this need for vengeance. I understand you were close to your sister, but revenge will not bring her back to you. I will not allow you to become the same as the one who took her from you."

While Mrs. Hurst glared at her husband for several moments, soon she wilted, and tears began streaming from her eyes. She sagged against him, and he drew her close, offering comfort and support. Then he looked up at Mr. Darcy and nodded, a clear indication that he should proceed. Elizabeth, who had never seen the man appear anything other than dull and uncaring, looked at him through new eyes. She had never held any great opinion of Mrs. Hurst, but she was suffering, and Elizabeth was happy she had her husband's support to help her through what must be a difficult time.

There was little to do but inform them of the situation, which Mr. Darcy did without hesitation. "Last night, Fitzwilliam and I discovered through various means that it is Mr. Collins who has been preying on us." Elizabeth noted his slight nod to her father and knew they had agreed Elizabeth's name would be kept from the rest of the company, as much as possible.

"We do not know everything, but we have pieced together a series of events and motivations for Mr. Collins's actions." Mr. Darcy turned a stern eye on them all. "I should not think I need to warn you, but I will be explicit: though this will need to be disseminated in court against Mr. Collins, as much of it as possible should be kept from society, lest our reputations all suffer."

So saying, Mr. Darcy explained the entire matter to them, including the progression of victims, the methods Mr. Collins had used and the outcomes of his attempts. Soon there were many shaking heads, as the company became aware of the man's bungled attempts to kill her father.

"A member of *your* family killed *my* sister," said Mrs. Hurst, as she glared at all Bennets once Mr. Darcy fell silent. "And in trying to kill your father, we are made to suffer when our only fault was to offer you shelter when you required it."

"Louisa," said Mr. Bingley, his tone chiding, "apportion blame to the one who deserves it—Mr. Collins. The Bennets are not at fault. They were just as much at risk as anyone else."

"I am sorry for your loss, Mrs. Hurst," added Mr. Bennet. "It *was* my cousin who took your sister from you, and for that, I cannot apologize enough."

"I will repeat," said Mr. Bingley. "It was not your fault, sir. I am certain Louisa will acknowledge this in time."

"Her resentment is understandable, Mr. Bingley," replied Mr. Bennet. "I do not take offense, for I know I might feel the same in her situation."

Mrs. Hurst sniffed in disdain and turned away, but at least she fell silent. Mr. Darcy, who had remained silent during the exchange, spoke up again to solicit any questions, and for a time he explained, to the best of his ability, anything they had not misunderstood.

"It is unfortunate, indeed," said Mr. Bennet, shaking his head in remorse. "It might not have quelled the gossip entirely had Mr. Collins perished, but it would be better than what we all face now with a trial for murder upcoming. I fear society will not be kind to us, regardless of our innocence in this matter."

"Heavens!" exclaimed Mrs. Bennet. "Whatever shall we do, Mr. Bennet? We will be shunned in Meryton! Our girls will never make good matches!"

"Mr. Collins's connection to you was distant, and he was unknown in Meryton," said Mr. Darcy. "This should allow you to escape the worst of the censure. It will not protect you from all gossip, but it would be worse if he were known to be one of the neighborhood."

Elizabeth watched her mother as she listened to Mr. Darcy's words. Mrs. Bennet was a flighty woman, one given to nerves and other such maladies, which Elizabeth had often thought were nothing more than her imagination. She did not think her mother would take it well, the first time she was subjected to the gossip of others.

But only time would tell in what form it would take. The Bennets had always had a good reputation in the neighborhood. Perhaps that would protect them to a certain extent.

Soon the party broke up, the Hursts returning to their rooms, while the others took themselves away, either to take time to themselves or to speak in whispered voices. Even the youngest girls remained largely quiet, the gravity of the situation affecting them as it did anyone else. Anne rose at the same time, Elizabeth assumed to return to her rooms. She hesitated, however, and after a moment's thought turned and approached Elizabeth.

"Elizabeth," said she in a soft voice, sitting by Elizabeth's side, "I wish you to know that I do not hold your family at fault for Mr. Collins's actions."

"Thank you, Anne," replied Elizabeth, accepting the other woman's offered embrace. Elizabeth did not know to what extent Anne was affected by her mother's death, but she was relieved her family had been exonerated.

"I do think much of you," said Anne, pulling away and directing a serious look at her. "We have not known each other long, but I hope we are able to put this behind us and become friends."

"I hope so too, Anne," replied Elizabeth. "I assume you will return to Kent with your cousins and your mother as soon as you can travel?"

Anne shot a look at her cousins, who were in earnest conversation with each other. "I have not spoken with them yet, but I assume we shall."

"Then I wish you Godspeed, my friend," replied Elizabeth.

They spoke for some few more moments before Anne excused herself to return to her rooms. Elizabeth was left in the company of her family and the gentlemen, Mr. Bingley also having left with the Hursts, no doubt to make his own preparations to return with his sister to his ancestral home. Jane sat nearby, immersed in her thoughts, and Elizabeth could not help but feel for her sister. Before Mr. Collins and his perfidy had come into their lives, she had never seen a more promising inclination. Now, she supposed, it would all come to naught.

With the improving weather, the roads became passable, first to horses, then to a carriage, and as such, contact with the outside world was re-established. First footmen were sent to the militia encampment to inquire about Lieutenant Wickham. The returning visit by Colonel

Forster was surprising in some ways, and less surprising in others.

"Wickham has been here all this time?" asked the colonel, almost the first words out of the man's mouth when he dismounted and entered Netherfield. "What in the blazes was he doing here?"

"He claimed you had sent him here, and his fellows to the other estates of the area," said Fitzwilliam. They had agreed he would take the lead, speaking one colonel to another. "He said you were concerned for the welfare of the people of Meryton when the Bennets did not return to Longbourn after the ball."

"I have a healthy respect for those who possess the rank of gentleman," said the colonel. "We have all experienced bad weather and know how to ride it out. I was not even aware the Bennets were missing."

Darcy and Fitzwilliam shared a glance. But Colonel Forster was not finished speaking.

"Wickham has been missing since that night. I had assumed he had deserted, though I could find no reason why he would do so."

"I believe he did, after a fashion," replied Fitzwilliam. "I have no notion what kept him at Netherfield, but it seems he sensed an opportunity here and acted accordingly."

"Then I believe I desire to see my lieutenant," said the colonel. "I believe there is, at the very least, time in the stockade in his future."

"I am afraid we cannot comply," said Darcy breaking into the discussion. "There are certain events about which you are not familiar."

When Darcy had explained what had happened at Netherfield, the colonel's silence for several minutes after the communication revealed his utter shock. When he finally did speak, his words were not what Darcy might have expected.

"It seems Wickham paid for his actions in a manner none of us might have expected."

"Given the kind of man he was, it is unsurprising to me he should end in such a way," muttered Fitzwilliam.

"We have called the magistrate," said Darcy. "Once he has been informed, and the constable has taken Mr. Collins away, we will, of course, release Mr. Wickham's remains to you."

The colonel shook off his shock and said: "Would you not, perhaps, prefer to inter him next to his father? He is also deceased, as I understand."

"That is true," replied Darcy. "I suppose I could arrange for it."

"I understand he was not a friend, sir," said Colonel Forster.

"No, he had long since lost all claim to such ties. But in memory of his father and mine, I am willing to do this."

The colonel nodded and soon departed. The next visitor was more difficult. Sir William Lucas was a jovial man, and though Darcy thought him more than a little silly, he had no true ill feelings for the man. When they explained the matter to him, his shock was akin to what the colonel's had been.

"This is most . . ." stammered the man. "Well, what I mean is . . ." Sir William sighed and looked to Mr. Bennet, who they had summoned due to his long acquaintance with the gentleman. "I sympathize with you, Bennet. Who could have thought your cousin was such a man as this?"

"Not I, to be sure," said Mr. Bennet. "I rather thought him far too silly for rational thought, let alone a proclivity for such heinous acts."

"Er . . . I suppose that is so." Sir William paused. "I suppose we must call the constable. Meryton is too small, but the constable from Stevenage may be called to transport Mr. Collins to the gaol there."

"That would be for the best," said Mr. Bennet. "The sooner he is removed from the neighborhood, the better."

Sir William gave a distracted nod. "Yes, I suppose that would be for the best. You and your family will have my support and that of Lucas Lodge. Though there will be whispers, I am sure you have apprehended, I know you were not at fault. Between us, hopefully, we can stem the tide of gossip."

"Thank you, my friend," was Mr. Bennet's heartfelt reply.

The constable arrived the next day, and Mr. Collins was escorted away. Though he had proven himself not to be a stupid man, he was also revealed to be a coward, for he departed, whimpering in fear, obviously understanding what his likely fate was to be. When he caught sight of Darcy and Mr. Bennet, watching him with implacable loathing, he attempted to break away and throw himself at their feet.

"Have mercy upon me, Cousin!" wailed Mr. Collins, pulling against the constable and his two burly deputies.

Mr. Bennet replied with a sardonic laugh. "I assure you, Collins, that I have none to offer. And even if I was, you have taken a family member of these two men, and another of our host. You will pay for your crimes."

"No!" screamed Mr. Collins. "I beg of you!"

By that time, the men had dragged Mr. Collins out, his gibbering sobs echoing back through the door. Soon he was enclosed in the prison cart, which pitched into motion, throwing him against the back bars. He continued to wail and plead with them, but none of the men gathered said anything. Within a few moments, the cart had pulled from sight.

"In the end, he is nothing more than a coward and not nearly so clever as he believes himself to be," said Fitzwilliam. "Even if we all spoke in his favor, he could no more avoid his fate than had he had wings to fly away to safety."

"We will all be required to appear at his trial," said Darcy. He turned to Mr. Bennet. "Have you any notion of when that will be?"

"I am not certain when the next assizes will be held," replied Mr. Bennet, rubbing his chin in thought. "Not likely until the New Year, I suspect."

"Sooner would be better," remarked Fitzwilliam.

"It will give him plenty of time to consider his misdeeds," said Darcy.

The other men grunted, and the subject was dropped. The very next day saw the first members of the party depart, for Bingley was for the north with the Hursts. Little was spoken between them, Bingley giving Darcy thanks for his role in solving the mystery. He also spent some few moments speaking with Miss Bennet in earnest, but Darcy had no desire to hear the results of that conversation. Given the serenity in Miss Bennet's countenance, she was not overly distressed by his going. Then again, she had always been rather inscrutable, and Darcy could not say how much he trusted his observation of her.

At the same time, the Bennets were preparing to return to their own home, as were Darcy and Fitzwilliam to return Anne and their aunt to Kent. Darcy watched Miss Elizabeth, thinking back on the time they had spent together, their joint attempts to solve the puzzle, her laughter and spirit. He knew he was in a fair way to being in love with her. As their departure approached, Darcy found that he was less willing to allow her to leave without some words passing between them. Thus, he used a moment when she stood alone to approach her with the intention of informing her of his feelings.

The smile with which she greeted him set his heart to soaring, and he bowed, saying: "It seems we are destined to part at present, Miss Bennet."

Her gaze clouded over a little at his words, and she nodded. "We must."

"I have obligations to my family," said Darcy. "I must inform my uncle of his sister's death and see Anne installed at Rosings as its new mistress. However," continued he, hoping she caught the expressive look he was directing at her, "just because we must part now, does not mean that parting must be of long duration. The mores of our society say I must mourn my aunt for three months. I will be half-mourning in six weeks."

Miss Elizabeth nodded, seeming to understand what he was trying to say to her. "It is, of course, necessary for you to show your respect for your mother's sister."

"Yes," replied Darcy. "This stricture must be adhered to, regardless of how trying I found the woman."

They shared a shaken head and commiserating smile, Darcy knowing how much Elizabeth had been targeted by Lady Catherine's insistence concerning his marriage prospects. Though he would not have wished to gain his freedom from such continual pressure by Lady Catherine's death, he was forced to conclude he was finding his freedom rather liberating.

"I shall be required to return for the trial, and Sir William has my direction to keep me apprised of that. But I have a more personal reason to return."

"You do?" was her arch reply. The corners of her lips rose, and the sight made him wish he could kiss her senseless if only to stop her teasing. Instead, he contented himself with assuring her of his regard.

"I have created a connection with a young lady of the neighborhood, one forged in trial, but sweeter for all we have endured. I should very much wish to continue that association, to call on that young lady when I return to the area."

"If you so wish it, Mr. Darcy," replied she, "I am certain she would be the happy recipient of your attentions."

"Thank you, Miss Elizabeth. When the time is appropriate, you may expect my company at Longbourn."

"I await that day with bated breath, sir."

EPILOGUE

$\mathcal{A}$s expected, the events which occurred at Netherfield Park those few days were on the tongues of every local gossip within days after the parties had departed it, leaving the manor empty and forbidding. While the Bennets were affected by the whispers of society, and some gleefully pointed out that it had been a Bennet relation who had been responsible for the murders, the more sensible among them held that the Bennets could not be held responsible for the actions of a man who had not been known to them, after all, before his unexpected arrival.

That did not stop certain comments, often within the family's hearing, or the whispered conversations which sprung up wherever they went. For the most part, the family accepted this change with philosophy, comforting themselves in the knowledge that they had truly done nothing wrong. The first few times they were subjected to such behavior, however, were trying, particularly for Mrs. Bennet, who had enjoyed a sort of reputation in the neighborhood by virtue of her position as wife to one of the most prominent gentlemen, as well as her reputation for being a consummate hostess.

"You appear to be taking Mrs. Goulding's incivility with patience, Lizzy," observed Charlotte Lucas one of the first times this had happened. They were attending the annual Christmas party only a few weeks after the events. Though Elizabeth had not been close enough to hear what had passed between the two women, she had noticed her mother stalking away from the other lady, her back stiff with affront.

At first, Elizabeth made mention of her ignorance of the particulars of the matter, but when Charlotte persisted, she could only shrug. "People will say what they wish, Charlotte. It will do little good for me to be offended every time someone alludes to it."

"Your mother should adopt a little of your philosophy," said Charlotte.

Elizabeth shook her head and watched her mother, who was now sitting close to Mr. Bennet, listening to whatever he was telling her. She suspected that her father was repeating the gist of what Elizabeth was currently engaged in telling Charlotte.

"Unfortunately, I cannot expect my mother to allow such slights to pass unanswered," replied Elizabeth. "You know how she is. She will almost certainly respond in kind when she hears such comments."

"I suppose you are correct," replied Charlotte. "It *is* unfortunate. For it will only make matters worse."

In time, after talk had died down, Elizabeth noted her mother did, indeed, begin to develop some ability to ignore when something was said. But that ability would depart whenever challenged, and she would respond in kind. There was no changing Mrs. Bennet, so the rest of the family simply adopted the practice of protecting her from it as much as they could. As for the sisters, they found they faced little overt censure, as their friends were, as a rule, much less inclined to meanness than the matrons.

Mr. Collins was tried at the next assizes in Stevenage and was found guilty of murdering the four people who had been staying at the estate. The women were not required to testify, for which they were all grateful. Mr. Bennet attended, of course, as did Sir William. Mr. Darcy and Colonel Fitzwilliam testified and ensured that Mr. Collins received the full penalty of the law in response to his actions. He was hanged only a few days later. The account Mr. Bennet bore back to his family was a surprise to no one, knowing that whatever cleverness and bravado the man had possessed, he was naught but a coward.

"You will be interested to know what your brother Phillips has discovered regarding the disposition of Longbourn," said Mr. Bennet one night when the family was sitting at dinner. It was only a few days after the trial of the insidious Mr. Collins. "As you know, I commissioned him to perform a search, as per the terms of the entail, for another heir of my great grandfather's line."

"And what did he discover?" asked Mrs. Bennet. While it was clear she was interested, she seemed almost fearful, for the entail was still a matter of great evil for Mrs. Bennet, especially given how Mr. Collins had turned out and how she might have been put in the man's power. The fact that Mr. Darcy and Mr. Bingley had not yet returned—ignoring the fact that both would still be in mourning for their family members—led to worry of her daughters all ending as old maids.

"Do not be cast down, Mrs. Bennet," said her husband, and Elizabeth detected a hint of actual compassion for her. "I believe this is good news. There are, in fact, no more living heirs of my great-grandfather. In short, there is no one to inherit Longbourn, and consequently, no one to cast you into the hedgerows when I leave this mortal life."

Mrs. Bennet blinked, her confusion showing in her stare at her husband. "Then who will inherit?"

"As there are no further heirs, the entail is broken, and the estate becomes mine to do with as I see fit. As I have no sons and no intention of breaking Longbourn up to leave to all my daughters, I shall instead leave it to my eldest daughter. Then when she marries, the estate will be the property of Jane and her husband and shall pass to their eldest son, or to another, however they see fit."

A gasp escaped Mrs. Bennet's lips, and she stared the length of the table, tears forming in the corners of her eyes. "I will not be required to leave my home?"

"No, my dear," replied Mr. Bennet, a tender note in his voice and in the look he bestowed upon his wife. "Longbourn is now *ours*, is not entailed, and will be your home for as long as you live, or as long as you wish it. You may put your fears of the entail to rest, for they no longer have any power over you."

Though her posture never altered, Elizabeth thought her mother sagged with relief, as tears streamed down her face. Dinner was finished largely in silence, even her youngest sisters realizing something momentous had just happened. Mrs. Bennet retired soon after dinner that night, but when she emerged the next morning, she was not a changed woman. She remained ever after silly, prone to gossip, and possessing only the faintest grasp of proper behavior. But the edge of her manic nervousness had been removed, and all her children found her much easier to tolerate. Even her husband found himself drawn from his library more often and was heard to say more than once that the companion of his early marriage had returned to him. But that was not the end of the changes for the Bennet family.

As he had promised Elizabeth, Mr. Darcy's horse was spied riding up Longbourn's fine driveway one afternoon not long after his official mourning was complete. Elizabeth, who had thought about the gentleman much in the months of his absence, was happy to receive him. Her sisters, or the observant ones, watched her with amusement, while those less observant were surprised. He was given a cordial welcome as one befitting his status—that being a suitor to one of Mrs. Bennet's daughters, which even she soon recognized. Between him and Elizabeth, the chance for a private discourse was requested and soon obtained, and they walked Longbourn's back lawn in earnest discussion.

"How are all your family, Mr. Darcy?" asked Elizabeth as soon as she had the chance.

"All well," replied he. "Fitzwilliam is, as I am sure you suspect, the same as ever. He has been assigned to a general's staff in London, which has made his mother happy, as it removes him from the likelihood of being assigned to the front. Though he has not caught the eye of any young lady yet, it seems to me he is cutting a swath through the young heiresses. Perhaps my aunt's wish will be granted this year."

"And Anne? How is she coping without her mother?"

"With a great deal of relief," replied Darcy. "She misses Lady Catherine, but I have spent several weeks there with her, reviewing the operation of Rosings. We have corrected some issues which bedeviled her mother's management of the estate and put an excellent steward in place. The new parson is a man of God, and she has the support of her family. I believe she will do very well."

"I am happy to hear it," replied Elizabeth quietly.

"Your family is all well, I presume?"

"Yes," replied Elizabeth, shooting him a smile. "We are all very well, indeed."

She explained to him some of the changes the Bennets had undergone during the past months, not excepting the news concerning the entail and how her mother had received it. Mr. Darcy was congratulatory as was proper, though they both felt keenly the sorrow which had occasioned those changes.

"Has it been very difficult for your family in Meryton?" asked Mr. Darcy.

"Not very," replied Elizabeth. "There were comments made at first, but most seem to understand we were not at fault. Mr. Forbes was the only long-time resident of the neighborhood to perish. As he was not a member of a genteel family, I believe that has lessened the impact."

"That, I believe, is a sad indictment on our society," said Mr. Darcy. "That a man's worth should be measured by his birth."

"I cannot say you are wrong, sir," replied Elizabeth. "Have any rumors followed you to town?"

"No. Or at least very few. Lady Catherine had been entrenched at Rosings for so long that only a certain subset of society even remembered her as a person. The announcement of her death did cause a bit of a furor, but the trial of Mr. Collins went largely unnoticed."

Elizabeth murmured her appreciation for that fact. For some time after they walked in silence, both lost in their thoughts. Primary among Elizabeth's thoughts and feelings was confusion. Mr. Darcy had promised to return to her, but his behavior thus far was not the close personal interest in her that he had displayed before he left. Had he decided against pursuing her? Though she found she hoped it was not the case, she would not blame him if he had.

At length, Mr. Darcy halted and turned to her, and Elizabeth could see an earnestness about him which she had often seen before. "Miss Elizabeth, I wished to stay away until my mourning was completed, for I worried what the gossips should say should I return early. Given the history at Netherfield, I do not believe this is an unwarranted concern.

"But I have never had so much difficulty keeping myself in check as I have these past two weeks especially."

Elizabeth gasped at the raw emotion in his voice, the longing he had suppressed. "You forced yourself to stay away?"

"I did, though I had no desire to do so. Every moment I was away, even when I was busy at Rosings, at Pemberley, or with any other matters which required my attention, you were never far from my thoughts. Dare I hope that I have been in *your* thoughts too?"

There was an eager sort of nervousness about him that Elizabeth finally understood. While she might have worried about his ultimate decision concerning her, he was terrified she would send him away. Her heart melted, and the smile she directed at him softened his brow and brought a measure of peace.

"I thought of you constantly, Mr. Darcy," said Elizabeth. "I will not vie for the greater share of longing, but I hoped you would return to me as you promised."

An expression of heartfelt delight came over his countenance, and he reached down to grasp one of her hands. "Nothing could have kept me away. Once the demands of propriety were met, I hastened here to be by your side."

"I am very glad you did," whispered Elizabeth.

They turned and began walking again, Elizabeth steps carrying her closer to his side than she might have had their mutual declaration not occurred. It was sublime, this feeling of belonging. Elizabeth hoped they would never be parted again.

"I have inquired into the possibility of leasing an estate nearby," said Mr. Darcy. "Bingley *does* still hold the lease of Netherfield and would allow me to stay if I asked. But I have no desire to be there."

"I can understand that sentiment, sir. I never wish to lay eyes on it again."

Mr. Darcy nodded. "With your permission, therefore, I shall sign the papers and take the lease of Pulvis Lodge, so that I may be close enough to attend to our courting."

Elizabeth turned a playful laugh on him. "As yet, you have not *asked* me for a courtship, sir. You have stated your intentions, but nothing beyond."

"At present, I only wish to call on you, Miss Elizabeth," said Mr. Darcy, returning her grin. "Everything between us must be done with the utmost in propriety."

"Then you may proceed, sir."

And proceed Mr. Darcy did. He proved to be an ardent suitor when the specter of danger did not hang over them. Elizabeth was well-pleased with his attentions and wished for them to proceed at a swift pace. She was to be disappointed in this, however, as while he did proceed, he did so in a manner which was far more deliberate than hasty. Elizabeth was certain this was a facet of his character, in addition to showing the neighborhood their courting was to be above reproach.

Their courting did excite the interest of the neighborhood, but most of her friends were supportive and happy for Elizabeth. She had always had the picture of him as a private man who did not appreciate his doings being fodder for the gossips. But she could see that he suppressed his usual feelings for her sake.

It was during this courtship that another large change for the Bennet family was made known, and it turned out to be a shock for the entire family. Elizabeth had watched her parents' closer relationship with approval. But while there had been no outward changes in her mother, she had noticed a glow settling about her which confused her.

In time, the reason was made known to them all.

"Your mother and I have an announcement," said Mr. Bennet one evening when Mr. Darcy had been dining with them. That in itself was no strange matter, as Mr. Darcy dined with them on an almost daily basis.

The company watched Mr. Bennet with interest, none of them having any indication of what he wished to say. It was strange, Elizabeth thought, but her mother's color was rather high. In fact, she realized, with a start, that her mother was blushing rather furiously. Elizabeth could not account for this behavior. A look at Mr. Darcy showed that he was watching her parents with what could only be termed a smirk.

"You see," said Mr. Bennet, before Elizabeth could question Mr. Darcy, "we have recently made a remarkable discovery. There is no way to say this to lessen the shock, so I shall come out and say it. Your mother is with child."

Silence reigned over the room, and for a moment Elizabeth thought her father was delivering a joke. But he watched them all, a hint of a grin playing about his mouth, betraying his enjoyment of their stupefaction. Mrs. Bennet, for her part, blushed even more furiously, if possible.

"But how is that possible?" demanded Lydia, the first among them to speak.

"I am sorry, Lydia," replied Mr. Bennet. "I shan't explain the mechanics of it to you. Suffice to say that in about another four months, you shall no longer be the youngest of the family."

"But Mama is so *old!*" cried Lydia with more emotion than sense.

This pierced Mrs. Bennet's embarrassment, and she glared at her — current — youngest with asperity. "I am not so very old, Lydia. I am one and forty, I will thank you to remember."

"Do you remember Mrs. Chambers?" asked Mr. Bennet. When they all nodded, he continued, saying: "Her final child was born when she was five and forty, as I recall. It is *not* impossible."

Lydia opened her mouth to speak, but the fierce look her mother directed at her silenced her, and she sat sullenly. Congratulations, though hesitant, were offered, and the family fell into an awkwardness rarely felt among the Bennets.

It was some time later when she noticed Mr. Darcy struggling valiantly to hide a grin, and as the conversation was now flowing a little more easily, Elizabeth turned to him to speak quietly. "Of what are you thinking, Mr. Darcy?"

"Just your father's announcement," replied he. If anything, his grin grew wider. "It *is* a surprise, is it not?"

"I can think of nothing more surprising, replied Elizabeth. "I cannot account for how this has come about. My parents have been indifferent to each other for years. As far as I know, they have not even shared a bed for more than a decade."

"They have not?" asked Mr. Darcy, one eyebrow raised. "They have if you recall, and the timing is perfect."

Elizabeth's eyes grew wide. "When we were at Netherfield."

"Exactly. Mr. Bennet, concerned for your safety, moved his wife into his room and you and your sisters into hers. Then, sleeping in the same bed for the first time in years, well, nature took over, and this is the result."

It was impossible for Elizabeth to reply, so she contented herself with nodding her response. The rest of the evening was passed on her part watching her parents, wondering at the changes which had come over them.

In due time, Mr. Darcy asked for a courtship, and then he proposed, both of which Elizabeth accepted with alacrity. In deference to her mother and her condition, they waited until after Mrs. Bennet was delivered to marry. And she was delivered of a healthy son, the long-awaited heir of Longbourn. The joy of both mother and father could hardly be described. When Elizabeth met her gentleman over the altar only a month later, the family truly felt they had been blessed, even after trials had threatened to destroy them.

Elizabeth and Darcy left for their wedding journey, and Jane, as her dearest sister, accompanied them. It was about six weeks later that a frantic letter from Mrs. Bennet arrived, imploring them to return to Longbourn, for Mr. Bingley had visited, apparently intent upon resuming his wooing to Jane. It was another occasion in which her husband regarded her with smugness.

"And why do you celebrate your own cleverness, Husband?"

"I have not been clever in the slightest. But I knew Bingley intended to return for your sister, as he informed me of it himself. I left instructions for him to be made welcome at Pulvis Lodge when he arrived, where I assume he is staying even as we speak."

Mr. Bingley was changed from the man he had been the previous year. He continued to be garrulous and friendly, but there was a hint of darkness in his eyes, and his demeanor was just a little quieter. It seemed he had suffered because of his sister's death and altered because of it.

But he was still an impetuous man, as his proposal to Jane attested, occurring only four weeks after his arrival in Meryton. Another celebration was, therefore, within Mrs. Bennet's purview, and she set to it with gusto. And when Mr. and Mrs. Bingley were joined in matrimony, they were quick to remove to the north, their new estate close to Pemberley where their close relations made their home.

In time, the events of that week at Netherfield Park were largely forgotten. Most of the rest of the Bennet sisters left for their own families, and though the next generation of Bennets was now assured at Longbourn, their border with Netherfield ever remained empty, for the estate slowly fell into decay. The owner of the place was content to collect what income it generated, but he was never able to lease it again. Netherfield obtained the reputation of a cursed house, and it lay abandoned for many years, as those who owned it let it fall further by the year.

The end came during a late November storm, on almost exactly the day when the ball at Netherfield had taken place. During the maelstrom, the house was hit by a bolt of lightning and burned to the ground

The End

FOR READERS WHO LIKED
MURDER AT NETHERFIELD

A Tale of Two Courtships
Two sisters, both in danger of losing their hearts. One experiences a courtship which ends quickly in an engagement, the other must struggle against the machinations of others. And one who will do anything to ensure her beloved sister achieves her heart's desire.

Out of Obscurity
Amid the miraculous events of a lost soul returning home, dark forces conspire against a young woman, for her loss was not an accident. A man is moved to action by a boon long denied, determined to avoid being cheated by Miss Elizabeth Bennet again.

In the Wilds of Derbyshire
Elizabeth Bennet goes to her uncle's estate in Derbyshire after Jane's marriage to Mr. Bingley, feeling there is nothing left for her in Meryton. She quickly becomes close to her young cousin and uncle, though her aunt seems to hold a grudge against her. She also meets the handsome Mr. Fitzwilliam Darcy, and she realizes that she can still have everything she has ever wished to have. But there are obstacles she must overcome . . . .

Netherfield's Secret
Elizabeth soon determines that her brother's friend, Fitzwilliam Darcy, suffers from an excess of pride, and it comes as a shock when the man reveals himself to be in love with her. But even that revelation is not as surprising as the secret Netherfield has borne witness to. Netherfield's secret shatters Elizabeth's perception of herself and the world around her, and Mr. Darcy is the only one capable of picking up the pieces.

The Companion
A sudden tragedy during Elizabeth's visit to Kent leaves her directly in Lady Catherine de Bourgh's sights. With Elizabeth's help, a woman long-oppressed has begun to spread her wings. What comes after is a whirlwind of events in which Elizabeth discovers that her carefully held opinions are not infallible. Furthermore, a certain gentleman of her acquaintance might be the key to Elizabeth's happiness.

What Comes Between Cousins
A rivalry springs up between Mr. Darcy and Colonel Fitzwilliam, each determined to win the fair Elizabeth Bennet. As the situation between cousins deteriorates, clarity begins to come for Elizabeth, and she sees Mr. Darcy as the man who will fill all her desires in a husband. But the rivalry between cousins is not the only trouble brewing for Elizabeth.

For more details, visit
http://www.onegoodsonnet.com/genres/pride-and-prejudice-variations

Also by One Good Sonnet Publishing

The Smothered Rose Trilogy

Book 1: Thorny

In this retelling of "Beauty and the Beast," a spoiled boy who is forced to watch over a flock of sheep finds himself more interested in catching the eye of a girl with lovely ground-trailing tresses than he is in protecting his charges. But when he cries "wolf" twice, a determined fairy decides to teach him a lesson once and for all.

Book 2: Unsoiled

When Elle finds herself practically enslaved by her stepmother, she scarcely has time to even clean the soot off her hands before she collapses in exhaustion. So when Thorny tries to convince her to go on a quest and leave her identity as Cinderbella behind her, she consents. Little does she know that she will face challenges such as a determined huntsman, hungry dwarves, and powerful curses . . . .

Book 3: Roseblood

Both Elle and Thorny are unhappy with the way their lives are going, and the revelations they have had about each other have only served to drive them apart. What is a mother to do? Reunite them, of course. Unfortunately, things are not quite so simple when a magical lettuce called "rapunzel" is involved.

If you're a fan of thieves with a heart of gold, then you don't want to Miss . . .

THE PRINCES AND THE PEAS
A TALE OF ROBIN HOOD

A NOVEL OF THIEVES, ROYALTY, AND IRREPRESSIBLE LEGUMES

BY LELIA EYE

An infamous thief faces his greatest challenge yet when he is pitted against forty-nine princes and the queen of a kingdom with an unnatural obsession with legumes. Sleeping on top of a pea hidden beneath a pile of mattresses? Easy. Faking a singing contest? He could do that in his sleep. But stealing something precious out from under "Old Maid" Marian's nose . . . now that is a challenge that even the great Robin Hood might not be able to surmount.

When Robin Hood comes up with a scheme that involves disguising himself as a prince and participating in a series of contests for a queen's hand, his Merry Men provide him their support. Unfortunately, however, Prince John attends the contests with the Sheriff of Nottingham in tow, and as all of the Merry Men know, Robin Hood's pride will never let him remain inconspicuous. From sneaking peas onto his neighbors' plates to tweaking the noses of prideful men like the queen's chamberlain, Robin Hood is certain to make an impression on everyone attending the contests. But whether he can escape from the kingdom of Clorinda with his prize in hand before his true identity comes to light is another matter entirely.

About the Author

Jann Rowland is a Canadian, born and bred. Other than a two-year span in which he lived in Japan, he has been a resident of the Great White North his entire life, though he professes to still hate the winters.

Though Jann did not start writing until his mid-twenties, writing has grown from a hobby to an all-consuming passion. His interests as a child were almost exclusively centered on the exotic fantasy worlds of Tolkien and Eddings, among a host of others. As an adult, his interests have grown to include historical fiction and romance, with a particular focus on the works of Jane Austen.

When Jann is not writing, he enjoys rooting for his favorite sports teams. He is also a master musician (in his own mind) who enjoys playing piano and singing as well as moonlighting as the choir director in his church's congregation.

Jann lives in Alberta with his wife of more than twenty years, two grown sons, and one young daughter. He is convinced that whatever hair he has left will be entirely gone by the time his little girl hits her teenage years. Sadly, though he has told his daughter repeatedly that she is not allowed to grow up, she continues to ignore him.

Website: http://onegoodsonnet.com/
Facebook: https://facebook.com/OneGoodSonnetPublishing/
Twitter: @OneGoodSonnet
Mailing List: http://eepurl.com/bol2p9